DEVIL'S DIARY

THE COMING

ANTHONY R HOWARD

WWW.ANTHONYRHOWARD.COM

Dedicated to the ladies of my life:
Jenjit, Jenetta Claire, Jaden, and Caren Howard.

BLACK FOX
IMPRINT

Devil's Diary: The Coming

Copyright © 2017 by Anthony R. Howard. All rights reserved.

Published and printed in the United States of America.

No part of this book may be reproduced, copied or used in any form or manner whatsoever without written permission, except in the case of brief quotations in reviews and critical articles.

Editor: Zoey Walls, Master of Theological Studies,
Harvard Divinity School

Paperback ISBN 978-0-9966397-2-9
eBook ISBN 978-0-9966397-3-6

www.anthonyRhoward.com

In the beginning God created the heavens and the earth. Now the earth was formless and empty, darkness was over the surface of the deep, and the Spirit of God was hovering over the waters. And God said, "Let there be light," and there was light.

Genesis 1:1–3

CHAPTER 1

There was heightened panic across America.

Amidst the unprecedented pandemonium, Oniva Mering was afraid. All she wanted was food. That was a tall order amongst the mayhem. She couldn't hear her stomach gurgle over the shouting. Piercing hunger pangs erupted again inside of her. She hadn't eaten today. She had money, but most stores now only accepted smartchips, and she refused to get one. Even after her three hour wait, banks were not giving out any more cash. In the last four minutes, three fistfights had already erupted beside her in the Safeway over bottled water and canned goods. The screaming and turmoil unnerved Oniva. She saw those who were able to fight their way to the register scanning the smartchips inside of their hands or foreheads in order to purchase food. As Oniva reached for the last box of pasta, another cart forcefully collided with hers, knocking her to the ground.

"Get the hell out of my way!" a large man yelled. "War is coming!"

He looked like an ox, his eyes blazing. Oniva was petrified.

"Please, don't hurt me. I just want to buy food. I don't have anything to eat."

The man looked down at Oniva, ignored her plea, and began grabbing food from her shopping cart in a frenzy. While he was preoccupied, Oniva scrambled to her feet and ran out of the grocery store, visibly shaken. Even the parking lot was in chaos. Car horns blasted amidst a chorus of obscenities. The desperate energy had shifted its focus from the last scraps of food to shopping carts and parking spaces. This was Washington, DC, but today, it seemed like a foreign country.

Oniva noticed a very thin man in a black suit standing just outside the perimeter of the chaos. He wore an archaic metal medallion. The man seemed oddly emotionless as he observed the anarchy. He nodded slowly to himself. Suddenly, he looked directly at Oniva and sneered. Oniva jerked her gaze from his, and in a moment, he was gone.

In the electronics store next to Safeway, CNN played on the window full of flat screen TVs, replaying the devastating news: The United States was under attack.

Oniva joined the group of frightened citizens listening to the newscast. "For the first time since September 11th, 2001, the United States of America has been attacked on its home soil. After today's crippling air bombing over Langley, Virginia, a secret alliance of over eleven countries and insurgent nations claimed responsibility for the attacks. Their primary target: The US." The crowd gasped in shock.

"Despite the United States' status as a world power," the CNN reporter started, "this alliance has declared war by the brutal attack of key forts and military bases nationwide."

"My God," Oniva said softly.

A woman next to her glanced sideways at Oniva and muttered, "Lady, we lost God a while back."

The TV screen flashed to a military officer reporting on the latest discoveries involving the terrorist plot. "It seems there are more German military forces in Canada now than there are Canadian military forces. Incredibly, the alliance has succeeded in bridging the gap between Siberia and Alaska through a vast underground tunnel. The Bering Sea between Alaska and Asia is some one hundred miles wide at its narrowest point. It is unknown at this point just how many war machines and weapons of mass destruction could be hidden underground."

"Is an invasion on the US imminent, commander?" the analyst asked.

There was an awkward pause. "I am not prepared to answer that question."

Oniva looked across the street at the bank. After her three hour wait, the bank announced that it was out of cash, but would happily load currency onto any smartchips. Lines at gun stores and pawn shops played across the TV screens as hundreds of people filled out paperwork to receive firearms. Anarchism had spread nationwide.

Feeling as though she was in a dream, Oniva turned to walk back to her car when a graph on the TV screen caught her eye.

"Look at the stock market!" a man yelled pointing at the screen. It showed the Dow Jones plummeting like a cinderblock in the ocean as the panic-stricken population liquefied any asset possible in preparation for war. "Banks are out of cash, and billion-dollar companies have been devalued almost instantly. We have no economy! This catastrophe will destroy the country overnight," the man in the crowd said, sounding stunned.

The US was ripe for invasion.

CHAPTER 2

Esau Rontrez stared at the two-hour wait ahead of him at the gun shop. He just wanted to buy ammo, not engage in all the madness. Might need a few more full clips for the chaos. Too late to get a gun. They were all gone, and he knew the backorders would never arrive. The US military would be taking all the shipments. The ammo he needed for his automatic pistol wasn't on the shelf, but he knew that it wasn't out of stock. Someone just scooped it up to hoard or to resell. He looked around. He saw a few folks watching a small TV detailing the recent bombing in Virginia. Will Baxter stood amongst the crowd by the TV, dressed in camouflage pants and a confederate flag T-shirt. "Hell, we'll show them what we've got!" he shouted to the TV.

As if on cue, the screen switched to footage of the US military mobilizing troops and preparing for retaliation. The oceans were filled with submarines and battleships, and a false move by either side could result in the first nuclear missile fired in World War III. The US had called for all offensive weaponry to be withdrawn immediately. The enemy alliance ignored the order, and now there was a standoff.

Rontrez looked into Baxter's cart and saw 20 familiar blue boxes of the ammo he needed. He sauntered up to the shouting man and said. "I'm gonna need some of those boxes, 'Patriot'."

"No can do," Baxter said adamantly. "Need these for my pistol."

"What kind do you have?"

"Smith and Wesson, 357."

"Then you won't be needing those. Those are 9 millimeter. They won't go into a Smith & Wesson 357. That's a revolver."

Baxter gave Rontrez a menacing stare. "These boxes ain't leaving my basket. And you best get from 'round me before things get ugly." Baxter's southern accent had come to the forefront of his tone.

"Well, we can do this one of two ways," Rontrez started. "You can give half of them to me, and hold onto the other half for resale later when you can triple the price. Or, I can wait for you outside and empty the last six bullets from my Glock into you the second you walk out that door. Then I take all 20 boxes, plus your smart chip, and then go on a shopping spree. Not the time or the person for games. The police are a bit too preoccupied with the riots to help you out on this one. Your move."

Rontrez saw Baxter sizing him up. He smirked. Rontrez knew Baxter was trying to figure out if he was joking. Rontrez had spoken casually, so that the threat on Baxter's life almost didn't seem serious. But Rontrez's words lingered, as did his indifference to them. From Rontrez's accent and appearance, Baxter could tell Rontrez was a Baltimore native with a hardened past. He noticed Rontrez did not have a smart-chip incision mark on his hands or his forehead. This meant there was a resilience and edginess about him. He was not a conformist, likely did need the bullets, and just might make good on his threat. Baxter couldn't tangle right now. He had to stay on mission. Baxter was a lethal member of the country's newest threat: The Bloodliners. Baxter jerked his head toward his cart. Without a word, Rontrez grabbed half the boxes. He hoped to get back to Oniva before it was too late. As a deeply spiritual and sensitive person, he knew she wouldn't be able to maneuver well in the dysfunctional unruliness.

Chapter 3

Oniva walked through the door, empty-handed. She was crying softly. Weeping for mankind.

"Stop all that," a smooth voice said from her living room.

She turned to see Rontrez laying on her sofa.

"Get your feet off my sofa," Oniva said. "Didn't you see the sign outside? It said 'No Riff-Raff.' Former pimps especially."

"I take it Safeway wasn't the safe way today?" Rontrez asked, seeing Oniva wasn't carrying grocery bags.

"It was a war zone," Oniva replied gravely. She took a deep solemn breath.

"I know, Niva. Gun shop was worse than our high school at lunchtime."

Oniva nodded her head sadly. "I was looking at some of the foreign news. Citizens on both sides are crying out for peace, but governments are bent on war. We need peace. People on both sides are pleading for an end to this."

"Begging for change won't help."

"What do you suggest? We need a solution. Time is of the essence."

"I suggest you get some rest. You look tired. I'm going to go find something for breakfast."

"Be careful, Esau."

"I don't need careful, Oniva." Rontrez winked. "I got ammunition."

Oniva couldn't sleep a wink. The world was in chaos. Rontrez was snoring loudly from the guest room. At about 7a.m, she got out of bed, famished. She didn't open the refrigerator. She already knew it was empty. She opened the freezer and pulled out some old asparagus. This would have to serve as her morning nutrition. The only breakfast she could find. She didn't have any oil left to stir-fry it, so she sadly put the asparagus into the microwave. On top of the microwave she saw a handwritten note from Rontrez: *Last box of cereal at Safeway. No milk.* She eagerly searched the cabinet and found the generic-brand corn flakes Rontrez had somehow managed to procure. As she poured herself a bowl, Rontrez entered the kitchen.

"Breakfast of champions," he said.

"And for lunch we have asparagus soup with a side of air pie. Served chilled with a glass of premium tap water," Oniva replied.

"I almost had to box someone last night for the cornflakes." As Rontrez spoke, the sky suddenly turned black. The sun disappeared and the moon went dark.

"What in the world?" Oniva muttered while turning on the lights. She walked outside with Rontrez to get a better look.

Though the clock read 7:06 a.m. EST, the sky read death.

A glowing, white cloud appeared in the sky. A blinding light appeared within the cloud. Although the phenomenon was the size of a house, it could be seen across the entire globe.

"What is that?" Oniva asked.

Rontrez had no answer.

The cloud was brighter than the sun, but as they gazed upon it, they both felt overwhelmed by peace and tranquility. Its radiance illuminated the sky brighter than daylight. Countless, scattered balls of light rained from the cloud as it sank lower to the earth.

Traffic stopped to admire the shimmering cloud. People beheld the sight from the windows of cars, trains, and buses. At once, every woman, man, and child was aware of the luminous being within. News crews rushed to film the cloud, but it did not register on their equipment. It could only be seen by a living soul.

Gracefully, the cloud continued to descend. The light inside spoke, but there was no audible voice. The being communicated without sound but with the celestial expression of thoughts. A parapsychologist might call it telepathy. Whatever it was, everyone could hear within themselves a gentle, kind voice overflowing with love and compassion.

"Behold, I am the Son of Man," the voice said. "Fear me not, for all knew this day would come. I am not here to bring vengeance. I am here to bring peace and love amongst the living."

As these words were spoken, countless separate clouds spawned from the original one. These clouds formed into winged beings with long golden trumpets, and the beings descended to the earth. When they stepped to the ground, the countless angels blew their horns at once, sounding a thunderous and awesome musical chorus. The angels stood erect and obedient, not moving or making a sound. The beings of great light seem to say, "Pay no attention to us. We are nothing. Listen to the words of the Messiah."

For the first time since the beginning of time, every living man, woman, and child on earth was awake.

Oniva was awestruck. She could hear the words, but could not believe what was going on around her.

"For all who may doubt," he said, "I deliver unto you the prophet Elijah. Upon my word, he will restore peace and prosperity to man-kind. I am sending my servant, and he will make ready the way before me, whom you are looking for. I will come to his Temple, and the angel of judgment, in whom you may or may not delight, is coming."

Oniva and Rontrez looked at each other. Rontrez shrugged his shoulders, indicating he too could hear the voice loud and clear.

"I say unto all, when you are taken and given up to be judged, do not be troubled about what to say: but whatever is given to you in that hour, say, because it is not you who say it, but the Holy Spirit who dwells within you. Judgment is swift and permanent, and the unclean shall be rebuked. Elijah will take his seat, testing and cleansing the sons of the first breath of life, burning away the dross from them as from gold and silver, so that he and his followers may make offerings to the Lord in righteousness. And I will come near to you for judging those who have been untrue in married life. I will bear witness against those who take false oaths, who keep back from the servant his payment, and those who are hard on the widow and the child without a father. Have no fear of me, I say, but fear the Lord of armies."

THREE DAYS EARLIER
(Three Days Before *The Coming*)

CHAPTER 4

"When is Jesus Christ coming back?" Minister Chris Justes repeated, unsure how to answer. The entire children's Sunday school class of the Mt. Olive Church of Jesus Christ fell unearthly silent. In all his years of ministry, no one had ever asked him this question with the gravity with which little Andrew now confronted him.

"That's a good question, Andrew. Let's see if I can help you out here, buddy. I can tell you've asked this question more than once."

Andrew nodded and gazed eagerly at Minister Justes.

"How many times have you asked this question?"

Andrew shrugged.

"That many?"

Andrew nodded.

"Well, turn your Bible to Mark, chapter thirteen," Justes replied. "Your question is answered in those Scriptures."

The entire Sunday school class followed the minister's instructions. All eyes remained on Justes as the children waited.

Justes read aloud: "But about that day or hour no one knows, not even the angels in heaven, nor the Son, but only the Father. Be on guard! Be alert! You do not know when that time will come," (Mark 13:32-33).

Justes looked at the class, then at Andrew. "Andrew, no one in the world knows exactly when the Son of God will return, because He doesn't want us to know. Let me explain it to you like this. Have you ever been home alone?"

"Just for a little bit," Andrew replied meekly.

"My mom left me home for a long time once," seven-year-old Philip blurted out.

Justes softly shushed Philip and continued.

"Do you remember wondering when your parents would come home?"

Andrew nodded.

"Well, if they told you they would be back in fifteen minutes, then you'd know you could be bad for fourteen minutes and fifty-nine seconds and not get in trouble. But since you didn't know when they would come back, you had to be good the whole time because you didn't want to get in trouble. It's the same thing with Jesus. If God told us exactly when he was coming back, we might act up until the minute he came back, then we'd be little angels when he was ready to pass judgment. That's not the way God wants us to live our lives. He wants us to obey all of his commandments, whether he's coming next week, next month, next year, or a thousand years from now. Got it?"

"Yeah, I get it now," Andrew said.

"Why doesn't God say he's going to come in the year 2035, but come in 2040? That way we'll be good for free, because we expect him to come back sooner than he really is," Philip asked.

"That's not the way God works. He is not here to deceive. He is here to love us."

Suddenly, a baritone voice cut in from the doorway. "Therefore keep watch because you do not know when the owner of the house will come back – whether in the evening, or at midnight, or when the rooster crows, or at dawn. If he comes suddenly, do not let him find you sleeping. What I say to you, I say to everyone: Watch!" (Mark 13:35-37). The voice came from Deacon Blackwell.

Justes didn't see any reason for Blackwell to come in and scare his twelve Sunday school students out of their minds, but the deacon seemed to enjoy it. Blackwell was a fire-and-brimstone minister who would tell the congregation they were going to burn in hell for eternity if they tried to cheat the Lord on their tithes – or if they parked in his parking space. Blackwell was once invited to speak at a church in a neighboring city. When he arrived, he saw his name listed second on the program, behind another deacon's. He refused to speak and returned home. Justes wouldn't call Blackwell an evil or dishonest person, but he definitely had his own way of doing things, and more often than not, Justes – and the church– disagreed with his actions.

Justes looked at his watch. It was time for the children to be dismissed. After saying a closing prayer, he dismissed the children and gave Blackwell a withering look.

"You scared those kids half to death," Justes said. "They'll go home and hide under the bed."

Blackwell shrugged. "The truth will set them free."

Justes brushed past the deacon, walked back to his small chambers, and closed the door. Sighing, he sat down behind his desk and looked out the window. Though it was a beautiful sunny day, times were chaotic. War raged around the globe. A secret society kidnapped, tortured, and murdered Christians every day. And everywhere he looked, someone claimed to be God.

Blackwell walked into Justes's chambers without knocking, as usual.

"Have you seen the news, Chris?" Blackwell asked.

Of course he had seen the news. Reports of the worldwide chaos appeared on any medium capable of delivering information. A widespread famine swept through war-ravaged countries, and earthquakes caused by shifting tectonic plates claimed thousands of lives in a three-month period. However, Justes had no idea what specific event Blackwell was referring to. He figured it might be the recent implementation of the smartchip law, which passed after the US had received intelligence reports of an upcoming attack.

A smartchip was a tiny microchip, approximately the size of an uncooked grain of rice, planted inside most human bodies. Touting the smartchip as a national security measure, the US government had urged all citizens to receive the implant as a means of global tracking and monitoring.

The smartchip held inside it a person's electronic identification code. In the right database, the code could pull up a person's credit history, what car they drove, their social security number, and any other personal information it had recorded from its host. Usually, smartchips were inserted into a person's forehead or hand. When the chip was scanned, money could be deducted from the person's account, food and services could be purchased or exchanged, and all transactions could be monitored and taxed accordingly.

Millions of Americans still refused to be implanted with the chip, which made it difficult for these outsiders to buy food and other necessities. After an attempt to stop food from being sold to those without smartchips did not result in total conformity, a new law was proposed and swiftly passed by Congress. The new law stated that every individual *must* have a smartchip implanted in them, or the offenders would be punished and imprisoned. Despite the initial outcry, the smartchip system became almost ubiquitous.

• • • • • •

Blackwell interrupted Justes's thoughts. "Now they're inserting smartchips in newborns."

"We all saw this coming," Justes said. "Once they crossed the line from animals to humans, it was just a matter of time until people started to believe the chips are valuable to society. People willingly bought into it, and gave up all their privacy because they told us it would stop credit card fraud. Idiots."

Blackwell almost rolled his eyes. "Yeah, the information age is truly an astounding revolution."

Suddenly, an explosion rocked the building, and Justes heard screaming. He ran out of his office to see a fire blazing down the hallway. He scrambled for the extinguisher hanging on the wall, but the fire was already out of control. Children—precious children—screamed for help.

He smelled the sickening odor of cooked flesh and burning rubber. The heat was suffocating, but he couldn't give up. He ran toward the flames, spraying the extinguisher while the fire danced around him. The flames seemed to laugh at his futile attempts to stop its destruction.

"Bomb!" a woman screamed as she ran down the corridor. Those who had escaped the flames stampeded for the exit doors, screaming for their savior.

Flames licked the walls and spread to the ceiling. Moments later, chunks of heavy debris began to fall around them. There were not enough exits to evacuate everyone safely. Some of the debris fell on top of parishioners scrambling to get out.

Justes ran to the sanctuary, smashed the antique stained-glass window with the fire extinguisher, and yelled for those around him to climb through the jagged opening. His face blackened with soot, the minister looked at the carcass of the burning church in horror and disbelief. His spiritual home had been bombed. A nightmare had come true.

Is this reality justifiable? Not one iota of it.

Undoubtedly, it's my world. Absolute pandemonium worldwide. The best part about it? Faith is on my side this time. Y2K, huh guys? You were all too busy putting your allegiance in your computers and your government and your damn self-interest. You should have seen it. You were filling up bathtubs, cleaning the stores out, cleaning out your bank accounts, swearing you would put the money back if everything turned out Y2-okay. You were scared to set foot out of the house because of the great Y2K scare. I guess you thought at the stroke of midnight a big wave of darkness would sweep across every city by time zone, and everyone would have to run westward. What a riot.

Then came 9/11 and the towers came tumbling down. Just another step in the perfect masterpiece. The fantastic, indestructible, incorruptible game plan that has come about through centuries of flawless planning. It has already been authored. My victory has already been written. I created it, you sealed it, and your almighty spook was too insipid to realize what the hell was going on. No pun intended.

I have existed since the beginning of time. I have stood as the most for-midable threat to those who would halt progress in the name of spiritu-ality. Those of my army are explorers on the untrodden paths of science, technology, self-motivation, humanistic mystery, and against all that is most truly occult.

I represent indulgence instead of abstinence. I embody vital existence instead of spiritual pipe dreams. I endorse undefiled wisdom, not hypo-critical self-deceit. I stand for self-acknowledgement instead of self-denial. I exemplify physical, mental, and emotional gratification, not the restraint of fundamental experience. I let an individual choose for himself, not twist his views into a warped religion. Man is hopelessness. Created in the image of Him? Hypocrisy at its finest. People need something to believe in. That is the secret. Something great happens, praise the Lord. Something bad happens, it's my fault, or he might "work in mysterious ways."

Through all the biblical charades, skyscraper churches, cabalistic orga-nizations, arcane literature, choirs, preachers, and mentors, only one thing separates every soul in existence from my ineffable presence. The key that time and time again has led many of the combatants' plans astray. The key that cannot be taken, but only pilfered: faith. But this time, faith can only work in my favor. I have been the best friend the Church has ever had. After all, I have kept it in business all these years.

The opening has now become ripe for righteousness to rise. The inge-nious plot designed to smash the hypocrisy and insanity that has ruled for too long shall finally commence. The elongated reign of senselessness has come to an end. So Praise him . . . or is it "praise her" this year? Halle-lujah. In God we trust, all others pay cash . . . that's the spirit of the age, and the time has finally arisen.

CHAPTER 5

Esau Rontrez drove his black E-Class Mercedes-Benz onto the exit ramp off of Interstate 495 and slowed to yield to the traffic before merging on Georgia Avenue. He looked at the car's digital clock: 1:32 p.m. Just when Oniva would be getting out of church. She kept urging him to attend with her, and he knew he should, but all the shouting and catching the Holy Ghost didn't excite him.

Ever since his health-conscious mother had suddenly died of a heart attack, he couldn't seem to understand how the faith thing worked. Experts on faith said you should believe in something with all your heart and continue to believe no matter what happened. Even when your beliefs crushed you underfoot without explanation, you just had to deal with your disappointment.

He knew it was odd that he had a grudge against God. He liked the music in the black churches, and there were a lot of pretty women at The Church of Zion, but that was nothing but temptation. Long ago, during his time as a pimp, Rontrez quickly learned that women were three capital T's: Taxing, Temptation, and Trouble. Women were taxing to the spirit and mind, but taxing was Rontrez's own euphemism for good, aggressive sex. If he slept in one day, and one of his colleagues called for him, he would say he was up last night taxing. His associates would understand immediately.

Though Rontrez had no serious romance in his life, he did have one strong, platonic relationship with a woman. Often, he would classify Oniva as his best friend – and he was her primary source of intellectual entertainment.

He had known Oniva for ten years, ever since they had graduated high school together. Oniva was always on the honor roll, but even back then, Rontrez was more interested in his money roll. An intelligent and streetwise hustler, Rontrez could shake down a crack dealer as well as debate various sides of political events.

Though Oniva was considered pretty by many, Rontrez never found her sexually attractive. Regardless, they were there for each other in every other way. Oniva found Rontrez's never-ending supply of comic relief delightful, and even though she knew he used to sell women, she loved him like a brother and never harbored any resentment when she realized some of his best moneymakers were people she knew. Rontrez had never forced anyone to do anything.

Rontrez pulled the Benz into the parking lot of The Church of Zion and found a parking space. He left the engine running. Oniva soon came strolling out of the church with a guy—handsome in a churchy kind of way. Rontrez sat back and observed the expressions and body language of the man, who was obviously interested in more than small talk. Disgusted, Rontrez flicked his lights at his friend. Oniva noticed, wrapped up her conversation, and headed toward the Benz. Rontrez rolled down his window as she approached.

"Hey, what are you doing out here? You should have been in there." Oniva grinned, pointing to the church.

"I must have made a wrong turn somewhere. Dang. Is church over already? Who were you talking to?"

"Just a friend of mine. His name is Ronald."

"Ronald is trying to throw dick in your direction," Rontrez replied.

"What are you talking about? We were just talking."

"I read through his act and mailed the script back to him. If that man ain't trying to get your panties off, then Toyota makes ice cream and Santa Claus weighs a buck twenty five."

"Whatever. What are you doing here anyway?"

"I'm coming from church."

Oniva looked excited. She had been trying to drag him to church for as long as she could remember. Since his mother passed away he had pretty much stopped going.

"Really, where did you go?"

"Bedside Baptist."

Oniva laughed. "Boy, you are too much."

"The sermon was all right, too, until the alarm clock woke me up. It was better than that church I went to last week though."

"Oh, yeah? What church was that?"

"Mattress Methodist."

Oniva laughed again. "You need to go somewhere and download some sense. It's the only way to deal with all this garbage going on in the world. Must be seven or eight different wars going on. Did you hear Israel was taken over in less than a day? Then the earthquakes, famines, and everyday some nut claims he's God. Rappers included."

"I think I'm gonna hide in my closet." Rontrez loved mocking Oniva's end-of-the earth speculations.

"This is not funny, Esau. You know about the Bloodliners!"

The Bloodline was an ancient, secret society that had recently emerged to violently persecute Christian churches and their leaders. They were responsible for dozens of worldwide church bombings, kidnappings, beheadings, and the torture of several prominent Christian figures. Anyone openly praising God was in danger. Race, creed, or denomination didn't matter. If you were a Christian and refused to give up your faith, you could be buried alive or even crucified. They had murdered or enslaved thousands.

Even more fearsome than the Bloodlines capacity for violence was the organization's uncanny ability to stay hidden. Not one major member had been caught since the wave of crimes had started almost two years ago, and their attacks increased every day.

"They supposedly have a terrorist cell right here in DC," Oniva continued, leaning on Rontrez's car.

"I did hear that on the news. That's why I came to see you." Rontrez covered her hand with his own.

"Why?"

"I want you to move to Baltimore for a little while. You can stay in my guest room. I don't like you living alone with all this mess going on. It's too crazy out here now, Niva."

"What makes you think the Bloodliners aren't in Baltimore?"

"Bloodliners don't come to Park Heights," Rontrez said, grinning. "If they do, we got something for them." Rontrez winked at her. "We'll blast the secret out of those cowardly sons of bastards."

Oniva thought for another moment. "That's a sweet offer, Esau. Thanks. I accept. It's pretty scary in my neighborhood right now. I stayed awake for hours swearing I heard noises outside my window. But watch your mouth, buster. You curse like a pirate."

"You really didn't have a choice. I didn't come here to ask you, I came to get you. I already spoke to your father about it."

"What!"

"Just playin'. Calm your nerves before you have a heart attack on the Lord's property. Someone might think you caught the Holy Ghost out here. Pass me a Martin Luther King fan. The one with the big Popsicle stick on the end."

Oniva laughed, but then her brow furrowed with worry. "It's like the end of the world is coming, Esau. I'm scared of all this madness. I don't even feel safe in church anymore. There have been two church bombings in DC already. We had four armed-security guards inside the sanctuary today. What is the world coming to?"

"I don't know what the world's coming to, but you're coming to Baltimore, end of discussion. I'll follow you home and help you pack. And look, don't pack like you're moving into my house. This is a temporary stay until they can take the blood out of the Bloodliners. And the only person that will be taxing in my house is me. You are now under involuntary celibacy until this madness is over."

Rontrez knew Oniva wasn't sexually active. She was a good girl all the way. A real straight arrow. Rontrez couldn't see her bringing a male friend over to his house anyway. Even when she tried to date, he would grossly exaggerate the man's every flaw until she fell over with laughter.

"Hey, who's that?" Rontrez stared at a woman, walking out of the church building. She was a tall woman with long black hair and a great body— two qualities Rontrez admired since he was tall and in good shape as well.

"That's Lisa. She's a nice girl. Leave her alone."

"I'm a nice man," Rontrez replied, flicking his high-beams at her. "She has got to be one of the finest women I have ever seen in my entire life."

"This is not a nightclub parking lot, you Neanderthal. Don't flash your lights at her! Go talk to her if you want to meet her."

"Too late. She's walking this way. Now watch my smooth operation, baby."

"You're impossible." Oniva sighed deeply.

Unlike that dude Oniva had been talking to, at least he was original when he talked to women. No corny lines, no lies, or phony impressions, just smooth conversation and an irresistibly mellow aura. In a way, she was sometimes jealous when he talked to other women when she was around. She would often criticize the women he spoke to, just as he would endlessly joke about the men who approached her. Though neither person had any desire to be intimate with the other, there was definitely a certain amount of guardianship they placed over each other.

"She's about as fine as I am," Rontrez said, grinning. "I'll suck her soul if she licks my lollipop emotions."

Lisa waved at Oniva as she came closer. Rontrez waved also, and Lisa returned the wave.

"Hey, girl, how you been?" Lisa gave Oniva a close hug. They had not had a decent conversation in a while, but not for any particular reason.

"Fine." Oniva replied, "I'm just here talking to this fool. This is my good friend, Esau."

Lisa extended a hand to Rontrez.

"What's the emergency, girl?" Lisa asked. "You're over here flashing the lights like you saw Bloodliners on the roof."

"Oh, that was me flashing the lights," Rontrez said. "The emergency was Lisa."

"I was the emergency?"

"Yup. You and that lovely outfit, confident stroll, and . . . will you look at that. Hey, Oniva, her Bible matches her dress. Lisa, you know you didn't do that by accident. Trying to come out the house matching the Lord's word."

"Actually, this is the only Bible I have. I didn't even notice it matched the outfit."

"Do you have a man to match the Bible and the outfit?"

"No," Lisa laughed, turning to Oniva. "I don't have a man. Oniva, your friend has no sense."

"I concur," Oniva said.

"Lisa," Rontrez continued, "Oniva was just telling me how flawless you are, and I know I'm at the top too. I think we should get together and marinate in our magnificence."

"How exactly would we marinate in our magnificence?" Lisa asked.

"Casual conversation, then perhaps escalation."

"Escalation to what?" Lisa replied.

"A movie, or meal, or even something more creative. I'm all about good times."

"You want to go out with all this wild stuff going on? The way the news sounds, we're about to be invaded, and we don't even know by whom."

"I can't live my life in fear," Rontrez said. "I love life too much. Fear is a disagreeable emotion. I prefer to indulge myself in life's pleasantries."

"So I suppose you don't get scared of anything, Mr. Invincible."

"I don't get scared, I get even. After I get even, I come for the enemy again and get odd. Then what. I can do square roots and exponents and algorithmic equations too. I'll get mathematical all over the presence of hostility."

"You're funny, but I still can't go out until things calm down a little."

"Let's stay in, then. How about a movie at my place—a bona fide Redbox night? You have to bring your movie card, though. I have fines on mine. I think I'm on their most wanted list." Lisa laughed. He was making progress. "I know you don't know me well yet, so you might feel uncomfortable, but Oniva will be there too. She is my official chaperone. I won't bite with her around."

"I think we'll be okay," Lisa replied. "We don't need a chaperone."

"I agree. We don't need a chaperone, but we do need to get together. So a movie at my place at your earliest convenience?"

"Sounds good, Esau."

CHAPTER 6

Vincent Minzano looked nervously around the dark room. He stood naked before an altar illuminated by candles, which cast a weak, flickering light on the upside-down crucifix on the wall of the chamber. Upon the altar lay a bloody, headless serpent, and the Holy Bible lay at his feet.

A man dressed in a hooded black robe stepped out of the darkness behind him. His face was painted an eerie white, with black ink surrounding his eyes and mouth. Veins of red dye streaked across his face, emanating from the black ink. Minzano had never seen this man before, but knew he was the Most Exalted Grand Archknight of the Bloodline Brotherhood. He would finally become a fellow Knight of the Bloodline.

The Archknight spoke in a low, booming voice. "My son, why is there now darkness around you?"

"To signify that in the beginning, the earth was without form and void, and darkness was upon the face of the deep."

"My son, why are you now divested of all clothing?"

"To show that I come before this brotherhood naked and penniless, just as the day I was born, as I am now born again through the brotherhood of the Bloodline as a fellow knight."

"My son, look at your bare feet. What do you see?

"A book of twisted lies and false prophecy."

"Then as your merciless and fearsome wrath shall pour down on the Christian and so-called holy men of this earth, so shall your urine fall upon the pages of these fraudulent bindings. Let it be done."

Minzano urinated on the Bible at his feet. After he was finished, Will Baxter, another Bloodline Knight, stepped out of the shadows in the corner of the room. He held a rod of iron, heated until it was white-hot. Baxter pressed the secret emblem of a Bloodline Knight into Minzano's flesh. Minzano heard his skin sizzle and gritted his teeth to keep from crying out. Baxter removed the brand from Minzano's arm, then cut his bicep. The pain from the brand was so great that Minzano barely noticed the sting of the blade. He watched as the Archknight placed a candle on the wet bible before speaking. The wick sputtered and began to burn.

"As your fellow knights illuminate the room, so will you illuminate the brotherhood with your strict obedience, dedication to the blood, and unrelenting execution of the ancient code. Your blood oath begins."

The Archknight soaked a cloth with the blood oozing from Minzano's bicep and passed it behind him into the darkness. Suddenly, a candle flame sputtered and grew to illuminate another robed man, his face painted black and white. It reminded Minzano of how his brother would tell him scary stories as a child, a flashlight perched below his chin to accentuate the hollows of his face. The knight slowly put the bloody cloth in his mouth.

The Archknight continued, "As your fellow knights drink of your liquid essence, all that is you is now inside the brotherhood, and all that is in the brotherhood is inside of you. These candles remind you, as do the smoldering pages at your feet, that your soul shall burn in the same manner, but a thousand fold for eternity should you ever turn your life to the evils of Christianity or spill the secrets of the brotherhood. Do you understand?"

"Yes," Minzano said. "With all my intelligence."

"Do you accept?"

"Yes, with all my soul."

"Will you protect?"

"Yes, with all my existence."

"Then I will now read the final oath. Take hold of it and walk in the presence of the light thereof, that thou may be illuminated."

CHAPTER 7

Oniva drove her gold Nissan Altima up the winding, forested road into the Meridian Place housing community. The alluring wooded acres surrounding the houses were calming and pastoral, and they were one of the reasons she had bought a home here. Rontrez followed the Altima in his Benz. Oniva was glad to be home, and relieved Rontrez was with her.

"Here we are at a Thousand Oaks again," Rontrez said. "Every time I come out here, those woods look darker and thicker. You ain't worried about the Blair Witch sneaking out of there?"

"They say there are king cobras living in these suburban woods," Oniva joked.

"Yeah, right. I'll take a king cobra and tie a knot in his ass and turn him into a necktie."

"Those woods are safe. Nothing but squirrels and deer live in there. Maybe a raccoon or two."

"That's what they told you at the real estate office. They didn't tell you about the hungry grizzly bears. I heard all the Berenstains live back there."

"There are no grizzly bears in DC."

"That's what they keep telling you to hold up the value of your property. I saw Bigfoot out there last time I was here. I think he was taking a dump or something."

Oniva laughed. "Shut up, Esau. You're scaring me. Come on, let's go to dinner."

"I don't get paid until next week." Rontrez grinned.

"Esau, you don't have a job."

"Then I definitely don't get paid till next week."

"I was treating you to dinner. It's my thank you." Oniva offered.

"I can get with that. Where are we eating?"

"Your choice."

"Let's swing by Dynasty's," he said. "I could use a good meal about now. I'm as hungry as a runaway orphan. Besides, I think you just want to be seen in your lovely, church outfit. You're trying to mess around and stumble into a husband."

She gave him the side-eye. "I'll drive, peanut head."

As Oniva started her engine and headed toward the interstate, she looked at Rontrez in the passenger seat. His body was in the car, but it was obvious his mind was not. Oniva knew he was daydreaming about being the President of the United States again.

"President Rontrez, I have to be totally honest with you."

"I can't have it any other way." Rontrez replied, climbing down from his thoughts.

"I don't want to stay with you in Baltimore."

"Why not?"

"Your neighborhood is too rough. There's always shooting and stuff going on. It's like Beirut over there. I don't feel safe. I don't know how you live up there."

"Look, when the bullets keep me up, I turn down the volume of the environment. If a bullet came near me, I'd tell it to turn around. I turn the burglars into gurglers and the winos into fine hoes. If I hear a strange noise, I'd tell it to identify itself immediately. If the noise isn't familiar, then I'm asking for ID. I'll build a house out of the homeless and tell the crime rate to bow to me."

"That's nice to know. But I'm still worried about it. I'd much rather you stay out here with me. You can sleep in my guest room and keep me safe."

"Well, dang, I'm glad I brought my clothes up here with me. You are about as predictable as yesterday and as brave as a baby squirrel."

"You're right, I'm a big chicken. But Esau, don't bring that gun in my house."

"It's a necessity, especially the way things are now. Times are unpredictable. You know that the righteous are heavily persecuted in these days of chaos. How can we have an offense with no defense? Without the item in question, we're like a herd of sheep. Prey just waiting for the predator. I refuse to play a professional victim."

Oniva glanced over at him, chewing on her bottom lip.

"Niva, you know the Bloodliners are breaking into houses and grabbing folks off the street. There's no way I'm stayin' in DC without my Glock. You've seen the news. They're animals. They have a big chapter down here. You'd rather stay near them than in my neighborhood, huh? I'll play by your rules about living arrangements, but you have to play by mine when it comes to protection. You know I don't engage in war, I elope."

"Okay, fine. Keep it. I just don't want to see it."

"Deal. Glad we could cooperate. I personally think you wanted me to bring it anyway. That little steel-phobia you are faking must be for the seatbelt."

"I have a question," Oniva said, ignoring him. "You've been unemployed for quite a while now. How do you manage to dress in those fine clothes and drive a Mercedes?"

"Girl, you're worried about the wrong things."

"I know you're not doing what you used to do, so where is the money coming from? I don't want to see you in jail, and I certainly don't want to be arrested as an accessory to some crime."

"Jail? Moi? The jailhouse is a fail house, and I am personally offended that you believe a man of my exemplary character would be seen in the general vicinity of such a place. I've been to jail, as a visitor to those less fortunate than me. To those who didn't have some of the chances I've had, or some of the talents I possess. Money doesn't grow on trees. Money grows on Esau Rontrez."

"Cut the crap, Esau. Where is the money coming from?"

"Oniva, it's coming from commissions."

"What commissions?"

"The young cats coming up wanted to get into the pleasure game. I wanted out, so I gave them my workers, and twice a month I get a percentage of what they make."

"What? You sold those women!" Oniva sucked her teeth and scowled at Rontrez.

"No. I didn't sell anything. I retired, so the women were out of work. Either they ended up crackheads, homeless, or someone's battered wife looking for love in the wrong place, or they continued to do what they do best. Don't knock their hustle. Some of them could have put you through college and graduate school. Do you know some of the women make more than lawyers? All nontaxable. Do the math."

"You're still making money on those women's backs. What kind of job security is that? What if those guys stop paying you?"

"They can't."

"Why not?"

"Because then the women stop working. Then the guys have nothing. The women aren't working for them because they want to. They're working for the new cats because I told them they need to. I didn't want the headaches anymore. The new boys don't want to kill the goose that lays golden eggs."

"How much do you get?"

"In the interest of national security, I must adhere to silence. But it's enough to treat you to dinner."

"I said I got it. It's the least I can do."

Oniva reached over and turned on the radio. A smooth hip-hop beat unfurled into the interior of the Altima.

"I feel it coming, baby," Rontrez grinned, closing his eyes. Since high school, he liked to recite impromptu rhymes off the top of his head. No rehearsal or preparation. Just the drop of a smooth beat set him to rhyming, and it was often comical. After hanging around him for so long, Oniva started to practice it, and now she considered herself as decent as Rontrez. Rontrez disagreed.

"Got an idea," Oniva said. "The winner of the flow treats the other person."

"Game on." Rontrez bobbed his head with his eyes still closed.

"You go first."

Rontrez opened his mouth and began to flow: "I bounce up in broads like basketballs, is it my solo style or is it because I'm tall? Sex in the Caravan, up in Maryland, with Carol Ann. Them ladies have a man steady telling me that they single. My dick talks while my mouth does so that means I'm bilingual. My flow remains acidic and my game stay sharp as needles. I'm in Jamaica with her cousin but she swearing that I need her. I walked through hell with arsenic draws. I spit game on the streets and dare for you to cross."

Oniva cut him off. "Time for me to testify, you just tried, you're denied. Let it slide I'm inside, you can cry, I know why. Acting like you're bullet proof, so I'll throw you off the roof. You can run but Oniva's quite speedy. You see me I'm straight 3-D. I know I'm gifted like Christmas, go head and put me on your wish list. Your princess—"

"Red light!" Rontrez yelled.

Oniva screeched to halt just as a bus crossed the intersection before them.

Rontrez grinned widely. "Dang, we almost got hit by Greyhound while you're over there, trying to go platinum. You lost because you almost killed us. And I *will* be getting appetizers."

CHAPTER 8

As he looked at the charred remains of his church, Chris Justes wept. This morning, it had been the largest and most prominent church in DC. The church he had helped build with his own hands. The bomb analyst said several plastic explosives were placed in strategic areas around the building and detonated remotely from a smart phone app. One had been placed in the pastor's office, two or more in the sanctuary, and one each in the hallway, the restrooms, and in the children's room. They were hidden in purses, musical instruments, hollowed-out Bibles, and plants, rendering them undetectable in the church environment.

The count was now official. Seventeen dead and sixty-six wounded. Children burned to blackened skeletons and many others charred beyond recognition. Justes already knew the organization that was behind this terrorist event: the Bloodline. They would pay. He would not turn the other cheek.

As Oniva wove through the crowded Georgetown area toward Dynasty's, a magic moment occurred. Her favorite song came on the radio, and she began to sing passionately along to its tune, increasing in volume until she almost drowned out the popular gospel artist, Aretha McKnight. Oniva's voice moved people. Her melody resonated within one's very being. It was magnetic.

Oniva sang a harmony to the melody of "Look to the Skies," and Rontrez remembered his mother. This was her favorite song. He drifted into his childhood memories when his mother would turn on the small stereo in the living room and sing vibrantly, her voice filling even the corners of the house and lighting them as if by magic. Rontrez used to wake up to her singing while she was cooking breakfast.

"You gotta believe . . . gotta believe . . . gotta believe in Him."

As Oniva continued to harmonize, Rontrez remembered when his mother used to drive an old Chrysler and Aretha's tape was stuck in the player for about six months. Every time she turned on the engine, Aretha McKnight's song serenaded them through the speakers. McKnight's voice flooded Rontrez's mind with memories of warmth and kindness, a mental oasis in this hostile present. Oniva's own voice accentuated these feelings – she was the only female outside of his family circle that he had ever trusted.

"He'll never leave you . . . through the storm . . . through the night . . . Grab His hand . . . hold on tight."

Rontrez felt like nothing could hurt him as he heard his mother's voice in Oniva's. He kept his eyes closed and let the moment take him to another reality. A world where there were no wars, no sadness, no hard times, and his mother was alive to enjoy it.

"Trust in Him . . . you gotta believe . . . through His love . . . you can achieve. . . Through the day . . . through the dark . . . Keep your Faith . . . inside your heart . . . "

Though Rontrez had heard the song dozens of times, he couldn't recite a single verse. As the radio station went to a commercial break, cutting the song off, Rontrez dropped from his memories like a brick onto asphalt. Oniva pulled into a parking spot near the restaurant, and they started towards the restaurant.

Oniva's eyes floated toward Nóir, an upscale clothing store that claimed to sell the finest of luxury goods, but which charged what seemed like one's unborn child for them.

Reading her mind, Rontrez spoke. "Niva, we can go in there, but you're on the clock. You have fifteen minutes before the referee calls a break in the proceedings, so we can get to eating."

"I appreciate it, ref," Oniva. Fifteen minutes was all she needed. The items were too expensive to consider buying, but it was a woman's right to browse. It would be almost unethical not to exercise her rights.

Oniva and Rontrez entered Nóir. In stark contrast to the chaos of the outside world, Noir's thick glass walls muffled all sound other than the smooth jazz that flowed through the speakers. This was a world of luxury and materialism.

Oniva walked straight to the women's shoes and gazed at them wistfully.

"Look, Esau, aren't these awesome?"

Rontrez looked at a pair of women's shoes. "I've never seen anything like them." He then looked at the price tag and chuckled. "Four hundred and fifty dollars, huh?" Rontrez pulled out a roll of cash.

"Esau, put that away!"

"I will if you stop screaming before you give someone in here a heart attack." Rontrez put his bankroll back into his jacket pocket.

"You put that money away, and I don't want to see it again. No one walking this earth needs a four-hundred-and-fifty dollar pair of shoes. Man makes the clothes; clothes don't make the man."

"Or woman. So if no one needs a pair of outrageously expensive shoes, why are you in here looking at them? I was just going to give you a token of our friendship."

"You have given me enough tokens. Why would you spend that much on a pair of shoes? You could put that toward someone's scholarship."

"My scholarship is in dollar-ship. You come in here and try these shoes on once a month, Oniva. Why not just buy them?"

"Because I can't afford them. And I don't need them. They're nice, but I couldn't ever walk out of this store wearing them."

"And why is that?"

"Because the shoes would be just the beginning. You know how it goes, brother man. First, the shoes. Then I need an outfit to go with the shoes. Then I need a purse to match the outfit that goes with the shoes. Then I need to wear this outfit and shoes somewhere, so I need to get my hair and nails done. Then I want to go out and look just as nice again, but I can't wear the same outfit, so I have to get a new one to match the shoes. The process will repeat itself when I decide to accessorize further. It's the start of a downhill path to materialism. A path I refuse to travel."

"That's a pretty interesting theory, Niva. I still think they're just overpriced shoes. Clearly overpriced, but that's the way things go these days. Everything has to be overpriced so people will think it's quality. That's another thing I'd change as President. No overpricing. You can only price things according to quality."

"And what happens when a store decides they still want to over-price? Who's to decide whether they're overpricing or not?"

"The OPC," Rontrez replied.

"The what?" Oniva laughed.

"The Overpricing Protection Committee. A subsidiary division of the Federal Trade Commission. Any establishment caught overpricing will be shut down and their merchandise seized. Think of all the problems this would solve."

"Esau, I am issuing you an official declaration of absurdity, because you are a certified fool."

"Seriously, think of the economic flow of money. Take discretionary income into consideration. If there was no overpricing, people would have more money to spend, thus strengthening our weak economy. Think of the tennis shoe companies that take five-dollar shoes, put an emblem on them, and charge over a hundred dollars a pair. Even after marketing, distribution, and all the other costs, the shoe still doesn't need to be priced anywhere near that amount to make a huge profit. They target their marketing toward poverty-stricken neighborhoods where the inhabitants can barely afford them. Think of the impact on self-esteem. No one would feel inadequate because of the way they dress. Everyone would buy what's comfortable and looks nice, not what's expensive. Teenagers would no longer feel deprived because of what they wear and would grow up into stronger individuals, both spiritually and mentally. No more teasing or bullying about clothes.

The list goes on and on for years. But you know I'm not long-winded, just recommended, and defended."

"Okay, you might have a debatable issue here."

"You know I have more than a few ideas. My mind is innovating twenty-five hours a day. The extra hour is to shake the haters off."

"And all of them are thoroughly amusing, Esau. Please tell me another one as I walk out this store and away from temptation. And I don't come in here once a month. This is only my third time."

"But the store has only been open for two weeks," Rontrez joked. Nóir had been around for years.

"Be quiet, clown. You'll be the first jester in the White House."

"And the next bill I will create and pass is that child molesters and child abusers get both their hands cut off. That way, they can't even beat the child who reported them."

"Makes sense to me," Oniva agreed.

"Yes, and one more. All crooked cops are to be put under the jailhouse, with the other worms, and the penalty for their criminal act is to be tripled. Cops are supposed to serve and protect the innocent from the criminals. If they are the criminals, then not only are they stealing taxpayers' money, but they're helping the criminals, further oppressing the innocent, and simultaneously placing the people in severe danger by actually heightening crime. Therefore, they get three times the penalty."

Oniva smiled, amused. "Let's go eat, fool."

CHAPTER 9

"Today will be different. Today is of great consequence." Chris Justes looked seriously at his wife as they finished their morning prayer. Each morning, their living room was a private sanctuary for worship and meditation.

"Did God speak to you again this morning?" Mary asked.

Justes nodded. "Not in the usual way, though. Today, it's a particular sensitivity – an awareness."

"What does it tell you?"

"That today is serious. Today will never be forgotten."

Mary was silent, and turned on the television just in time to see a shocking news report.

The United States had been attacked. As soon as the bombing occurred over Langley, VA, a strike began on key military installations across the globe. A conglomerate of over eleven countries revealed themselves. Vietnam, China, Japan, Afghanistan, Iran, Russia, Germany, Iraq, Italy, Romania, North and South Korea, Austria, Hungary, and several other smaller insurgent nations were part of the alliance.

"Chris, look!" Mary gasped. "We missed this because of our media fast yesterday."

Justes looked at the screen with disbelief as it displayed the pandemonium that had spread since only the day before.

"I thought today was the big day," Mary said quizzically. "This happened yesterday."

Justes nodded thoughtfully. "Today will be a momentous occasion. What you see is not even the tip of the iceberg."

"Is this why you insisted I go grocery shopping two days ago, just before the fast? So I didn't have to deal with *that*?" Mary motioned to the TV, flooded with reports of riots and anarchy. Grocery stores nationwide were faced with stampedes, violence, and looting as shoppers fought each other over as little as a box of cereal.

Justes nodded. "I'm just a servant. I didn't save you from anything. I just passed a message. I didn't want to worry you."

If he put society's plunge into absolute chaos out of his mind, Justes thought that the morning was particularly serene. Almost perfect. Rustling green leaves framed the soft clouds suspended in the seemingly endless blue sky. Tranquility seemed abundant, as if this moment were an oasis within the chaotic world.

Suddenly, the sky darkened. A large white cloud appeared, bringing with it a deep sense of serenity. Though it was hard to estimate its size because of its brilliance, the cloud seemed as big as a planet, and it lit up the sky brighter than day. As the cloud brightened, the world around them went quiet, as if blanketed by a layer of temperate serenity. Justes watched, awestruck, as thousands of balls of light shot out from the radiant cloud in all directions. Mary looked on next to him as these balls morphed into winged beings with long, golden trumpets, and the beings descended to the earth.

Across the world, everyone froze. Indescribably, Justes understood that every soul on the planet was now aware of the shining phenomenon. Traffic stopped on roads all over the world, and people fell silent midsentence to watch the cloud descend lower to the earth. As the beings of great light floated towards Earth, they assembled opposite themselves into a sloped horizontal formation, floating in the air silently at attention, almost like the two rails of an invisible slide. The formation seemed to indicate: "We have come to change this world. Special Delivery."

Without an audible sound, the light inside the cloud began to speak directly to the minds of all who watched, its gentle voice emanating love and compassion. Justes studied the bright cloud and listened intently as it spoke.

"Behold, I am the Son of Man. Fear me not, for all knew this day would come. I am not here to bring vengeance. I am here to spread peace and love amongst the living."

Justes and Mary ran outside to get a better look. As the angelic beings stepped to the ground, the countless angels blew their horns at once, creating a thunderous but wondrous musical chorus. The world stopped what they were doing and looked toward the skies as the Son of Man spoke again. "For all who may doubt," he said, "I deliver unto you the prophet Elijah who upon my word will restore peace and prosperity to this region upon man. I will send my messenger, who will prepare the way before me and the Lord you seek. Then suddenly I will come to his temple; the angel of judgment, whom you may or may not desire, will come."

Mary didn't understand how she could hear the brilliant cloud. She looked to her husband for his response. She expected something cool, thought provoking, and deep. Justes said only, "See, I told you today would be different."

The voice continued: "I say unto all, when you are taken and given up to be judged, do not be troubled about what to say: but whatever is given to you in that hour, say, because it is not you who say it, but the Holy Spirit who dwells within you. Judgment is swift and permanent, and the unclean shall be rebuked. Elijah will take his seat, testing and cleansing the sons of the first breath of life, burning away the dross from them as from gold and silver, so that he and his followers may make offerings to the Lord in righteousness."

Justes closed his eyes in order to focus on the message.

"And I will come near to you to judge those who have been untrue in married life. I will bear witness against those who take false oaths, who keep back from the servant his payment, and those who are hard on the widow and the child without a father. Have no fear of me, I say, but fear the Lord of armies."

Two angels emerged from the cloud, bearing a man of flesh, and the cloud began to ascend into the sky. The Son of Man spoke his last words before leaving sight.

"From the days of your fathers you have turned away from my rules and have not kept them. Return to me, and I will return to you. And you will be named happy by all nations for you will be in a land of delight. For you see, the Day of Judgment is coming; it is burning like an oven. All the men of pride and all who do evil will be dry stems of grass, and in the day which is coming they will be burned up till they have not a root or branch. But to you who give worship to my name, the sun of righteousness will come up with new life in its wings, and you will go out, playing like young oxen full of grain."

Just as the being came, it was gone. Where it was day, the sun reappeared, and where it was night, the moon shone vibrant once again.

"Is this for real?" Oniva asked Rontrez. "You heard that too, right?"

Rontrez emerged from his silent moment of reflection. "Yeah. Heard everything. Saw the shiny talking cloud too. It's a new day."

"I really don't believe I just saw God come back down from the heavens, drop his boy off, and dip out," Oniva replied.

"New Sheriff," Rontrez answered.

Oniva looked astonished. "This is crazy. I have to call mom."

She picked up the phone and put her ear to the receiver. "The phone is dead."

"That's because the world just went crazy." Rontrez looked out the window at the sky. "Everyone is trying to use the phone right now to confirm that our fragile reality has just been shattered. But that might be the least of our worries. I might have to stop taxing. I need to totally rethink this salvation thing."

Justes looked out from his living room window and ran his fingers through his hair. He could barely believe it.

"Am I insane? Did we just see what I think we saw?" He looked to his wife for reassurance. Though he had known this day would come, somehow he never figured that the time would feel so mundane, so earthly – a few minutes past seven AM on June 6.

The Son of Man spoke once again from out of sight, seemingly for the benefit of those who still stood paralyzed with amazement.

"I have held back the locusts from wasting the fruits. I have given you rule over the fish of the sea, over the birds of the air, over the cattle of the land, and over every living thing. I have given you every plant producing seed and allowed them to prosper and grow so you may feed yourselves. I have held back the storms and wind from leaving not one stone resting upon another. I have kept the sea at bay from uprisings threatening to wipe your land clean. What I ask is that you follow my servant."

"He's giving everyone a second chance." It made sense to Justes. God was kind and loving. But then again, it didn't make sense at all.

He thought back to what he had told little Andrew two days earlier in Sunday school: *If God told us exactly when he was coming back, we might act up until the minute he came back, then we'd be little angels when he was ready to pass judgment. That's not the way God wants us to live our lives. He wants us to obey all of his commandments whether he's coming next week, next month, or next year.*

But now it seemed as though the Lord was doing the exact opposite. Justes knew better than to question the Lord, but a part of him could not help wondering: if the plan was to take everyone up to heaven, then what was the point of faith? He looked to his wife, who stared back at him with the same curiosity.

"The time of peace has finally come, Mary," Justes whispered.

"How long do you think until he comes back?" Mary asked.

"According to Revelation 20, verses five through seven, it's going to be a thousand years or so."

Justes suddenly thought back to another moment in Sunday school, when Philip had asked, *"Why doesn't God say he's going to come in the year 2035, but really come in 2040? That way we will be good for free."* Justes had replied, *"That's not the way God works. He is not here to deceive."* But wasn't that what the Lord was doing? How could he reconcile Scripture with what he had just witnessed?

"A thousand years?" Mary asked.

Justes nodded. "There have been thousands of interpretations of this passage. In my opinion, some translations are out in left field. I remember one movie whose plot was that Satan could be let loose at any time after any random set of one thousand years had ended. I don't think that's the case. Anyone who knows the Bible will tell you, there will be a thousand years of peace before Satan is released," (Revelation 20:1-6).

"What does the book of Revelation say?"

"It talks about the second coming, mostly. Some of the blessed reign with Christ for a thousand years, but many of the dead do not come to life again till the thousand years were finished – until the second resurrection," (Revelation 20:4-7).

"But what exactly does Revelation say, Chris?"

Chris Justes took his Bible from the nightstand and thumbed through its pages. "Revelation 20, verses six and seven. Here we go: 'Blessed and holy are those who share in the first resurrection. The second death has no power over them, but they will be priests of God and of Christ and will reign with him for a thousand years. When the thousand years are over, Satan will be released from his prison'. Then, in chapter 21, God says He will create a new heaven and a new earth, removing certain vile elements, so that righteousness may truly shine."

"So Satan's not coming out of his prison yet?"

"I'm not sure. According to the Bible, we're supposed to have a thousand years of peace first, but that has never happened in human history. Our Lord is supposed to rule for a thousand years. This is my interpretation of the Bible, but I'm only a man. I've been wrong before. Satan could rise tomorrow. Only God knows for sure."

"I thought the Lord was coming like a thief in the night. It's still morning," (1 Thessalonians 5:2).

"It's night somewhere in the world. Besides, it's a metaphor," Justes smiled.

"Was the prophet in the Bible too?" Mary asked.

"Yes – in fact, the cloud referenced it directly. He said, 'I will send my messenger, who will prepare the way before me. Then suddenly the Lord you are seeking will come to his temple,' or something like that. It's in Malachi. The cloud even spoke of the angel of agreement, or the angel of Judgment. I hadn't quite interpreted the meaning the way it was just presented. Then again, there are lots of interpretations. Everything that's happening right now is foretold in the Bible. Wars, rumors of wars, earthquakes, famines, revolutions. And the merciless persecution of Christians, such as what happened at our church. The Bible also speaks of a general increase in moral bankruptcy. This is also happening," (Malachi 3:1, Matthew 24:6-9, 2 Timothy 3:1-5).

Mary picked up her own Bible and stroked the worn cover. "I should know this. How many Bible studies have I taught? Does the Bible say Elijah is coming back?"

Justes thumbed to the book of Malachi. "It says here that the prophet Elijah will be sent before the Lord's coming. It also says that the day was greatly to be feared. A day when evildoers will be burned up."

Mary sat down on the bed. "What is Elijah supposed to do?"

"Specifically, he's supposed to turn parents' hearts to their children and children's hearts to their parents. Families will be restored. But if the people refuse, God will bring destruction," (Malachi 4:1-6).

Mary was silent, considering the gravity of what they had just witnessed.

"In the Bible, Elijah never actually dies. Instead, he's taken up to heaven by a giant wind," (2 Kings 2:11). Justes closed his Bible and sighed. "I guess he's here for round two. I wonder where he is."

"I'm still confused," Mary said, and snuggled under her husband's arm.

A knock sounded on Oniva's apartment door. She glanced at the clock on her nightstand and put on her robe. Who on earth would be knocking on her door this early in the morning?

Oniva walked to the door. "Who is it?"

There was no response. She looked through the peephole, but saw only the empty stoop. She turned to go back to bed, but someone pounded on the door with such force that the frame rattled. Oniva looked through the peephole again, but still she saw nothing. A shudder of fear shot up her spine.

"Well, woman, who is it bringing all that ruckus?" Rontrez groggily poked his head out of the guest room door.

"I don't see anyone."

Rontrez thought back to his hustling days, when an unexpected knock at his home meant trouble. People coming to kill him, rob him, or maybe just someone trying to get even for something he didn't even remember. Nobody like that would knock on Oniva's door.

"Stop that damn racket!" Rontrez shouted. He walked to the door and threw it open.

Standing before him was a tall, older man clad in a coarse cloth robe, unfamiliar to both of them. He had short, black hair, a thick beard, and wise, dark eyes.

Rontrez looked him over before speaking. "Are you looking for the Ark? What's with the wizard robe, Gandalf?" Rontrez looked to Oniva. "Who is this guy?"

"I am Elijah the prophet," the stranger said.

"What? You're the cat God just dropped off?" Rontrez scratched his head. Oniva peeked around her friend's shoulder.

"Yes. I am the Lord's servant, here to deliver this land unto peace and prosperity."

"How do I know you're not some nut dressed up like Moses?"

"Would you like me to do a magic trick? I am shocked that there is still doubt amongst man."

"Oh, I have faith in no man. Man will let you down every time. Do a miracle or something."

Elijah stepped closer to Rontrez and spoke softly in his ear. "Esau Rontrez, if you do not stop taxing, you will catch a disease for which there is no cure."

For a moment, Rontrez was silent. "Do I know you?"

"No, but the Lord knows all."

"Do something else. Tell me something that only Kelly and I know," Rontrez said pointing at Oniva.

"Her name is Oniva Mering, not Kelly, and I know all about you, Esau. In your spare time you daydream about being the president of the United States. The Overpricing Protection Committee might actually do some good. That other idea from last week would be tough. It will be very hard to legalize marijuana nationwide, my son. The billion-dollar tobacco companies will continue to fight tooth and nail to stop that from happening."

"That makes sense. Who wants to smoke a cigarette when you can get high?"

"Very good, Esau."

"What can I do for you?" Rontrez asked.

"I need to be taken to the leader of this kingdom."

"Well, he's downtown. Let me get dressed. Oniva, you want to come with me to take the prophet to Pennsylvania Avenue?"

Oniva, speechless with awe, nodded, backed into her bedroom, and shut the door. She had no idea how Rontrez could be so nonchalant about a true to life prophet knocking on her door. Then again, Rontrez seemed to be cool about everything.

Once they were ready, Rontrez picked up his keys, and the three of them walked outside and climbed into the Mercedes. It seemed that Elijah knew which vehicle to walk to before Rontrez even started toward it.

Rontrez started the engine and pulled out of the parking lot. He looked in his mirror at Oniva in the backseat. She hadn't said a word since Elijah showed up at her door.

Though the car was silent, Elijah looked at Rontrez and said, "Esau, do you know that hardcore rap music can tear your spirit in half?"

"Yeah? I guess I better take care of business, then. I didn't really think it was that deep, Elijah."

"Deeper than you can imagine."

"A little rhythm and blues moves me now and then." Rontrez grinned at the prophet.

"It moves you in the wrong direction. Trap music could trap your spirit."

Oniva, sensing a possible debate between Rontrez and the prophet, stepped in. "Elijah, I have a question for you."

"Yes, Oniva."

"Why is there so much suffering in the world? Poverty, diseases, violent crimes, wars, and all those things. I know everything happens for a reason, but I don't understand why suffering is so extreme right now."

"That's a fair question, Oniva. I do not sense hostility in your spirit, but curiosity, which indicates that you are eager to learn. Suffering happens for a number of reasons. Most suffering comes from man's foolishness. For example, fault lines are necessary to keep the earth from falling apart. But when people construct buildings upon fault lines, they inevitably suffer when an earthquake comes. Man knows of floods and high tides, but yet for profit builds homes by the water."

"How do we end the suffering?" Oniva asked.

"We can either cooperate and accommodate nature, or we will be destroyed by it. Many sicknesses, too, are manmade. Some because of improper nutrition. People do not eat right. God gives us natural sugar, but man bleaches it to make it white. We eat white bread, when whole wheat is much better for us. We are given natural fruits and vegetables, but man boils away their nutrients. People squeeze the juice out of oranges and throw away the pulp, which is the good part. Cigarettes, alcohol, and drugs harm the body's temple in dozens of ways."

"Are you saying it's our own fault we're suffering?" Oniva asked.

"Oniva, eighty percent of the illnesses in most of the world are caused when the mind and body interact in the wrong ways. People literally worry themselves to death over careers and worldly things. Now examine the technology you have developed. If there were no cars, there would be no car accidents. If there were no industry, there would be little air pollution. Instead of talking with each other, individuals are now dependent on technology."

"How do you mean?"

"People used to talk, but now all their interactions are mediated by the internet. Many people just text and tweet. Social media gives you a massive shallow network of 'friends', but no depth and no devotion or fellowship. The emergence of this new kind of relationship promotes viewing individuals as something other than a kindred spirit to be loved."

"Deep insight. What about worldwide poverty and hunger?"

"Another good question. There is enough money and enough food on this planet to feed, clothe, educate, and assist everyone on Earth a dozen times over. Even when the technology you create benefits humanity, it is privatized and withheld. Your resources are ill-distributed. Look at the environment. Man has disturbed the ecological system so terribly that the balance in nature has been all but destroyed. Look at manmade diseases: AIDS—"

"AIDS is a manmade disease?" Rontrez asked.

You know about sexually transmitted diseases, don't you, Esau.

Elijah paused. "All things shall be revealed to you in time, Esau Rontrez."

"What about crime?" Rontrez waved his hand in the air. "Why do innocent people get caught up in the rugged, the rough, and the real? Look how messed up everything is."

"Esau, God has given man a certain amount of freedom. Some suffering is a result of this freedom. If you and Oniva were simply robots, or automations, then you could be programmed or forced to do what is right. But then, to follow God and have faith would not be a choice. God gives man the free will to stay with Him or rebel against Him. Hence, we have crime. Evil has a tendency to multiply itself, and many evils lurk in the hearts of men."

Don't you agree, Esau?

"How'd you do that?" Rontrez asked.

"How did I do what?" Elijah answered.

"You know. You can talk without opening your mouth. You asked me if I agreed. I heard you as clear as I heard them trumpets a while ago."

"There are more types of communication than you will know in your lifetime, Esau. It is not of great importance right now. What is important is that you can hear and understand me."

"There is our stop," Elijah said, pointing to the White House. "Drop me off here. I'll be fine."

Oniva gasped. "How did we get here so fast?" The drive to downtown DC, which usually took twenty-five minutes, had taken only five. They looked back at Elijah for an explanation. Somehow, the prophet had exchanged his cloth robe for a sharp, hand-tailored suit. Elijah looked sharp.

"Can you teach me to change clothes like Clark Kent too?"

I didn't change clothes, Esau. I changed your eyes.

CHAPTER 10

By noon Elijah had appeared on television, making major news. Out of all the people claiming to be Elijah, somehow *this* Elijah managed to make it inside the White House and onto national TV.

Most people stayed home from work. Everyone's eyes, including those of Oniva and Rontrez, were glued to their televisions, watching Elijah share his plans with the public. The prophet appointed heads of state and implemented the United States' smartchip system worldwide. There would be no more robberies or killings over a purse or a wallet. Those people who went against the Word of God could be easily found.

"I don't care what he says. I'm not getting a chip in my head," Rontrez said to Oniva.

What's wrong, Esau? You don't want to be found?

Rontrez spoke back to Elijah in his mind: *If you need me, you know where I stay.* He turned to Oniva, but decided not to tell her what he had heard in his thoughts.

Chris Justes stared at his television screen in amazement. Elijah had stopped all wars in a matter of hours. He initiated a cashless society and crushed the Bloodliners by sending the authorities their names and addresses. It turned out that some of the most powerful and devout members of the Christian society were far up in the Bloodline hierarchy. Members were imprisoned without any trials.

Amidst throngs of followers, Elijah greeted his supplicants and publically healed the sick and the blind by the thousands, including those paralyzed from birth. He performed other curative miracles for the public including a celebrated relationship with the National Breast Cancer Foundation. Elijah humbly walked down the street in DC, with the thousands of breast cancer patients he had instantly cured simply by touching them. Many had been diagnosed with terminal cancer before being healed. All of the patients gave personal testimonials, praising Elijah. He instructed his followers to begin work on a statue in his likeness.

The prophet eliminated all taxes and tariffs before he laid out a plan for the distribution of all monetary funds. It baffled economists. The plan seemed to be a derivative of socialism, where the government controls most of the funds and distributes them equally, serving the needs of all people at one time. He created a classless society, without hierarchy, but still allowed personal property, and did not seize control of production. He integrated the government with the church. No more poverty or war. Peace reigned.

⋯⋯•◦●●━━━ ⬤⬤⬤ ━━━●◦•⋯⋯⋯

"Boy, he didn't waste any time cleaning up society." Mary set down a glass of orange juice in front of her husband.

Justes was silent as Elijah spoke directly into the camera, his gaze piercing. "Peace has settled upon the world through your cooperation. By tomorrow the nations and kingdoms will be as one, and every living man, woman, and child should have a chip implanted in his or her brow or hand. There will be no more starvation. The chip will allow everyone to pay for their needs. My servants and I have wasted no time in transforming the old earth into a new earth. I will wipe every tear from your eyes. There will be no more death, or mourning

49

or crying or pain, for the old order has passed away. I make all things new. Write this down, for these words are trustworthy and true. It is done. I am the First and the Last, the Beginning and the End. All shall now work seven days a week to restore the new earth in all its fullness. All shall work and enjoy the fruits of every laborer."

Mary looked at Justes. "On the news this morning I saw that some people were not happy about Elijah. What do you think will happen to them?"

Justes silently gestured to the screen. "For those who oppose me: The cowardly, the unbelieving, the vile, the murderers, the sexually immoral, those who practice magic arts, the idolaters and all liars — they will be consigned to the fiery lake of burning sulfur."

CHAPTER 11

Rontrez awoke suddenly from his sleep. He felt a presence in the room, but it was too dark to see. Reaching over to his bedside table, he quickly pulled out his Glock pistol and gently removed the safety. The gun was ready to fire.

"Oniva, is that you?"

Silence.

Rontrez turned on the bedside lamp, partially illuminating the room. He saw the outline of a woman in front of his bed. His sleepy eyes adjusted to the dim light. It was Lisa, the woman he had met outside Oniva's church. She was wearing lacy red lingerie and her body glistened in the light of the lamp. Her curves aroused Rontrez immediately. Her sensual fragrance filled the room, tantalizing him further.

"Hey, what are you doing over here? It's two in the morning. I could have shot you."

"I heard you were a night owl. Oniva let me in. Sorry to wake you, baby."

"It's been a busy day."

"Turn the light off for a minute, baby. And close your eyes."

Mumbling tersely that she almost had gotten herself shot, Rontrez complied, putting his pistol safely back in the drawer. He soon felt Lisa slide underneath the covers from the foot of the bed, then moments later felt a sensuous warmth around his manhood. Rontrez opened his eyes to see Lisa's head bobbing up and down underneath the covers, so graceful as to seem professional. Lisa's hand and mouth aggressively stroked and teased Rontrez until he let his bodily fluids ooze into her mouth. Lisa did not stop after the fluid entered her mouth, but only became more aggressive. Rontrez grabbed his pillow and pressed it over his face, hoping Oniva couldn't hear him screaming. Lisa gradually slowed to a halt as Rontrez became soft again. Without a word, she got up, went into the bathroom and came back with a warm red washcloth to clean Rontrez with.

"How was it?" she asked smiling.

Rontrez felt as if he were truly in another world—relaxed, calm, comfortable, and definitely pleasantly surprised. "Look, kitten, just tell me when the wedding is, and I will be there in my tux."

Lisa smiled suggestively. "I'm glad you enjoyed it. I didn't think I was going to get that whole thing in my mouth, Esau."

"Just tilt your head to the side, baby. It works every time."

"I have to go now. I have to be up for work tomorrow morning," Lisa winked.

"I thought you were scared to leave your house. I'm glad you overcame that fear."

"I decided to take your advice. I can't live life in fear."

"You're a soldier. All you need is fatigues and a battle helmet."

Lisa smiled and started down the steps. Although she brought a small bag with her, Rontrez noticed she didn't get dressed before heading downstairs.

"Call me when you get in," Rontrez said to her.

"We'll definitely be in touch," Lisa answered, already out of sight.

The next morning, Rontrez woke up to the smell of an omelet and pancakes. Oniva knew that was his favorite meal.

"Way to go, champ," Rontrez said coming down the steps.

"I thought it was the least I could do for your companionship, slim," Oniva answered. "It's almost ready."

"I'm not talking about eggs, woman. I'm talking about the promotion you earned last night."

"Promotion? What are you talking about?"

"Hear ye, hear ye. Thou hast hereby been declared archbishop of my inner circle of friends. Effective immediately. Thou hast been knighted…Withforth."

"Why is that?"

"Why do you think? For letting Lisa up in here last night. Tell her she is welcome here anytime. I mean absolutely anytime."

"I didn't let anyone in here last night, I went to sleep. You must have been dreaming."

"Be for real, Niva. Lisa was up in this palace last night taking care of business."

"She was?"

"Yeah she was. She said you let her in."

"Shut up, stupid," Oniva was laughing now, "See, that's how rumors get started."

"What are you laughing at? I'm not lying, she was here. She said you let her in."

"So," Oniva smirked, "What happened after she came to the door butt naked? She went upstairs and rocked your world, I suppose." Oniva tilted her head sideways in disbelief.

"Something like that."

"I know you have dexterity with the women, but never that," Oniva remarked.

"Why not? Am I not gifted with magnetic appeal flowing through my ambrosial veins?"

"Have you even spoken to Lisa yet, blockhead?" Oniva asked.

"Nope."

"Well then, your lie isn't even making sense. How does she know where I stay? She's never been here. And furthermore, I guarantee you Lisa did not come down here by herself at – hold on, what time was this?"

"Around two A.M."

"Two A.M!" Oniva broke out in laughter. "Lisa is home in bed by ten on weeknights. And as for sex, not a chance. Lisa doesn't sleep around."

"She was here last night, and I didn't say we had sex."

"Oral sex?" Oniva exploded with laughter again, "Oh, this just gets better and better. Nonstop comedy at its climax. Oh, you fool. Shut up and eat."

"It's the truth," Rontrez insisted.

"Look, shut up about my friend. You're getting on my nerves now. Eat before your food gets cold."

Rontrez started to fix his plate, but couldn't help but mumble a final remark. "Hey, Niva. Your friend was absolutely spectacular. You need to take some notes or something. Bet you won't ever have a problem finding a man in life."

"Not that I do now, bozo the clown. So where is Lisa now, if she was so spectacular?"

"She left. She said she had to be to work in the morning."

"Um, Pinocchio, your nose is now all the way out to the neighbor's living room, trespassing in their personal space. Lisa doesn't have a job, she's in graduate school full-time."

"For real?"

"Yes, for real, Aesop. You need to stop spinning those fables before your tongue rots out. To think that Lisa drove over here from across town at two AM, sucked on you, then dipped out the door and drove back across town is totally ridiculous. It's a 25 minute drive each way, Esau. It was funny at first, but now it's not. You have played it out, and played yourself along with it. Besides, I'm sure if Lisa was over here, you would be the one with your head down south, Mr. Nasty."

"Girl, you indecent. Not as raw as Lisa, though."

"That's it! You have one more time to try me before you pluck my last nerve and I become devious. I'm not kidding. Don't try me."

"Yes, I see. You even have your serious face on." Rontrez playfully mimicked Oniva's grin.

Oniva tried to hold back a laugh but couldn't. "Stop it, Aesop," Oniva laughed.

"Stop calling me Aesop."

"Stop telling fables, then. Lisa's a sweet woman. I didn't like it when you were demeaning her like that. Well, it was funny at first because it was you, but it dried out quickly."

"I bet it wasn't as dry as these pancakes," Rontrez winked. The pancakes were delicious.

"That's it, Aesop. You're busted."

Oniva pulled out her smartphone from her pocket. She didn't have Lisa's number memorized, but that didn't matter to her now. She began to search online and through her contacts to find Lisa's number.

"Call Lisa," Oniva said to her phone hoping it displayed Lisa's number. It didn't work.

"No, you don't even have to beg your phone for information or be all on the internet going insane. I'll give you the number myself." Rontrez found her contact information in his phone, handed it to Oniva, and walked back to the table to finish his omelet.

"Dial, chump," Rontrez grinned.

After two rings, Lisa's voice echoed through the speakerphone. "Hello?" Rontrez put his index finger to his lips, signaling to Oniva not to say a word.

"Good morning, may I speak to Lisa?" Rontrez asked.

"This is she."

"This is Esau. I just wanted to tell you what a wonderful time I had last night. You are definitely the prize."

"Esau who?"

Oniva struggled to contain her laughter.

"From last night. Oniva's friend."

"Oh, from yesterday, after church. I'm sorry, Esau. I'm a little tired. My mind's not with it just yet this morning. Long night."

"Yes indeed," Rontrez replied, grinning to Oniva.

"Yeah. I was studying all night for my Theory of Finance final exam. I'm about to step out of the door right now. I'm sorry I couldn't place the voice. I'm just exhausted, Esau, and you sound really far away. I hope you don't have me on speakerphone. Anyway, I'm going to go take this final, come back here and sleep for ten hours. I will call you when I awaken from my well-deserved slumber."

"You're not going to work this morning?"

"Nope. I'm in graduate school. It's very demanding, I don't have time for a job. Barely any time for a social life."

"I'm sure you can pencil me in somewhere."

"I'll try. It would be good to at least see you."

"That would be great, looking forward to it. Take care until then."

"Goodbye," Lisa replied, "and please don't put me on speakerphone anymore, I can barely hear you."

Rontrez hung up, stunned, as Oniva looked at him with disgust. He went upstairs, desperately looking for any evidence that Lisa had been there. There, on the floor beside his bed, was a small rag, still wet. It was the red washcloth Lisa had used to clean him off.

CHAPTER 12

Only two days later, Elijah and his army had already completed miraculous feats of labor. The nation-state as it once was defined ceased to exist. Every head of state had been taken down, and Elijah's armies quickly overcame those dictatorships that resisted. He brought about a peaceful resolution in the Middle East. Particularly impressive was his charismatic negotiation of the Israeli-Palestinian conflict. Elijah had granted fair use of water rights, preservation of historical landmarks, right of free passage, while taking a zero tolerance policy in regards to the violation of human rights. He had promptly designated heads of state to take over the conquered territories, and had even created a flag for *The New Order of the Age,* commonly referred to as the New Global Order by the media. He had used the American symbols from the back of the one dollar bill: on one side of the flag was the pyramid, and on the opposite side, the eagle.

Even in the end times, there was still merchandising. One TV network even tried to make an Elijah reality TV show. 'Elijah' t-shirts, sweaters, tennis shoes, bumper stickers, and even an Elijah brand of clothing was launched. The Elijah jacket had a gaudy, golden E on the back of it, and the new global flag emblem on the front. Even mugs and key chains had been created to make a dollar – or smart-chip credit, that is. The economic system as it once was, was now extinct. There was no paper currency anywhere that was worth anything. Everything was done by smartchip, which Elijah's armies had delivered to three quarters of the world in two days. A colossal statue had been created in the image of Elijah and erected in Washington, DC, in very close proximity to the White House, and people from all over the world flocked to it. It was built in the well-kept grassy plaza just north of Pennsylvania Avenue, in Lafayette Square. It was now the most famous tourist attraction in the world.

Elijah once again appeared before the entire world, this time on his own TV network. The Bloodliners were still held in captivity waiting to be executed, and the heads of state Elijah appointed claimed they would stop any rebellion that threatened the new world peace. Religion had almost standardized to a form of Elijah worship – not by any move of the prophet, but because everyone now believed. Elijah and his ministers had healed thousands of the sick, blind, and wounded, and the world welcomed him and his vision with eager, open arms.

Justes walked to his desk, sat down, and started to pray for the second time that morning. He prayed for direction, and prayed for the Father to give him instructions on how he could assist in the plans of the Coming. Upon speaking with the Lord, he received a strange sense that something was not right. He opened his eyes suddenly, and turned back his clock to the exact time and date the Son of Man appeared. On his digital clock before him was the nightmare, plain as day. He grabbed his Bible and turned to the book of Ecclesiastes, then turned to chapter three. His eyes widened in shock. He then turned to Second Corinthians, chapter 11 verses thirteen and fourteen. After reading the passages, Justes ran to the bathroom and vomited. Kneeling on the bathroom floor, he looked upwards and whispered, "Heaven help us."

Vincent Minzano glared at the council before him. He had called an emergency meeting and insisted that all the administration be in attendance. Minzano, one of the best undercover agents in existence, had penetrated societies from underground gangs to Mafia clans. Now, as they all knew, he was a well-respected member of the Bloodline, or what the papers called "the Bloodliners".

"We have a problem, gentlemen. A serious fucking problem," Minzano started.

"What is it, Agent Minzano?" Leo-Shey Caviant, the director of the FBI, asked.

"This prophet guy, Elijah, is appointing the heads of state like it's going out of style. All the heads of state have two things in common."

"What are those?"

"One, they all report directly to him. Two, they are all Archknights or above in the Bloodline hierarchy."

"The Bloodline has been caught. They are in an underground prison at an undisclosed location," Caviant retorted.

"No, Leo. That's what I'm trying to tell you. All the people that Elijah reported that were supposedly down the Bloodline, I've never heard of them or seen them. I know all the knights. I've met several of the Archknights. The men he is appointing to the heads of state are definitely deep down the Bloodline. I've met them! The people in prison are legitimate Christian leaders."

"What are you trying to say, Minzano?" Caviant asked.

"I'm saying that this prophet is as crooked as a candy cane. I'm not a religious man, but it doesn't take a genius to see what the hell is going on here."

"Are you saying Elijah is down the Bloodline?"

"No. I'm saying the Bloodline is down Elijah. If we don't act now, we will never have a chance to get this situation back under control. Within two days, Elijah has taken control of the entire world's government and economy. This man is now the president of the Earth, and I promise his intentions are not godly, even if there is such a thing."

"I assume you have evidence to substantiate this."

"His affiliation with the Bloodline proves this. You know what I had to do at my birth into Bloodline knighthood. I had to piss on the Bible, Leo! How can you tell me this man is of God when he appoints the Bloodline to help him rule? Listen to the wiretaps. Look at the pictures I've submitted from the Bloodline family. They are the same people this fraud is appointing to lead his New Global Order."

"Did you not see the man come out of the sky?" Caviant asked.

Minzano was silent.

"Did you not hear trumpets?"

"Yes, I heard them, but I also know that the Bloodline Archknights are now in charge of the nation. Leo, we're not asking enough questions here. How can one man end the world as we know it in two days? How did he get smartchips into three quarters of the people on the earth in a day and a half? How did he build a hundred foot statue in two days? How did he repair and revolutionize the economy in forty eight hours? Where did he get an army from? He just got here! How does he know who to appoint to the heads of state? He took over more than 10 dictatorship countries that gave him resistance! He fought ten wars in two days, while organizing the rest of his order. One man can't do that. Especially not while he is on TV, on his own TV network. We just let him lock up some of the most prominent Christian leaders in the world, and we don't even know where they are. We just let him do it. I admit it, someone does not come out of the sky every day, but we are ignoring our common sense here."

Caviant paused before responding. "As far as I can see, the man has brought peace to the nation and to the world. As far as any eye can see there is nothing but peace. Do you know that within the last two days not a single crime was reported worldwide? That has never happened in the history of human existence."

"Not a single crime has been reported because we're too blind to recognize it. He's committing all the crime! The man has put people on death row with no trial, and we let him. How did he spread the smartchip system across the world? How did he do it so fast? How can the entire globe now be under the dictatorship of a man nobody knows? Because he fell from the sky, we have given him absolute power over our existence."

"Minzano, what you are saying is ridiculous. Have you ever actually read the Bible? I mean, before you urinated on it."

"No."

"I have, and everything in Revelation is happening verbatim. A prophecy about the end times is written, and now the prophecy is coming true. The very little known first coming has arrived, Vincent. In Revelation 11, Two Witnesses are appointed by God, and they stand before the Lord of the Earth. They have great power. Even hundreds of years before now, many people believed that Elijah is to be one of the two witnesses. In the Bible he did not die, but was taken up to heaven in a whirlwind. Revelation 11 also states the witnesses would be dressed in sackcloth, which is what Elijah was wearing the day he appeared. And that anyone who tries to harm these witnesses will be destroyed," (Revelation 11:1-5).

"You mean destroyed like anyone going after the New Global Order?"

"Yes. Personally, I am mesmerized by Elijah. The man has taken the worst times we have ever seen and changed them into the most peaceful times we have ever known. Who cares if he changed the economy and made everyone get a smartchip? No one can rob anyone if there is no money to take. He has given every person over 18 an allowance through the smartchips. He has single-handedly eliminated the concept of poverty. So he built a statue. Heck, I would too, if I were a prophet. And the dictators he ran over were merciless, greedy, immoral tyrants who oppressed those who could not defend themselves. If I could have been there to help him run them through, I would have. All the respectable countries went along with the program. Everyone saw and heard the Son of Man. How can you question his methods?"

Aaron Bryant, Minzano's direct supervisor, cut in. "Vincent, I think you have gone too deep down the Bloodline. They have brainwashed you into a real part of the Antichrist. I think you should relax and step back. Disappear for a minute if you need to. This has gone too far. You are disputing God."

"He's not God!" Minzano shouted. "This guy is bending us over right now. There is only one reason you bend someone over – to screw them! He is bending the entire globe over the bed rail. He's not using Vaseline, he's not using a condom, and gentlemen, and I promise you he will not be gentle. The least you can do is check into the evidence I sent you about the new heads of state."

"We'll do so and get back to you. In the meantime, I want you to take a vacation. Stay away from the Bloodline for a moment. That's an order. Vincent, I'm worried about your mental health. There are a number of symptoms that occur when an operative has gone too far undercover, especially in a religious organization like this. I'm considering pulling you out. We have another man inside the Bloodline as well."

"He's not a knight," Minzano said. "Let me explain to you how the hierarchy works. They have a nursery level. The blind operatives. The ones who do what they're told like toy soldiers in one nasty military. The knights are the ones who make the decisions. Having someone on the nursery level means nothing. That level is considered expendable, Leo. I'm the only man you have. I'm not ready to jump out. I'm fine. It's you guys that need to jump out of this fantasy before it becomes a nightmare!"

"You are dismissed, Vincent. That will be all," Caviant answered.

In a rage, Minzano threw his documents on the table and stormed out of the room. The others present did not move.

"That's the price we pay for a darn good operative," Bryant reflected. "Sometimes he gets too far into the role and starts to believe that he is actually the fictitious character we created. In the end it always works out for the best, gentlemen. A belligerent attitude is a small price to pay for his level of quality service. He's done what no agent in the world has been able to do. He's fooled the Bloodline. And he was right about Greg. Greg has not penetrated the organization. He's still running around doing errands. The least we could do is check out Minzano's photos and cross-reference them with the heads of state."

"We will do no such thing," Caviant rejected. "His allegations are ludicrous."

"I believe we owe it to him. Just to ease his nerves. If he's in a state of paranoia, this might ease him out of it. Greg has been reporting to me daily, and Greg's reports lack substance and useful intelligence. As you know, Vincent does not always submit his daily reports, but when he does, they are full of key information. He's uncovered extremely complex plots, strategies, and ceremonial procedures. Because of Vincent, we now understand this organization. With him on the inside, he can vouch for other potential agents we place within the Bloodline organization. He can even speed Greg's ride to the top. We need him in there, and it wouldn't hurt things to have him happy while he's in there. A couple hours worth of research is a very small favor to ask for his time and effort."

Caviant was silent. He knew the full story on Vincent Minzano. Ex-convict with several uncanny abilities, the most impressive of which was the ability to attract the bad guys. Bad guys flocked to him. Whether he was in prison, in a bar, or on the street, the bad guys would somehow always end up talking to him, and, eventually, respecting him. Another exceptional talent Minzano possessed was the God-given ability to act. It seemed to Bryant that Minzano could be a Broadway stage actor or perhaps a movie star if he had put his mind to it. Bryant had heard Minzano on the tapes hundreds of times, and Minzano sounded like a bona fide gangster. Minzano could make up a story, and tell it like it happened to him yesterday, details and all. Minzano had penetrated Mafia families, gangs, the Ku Klux Klan, and now he had accomplished the unthinkable: A Knight in the Bloodline. Minzano was officially 'down the Bloodline,' a decision maker in the most fearsome organization since the reign of Hitler.

Secretly, Bryant believed that this ability was in part because Minzano wasn't entirely acting – part of Minzano was a thug. He had been arrested in 2009 for large-scale narcotics distribution, and the bureau had fake criminal charges pasted to his record to make him an official bad boy. On the streets, Minzano's name was Dax Cameron, and Dax Cameron looked, talked, walked, acted, and fought like a mobster. You crossed him, you paid the price. You talked to him wrong, you paid the price. If you came after him, you'd better kill him, because he would come back for you until there was a funeral – whether it was his or yours. Many members of the bureau considered him out of control. Bryant disagreed; his recklessness was necessary to ensure success.

Bryant had once known the famous agent known as Donnie Brasco, who successfully penetrated the New York Mafia. When Donnie went too deep and turned to the other side, agents were sent to the heads of his Brooklyn family. The agents carried evidence linking Donnie Brasco to the FBI. They showed the family pictures of Donnie surrounded by FBI agents taking his oath. His hand was on the Bible, his face clearly visible. The family claimed the picture was fake, and gave it back to the agents without another thought. Minzano was a hundred times better than Donnie. Bryant could give the Bloodline a picture of Minzano taking his oath and Minzano could tape the picture to his shirt collar and laugh, "Hey guys, look, 'In God I trust.'"

"All right," Caviant said to Bryant. "You conduct an investigation. Keep it quiet, keep it small. If it's discovered, I know nothing about it and the matter will be conducted as such."

"Nice to know I have your full support, Leo," Bryant answered.

"These circumstances are unprecedented. Never can be too careful," Caviant replied. "Get back to me when you have the results. You have 48 hours."

· · · · · · · · · · · · · · · ·

Rontrez pulled off the boulevard to the gas station. The gas light had been on since he had gotten off the interstate. He got out of the car, passing by the grids on the gas pumps for those with smartchips, and walked into the gas station with a handful of cash. When he entered he saw the sign: "No Cash Accepted." This was the same sign he had seen everywhere he looked. It was becoming increasingly harder to buy food and other necessities without the smartchip inside of his body. Rontrez knew he could not make it home with the little bit of gas he had in his Benz. He was past driving on fumes now and riding on faith. Credit cards were no longer any good, nor were checks, debit cards, or money orders, or anything else. Rontrez smiled to himself as he realized that the United States chip law could no longer be enforced by punishment – with the initiation of the New Global Order, those without chips simply couldn't buy anything.

"This is ridiculous. I can't put gas in the car without a barcode in my head?" Rontrez muttered to himself. He opened the trunk and pulled out his one gallon emergency fuel canister. He poured it into his tank, hoping it would be enough to get him home. He looked at all the individuals at the gas station who scanned their hands against the panels as if they were robots. Rontrez didn't care what everyone else was doing. He was not going to get a chip in his body.

• • • • • •

A couple hours after their meeting, Minzano barged into Leo-Shey Caviant's office with no appointment.

"Here is more evidence of Elijah's affiliation with the Bloodline."

"The New Order flag?" Caviant asked Minzano.

"It's not a flag. It's a symbol."

"A symbol?" Caviant repeated.

"Yes. Illustrations or reasonable images used to convey a hidden meaning. A symbol."

"I know what a symbol is. A symbol of what? It's the same thing that has been on the back of the dollar bill for generations. The dollar bill we used to have."

"No. These are symbols of the Bloodline."

"The eagle and the ancient Egyptian pyramid," Caviant replied dryly. "I thought I told you to take a rest, Vincent. Stay away from the Bloodline. Has the Bloodline even met since Elijah has come?"

"No, we haven't."

"Because all of them are in prison," Caviant replied.

"Then how come I'm not in prison? I haven't been arrested and I'm a knight. The knights are one of the deepest levels. The knights make the decisions. Elijah didn't send men to my house. I checked on Greg, he's not in prison either. Why are we not in prison if all the Bloodline is supposed to be locked up?" Minzano asked.

"You and Greg are supposed to have absolutely no contact. You have violated a direct order," Caviant replied.

"I'm a knight. Greg is in my district. I'm supposed to keep tabs on him. I also know the knights have no plan of bringing him down to the next level. They really haven't even heard of him."

"Explain this symbol to me, Vincent. How do the eagle and the pyramid relate to the Bloodline?"

Minzano pulled out a wrinkled one-dollar bill and placed it beside the flag of the New Global Order. "The pyramid is the Bloodline's organizational structure. Look at the layers of the pyramid. Each layer of the pyramid represents a different rank in the Bloodline." Minzano spun the dollar upside down, so that the point of the pyramid was facing Caviant. "Remember, down is up in the Bloodline veins. When someone is moved 'down', it means they've received a promotion. From the widest levels of the nursery, down to the Watchmen, to the Shepherds, and all the way down to the Knights, the Archknights, and such, and then down to the Warlocks and Witches. And look behind the pyramid, Leo. . . there is nothing but darkness all across the land all the way to the horizon."

"And what about the eagle? The American symbol of our new republic. Many would say the eagle used to be our national symbol of freedom and equality."

"It's not an eagle. If you look at it closely, it doesn't even look like one."

"It looks like one to me. I think you need a rest. Take a break from the case for a while."

"No! I'm not taking a vacation," Minzano shouted. "You're going to sit there, and you're going to listen to me. It's not an eagle, it's a phoenix. The phoenix was a mythical creature that was reborn from its own ashes. It's the symbol of an uprising. The satanic uprising that's happening right now."

"We have experienced nothing but peace since Elijah's arrival. How have you come to this conclusion? This is preposterous."

"From deep down the Bloodline. It's not written anywhere. Do you know why? Because it's against the blood oath. It's information that's passed down, revealed to all the knights during the ceremony."

"Before or after you pissed on the Bible?"

"Look, do you think I wanted to do that? It was part of the ceremony! Dax Cameron pissed on the bible. Vincent Minzano did not."

"There is no such thing as a phoenix, Vincent. Calm down. I'm very worried about you. I'm seriously considering pulling you."

"Of course there's no such thing as a phoenix. I told you, it's a symbol. In Greek mythology, the phoenix was a legendary bird that was reborn from its ashes, and gave itself a new life. That is what the Bloodline has done. They have gone from the bowels of the underground occult to the top ranks of this New Global Order overnight. They have given themselves a new life!"

"Really."

"Look at the pyramid on the dollar. The top layer isn't connected — it's suspended above the rest of it. Do you know why?"

"No, but I suppose you're going to tell me."

"Because that part of the pyramid is not of this earth. All the way down the Bloodline hierarchy is made up of men, but the final piece is no human."

"And what is the final piece of the pyramid?"

"The sheep have several names for him." Minzano's heart thumped as he had realized what he said. He had used the term "sheep" outside of his life as Dax Cameron.

"Sheep?" Caviant remarked.

"Sheep is what the Shepherds call anyone outside the Bloodline."

"I suppose you call yourselves shepherds?"

"No. It's what the Bloodline calls themselves. I am an agent of the Federal Bureau of Investigation."

"So what would the shepherds call the top piece of the pyramid?"

"Great One."

"This is sickening," Caviant growled.

"No. This is the tip of the iceberg. A tiny bit of the crown. Look at the phoenix's breast."

"I will look at the *eagle's* breast." Caviant looked closely at the image. "I see a breastplate shield. With stripes on it."

"There are six sets of dark lines placed above a field of white that is divided into seven sections. Each of the six sets of lines contains three lines, or three sixes. You read the Bible Leo. Six is the number of man and seven is the number of God."

"That's not in the Bible."

"Okay, it might not be. I've never read it, but it is in numerology. Six is the number of Man and seven is the number of God, or spiritual completeness. Man's number is six because we fall short of perfection."

"Some fall shorter than others," Caviant replied dryly, looking Minzano in the eye.

There was a tense silence, in which Minzano briefly considered smacking him.

"What is this supposed to signify? Are you saying that this shield is a mathematical algorithm?" Caviant asked.

"No, it's a hidden meaning. The six black stripes are placed over the seven sections. The symbol places man above God."

"Why can't it be man and God working together in harmony, Vincent?"

"Leo, the world is worshiping the messenger, rather than the person who sent the message. Where is God on the flag? He's not there. Where is the Holy Cross or anything else on the flag? It's not there. It's as clear as day. Look at the inscription around the pyramid."

"It says, *Annuit Coeptis Novus Ordo Seclorum.*'"

"It's Latin. It's two phrases: 'He has favored our undertaking' and 'A new order of the ages.' Who exactly favors this new order?" Minzano said. "If you remember what Elijah called his new form of government it was specifically 'A New Order of the Age'."

"This is foolishness, Agent Minzano. Elijah has begun a New Global Order."

"Then why was it on the old dollar bill?" Minzano forcefully tapped the bill with his middle finger. "The New Global Order began three days ago. How can the inscription, the pyramid, and the phoenix be here, when this bill is dated 1988? Where is the 'In God we Trust'? On the old dollar bill, people thought the one who 'favored our undertaking' was God. But God's not on your new flag anymore. Open your eyes, Caviant. There's a train coming, and we're standing right on the tracks."

"This is outrageous. I'm not listening to another word. You are to take a paid vacation starting right now."

"Leo, look at this pyramid, it has three sides."

"All triangles have three sides, agent Minzano."

"The sides represent the Trinity."

"Yes. The Father, the Son, and the Holy Spirit. Vincent, I want you to take a break. Come back in two weeks. That's an order. You are off the assignment for a while. You're talking crazy. You are not to affiliate with the Bloodline. I'll let your supervisor know."

"No. It's the Bloodline trinity, Leo. The Antichrist, the False Prophet and-"

"No more!" Caviant shouted. "You've gone too far down the Bloodline. You are to refrain from this assignment until further notice. Is that clear?"

In a fit of rage, Minzano shoved Caviant's computer and flat screen monitor over his desk onto the floor, where they crashed to the linoleum behind him, scattering papers everywhere.

"The false prophet. He's here! Why aren't you listening to me?"

"Get out before I have you brought up on charges. Do you hear me, Agent Minzano? Get out!" Caviant picked up the phone to call security.

Minzano slapped the phone out his hand. Caviant looked up in shock and realized that it was not Agent Minzano who stood before him, but the violent thug he had always pretended to be. Agent Minzano had left the room.

"You're one of them, aren't you? Are you with the false prophet?" Minzano lunged across the desk and grabbed Caviant by the collar as he screamed for help. "Is that why you're taking me off this assignment when you know I'm the best man you've got?"

Three armed security guards burst through the locked door and tackled Minzano to the ground. He fought wildly as the guards tried to subdue him, but there were too many of them. As Minzano was carried off, his cries echoed down the hallway in his wake. "You're one of them! You're one of them, Caviant. You work for the false prophet. You'll burn in hell, you son of a whore!"

As soon as Bishop Dr. Bo Pathem answered the phone, Justes barked hurriedly into the receiver. "We need to assemble the members for an emergency meeting. Now."

"I agree," Pathem replied. "One has already been scheduled. You were my next phone call. I'll gather the members and meet you in the chambers in one hour."

Rontrez thought about how he was going to buy food with no money. He jingled the change in his pocket, and knew he couldn't find even a vending machine that still accepted change. Suddenly, there was a voice in the back seat of his car.

"Rontrez, you haven't gotten your smartchip yet. What's the problem?"

Rontrez glanced in the rearview mirror to see Elijah looking back into his eyes.

"I told you, I'm not really feeling that subdermal implant madness," Rontrez replied.

"Are you scared it might hurt? It doesn't. You will not feel a thing, I promise."

"I've got enough things running around in my head already. I don't need something else. Whenever you need me, just give a holler."

"Come on. Everyone else is doing it."

"You know that peer pressure thing never worked on me."

"Yes, I know. You went all through high school without getting high one time. I'm very proud of you too, son. Drugs were really not your mode of operation."

"Did you beam by here to ask why I don't have a barcode yet?"

"Well, Esau, it's my duty to check on people. I feel a rebellion coming soon, and I wanted to make sure you're on the right side."

"Which side is that?"

"The winning team, Esau. The winning team."

"Whatever team I'm on is the winning team," Rontrez responded.

"I love the attitude. There's only one small problem. There's only one path to salvation, and that is through me."

"Yes. There is one way to peace: through the power of the cross. My mother used to tell me that."

"Mm. I remember your mother, Esau. Rebecca was such a beautiful woman. Such a beautiful soul. Truly an angel on Earth. Esau, believe me, she made a difference everywhere she went. She touched so many lives in so many ways, it would lead one to think that she truly was a product of divine glory."

"Then why did you take her?"

"Esau, believe this when I tell you. There is a time for everything. Everything under the sun has a time. Just as you will have a time to reign supreme, there was a time that your mother was called home."

"Why?"

"The design is very complex, which is why the plan is difficult to perceive. Think of the good that happened when Rebecca passed."

"What? There was no good. I cried my eyes out every day for a year. I didn't care about life, I didn't care about people. I didn't care about myself. I lived like an animal, I treated —"

"There you go. I, I, I. Look beyond yourself for a moment. It's not always about you, Esau. It's about the plan."

"When Ma died, the family was in shambles. She was the one everyone went to for help, she was the one that held the family together. She made miracles happen for everyone around her."

"Yes, then what happened? You hated your father. You hated him because he caused your mother so much pain, and you blamed him for all her pain. There was hate in your heart, Esau. It was there and it consumed you. You wished it were him, didn't you? You wished I'd taken him instead of Rebecca."

Rontrez was silent.

"Look at things now. You are the man. You and your father get along great, and you were there to step in and make sure your little siblings weren't falling in with the wrong crowd, some of whom may have resembled you. And they love you for it. They absolutely love you for it. If you hadn't kept sending money to the family, they would all be homeless. Did you know that? Your family is now closer than it has ever been. You can talk to your father about anything under the sun. All because you saved the day by standing strong. I need an intelligent and unwavering man like you to help me, Esau. I'm convinced there is no other man for the job. You have stood courageous and resilient in the face of adversity, and have overcome countless obstacles thrown your way."

"What job are you talking about? You said something about me reigning supreme."

"You liked that, didn't you? What job am I talking about? The plan, my child. The big plan where you reign supreme in my kingdom. There's really not too much to think about here. Your choices are salvation or no salvation. But we'll keep in touch. Have your people call my people. We'll get together as soon as you want."

Minzano sat in his living room, frustrated and numb. He stared at his TV, which displayed televangelists praising Elijah on every channel. The telephone rang, breaking the television's repetitive monologue.

"Yeah," Minzano grumbled into the phone.

"We have to move, it's raining," the voice said. Minzano knew it was Will Baxter, one of the dedicated knights down the Bloodline. 'It's raining' was code for an emergency. "I'm already on my way. I'll pick you up in three minutes."

"I'm ready," Dax Cameron replied.

CHAPTER 13

An hour later the twelve members of a religious fraternal order known only as the Order of the Temple had assembled inside of Bishop Pathem's living room. Many of them had traveled across the country for this emergency meeting.

"It's as clear as the glory of God could allow," Justes said. "Everything is here. It hit me like a ton of bricks. Everything about his coming spells out the Evil One." Justes looked to Pathem and saw that the seats on either side of him were empty. Usually, the elected secretary and the treasurer sat at Pathem's left and right, recording minutes and taking notes. Justes hung his head as he realized their fate. "We are all that's left. All of our brothers have been captured by Elijah's armies and imprisoned as part of the Bloodline."

"We have known for some time that this might happen," Bishop Pathem stated, looking westward at Justes from his large throne-like chair in the front of the room.

"We have known for some time? I sure didn't know," Justes replied, looking eastward into Pathem's eyes from the back of the room. Shock was drawn across his face. "I sure wasn't aware that someone was going to come from the sky claiming to be the Son of Man."

"It's not that simple," Pathem replied, "As you read in the Bible before you called me, for everything there is a fixed time. A time to be born and a time to die, a time to plant and a time to uproot, a time to kill and a time to heal, a time to tear down and a time to build. A time to love and a time to hate, a time for war and a time for peace," (Ecclesiastes 3:2-3, 8). Pathem picked up his Bible. "Presently, we are upon the time for hate, and the time for war. In Second Corinthians, Paul warns us of false Apostles, workers of deceit who will make themselves seem like apostles of Christ. This is why we are here today." Pathem read aloud to the twelve men: "And no wonder, for Satan himself masquerades as an angel of light. It is not surprising, then, if his servants also masquerade as servant of righteousness," (2 Corinthians 11:13-15).

"Everyone knew about this except me?" Justes said, looking around the room. Everyone was silent.

Pathem responded. "Chris, you are our youngest member. There are many things that you haven't been exposed to. We did not know it was going to happen, but knew only that it was a possibility. Most of the others who studied this have been locked up by the false prophet. We are all that's left of the Order."

"Well since you've been studying, I suppose you've come up with a strategy to overcome this absolute catastrophe."

The room fell silent again.

"You mean you have no plan? This is absurd. We need to start strategizing this minute, before it's too late. How much time do we have?"

Reverend Prince Hall spoke up from his seat to the far right of Pathem's chair. "In Revelation, the Bible speaks of many things that are to happen before the Evil One reveals his true self. First, chaos increases in world. Even before the false prophet arrived, we were experiencing unprecedented wars, famines, earthquakes, and disease," (Matthew 24:4-15, 24, Luke 21:7-19). "Second, a beast will be given great authority in the world, as Elijah has already been given control of the New Global Order. Third, the dictator is supposed to appear as a great leader, and draw both non-Christians and Christians to worship him. To the public he will perform great wonders. This has indeed occurred. Fourth, all are supposed to wear the mark of the beast, 666. Only those who have the mark of the beast are allowed to barter and trade," (Revelation 13:2-8, 16-18).

"I assume the smartchip is the mark of the beast. But how does this fit? There is no number associated with the chip," Justes argued.

"Wrong," Reverend Hall stated, looking at Justes. "Some time ago I used to manage a retail outfit. Stores use a standardized barcode system to scan items at the register. They call it the Universal Product Code, or UPC. There are three sixes embedded in every sticker. Two thin lines to the far left, two thin lines in the middle, and two thin lines to the far right. Each thin pair of lines always represents a six. Three sixes appear in every UPC bar code, just as in every smartchip. Look for yourself."

Justes grabbed a can of juice on the table and examined the UPC bar code closely. He and saw that Hall spoke the truth.

"So three fourths of the world is wearing the mark of the beast," Justes said gravely.

"That is correct," Hall answered. "The forehead represents our will, our hand represents our actions. The Evil One has planted his mark in our wills and actions worldwide. The Bible also warns us if we have the mark of the beast, then we shall share in the fate of the Evil One as the Lord should see fit," (Revelation 14:9-11).

"What else is supposed to happen before Elijah turns on us?" Justes asked.

"Second Peter predicts that 'in the last days scoffers will come, scoffing and following their own evil desires. They will say, 'Where is this "coming" he promised?'" (2 Peter 3:3-4).

"This was the famous Y2K fraud, correct?" Justes asked. "People put their faith in machines, rather than in God. When the world didn't end, unbelievers used that as proof that the end would not come as we knew it would."

"Exactly. Very astute, Chris. The things I hear about you must be true."

"That depends on what you've heard, but continue."

"The Bible also says that a statue is to be constructed in his image – the image of the beast – and that people would worship the image," (Revelation 13:13-15). Hall turned on the large flat screen television to see people bowing down to the statue that had been crafted in Elijah's image. "A wondrous worldwide tourist attraction and public relations tool. What everyone fails to see is the dimensions of the statue."

"One hundred feet tall," Justes responded.

"That's what Elijah wants you to think. The statue is 99 feet tall," Hall remarked. "In ancient times, they did not use the metric or the imperial system. There were no inches, yards, feet, or meters. Everything was measured in cubits. The statues are 99 feet tall, by nine feet across. This is 66 cubits tall, and six cubits across. Another 666. His number is etched in everything about his coming. We have the time he came. We know his target was the most powerful nation. He first appeared physically in the United States capital, so we will use Eastern Standard Time, 7:06am. The sixth hour and sixty sixth minute of our day. If I had a stopwatch, I'm sure it would have been sixes all the way down to the nanosecond. Furthermore, he came on June 6th, the sixth day of the sixth month, which is the 6th day of that week. The year might not be the 666th year as far as we are concerned, but the Evil One does not acknowledge our years. Remember, that would be acknowledging the birth of Christ. There is no B.C. or A.D. for the adversary. The birth of Christ on which our date system is based is meaningless to him, and he has existed for time far beyond our own."

"His mark is painted everywhere," Justes thought out loud.

"Indeed it is. Even from what he uttered as he appeared in the sky: 'All shall now work seven days a week to restore the new Earth in full.' Elijah's command contradicts His third commandment, which is to remember the Sabbath and keep it holy," (Exodus 20:8, 35:2).

"He left another mark on the flag of the New Global Order," Hall continued, laying out a copy of the flag on the table before him.

"I know about the symbol already. The pyramid, the phoenix and so on," Justes nodded.

"Yes, but do you know about the key?" Pathem asked seriously.

"The key? The key to what?" Justes asked.

"Look about the phoenix," Pathem instructed.

Justes looked at the phoenix and saw the phrase 'E PLURIBUS UNUM'. Justes was urged to take Latin by one of his mentors in seminary. Though it was a dead language, he now found it useful.

"It's the Latin expression, which in translation, means "One out of many.""

"Very good, Chris. The question that must be asked is; One out of many *what*? That is the key."

"Well, what's the answer? What's the key to this prophecy?" Justes asked.

"We don't know. We can only speculate the meaning. Nowhere in the Bible is the phrase even remotely mentioned or referred to. It has baffled us for years now. I was hoping you had a clue. You know the Bible as well as any of us. Your spirit is definitely strong; your relationship with the Lord is healthy and wholesome. I've heard you give direction and advice just as I would myself. You are the most promising member of this organization, Chris. I was hoping you could shine some light on the situation."

Justes was silent for moment as he mulled over the puzzling phrase. He prayed to God. Then he fell silent and listened. Almost instantly, he had an answer.

"I've pondered on the coming of Christ many times before. It's discussed deeply in Matthew, Mark, Luke, and most extensively in Revelation. In those four books of the Bible, I always wondered how these events would appear in the modern world. Where is the United States in all of this? Where is the superpower that is conquered before havoc can break loose? At first I had speculated that America's absence in the prophecy could be explained by its being physically destroyed or economically devastated before Christ returns. Now the plan is clear. There was no mention of a supreme kingdom, nation or state in the last times because Evil has broken down borders and constructed a new order so he may reign over the United States while ruling over all. It makes perfect sense that the United States be the primary target for Evil. Despite the growing moral decay in the United States, it still has the largest Christian population in the world. At least forty percent of the population claims affiliation with a Christian church. The true "Born-again Christians" that is, Christians like ourselves, who believe in Christianity, practice the ways of Christianity, and actively spread the

Gospel of Christ through actions or voice, number between fifteen and twenty percent of the United States, if that. This means that when the Lord calls those true to Him, the United States will suffer the sudden removal of forty or fifty million Christians. I believe this is the 'Many' the Latin phrase refers to: the many Christians in the most powerful nation. From this population, the Evil One will select the 'one' from the 'many.' He would choose someone who professes to be a Christian. A good person at heart, but they might not be a regular church-goer. Then again, they might be. A person who would lend you a hundred dollars, but might beat you if you stole it."

There were murmurs around the room as Justes stopped speaking. Justes could not tell whether they were murmurs of approval or dismay. He glanced at the faces around him for any indication that his interpretation had been accepted.

Pathem spoke. "Justes, you are the youngest man ever to join this organization. Though I was initially against it, now I know why I was instructed to take you. Only the Lord knows if you are right or not, but I have a few more questions. You didn't quite finish the explanation. What is the significance of this person? What is so special about him? What are they going to do? Where would we find them?"

Justes prayed again, but he did not receive an immediate answer. Justes looked Pathem in the eye. "I don't know," he replied, "But I do know this. The 'one out of many' is definitely the key to Evil's plan, and I don't think it has much choice in the matter. Evil can not choose its own deliverer. Do we know anything else? You've said you speculated on this for years, correct?"

"I'm afraid our hypotheses haven't been much assistance. We do know Elijah will not reveal his true self until the very last moment."

"How do we know this?"

"Because he doesn't want to instill fear until he has conquered all. This is not the first time the Evil One has been upon the Earth. He has already tried to rule by force and fear in the image of man. He is now going to bring destruction to man by pretending to love."

"When was he here before?"

"He came in the form of Joseph Stalin, Ghengis Khan, and Mao Tse-Tung. We believe these attempts were made by the Evil One's most powerful archdemons, mainly Apollyon, also known as Asmodeus. His name means 'destruction.' One of Evil's most powerful attempts of destruction was that of his appearance of Adolf Hitler. Notice he has a slightly different approach each time, but he is always totally merciless and unpredictable. Each time he has caused the deaths of millions without hesitation. When he appeared in the form of Adolf Hitler, he attempted to take over the world, leaving the United States for last. He knew that by the time he had conquered every other country, he would be strong enough to defeat the United States. Now he has decided to start here, and the rest of his quest is a ride downhill. In two days, the enemy has broken down our entire way of living, and twisted it to fit his ways. Three fourths of this world now wears the mark of the beast. Those who are holding out are finding it increasingly harder to live. You can't buy anything without the chip. No one in here is marked with the beast, are they?" Pathem asked.

There were murmurs of confirmation from the group. No one had a smartchip.

"Well, gentlemen, we are in dire circumstances. Here are chips to use only in case of emergencies," Pathem handed out microchips, hardly the size a grain of uncooked rice, to each member. "These are smartchips. Do not let anyone see you with them. If your family is hungry, use these to feed them. Considerable amounts of credits are already loaded on them. Don't let anyone see them."

Though Justes was curious, he did not want to ask where Pathem had gotten the chips. Maybe it was better that he didn't know.

Another man, whom Justes had never seen before, spoke. "Why don't we have faith that this is the Lord's plan? Faith is the strongest weapon we have. The Bible speaks of a period of suffering in which some of us are imprisoned," (Revelation 2:9-11). "Sometimes we must be persecuted for our faith. In the Bible, it says that the Lord will destroy the devil, the beast, and the false prophet. Why don't we let him do it?" (Revelation 20:10).

Pathem replied. "Brother Payens, Faith is indeed the most power-ful sword ever forged, but you have to understand Evil's plan. His plan is to capture *all* souls on earth, so there will be no saved ones. He has already distributed his mark upon the people, and the Bible clearly states that those who wear the mark will not enter the kingdom of Heaven, but share the fate of the Beast," (Revelation 14:9-11). Payens nodded as Pathem continued. "By appearing to be a messenger of God, Elijah is using Faith to his own advantage. People worship idols and praise his name. They put statues of Elijah in churches worldwide. Evil is using the sword of Faith to slice through salvation – and this is just the beginning. If we do not act now, there will be no souls left to save! The ultimate Evil deals with three kinds of people. The lost, the saved, and those who only think they are saved. The first and last belong to the devil and he will do anything to keep them. The second belongs to God, and Evil will do anything to defeat them. Do you see now? His plan is to bring an end to all souls. He has already won three fourths of the battle. The angel of the bottomless pit is greedy. He will not rest until all souls are his."

Elijah now stood before the world as supreme dictator of the New Global Order. In his televised speeches to the world, he made it clear that he would crush any rebellion against the new system. Coopera-tion, he insisted, would bring upon mankind the glory and honor of all nations. Churches across the world were praising the prophet's name, bowing before the statue of the man who brought peace to the world in three days. There was no more war, no more crime, no more sick-ness, no more poverty, and no more rebellion. Both non-Christians and members of Christian churches became his servants, preaching his gospel worldwide.

Standing before the world, Elijah began to speak. "For the righ-teous said, reasoning with themselves is part of wisdom. My children, our life is short and tedious, and in the death of a man there is no remedy, neither was there any man known to have returned from the grave. For our lives are given to us for a great adventure, and we shall hereafter be as though we had never been: for the breath in our nostrils is as smoke, and a little spark in the moving of our heart. Or like as when an arrow is shot at a mark, it parts the air, which immediately comes together again, so that a man cannot know where it went through. Upon each of us embracing death, our body shall be turned into ashes, and our spirit shall vanish as the soft air. My children, our name shall be forgotten in time, and no man shall have our works in remembrance, and our life shall pass away as the trace of a cloud, and shall be dispersed as a mist. Our time will be driven away with the beams of the sun, and overcome with the heat thereof. Our time is a very shadow that passeth away; and after our end there is no returning: for it is sealed, so that no man cometh again.

Justes and his colleagues watched Elijah's televised appearance, speechless.

"Come on therefore, let us enjoy the good things that are present: and let us speedily use the creatures like as in youth. Let us fill ourselves with costly wine and ointments: and let no flower of the spring pass by us. Let us crown ourselves with rosebuds, before they are withered. Let us leave tokens of our joyfulness in every place, for this is our portion, and our lot is this. Let us not spare the widow, nor revere the ancient gray hairs of the aged."

Oniva listened carefully from her sofa. "It's happening," she said softly.

"Let our strength be the law of justice: for that which is feeble is found to be worth nothing. Therefore let us lie in wait for the unjust; because he is not for our turn, and he is contrary to our doings. He upbraideth us with transgressions of the law, and objects to our way of life."

Minzano heard Elijah's words through Will Baxter's radio. Though it sounded as though the prophet was now telling everyone to run wild, Minzano was careful not to react. A pair of Bloodline Knights had been assigned to each man leaving the gathering led by Bishop Dr. Bo Pathem – a gathering that now threatened rebellion against the New Global Order. Bishop Pathem had long ago stopped actively spreading God's word and disappeared underground in order to dedicate himself to religious study. Minzano and Baxter's target was Chris Justes, a promising young minister who had joined Pathem's group of religious leaders.

Minzano glanced sidelong at Baxter, whose eyes were fixed on the large house. Baxter was the only urban redneck Minzano had ever known, a good ol' boy who didn't like any race but pure Caucasian. Baxter didn't know that Minzano was Italian, and would have had some choice words for Minzano if he knew. Baxter was an atheist before he was born into the Bloodline. Ever since there had been a fire in his old trailer, the Bloodline brotherhood was the only family he had. Though Baxter had vouched for Minzano to become a knight, Baxter was a murderous man that Minzano truly could not stand. Baxter's dirty appearance also turned off Minzano. Even physically, Baxter was repulsive – he stank. He would often wear the same clothes several days in a row, and his matted beard suggested he was allergic to grooming.

"I remember him," Baxter said, peering at Justes through his binoculars. "We got his church last Sunday. He was crying like a wounded whore watching the building burn to ashes."

"Why can't we just bomb the house?" Minzano asked.

"We can't get near it, Dax. It's like Fort Knox over there."

"How many of them is it?"

"Twelve in all."

"I guess they think they're disciples," Minzano muttered. "How are we going to get Pathem? He's not going to leave the house."

"We can't get him now. When he finds out his boyfriends are dead, he'll double his protection, and we won't be able to get to him at all. Eleven out of twelve isn't too bad."

"Let me see the target. And you were supposed to come with a lot more ammo than these pitiful boxes, buzzard. What happened to your ammo run?"

"Store was out. Quit 'yer whining." Baxter said, handing Minzano the binoculars.

Minzano put them to his eyes. "Which one is he?"

"The one with the blue tie," Baxter answered.

"He looks like he just graduated from college. Who gave the order?"

"Beats me," Baxter shrugged, "A.K. called me a half hour ago and told me to move now."

"Wish we had a rifle," Minzano stated.

"Bad idea," Baxter replied. "As soon as we hit one, the rest would scatter back in the house."

"Yeah, but we'd be done, and I could go home and beat off."

Baxter chuckled. "Hey Dax, we're all a team. There's no 'I' in team."

"But there's an 'M' and an 'E,'" Minzano grinned.

Justes pulled out of the driveway of Pathem's heavily-guarded estate and onto a small road, headed toward the interstate. Baxter motioned to Minzano. "He's moving, let's go."

Minzano and Baxter got into the truck, headed down the hill, and pulled onto the road, blocking both lanes. Baxter shut off the engine, put on his hazard lights, and reached behind his seat for the shotgun. After checking it, he handed it to Minzano and got out of the truck.

"I'm sure you know how this goes. When he gets out of his car to help me, blast him and let's go home."

"Great. Tutorials from the trailer park ranger," Minzano grumbled.

"Get your ass up there," Baxter replied, gesturing to the forested slopes that rose around them. "Head to the right. As soon as you have a clear shot, get him."

As he trudged into the woods, Minzano wondered how he was going to get out of this one. He had been in worse predicaments deep in the ranks of the La Cosa Nostra in New York. He thought back to the time when he went with Sonny the Axe to take care of some two-bit thugs who had ripped off the family. The thugs had put up more of resistance than anticipated, and Minzano and Sonny had gotten into a gunfight. As a federal agent, Minzano was allowed to shoot as long as the person was posing an immediate threat. Minzano shot one of the thugs and returned to the family to get his stripes.

This time, it was different.

He doubted the minister would pull out a gun and go to war. Minzano thought about missing on purpose, but he knew Baxter wouldn't buy it, and his cover would be blown. Right after Baxter contacted him, he had called Bryant, but Minzano hadn't been able to tell him much. He tried, but at the time, Minzano didn't even know what was going on. Minzano had a transmitter with him so that headquarters would know where he was, but it didn't look like anyone was going to show up before Justes did. Baxter had checked the gun, so he couldn't pretend it didn't work. Minzano checked the chamber and saw that although the weapon was capable of holding five shells, there were only four loaded into it. Minzano knew that three or four shots with a shotgun didn't make a difference at close range, but he removed one of the shells and threw it far into the woods. In order to avoid blowing his cover, he would have to kill the target.

A moment later, Justes screeched to a halt at the disabled vehicle. The old pickup truck had its hood open and its hazard lights flashing. Justes eyed the truck carefully and unlocked his door to get out. He began to open his door, but he suddenly paused. Justes then closed the door. Many of Justes's respected associates said that he had the ability to communicate directly with God, sometimes on a moment's notice. They often joked they wanted to take him to Vegas and clean up, but Justes had never paid special attention to it. Justes considered himself God's servant, and sometimes his prayer was rewarded with convictions that felt as though they were sent by God. This time was different. He had been given a direct order: *Stay inside of the car.* Justes was confused. How was he going to get home if he didn't help the man in front of him? Before he had even finished the thought, the voice repeated, with the gravity of an eleventh commandment: *Thou shalt not get out of the car.*

'I hear you, Lord. I will do as you wish. I am here to serve you,' Justes thought to himself, and pulled his door shut.

Justes looked at Baxter, who was frantically waving for him to get out of the car. He pulled closer to the disabled vehicle and rolled down his window, but remained inside of the car.

"What's the problem?" Justes asked.

"I think I just need a jump start," Baxter replied uncertainly, confused by Justes's decision not to exit his vehicle.

"No problem. I have some jumper cables in the trunk." Justes leaned down and pressed the trunk release button. "The trunk's open. Go ahead and grab them."

"Thanks, pal," Baxter replied, walking to the back of the car.

"I forget where these things go," Baxter said to Justes as carried the cables to the hood of the car.

"Right on the battery. Positive to positive, then negative to negative," Justes replied.

"Okay, thanks." Baxter silently cursed himself for being unarmed. There was no way to get a clear shot at the target unless he got out of the car.

Baxter connected the cables to each vehicle as he debated what to do next. Shielded from Justes's line of sight by the hood of his car, Baxter signaled Minzano.

Minzano reacted immediately. From the hill above, he aimed for the rear door of Justes's car and fired. A deafening burst erupted from the shotgun. As the window of Justes's car shattered, he threw the car into reverse and punched the accelerator with all his might as Minzano let off another shell from the shotgun. Minzano pumped the shotgun again and fired at the car as it sped up the road in reverse, succeeding only in cracking the right headlight.

Minzano leapt out of the woods and started towards the truck at a dead sprint. "Come on, Baxter!"

Baxter threw the jumper cables aside and slammed the hood of the truck closed. Minzano knew that he was extremely lucky to get off three rounds and not hit Justes. He had missed all three times on purpose, but Baxter would never figure that out. After all, the target was in a moving vehicle, protected by glass, metal, and the car's raised hood.

Baxter started the vehicle and raced up the road. Baxter had no idea that the shotgun Minzano carried was now empty.

"What the hell happened? Why wouldn't he get out of the car?" Minzano yelled at Baxter as they accelerated.

"I don't know, he just wouldn't get out."

"I'll finish it then! Catch him, ram him off the road, and I'll finish him!"

Baxter raced up the road as quickly as the truck would allow. As they sped around a curve, the truck lost its grip on the road and slammed into a tree. Baxter's head hit the windshield, and he was knocked unconscious. Minzano, shaken, got out and stretched, feeling for aches and pains. Nothing was broken, and he didn't hurt too badly. He had learned long ago that any fight where nothing was missing, broken, or riddled with bullets was a victory.

CHAPTER 14

Rontrez closed the door to the empty refrigerator and looked at Oniva, who was laying on the sofa in the living room. He had barely eaten all day, was ravenous, and even though he had expected it, he was still disappointed to see there was no food. Oniva was stretched out on the floor reading her Bible intently and scribbling notes on a small pad as she went along. She wore a long purple sweater and skin-tight black pants that hugged her muscular thighs, still seemingly intact after running high school track years ago. If it had been any woman other than Oniva, Rontrez would have made a comment about her body. Instead, Rontrez walked into the living room and muttered, "You ain't cook. You trying to catch the Holy Ghost or something?"

"I'm reading. This stuff is making me think on another level. The things in the book of Revelation are happening right now. I remembered something about the mark. The mark of the beast, as the Bible called it. It says that we won't be able to buy anything unless we have this mark. Today I tried to go grocery shopping and I couldn't buy anything. That's why there's no food. I mean, they would not accept credit, check or money order. They wouldn't even take cash."

"I remember hearing something about that when I was in diapers or something. Is that for real? Where does it say that in the Bible? I missed Bible study last week."

"Revelation," Oniva replied.

"Let me see that, Pastor 'Niva," Rontrez said, reaching for the Bible. The passage she had just highlighted read: "It also forced all people, great and small, rich and poor, free and slave, to receive a mark on their right hands or on their foreheads, so that they could not buy or sell unless they had the mark, which is the name of the beast or the number of its name," (Revelation 13:16-18).

"See?" Oniva asked Rontrez.

"But it's a microchip. How is it the mark of a beast, oh wise one?"

Oniva started flipping through the pages again.

"Look, woman," Rontrez started, "This isn't Sunday School. I see you have taken notes until no more notes can be taken. Matthew, Mark, Luke and John called for you an hour ago. They forgot what in the world they wrote, and they need to hold your notes for a minute. You don't have to find any more verses for me. If you say it's in there, I believe it."

"Earlier in the chapter, it says the number of the beast is 666. Six in biblical numerology is just short of perfection. Perfection is represented by the number seven. Six is the number of man, so it makes sense that a man is now in charge of the world. All he preaches is man. Man this, man that. He never gives glory to God. Never! He builds statues of himself and people bow down and worship them like he's God."

"You're reaching, big time. And all the numerology. You know I hate math. I couldn't add water."

"Well you don't have to take my word for it. Six. Just short of perfection. The devil was an angel that was kicked out of heaven because he wanted to be as powerful as God. He was cast down, and it says that – no! I'm not telling you this! I want you to read it for yourself." Oniva rapidly flipped through the pages. "Here it is."

Oh, give me a break, I don't believe this. This cannot be happening. Is this guy really reading the Bible? This has got to be an official Red Alert. I can not believe that this strumpet is interpreting the Bible for him. Send in the Marines.

Rontrez took the Bible and read: "A third angel followed them and said in a loud voice: 'If anyone worships the beast and its image and receive its mark on their forehead or on their hand, they, too, will drink the wine of God's fury, which has been poured full strength into the cup of his wrath. They will be tormented with burning sulfur in the presence of the holy angels and of the Lamb. And the smoke of their torment will rise for ever and ever. There will be no rest day or night for those who worship the beast and its image, or for anyone who receives the mark of its name,'" (Revelation 14:9-11).

Rontrez paused in deep reflection before he spoke. "Wow. Big man isn't joking with this mark thing, is he? You have my word I will never get a chip. That torment with burning sulfur kind of caught my attention. It doesn't look like God is playing. It's funny that Elijah just asked me to get a chip though."

"What?" Oniva's jaw dropped.

"Yeah, he appeared in the back seat of my car and asked me why I hadn't got a barcode yet."

"Are you serious?"

There was a knock at the door.

"Hold up," Rontrez said before he walked over to the door and looked through the peephole. It was Lisa.

"It's Lisa. I told you she knew where you stayed," Rontrez grinned opening the door.

"Rontrez, I need to speak with you," Lisa said. "It's urgent."

"What's the deal, baby? Come on in."

"No, I need to take you somewhere private," Lisa winked.

"Alright, what did you have in mind? Creativity scores a few points over here."

"I have just the place."

Rontrez turned to Oniva. "I'm going to go check out this urgent situation this lady is talking about. You be good until I get back."

"What's wrong, Lisa?" Oniva asked.

"Nothing your friend can't handle, Oniva."

"Well I hope everything turns out alright. If there is anything I can do, let me know."

"Thank you. I might be talking to you soon," Lisa smiled.

Rontrez followed Lisa outside to a luxurious black stretch limousine. As they approached, a chauffeur dressed in a black tuxedo pulled open the door.

"Who's in there?" Rontrez asked.

"Compassion, faith, and love is in there," Lisa replied with a peculiar and impelling look on her face. It was as if she knew the world was going to change, again…and Esau was of momentous importance.

"Is that for us?"

"No. It's for you, Esau."

"I'm impressed. Is there food inside?"

"There is food for the body, provisions for the mind, and cuisine for the spirit."

"Who's in there?"

"Your life is in there."

"Well tell life to hold up, let me go give some food to Oniva before we leave. We haven't gone grocery shopping."

"I'll take care of Oniva. You get comfortable."

Drawn to the hint of the vehicle's luxe interior, Rontrez let the chauffeur usher him into the limo. The inside of the limousine was as magnificent as the outside. The spotless interior contained a bar, a television, and a gleaming refrigerator. Across from Rontrez was Elijah, dressed in a designer pinstripe suit, sitting between two beautiful women. A woman with honey brown skin clothed in a black pantsuit sat to Elijah's right, and a Caucasian woman in a black skirt sat to his left. Rontrez sank deep into the plush leather seats and opened the refrigerator. Rontrez grabbed several delicious-looking pastries and sandwiches, placed them on a glass plate, and gave them to Lisa. Lisa carried the plate back toward Oniva's house as the chauffeur shut the door behind her.

"Welcome, Esau," Elijah grinned. Elijah seemed to be looking through Rontrez. Elijah leaned back on a leather headrest attached to black dividing glass, which partitioned the chauffeur's driving compartment off from the large seating area. "These are some friends of mine, Mona and Jade." Rontrez shook hands with Mona, the brown-skinned woman in the pants suit, and then Jade.

"This is nice. I wouldn't mind having one of these in the garage," Rontrez admired.

"This is only where it starts, friend. Now, you'll excuse me for not asking how your day was, but we're running a little late." Elijah withdrew his right arm from around Mona and rapped twice with his knuckles on the glass. The vehicle began to move.

"What about Lisa?" Rontrez asked.

"Don't worry about her, Lisa's a big girl. She is going to spend a little quality time with Oniva. She'll catch up later." Elijah then pointed to the television. "I love this part."

Rontrez looked at the TV to see the movie *Kings,* about life in tribal Africa before the slave trade began in the Americas. Mona moved opposite Elijah to sit on Rontrez's right. They listened to the vibrant music as a boy was brought before the head of the African tribe to become a man. Simultaneously, an enemy clan prepared for war with the tribe, painting their faces with the blood of their enemies.

"You watch movies often?" Rontrez asked Elijah.

"Every once in a while. When one worth watching comes along."

"This was my mother's favorite movie. She said she would cry, laugh, and learn from it every time."

"It is a powerful masterpiece of emotions," Elijah replied.

"I didn't think I would be seeing you again so soon."

"Me neither, honestly. Sometimes things happen sooner than we expect."

"Ain't that the truth," agreed Rontrez, thinking of his mother's death. "What is this emergency that Lisa was talking about?"

"Everything will be revealed to you very soon, my friend. I see you still don't have a chip."

"No way. I read something just before I left the house. It was deep, too." Rontrez looked out the window. He saw several police cars escorting the limousine. "Where are we going? There's an army behind us. Where's the war? Or is that just how you prefer to travel?"

"We're going to the cemetery."

"Why are we going to the cemetery? Who died?"

"A good friend of mine, Esau. I'm going to pay my last respects."

"He must have been important. We have a whole entourage out there escorting us."

"Very important indeed. The thing is, he didn't understand how important he was. He didn't understand how to make the right decisions and take advantage of the opportunities he was blessed with. It's a shame when that happens."

"I feel you. A good mind is a terrible thing to waste."

"A good soul is a far worse thing to waste."

"How long did you know him?"

"All his life, really. I was right there when he took his first steps, his first kiss, to his first fight, to his last breath."

"So you grew up with him?"

"Something like that."

"How did he die?"

"He killed himself."

"Dang."

"He didn't kill himself like you're thinking. He didn't put a gun to his head, or take pills or jump off a building. No way. This man was entirely too strong for that. He didn't take his own life by something he did to himself. He lost his life because of something he didn't do for himself."

"Didn't exercise or something?"

Elijah laughed. "This is on a different level entirely. He was a good man. Just a little confused about where to go."

"Well he's up there now looking down on all circumstances," Rontrez said jerking his head toward the sky. "I'm sure he's realizing some things now."

"Unfortunately, he's not up there," Elijah replied. There was sadness in his eyes. "He chose to follow another path."

"I assume you tried to put him on the right path. What happened?"

"He was too afraid to follow his heart. He listened to the external environment. He wanted to do the right thing, but he was a little confused."

"Well you're here to change things. Hopefully you can put everybody on the right path."

"Well spoken, champion," Elijah replied. "That is exactly the plan."

Mona whispered in Rontrez's ear, "Slide to the edge of the seat, Esau."

"I would listen to her if I were you," Elijah grinned, taking a sip from his champagne glass.

Rontrez obeyed, and Mona gracefully maneuvered behind him and began to massage his neck and shoulders. Rontrez felt more relaxed with every passing second. "I'm a little underdressed for a funeral, aren't I?" Rontrez asked with his eyes closed.

"Don't even worry about it. No one will even know you are there," Elijah replied.

————

The limousine pulled into Columbia Community Church. Rontrez felt sick as he remembered vividly that this was where his mother had been buried six years earlier. The vehicle pulled around a stone building and slowed to a stop. The chauffeur then opened the door, and Elijah and Rontrez got out.

As he followed Elijah into the building, Rontrez recalled the dim corridor they now walked. He looked into the sanctuary, which didn't seem to have changed a bit. He glanced at the crowd in the sanctuary. All he could see was the backs of heads, and Rontrez saw that the service had already started. Rontrez rotated his shoulders, feeling the tension continue to leave his muscles from the massage.

"You like her, don't you?" Elijah asked loudly. Rontrez looked to the mourners, but Elijah said, "Don't worry, they can't hear us."

"You mean Mona? She's alright. The massage was tight work. Is she a professional?"

Elijah smirked. "She is definitely a professional."

"I'll wait here while you pay respects to your friend," Rontrez offered.

"You should come with me. I know it brings back painful memories, but you might learn something."

As he followed Elijah down the aisle into the sanctuary, Rontrez recognized the minister. It was the reputable pastor from his youth, Reverend Reginald Elliott. This is where he was baptized. He still shivered thinking about the ice-cold water he was dipped in. He had attended

Columbia Community Church from early childhood until he had graduated high school, where Reverend Elliott had been preaching for as long as he could remember. Rontrez didn't have a personal relationship with the reverend, but his mother had, which was why he had presided over her funeral. As they walked down the aisle, Rontrez glanced at the crowd. Just as at his mother's funeral, he recognized many of their faces.

"They can't see us, Esau," Elijah said.

"What's going on?" Rontrez asked as they approached the casket.

Elijah looked down in silence. He put his hands together and bowed his head for a few moments, then stepped back and dropped to his knees.

Rontrez put his hand on Elijah's shoulder as a measure of comfort. He stepped forward and looked into the casket.

Nothing Rontrez had ever experienced prepared him for this moment, which changed him forever. Lying in the casket, clad in a neat black suit, was Rontrez himself.

Rontrez squeezed his eyes shut and opened them again in disbelief. It was his body in the casket, lying still as if in a deep slumber. His looks had not changed – it was as if he had died that very day. Rontrez looked back to Elijah, who now stood behind him.

Elijah spoke softly. "Death is a judge that no king or emperor can corrupt."

Rontrez turned to look to the audience. When he looked into the audience and realized that he knew almost everyone, he almost lost consciousness. He saw his little brother and sister, Crystal and Jacob, sobbing in the front row. Rontrez's heart sank into his chest. He was attending his own funeral.

"This is the wake up call. It's inevitable. Everyone dies, Esau, but there is more than one way to do anything. You can either follow me, or undergo the alternative," Elijah warned, motioning toward the casket. "It's your choice."

Rontrez was silent.

"I will ask you only once. Will you follow me?"

"What do you mean, follow you? I still don't understand. What do you want me to do?"

"Three things. One, I want you to recognize the almighty as authority."

"I do. He is all powerful."

"Two, I want you to respect that authority."

"I do."

"Three, I want you to respond to the authority. I want you to recognize your calling and act accordingly. It's actually very easy. You play cards, Esau. All you have to do is follow suit."

"How do I do this?"

"By accepting it."

"I have already accepted it. I remember doing it a long time ago. I confessed in my mouth and believed in my heart."

"This is something different. This is another level."

"Another level. What are you talking about?"

"I'm talking about enjoying the pleasantries that I have put here on earth for you."

"That sounds pretty easy."

"All I want to do is give you the world. I can't do that if you don't have a way for me to give it you."

"Are you still talking about that mark?"

"What mark are you talking about? I'm talking about a small microchip."

"Nowhere in the Bible does it say I have to have a chip to get to heaven. How are you going to make up new rules?"

"In Deuteronomy, right after the Ten Commandments. 'Tie them as symbols on your hands and bind them on your foreheads,'" (Deuteronomy 6:8).

Rontrez reached for a Bible on the small table by his coffin and started to flip through the pages.

"Allow me," Elijah offered. He waved his hand in a semi-circular motion. As if picked up by a wind, the pages flipped to Deuteronomy 6:8 by themselves.

Rontrez read the verse. It stated exactly what Elijah had recited. Rontrez looked at the first and second verses of Deuteronomy. They explained that these were indeed the teachings and instructions of the Almighty.

He flipped the Bible some pages back, and there he saw the Ten Commandments. Rontrez looked back at his own corpse and felt sick.

"There are many that pose as friends that will try and turn you against me, Esau. I ask you to stand strong."

"I have to go. I don't feel too well," Rontrez replied.

"I need a decision."

"I can barely think right now. I need some rest."

"Let's get out of here. A nice massage will do you well. Mona will fix you right up."

Elijah led Rontrez back down the aisle. While Rontrez looked among the audience again, he saw his friends from grade school and people from his old neighborhood. He saw his good friend Gypsy, who he had not seen in years. He remembered back to when he and Gypsy used to take care of everything together when he was selling women. Gypsy was the muscle of the operation, and Rontrez was the charm and brains. Gypsy got his nickname because he wore a headscarf every time he set foot out the house, and Rontrez would comment that he looked like a gypsy. Rontrez was glad Gypsy didn't mind brawling, because Rontrez didn't care too much for it. Gypsy was over 300 pounds, but brawny and mobile as a panther, notorious for putting men to sleep with one punch. Gypsy had been one of Rontrez's closest friends, but they had fallen out of touch when Gypsy went to federal prison, then was transferred across the country.

Rontrez's stomach churned as he glanced at the casket again, and rushed out of the sanctuary.

Back in the limousine, Mona began to give him a wondrous shoulder massage. Rontrez closed his eyes and began to drift on the waves of his imagination.

He dreamed he was back at his house, sleeping soundly. It was night, and everything was quiet. Someone was creeping up the stairs. The shadowy figure opened his bedroom door without a sound and crept toward him, brandishing a knife. The figure stepped out of the shadows, and Rontrez saw its face: it was Oniva. She crept stealthily toward the bed before raising the knife above his head. She then smiled grimly and brought the knife down toward his chest—.

Rontrez snapped awake to see Elijah looking at him with concern. Rontrez noticed immediately his clothes had changed. He was now wearing an Italian pinstripe suit, with shining sharkskin shoes. The suit fit him as if it was tailor-made, and his new watch looked like it cost a fortune. His hair was neatly brushed and his hands were manicured. He definitely looked like a gangster. He felt more relaxed than he had ever been before, especially considering he had just come from his own funeral.

"You look sharp, buddy," Elijah smiled. "You look like a million bucks. We're going to knock 'em dead."

"Knock who dead?" Rontrez asked.

Jade smiled at Rontrez as Elijah motioned to the television. Rontrez saw a newswoman standing in front of the Supreme Court, surrounded by throngs of people. With the remote Jade turned up the television and Rontrez listened to the newswoman as Mona continued to massage his shoulders.

"We're gathered here live in Washington, DC, in front of the New Global Order Supreme Courthouse for what could very well be the trial of the millennium. An unprecedented turnout for the Rontrez hearing is gathered around the courthouse ensuring certain pandemonium if an unwanted verdict is given. One can feel the tension building as the Tri-State versus Esau Rontrez case is scheduled to begin in less than twenty minutes. The verdict will indeed decide where Rontrez is to be placed. The Tri-State seeks the maximum charge in the upcoming hearing, which is an eternal penalty of indescribable horror. The defendant's attorney's attempts to decrease the charges or dismiss the case have been unsuccessful. The Tri-State still seeks the maximum penalty. With the overwhelming amount of evidence presented by the prosecution, things look grim for Esau Rontrez."

"What's going on? What are the charges? It looks like they're throwing the book at me. For what?"

"They're throwing the book at us alright. The book that has been thrown at you too many times, but you never caught it. You just let it fall to the ground."

Rontrez turned his attention back to the television. "Time and time again Rontrez has claimed to be a prisoner of circumstance, but the District Attorney is unforgiving, and is determined for Rontrez to serve time in a different kind of prison."

The limousine slowed to a stop, and through the tinted windows, Rontrez saw the crowd start to mob the vehicle.

"It seems you're pretty popular, kid," Elijah winked.

"What's going on? If I'm being sued, you're the president of the world. Get me out of this."

"I'm afraid there are no back door politics for this kind of court, Esau. For there is a time when every man must come before the angel of judgment."

Crowd control officers cleared a path to the door of the vehicle. The chauffeur opened Rontrez's door, and the roar of the crowd almost knocked him back into the car.

The rambunctious crowd cheered as Rontrez stood erect and looked at the building ahead. Rontrez recognized the gray towering façade before him as the United States Supreme Court. Today it was the Supreme Court of the New Order.

Elijah started toward the marble staircase. "Don't say anything to the reporters. They'll twist your words. Let me do all the talking," he instructed.

The reporters attempted to shove microphones in Rontrez's face, but the crowd control officers forced them back. Many of those in the screaming crowd waved signs and posters featuring his picture. As he stared over the crowd, one sign came into focus. A silent old woman was holding it as high as she could: *Free his soul*, it read. Rontrez flinched.

He looked back to Elijah to find that a reporter had gotten through the guards.

"How do you plan to prove Rontrez is innocent in the face of the tremendous amount of evidence the DA has against your client?"

"As far as I'm concerned, the crimes that have been committed are all *against* the innocent Esau Rontrez by the District Attorney. The DA's diabolical methods to convict my client are a travesty to our entire justice system."

"How do you figure that?" the reporter asked.

"His lies, his creation of a false image of my client, then his worship of the image. The way the DA has committed adultery on righteousness, the treacherous tactics the DA has used to steal my client's innocent reputation from the minds of his community, and slaughter it in the streets by way of the media. He covets my client's confidence, and he has and his grossly falsified my client's crimes. The entire system should be on trial, not Esau Rontrez."

Rontrez followed Elijah into the building. Rontrez could feel the hostility towards him as strongly as if the building were alive. The interior was entirely gray, and the dull gray floor seemed to stare back at him. Rontrez walked through a metal detector, and Elijah placed his briefcase onto an x-ray conveyor belt and waved his thanks to the guard as it came out of the other side. They passed between two pillars, and headed toward the end of the wide hallway. The whole place gave Rontrez the creeps. Elijah stopped abruptly, turning left to face a large double door with an engraved image of a pyramid.

"What does that mean?" Rontrez asked.

"It's the Tri-State emblem."

"The news lady said something about the Tri-State, too. What is that?"

"The Trinity, kiddo. You're being tried by the Trinity."

"The Holy Trinity?"

"Call it whatever you want. In here, it's called the Tri-State."

Elijah pushed open the courtroom doors. As they entered, the room erupted with murmurs.

"The dapper Don has arrived," Elijah whispered to Rontrez. "I haven't seen such a commotion since the O.J and George Zimmerman trials."

They both took their seats and faced the judge. The judge was a powerful being. It didn't look threatening, but something about its presence humbled Rontrez completely. The judge appeared to Rontrez as a large vertical slice of light that emanated a soft white mist. It was an indescribable being of decision. The mist seemed to bring peace about the room, but the judge was still more intimidating than any other being Rontrez had ever encountered.

"That's the judge, right?" Rontrez asked Elijah.

"That is the judge of all judges."

"That's God?"

"No, Esau. That's the angel of judgment."

Rontrez looked again. Though it had no eyes, the angel seemed to be looking right through him. For an instant, Rontrez thought back to the crowd outside the courthouse cheering his name and begging for autographs. The angel of judgment seemed to know this, and its light pierced to Rontrez's core.

It spoke to Rontrez without sound. *One wise man's verdict outweighs all the fools.*

A hybrid between an unbearable chalkboard screech and a tortured moan suddenly tore through the courtroom. Rontrez clenched his teeth and put his hands over his ears to protect himself from the horrifically unpleasant sound. There was suddenly the odor of cooked flesh, and Rontrez felt the overwhelming urge to vomit. He held his breath.

"What's going on?" Rontrez asked.

"That's the District Attorney," Elijah replied. "Don't look behind you."

The courtroom door opened with a thunderous clang, and the noise and smell ceased upon the DA's entrance into the courtroom. Rontrez looked back to see the most hideous creature he had ever laid eyes on. It was a black horned creature with six heads, each faintly resembling the structure of a horse's head, and six eyes on each head. The beast had two muscular legs with a horned toe on each hoof. Rontrez had to repress a shudder of disgust as he ripped his eyes from the beast's heads and looked down at its body. It didn't seem to have any skin, and it looked as if its innards were writhing with wretched animals. Two tails dragged angrily behind him. When the beast looked at Rontrez with all six of its heads, its pulsating organs churned, producing a high-pitched screech that resembled laughter.

Rontrez looked back to Elijah.

"I told you not to look back. Now he knows you're scared. He can read minds, if you let him. It's important you follow my every instruction, Esau. I will never lead you astray. You have my word."

"Alright, you got it. I'll do everything you say from now on, man. Just keep that thing away from me."

"That's the plan, Esau. All you have to do is follow me."

"What are the charges?" Rontrez asked.

"What's the basis of the trial, you mean? The seven deadly sins."

"The seven sins. The DA says I'm one of the worst cats walking the planet? He's got to be kidding!"

"He's anything but kidding. I'm afraid he's very serious. *Dead* serious. He's after your soul, and from what I hear, he has enough evidence to claim it."

"What! What kind of evidence does he have?"

"He has your life. He holds the reality of your being."

"He holds the reality of my being? I don't even know the seven sins. I saw a movie about them once, but I didn't do any of the stuff that they did in that movie. What are the seven sins again?"

"Pride, Wrath, Envy, Lust, Gluttony, Sloth, and Avarice."

"What is Avarice?"

"Greed. The love of money, in your case."

"I do like money, but I don't worship it or anything. Everybody likes nice things."

"The DA has massively exposed your prostitution operation. That didn't help any. It practically covered all seven sins at once."

"What about envy? I don't envy anyone. What does he have for envy?"

Elijah gave a sadistic laugh. "Esau, the DA sees through all that. He knows you don't really need billions of dollars, or twenty cars, or a fifty thousand dollar watch on your wrist. He knows the daydreams you have of the presidency don't classify as true envy. But he knows what you *do* want. You've always liked women, but always wanted something else – something more complex than women. Something was missing that could not be bought. It cannot be found, it cannot be asked for, it cannot be paid for. It must be usurped."

"What's that?"

"Power." The word slid off of Elijah's tongue like oil. "The DA saw your face when you stepped out of the limousine. He knew how you felt when you saw the crowd screaming your name. He knows how you felt every time those crooked cops illegally searched you and your vehicle, time and time again, and found absolutely nothing. You wished you could put an end to that. You wished that you could have those cops come up missing and there wouldn't even be any paperwork. He remembers the way you felt when your mother was dying and the paramedics were more worried about their lunch break. You knew if you were someone else, it would have mattered to them. He saw you when you were little, watching all the women flutter to the local gang lords. You liked that, and he knows you liked it. You want the jurisdiction to influence other people's actions according to your will, Esau Rontrez. You want power."

Rontrez was silent. "What happens if I lose this case?"

"The unthinkable."

The hideous district attorney stood, and Rontrez knew it was time to start. Its horrendous voice was as frightful as its appearance. The DA spoke in a murky, staccato baritone, punctuated by chillingly high-pitched screeches. It sounded as if radio static was mixed into his speech.

"I present to you: the reality of Lust," the beast declared. At once, the open area of the courtroom turned into a stage of Rontrez's life. Everything from Rontrez's first sexual experience at thirteen years old to the present day was cast before the courtroom. The beast ran endless holographic footage of Rontrez's fornication with hundreds of different women, sometimes two or three at once. There was no sound from the angel of judgment as Rontrez's X-rated life played before the courtroom.

"Can't you object?" Rontrez whispered to Elijah.

"Object to what? It's you. It's a rule in here. You can't object the truth."

"This is crazy," Rontrez cried. "How much more of this does he have?"

"You tell me, kid. It's your life."

The pimp era was coming up, and Rontrez closed his eyes. Rontrez himself did not like sadomasochism, but many of his clients did, and the activities he oversaw were shown before the angel of judgment. Rontrez opened his eyes briefly to see his hookers urinating on individuals, and men eating dog food while being whipped bloody. He shut his eyes again as more obscenities played. After what felt like an eternity, there was the image of Lisa giving him a blowjob a few days before.

Elijah stood up and grinned at the DA as if they had known each other for years. "I object to that one," Elijah announced

"Withdrawn," the beast howled. "The prosecutor rests in torment."

"One down, six more go," Elijah informed Rontrez.

"What are you, the narrator? You barely said anything. What are you here for?"

"There was no way I could have proven you innocent of lust. God couldn't even do that."

"God can do anything."

"Anything except that. I promise."

"I just thought of something. Can't I get off on a technicality or something? Wasn't I or someone supposed to swear on the Holy Bible or something to tell the whole truth and nothing but the truth?"

Elijah was silent for a moment. "You can't lie in here, Esau."

"I present: Avarice," the beast howled.

Rontrez's greed was shown before the courtroom. The way Rontrez would make up to $10,000 off a single John, but sometimes give his workers less than $500. The beast showed him counting money every night and stashing it away.

After envy, sloth, gluttony, and pride came wrath. The beast showed an image of Rontrez creeping through the darkness. He remembered the incident clearly. Rontrez was sneaking through the darkness with his Desert Eagle, looking for revenge. Rontrez did not like violence, which is why he chose never to enter the drug game. There was not enough money in violence to interest Rontrez. But on this occasion, his good friend Gypsy crept beside him. The blood drained from Rontrez's face as he realized what the DA was about to show. Rontrez now feared for his life.

"You have to stop this!" Rontrez gasped. "If you don't, we'll lose the case."

"Esau, I can't stop reality." Elijah continued watching the incident as if it were a movie.

"Do something!"

"What do you think this is, a sitcom?"

Rontrez began to look frantic. "I'm not kidding. Object, strike, petition, protest, march, have a sit-in – something! If the judge sees this scene we can't win. It's worse than all the others!"

"It's worse?" Elijah asked with shock. "Shoddier than the beguiling lust expeditions?"

"Yeah. It's worse than anything else he showed us. Now you have to pull some strings. You're the president of the world. Get him to stop!"

"You can end it all," Elijah informed Esau.

"How can I stop it?"

"All you have to do is say the words."

"Say what words? What do I say to get him to stop?"

"All you have to do is renounce."

"Renounce? What do you mean, renounce? Renounce what, renounce how?"

"Just say you renounce."

"I renounce."

"Louder, they can't hear you."

"I renounce!"

The image of Rontrez's form in the darkness continued to flicker before them.

"It didn't work, he didn't stop!"

"That's strange. That usually works. Well there is only one thing left to do now."

"What's that?"

"We have to wait until the trial is over, and before he's about to render the verdict you can ask for a dispensation."

"What's that?"

"An exemption. You're asking him to let you slide by."

Rontrez looked at the angel of judgment. "He doesn't look like he's going to let anyone slide by. Has he ever given a dispensation before?"

"Of course not. Don't be ridiculous."

Rontrez felt the bile gurgle in his stomach again. He watched as he and Gypsy entered an old apartment building. They were looking for Sheek, a low-life drug dealer. Sheek had raped and beaten Dina, better known as 'Strawberry,' nearly to death, and run off with her earnings. Rontrez and Gypsy had come to settle the score. Not because Rontrez cared about Strawberry, but because his reputation was on the line.

"Come on, 'Trez," Gypsy urged, "we got to handle this, baby."

Rontrez knew two things: that Gypsy had always had a liking for Strawberry, and that Sheek was about to catch a wrath like he had never imagined.

Gypsy knocked gently on Sheek's door.

"Who is it?" came a voice from behind the door.

"Cash," Gypsy replied.

"Cash who?" Sheek replied.

"Cash Money," Gypsy answered, waving a hundred dollar bill in front of the peephole. "I need some of that good stuff, baby."

Sheek unlocked the door and opened it as far as the chain bolt would let him. "Man, do I know you?" he asked.

Rontrez stepped into Sheek's view. A look of shock came over Sheek's face. Ferociously, Gypsy charged into the door shoulder-first, snapping the thin chain, and the door swung open with a loud crash.

Sheek raced to the back room, and they knew he was running for his gun. Gypsy grabbed a lamp from its stand and threw it at Sheek with such force that it shattered upon impact with Sheek's back. As Sheek stumbled, Rontrez sprinted to him and tackled him against the wall, knocking a large hole in the flimsy sheetrock. Sheek was a big man and gave fierce resistance. As Rontrez and Sheek wrestled on the floor, throwing random punches at each other, Gypsy approached them.

Rontrez slapped Sheek, then pushed himself off of him. As Sheek scrambled to his feet, Rontrez remembered that Sheek probably had a gun in his bedroom, so he stood in the doorway, blocking any attempt to enter.

Gypsy came at Sheek with a series of fierce punches, and caught him with a right and a left. Rontrez heard the smack of the flesh, and heard the crack as Sheek's jaw snapped out of place. Gypsy continued to pummel Sheek until he was on the floor, covered in his own blood.

Rontrez knew Gypsy's stories as a former bounty hunter, but Gypsy had no idea what methods of vengeance Rontrez had in store for his new enemy.

"Where is the money," Rontrez growled.

"In the freezer," Sheek replied, wiping some of the blood from his face.

Rontrez realized that Sheek could be attempting to clear a path to his bedroom so he could grab a gun.

"Where in the freezer?"

"In a red pizza box, second to last shelf."

"I'll make sure he doesn't get up," Rontrez told Gypsy.

Gypsy walked to the kitchen and opened the freezer. Sure enough, there was a red pizza box with money in it. Though it was more in it than what Sheek had taken from Strawberry, Gypsy pocketed all of it. It looked to be about a couple thousand. Gypsy returned to the living room to see Rontrez urinating on Sheek. Sheek was lying still on the carpet, unmoving, as the yellow liquid streamed down his face. After Rontrez had shaken the last drops on him, he kicked him and ordered him to kneel.

"That's right. Now bow to me, whore," Rontrez ordered.

Sheek didn't say a word. Rontrez began to slap Sheek's face with his phallus and forced it into his mouth. Gypsy laughed out loud as Rontrez ejaculated onto Sheek's face, than hit him again a few more times before putting himself away and zipping his pants. Rontrez looked back at Gypsy.

"You got it?"

"Everything is cool, 'Trez. Let's bounce," Gypsy replied.

They both left the building quickly. Gypsy didn't even ask him about what happened – he already knew. Gypsy recognized that even though Rontrez wasn't a homosexual, he made Sheek perform those acts because they humiliated him. Sheek wouldn't come running after them not because he was physically hurt, but because he was ashamed. Gypsy didn't even have to ask him where he learned the tactic. Prison taught a man things that no classroom ever would. Rontrez had never been to prison, but when those around you talk, it isn't hard to listen.

"For real. That's what you do to take a man downhill?" a younger Rontrez remembered asking his cousin Kedar, who had described what he did to survive behind bars.

"Nah. Actually, what the tall numbers do is make him take it up the ass, but I ain't with all that." 'Tall numbers' was Kedar's term for anyone in prison with a long sentence – usually anything in the double digits.

"You didn't feel strange with a man sucking on you? I couldn't do that, man," Rontrez had replied.

When it was safe to talk, Gypsy spoke. "Never thought he had that coming. I ain't think you would do nothing like that. You're quite creative with the revenge, baby. You ain't feel weird or nothing?"

"I know I ain't gay. Nothing else matters. That bastard definitely won't tell anyone I made him speak into the microphone. He's too embarrassed. That would ruin him, you feel me? He can't tell his homeboys he was on his knees doing favors for me. He can't rally his crew to come get at me because my sperm was in his eye. He's not going to tell anyone why his throat hurts tomorrow. That's a secret he can't tell. No one saw me do it but you, and you know I ain't gay so it's all good."

Rontrez was light years from that life now. He was a totally different man than in the years when he ran the streets. Rontrez had reformed himself, but it didn't look like it mattered now.

The beast howled Rontrez back from his thoughts. His past had finished playing, and Rontrez could not even look at the angel of judgment.

"I have presented to you all seven sins in the past reality of wrath. There is no decision to make," the beast continued. "His soul is mine." The beasts' eyes began to glow red.

"Hey, what about the defense?" Rontrez cried to Elijah. "I've done a lot of good things in my life. I've helped a lot of people. Show some other parts of my life. Show the judge I'm a good man at heart. You're sitting here like this is a cinema!"

"The basis of the trial is the seven sins, Rontrez." Elijah's voice softened to a whisper. "You are guilty. There is no plea bargaining in here. It's either innocent or guilty."

"Then why are you here? Why are those people outside of this building if the verdict was in before I set foot in this courtroom?"

"I am here to facilitate the experience. There is no way I can change what you have done in the past. I could show anything you've ever done in your life and the DA would show something that would sink you deeper into the grave."

Without a sound or a movement, the angel of judgment declared it was ready to give its verdict.

"Already?" Rontrez's heart skipped a beat as he felt adrenaline flood his body. His breathing got heavy and he began to get dizzy.

The judge began to render his decision. The voice was thunderous, fearsome, and final.

"For the sin of Lust, I find you guilty."

The image of his own body in the casket flashed before Rontrez's eyes.

"For the sin of Envy, I find you guilty."

Rontrez looked at Elijah for help. Elijah sadly looked at the floor, for he could offer no assistance.

"For the sin of Sloth, I find you guilty."

Rontrez felt tears come to his eyes. "Stop this, please stop this! I'll change my ways, I'm serious. Give me another chance! I was a victim of circumstance. I didn't have anything when I was growing up. The only way I knew how to survive was on the streets."

"For the sin of Gluttony, I find you guilty."

Elijah replied. "Esau, you can't sing the same song as everyone else. It has been heard before too many times to count. You can't tell the angel of judgment you've been framed. Everyone who comes into this world is dealt a certain hand. The hand you are dealt is part of the plan. It is your free will that determines the outcome in the end."

The far wall on the courtroom slowly fell away to reveal a world of fire. Tormented souls grabbed at the air, clawing for the same second chance that Rontrez was begging for. They screamed in terror and cursed in rage.

Rontrez shuddered with fear. "This is crazy! Please, get me out of this. I'll do anything! Anything! Whatever you want, I'll do it! Stop this! I'm sorry."

"For the sin of Pride, I find you guilty," the angel of judgment continued.

Rontrez knew he was moments away from the fiery dimension before him.

"Stop this!" Rontrez cried.

"Are you willing to humble yourself before me and do the work you were meant to do?" Elijah asked.

"Yes!"

As the judge spoke his last words, Rontrez was lifted off the ground and thrust toward the flames by an invisible force. He could feel the heat singe his skin as he approached the furnace-like pit. He smelled the cooked flesh, and saw the angry orange, red and white-hot flames. He yelled at the top of his lungs in fear, sorrow, and despair.

"Esau Rontrez, for the sin of Wrath, I find you-"

"Hold!" Elijah shouted.

Rontrez suddenly stopped in midair, and everything was still. Rontrez twisted, his body in midair, and looked at the DA. His eyes glowed bright red, and though his mouth was still open, the sickening howl had ceased. Time had stopped. Rontrez looked back at Elijah, whose face was void of expression.

"Hell is only the truth seen too late, Esau."

"What do I have to do to keep from going in there?" Rontrez asked desperately, still suspended in midair. He looked back at the fiery dimension. Time had not stopped there. Screams of pain, shrieks of horror, and shouts of anger still echoed in his ears.

"Submit," Elijah replied.

"I submit!" Rontrez exclaimed.

"Well then your life starts right now, son. Born again. A fresh start like no other. Are you ready?"

"I'm ready," Rontrez replied.

"Are you ready to rule?"

"Yes."

"Are you ready to run the show like you've always wanted?"

"I'm ready."

"Then let's get started. Just obey orders, and everything will fall into place."

CHAPTER 15

Minzano and Bryant drove up to the gate to Bishop Pathem's estate. After the guard closely examined their identification, they were allowed inside. Bryant did not want Minzano with him while he talked to Bishop Pathem and Minister Justes. Minzano's arrogance might cause problems among the grieving clergy. Plus, there was the possibility that the clergymen would frown upon Minzano for letting ten of their colleagues be gunned down in broad daylight. Bryant knew that if either of them mentioned his failure to protect the other clergy, Minzano would explode.

Minzano hadn't always been like this. When Bryant was first introduced to Minzano, he was a professional. He was timely, respectful, and cooperative. But now, Bryant knew Minzano was being consumed by his role as a criminal. Although this created a more convincing cover, it was bad news for the agency. Minzano had long ago turned from a professional to a thug. He was never on time for any meeting, if he showed up at all, he refused instructions on strategy, and missed daily reports on a regular basis. Bryant could remember times Minzano went weeks without reporting. Minzano's mindset had changed as well. Instead of having an upstanding outlook on life, he now possessed a firmly rooted criminal mindset. Minzano had committed several minor crimes, forgetting to include them in his reports, and many times his reports were evidence of his psychological changes.

Bryant thought back to when Minzano was Joey "The Stick" Petrella, a New York Mafia henchman. His assignment was to collect evidence to bring down the nefarious mob boss Sam Corleone. Minzano sounded shockingly at home in the family of crime. In the tapes, Minzano's voice, diction, ideas, humor, and slang were identical to the authentic gangsters he was surrounded by.

When submitting his intelligence reports, Minzano had been picture perfect at first. He gave accounts of criminal activities of several of the most prominent family members. He also gave information on new and unknown players from different families and rivals. Their plans and strategy of the gang were described in great detail, and Minzano's undercover operations were going smoothly. By the end of the operation, Minzano's reports were only two or three lines:

"Sam told Stickman to whack Sonny because Sonny is skimming off my family's profits."

Minzano's reports had begun to indicate that he was in too deep – he called the mob family "his family" and referred to rival families as bastards, even in official reports. He had refused the agency's requests to see a psychiatrist, despite the drastic changes in his behavior. If he were forced to go, he would make the appointment, then find a reason not to show up. Bryant knew some of the supervisors considered Minzano a walking time bomb, and were ready to sever connections with him as soon as he had gone off the deep end.

Bryant pulled up to the valet and got out. Through a wrist radio, the doorman alerted Pathem that there were federal agents waiting to see him. After they had shown their badges, the doorman led Bryant and Minzano into a small back room where Pathem and Justes were sitting, talking quietly.

"Dr. Pathem, these are the men are from the Federal Bureau of Investigation. They have come to talk to you about the incident this afternoon."

Pathem and Justes stood up and greeted Minzano and Bryant as the doorman left quietly.

"I'm investigating what happened today," Bryant assured Pathem. "In light of today's events, I've decided to reveal some important information to you. Because you are each members of the clergy, I am asking for your word that everything we speak about here is to remain absolutely confidential."

"Of course, Agent Bryant," Pathem replied.

"For some time now, we have been tracking the organization known to civilians as the Bloodliners. They are an ancient secret society that has recently reemerged, encouraging violence and callous hate crimes. Their true name is unknown, and the organization is possibly Satanic. This is the organization that targeted your friends. An undercover agent has infiltrated their ranks and become one of their higher officers."

"Where is this agent?" Justes asked.

"You're looking at him," Minzano said, looking Justes in the eye.

"Were you outside these premises today?" Justes asked.

"Yeah, I was the man that tried to kill you this morning. Well, one of them."

"And now you're coming to ask for forgiveness?" Pathem asked.

"Look, I don't ask for anything. I've come to tell you that you're a target. What you want to do about it is up to you."

"Why are you just now telling me I am a target? What about my ten colleagues that were murdered earlier today?" Justes asked.

"We couldn't save them," Bryant answered. "It was impossible. We got the order to move twenty minutes before it happened. By the time we got there, it was too late."

"Well, what do you suggest I do now that I'm a target?" Justes answered.

"I was hoping you could give us some answers," Minzano said.

"What do you want to know? The Bloodliners kill any Christian they can get their hands on," Justes said despairingly.

"This is true, but this time it seemed different. More urgent. What were you all meeting about?"

"My organization's communications are strictly confidential," Justes replied.

"Look, Reverend," Minzano mumbled, "There aren't too many members of your organization left to get mad at you, are there? I'm trying to see why the hit was put out on you. Any other hit is routine. The assignment is given, the target is traced, then attacked. This time was a total breach of protocol. I was called less than a half hour before the shootings. It was like your organization was a threat to something. I think you know what that something is."

"I am under oath not to spill the secrets of the brotherhood," Justes replied.

"Fuck your oath. If you set foot out of this house again they will kill you. That is a fact. If you tell me what's going on, I can help you."

"Only Bishop Pathem can give me an allowance to speak."

"Okay. I see you're a little wrapped up in this protocol thing. Am I not getting through to you? If you do not tell us what was going on in the meeting, you will die."

"You may speak freely, Chris," Pathem stated.

"Great. You now have permission to talk. Now what were you talking about in this super secret meeting that was so important that the whole Bloodline chapter had to come down here to try to silence you?" Minzano inquired.

"Your arrogance hides something. What is it?" Pathem grinned at Minzano.

"Now he's a psychologist. This is great. Hey, Uncle Moses, don't quit your day job, or night job, or any jobs you have in between. Chris, what were you about to say?"

Minzano reminded Justes of a Mafia gangster he once met in Chicago. His tough-guy charade, wrapped tightly in machismo, and the fearless act was enough to intimidate anyone who didn't know better.

"The Order was speaking about the false prophet," Justes answered.

Minzano was silent. He glanced at Bryant, barely able to contain his smug expression.

"It's true, isn't it? Elijah is a phony," Minzano looked at Bryant. "I knew it. I knew the bastard was shady. I knew the whole thing was a sham. I kept telling you and telling you, but you wouldn't listen! So Justes, what's the plan? What's the great plan you guys came up with before you left the house? How are we going to take this son of a whore down?"

Justes and Pathem were silent.

"There's no plan. The top twelve priests in the region are here together and can't come up with a plan before they get wiped out? That's pretty sorry, if you ask me. Can't we just sprinkle some holy water on him or something?"

"He is not a vampire," Pathem snarled. "Nor is he some villain out of a comic book. He is the greatest peril of all time: *The ersatz prophesier.*"

CHAPTER 16

"How did you get me out of there?" Rontrez asked Elijah as they walked through a cheering crowd back to the limousine. Though the crowd around him was ecstatic, Rontrez felt the lowest he had ever felt in his life. The experiences he had been put through were enough to drain him mentally, physically, emotionally, and spiritually.

"I didn't do anything. Just consider me a facilitator. You have the power, Esau. You have the power."

"I feel like dirt. I feel like absolute filth. I think I just saw every wrong thing I've ever done flashed before my eyes in front of the judgment angel."

"For all have sinned and come short of the glory. Every man is dirty, Esau. No man is free of sin."

"What about you?"

Elijah smirked. "It depends who you ask."

As the two approached the limousine, the chauffeur opened the door for them. Mona, Jade, and Lisa were waiting for them, scantily clad and sipping champagne.

"I don't understand," Rontrez whispered to Elijah as they got in the car.

"No need to whisper, my friend. We're all very close here," Elijah replied.

"Okay. What exactly do you want me do?" Rontrez asked Elijah.

"You've already done it. You have confessed, and I have cleansed you."

"So where do we go from here. What's the plan?"

"Let me worry about the plan, Esau, you worry about what life has to offer." Elijah pointed to Lisa, Jade, and Mona.

"Isn't that lust or something? I want to start off taking care of business on the right foot here."

"That's the thing. You are taking care of business. And you will rule on high for it. You will look out over your kingdom, and realize what your purpose of existence is."

"What is my purpose of existence?"

"To become the Prince of the Earth."

"How am I going to become the Prince of the Earth?"

"Through your own will. Do you want to become the almighty ruler of all kingdoms?"

"Sounds pretty cool. But I've been in the game long enough to know ain't nothing free. Everything has a price tag on it. If you're doing all this for me, something's got to give in the end. What is it? What do you want?"

"You still don't understand. In your old life everything had a price tag. The new life you have started, the new life I have given you, is something totally different."

"What am I a part of now?"

"You are a part of righteousness and allegory."

"What?"

"But fear not. All will be revealed in time. There is a new way of doing things to reach the real eternal life that is above all."

"Well what do I have to do? I'm with it."

"First, I will give what you desire. I will give you authority, command, control, domination, jurisdiction and mastery over all. You will be the Mighty Prince of the Earth. Second, I will give you flesh."

Mona began to slowly undo his zipper. When she saw he was ready, she began to ride him gently as Lisa rubbed his back. Across from Rontrez, Jade hiked up her thin skirt and started to masturbate.

Elijah looked on and smiled. "A new life that plays by different rules, Esau. Yours to enjoy forever."

Chapter 17

"We need a plan," Minzano uttered to Pathem and Bryant. "The first thing we need to do is hold a funeral for you, Chris."

"What?" Justes asked.

"I was supposed to kill you. If there is no funeral, they'll know you're alive and you will still be a target. The Bloodline doesn't target dead people."

"Will they buy a cremation ceremony?" Bryant asked.

"Unfortunately not. They're a little too thorough for that. We need to stage an explosion. Right here."

"Blow up my house?" Pathem gasped. "You're absurd. I find it hard to believe that you actually work for a law enforcement agency."

"Well that's why I'm so good, Reverend. No one believes I work for a law enforcement agency. The only way to get the Bloodline off of you is to stage a high impact explosion. I was thinking of a boating accident earlier where you could be lost at sea or something, but I checked your records. You don't even own a boat, and you don't sail."

"I go fishing," Pathem said indignantly.

"You go fishing in some mud puddle lake. It's about twenty feet deep at the most. You can't be lost at sea in a twenty-foot-deep lake. The Bloodline would be out there with divers and sixty-foot fishing nets trying to find your body. This organization doesn't leave anything to chance. If you have a better idea, I'm open to suggestions."

Everyone in the room was silent. Then Pathem spoke.

"How do we know that they'll believe I'm dead just because there was an explosion in my house?"

"Because only I'm crazy enough to think of an idea like this. We need a body. If no body is found, they'll assume you're alive."

"And where do you suppose we get a body from?" Pathem asked.

"The morgue. We need a John Doe. The Bloodline has members on the police force. If the forensic analysts don't see what they are supposed to see in the debris, then you will remain a target. The bomb will be in your bedroom, the John Doe will be sleeping in your bed."

"What about DNA?" Justes asked. "The Bloodline police can collect DNA samples from the charred remains of the John Doe. It won't match up with our Bishop."

"Oh, been watching CSI, huh?" Minzano said sarcastically. "Got that taken care of. Before the local police can collect anything, the FBI will be on the scene, taking control of the investigation. This will be deemed a domestic terrorist incident. Our jurisdiction."

"What do you mean 'will'? I haven't agreed to this yet. My entire estate could burn to ashes. This idea is ludicrous. There has to be another way."

"I'm listening," Minzano offered.

No one said a word.

Minzano spoke again. "Since the vote is unanimous, we need to get a body. There won't be enough left for anyone to figure out this is a hoax. And you two need to get out of town now."

"We can't do that, Agent," Justes said.

"And why is that?" Minzano asked.

"You're a member of the Bloodline, correct? I would assume you know already."

"Yes. I am down the Bloodline, but what are you talking about?"

"Can you interpret their symbol? The symbol that Elijah has placed on the new world flag."

"Most of it."

"On the eagle, it reads *E Pluribus Unum*. Do you have any idea what that means?"

"No. How would I know what that stands for? I don't speak hieroglyphics."

"It's not hieroglyphics. It's Latin—"

"Whatever. What does it mean?"

"When translated, it means 'one out of many.'"

"One out of many. One out of many what? One out of many who? Please say you have some insight to this encrypted message. Or is that something else you guys forgot to do?"

"Perhaps if you had not allowed all my brothers to be murdered in broad daylight we could have come to a conclusion," Justes retorted.

Bryant motioned for Minzano to calm down. Bryant was certain this would happen as soon as Minzano had entered the meeting. Minzano was known inside the agency for his abrasive attitude, blatant arrogance, and lack of compassion for his environment. The tension in the room that had been present from the very beginning had inevitably started to bubble over.

"Look, gentlemen," Bryant jumped in, "Jumping down each other's throats is not going to help anyone. We need to focus on a solution, not the problem. The blame game is not going to help anything. We tried to prevent what happened this afternoon, but they moved too quickly. If you tell us what we need to do to help you bring down the Bloodline, then we'll do it."

"You are one of them," Pathem stated, looking coldly at Minzano.

"What? What are you talking about?" Minzano shot back.

"What is inside your brow?" Pathem asked, pointing to his own forehead. "A chip," Pathem continued. "The mark of the beast indeed. You shall share his fate."

"I didn't want this chip inside my head, but we have to get one. If not, I blow my cover."

"A cover indeed," Pathem replied solemnly. "A cover of thy spirit."

"Look, we're overreacting," Bryant cut in. "One out of many. It obviously means one out of many colonies or nations. Think when the dollar bill was founded, then look at the eagle of freedom. I want everyone to realize the Almighty has come from the sky, what more evidence do we need? He revolutionized our economy and stopped all wars and violence in about two days. That's a miracle if I ever saw it. How can you claim this man to be a false prophet?"

"He's a vessel of the unimaginable," Pathem warned. "You have the mark also, and will soon feel the mighty wrath."

"How else am I supposed to eat?" Bryant asked. "And Minzano has to get one because all the Bloodline has them. I know who I am inside. I know I'm a good person. Just because I want to eat doesn't mean I'm a bad man. You're not making sense."

"Hey, back to the one of many," Minzano started, ignoring Bryant. "What does it mean?"

Justes looked to Pathem, who nodded in agreement.

With Pathem's permission, Justes began to speak. "We believe that Elijah has to find a certain person to carry out his plan. A keystone individual."

"Who?"

"We're not certain at this point."

"I think I'm going to vomit," Minzano grumbled. "How can you all just not know *anything*? No name, no description—I mean dang, can I get a shoe size? This is past ridiculous. Instead of worrying about microchips and dip, you should be trying to find the one of many."

"Wait a minute, you two are not about to go on a hunt for the 'chosen one,'" Bryant reminded them. "It's safest for you to leave town as soon as possible. Remember, you are both targets."

"Agent Bryant," Pathem started, "You don't seem to understand the severity of this issue. The false prophet is here, and Chris and I are the last members left to take care of the matter. Everyone else is locked up as a supposed Bloodline member or dead. If we run from Elijah and his men, he will win. You can bomb the house if you're sure it'll work, but we can't run and hide."

"How are you going to find the keystone person anyway?" Minzano asked. "You don't know who it is or what they look like."

"We are taught to walk by faith and not by sight," Pathem replied. "We'll find the key."

"Well where do we start looking? Or is that in the 'I don't have a clue' category with everything else?"

"You being a member of the wretched Bloodline organization should perhaps shed some light. Ponder who is truly clueless before responding," Pathem answered.

"There have been no bombings or hits except for you guys. That's why I know whatever you were in here talking about was a serious obstacle to their mission. The Bloodline hasn't been after anyone like that before, and this is the first I've heard about a one of many," Minzano said.

"The Bloodline is an ancient evil, part of this world, part not of this world," Pathem declared. "You don't really have a clue what kind of organization you are truly dealing with."

"I think if I'm in the organization, I have a better clue than you do."

"Or perhaps not. How deep are you, Agent Minzano? With all your arrogance and glass confidence, how deep have you penetrated into evil? A warlock, maybe?"

"I'm a knight."

"A lowly knight. Even less than I expected. You have not even been exposed to the unearthly powers that the organization has desecrated. You are merely a Bloodline pawn. It's easy to tell."

"What do you mean?"

"Your soul has not been entirely corrupted . . .yet," Pathem spat. "The Bloodline has been blackened a thousand times over by centuries of untold evil. You are not quite there, Agent Minzano. Through your gangster facade, I still see a decent heart in front of me. You would not be here if it were otherwise."

"So you're an oracle now?"

"No. Merely a man. A mortal whose time here is as long or as short as a mystical rainbow, and whose knowledge spreads as far as the sands of the desert."

"Well, rainbow, where do we start looking for the one of many?"

"All we know now is that he cannot have the mark. We'll start from there."

"I'll keep an ear inside the Bloodline. I'll see if they're looking for anyone," Minzano offered.

"I can't believe this is happening," Bryant interjected. You're searching for someone who could be anywhere in the world. There are thousands of people worldwide who don't have the chip yet."

"We are guided not by what seems impossible, but by the evidence of things not seen, and things hoped for," Pathem replied.

"Yeah, what he said," Minzano agreed.

"Agent Bryant," Justes started, "a man is either for the conspiracy or against it. There is no neutral ground in this kind of war. One cannot serve two masters. Are you with us or against us?"

"How can you be so sure that you are right? Have you considered the consequences if you're wrong?"

Justes answered him. "Agent Bryant, I'm not sure you understand who we are. We are more than clergyman. We are the keepers of many secrets. We guard many ideologies and sacred truths that are unknown to the common man. We have studied Christianity from every angle. You can consider us elite Biblical scholars, for lack of a better term. Everything that has happened so far has been written. If time were not of the essence, I could cite the verses. Everything has been foretold. We cannot be wrong."

"If everything has been foretold, why don't we just let everything fall into place the way it's supposed to?" Bryant asked.

"If Elijah has his way, *everyone* will turn towards evil, and the prophecy will thereby be tainted," Pathem explained. "If all is evil, then evil triumphs. Our resistance to evil has also been foretold. I don't believe you understand the gravity of what's going on. We need to act now."

"What do you need from us?" Minzano asked.

"To start, we need a list of all male individuals in the United States who do not have the mark, and are not active in any church organizations," Pathem instructed.

"Men only?" Bryant asked.

Pathem looked at Bryant. "For reasons not explained nor revealed I know that the one of many is not a woman. Elijah's keystone must be a man. A man with not only great potential, but limitless aptitude."

Justes turned to Minzano. "Agent, I need you to gather as much intelligence as you can from the Bloodline. They have to be searching for this person. Someone has to know something."

"So the keystone guy is just an ordinary Joe? I mean, he's not some superstar or anything. Not a renowned criminal or a bastard politician, no one important?"

"Not important in the earthly world," Pathem answered, "but in the dimension of good and evil, he is priceless. He is the only key to unlock darkness, and the only key at this present time that separates good from becoming evil."

"So if the Bloodline or Elijah finds him, then evil will win over good?" Minzano asked.

"No. There would be no war to fight. Good would not be in existence."

"If he's an everyday guy, how do we know when we find him? Does *he* even know he's the keystone? I don't suppose he has a keystone shirt on."

"No. As far as I know, Agent, you could be the keystone," Justes replied.

"Well, damn. I don't suppose the Bloodline knows who he is then either, or do they?"

"I'm not quite sure," Pathem answered. "But I do know this. Evil in its present form does not have patience. As we speak, it is either diligently looking for the keystone, or has found him already."

"What happens when evil finds him?" Bryant asked.

"If he is converted through his free will, then darkness will be upon the face of the earth, and mankind as we know it shall end. Anarchy will rule, terror will run rampant, death will—"

"Alright, stop it. You're going to give me nightmares," Minzano interrupted. "Let's hit Elijah. If we get him out of the picture, everything else will be alright. He's the ringleader of this mad circus. I could get close enough to do it."

"No," Pathem declared.

"What do you mean, no? I wasn't asking you anyway."

"Elijah is not of this world. Though he looks like a man, he possesses powers far greater than any warlock in fact or fiction."

"Are you saying the man is invincible? No one is invincible. He's the ruler of the world, but he ain't got no cape. He can go down with a bullet just like anyone else. I know you two are preachers and everything, but today is not the day to turn the other cheek. That never made much sense to me anyway. Where I'm from, if you turn the other cheek, you get a broken jaw. They need to modernize church or something. It should be 'turn the other barrel.'"

"Elijah is not invincible, but earthly weapons can not harm him. Evil can not be shot or wounded."

"So how do we get him?"

"You can't fight evil with evil, Agent Minzano. That's basic theology. Only good can overcome evil. Since we can not defeat Elijah ourselves, we must get to the keystone first."

CHAPTER 18

Rontrez reclined opposite Elijah in a large Jacuzzi, sipping an exotic juice while soothing music streamed through the speakers in the ceiling of the large mansion.

"Do you like your new house, Esau?" Elijah asked.

"Yeah," Rontrez admired, looking around. "I'm really feeling this. This place is laid out. You have good taste, E."

"Thank you. If there is anything else I can get you, let me know."

"There is. You can get me the bill."

"Excuse me?" Elijah asked.

"Check, please. I told you before, everything has a price tag. You gave me a new life, you gave me these nice things, you gave me the women, the food, the house and everything else under the sun. Eventually it's going to come time to pay the piper. What does the piper want?"

"I keep telling you, all will be revealed. Most men would enjoy things as they come and not ask questions every third minute."

"I'm not most men. What happens if the stakes are too high? I'm not sure what kind of game we're playing here."

Elijah chuckled. "Game? No, Esau, this isn't a game at all. This is anything but a game. Perhaps you would like to journey back to the courtroom."

Rontrez was silent for a moment before responding.

"Look, I'm thankful for the second chance. I'm here to live life like I'm supposed to. I just don't see you giving everyone else the VIP treatment. Everything in my life that my mother didn't give me had a price tag on it."

"What is the price of your soul, Esau?"

"It doesn't have a price, it's not for sale."

I beg to differ.

"So it's priceless. Without price, correct?" Elijah clarified.

"Yup. I'm my own man."

"Whom does your soul belong to?"

"It belongs to me."

"Truly a master of self?"

"Yes."

"Well then there it is."

"What?"

"In your new birth, your soul is yours completely. You are the master of your life. That is all I wanted you to see. From now on, you are to do what you feel is right. I know you want Lisa, I know you want Mona. You may have them. You are master of yourself, correct?"

"What is this, a trap? I don't want to end up back in that courtroom, in that other place. It looked kind of hot and painful. I'm on the straight and narrow."

"God is within you. You are a temple unto yourself. A true master. All I am here to do is facilitate the experience and make it joyful as possible."

"Why are you doing all this? I don't see anyone else getting this treatment."

"There is a lot going on that you don't see. Call it bounded rationality. The largest human flaw. In short it means that you don't ever know what is really going on. A powerful symptom of your imperfection. You don't see reality, Esau. No human can ever see reality, they just interpret what they see and call it reality. But I'm here to change all that."

"You're going to make me perfect?"

"Indeed."

"How?"

"By your own free will and desire, Esau. Would you like to become a god?"

"What?"

"Your ears seem perfect to me. Why is it that you have such a hard time understanding what I say? I asked if you would like to become a god."

"A god? There's only one 'God'. The god that sent you."

There was a grim smile from Elijah. "You speak the truth. But Esau, all things must change. It's the law of nature. All things must come to end. Adaptation is only natural. Everything living creature must adapt to its environment to survive."

"God doesn't come to an end. He is the Alpha and Omega. The beginning and the end."

Oh, give me a break. I think I'm going to go into conniptions.

"Do you believe in change?" Elijah asked

"As long as it's for the better. Most things change at some point."

"Exactly. It's time for change to occur now. Do you think that anything can be done without help? Everything needs help, Esau. Nothing is a closed circuit. I need you to become change."

"So what do you want me do? What am I supposed to change?"

"Everything. I want you to change absolutely everything. This world has been so corrupt. The good have been suffering for the actions of the evil. There is pollution, terrorism, disease, murder, molestation, sickness, pain, war, disasters, poverty and everything else in between. I could go in alphabetical order, if you want me to. I want you to change all this."

"Haven't *you* changed all this? You've solved the world's problems in a few days. What makes you think I can do better than that?"

"Because I know you can. How long do you think this little fantasy world will last? Until some clown decides he is tired of peace and wants to start war again. It's only a matter of time. It's in man's nature to screw things up royally. You can stop all that by accepting what you have always wanted."

"And what is that?"

"Power. Absolute power and dominion over all things, living and non-living."

"How are you going to do that?"

"By granting it to you. It's time for a change."

"What happens if I say no?"

"*No?* I ask you if you want to become a god and you say no? I say that's pretty unheard of. You have got to be kidding me."

"There is only one God. Only one Supreme Being. Yes, I want power, but I'll stay away from becoming a god. I don't want to step on anyone's toes. If it is in the plan, I'll take the power part of the deal."

"If I were finicky, I would say it's a package deal, but I guess I'll have to find someone else for the job."

"I guess so. Man can't be above God. It doesn't make sense."

"What if I were to prove otherwise? You're not even curious what being omnipresent would feel like? I find that hard to believe. Who doesn't want to be the ruler of all things? Who could refuse to administer justice, consequences and judgment on all living matter? Who doesn't want to know what it's like to be the one that controls all destiny?"

"Of course I'm curious what it's like, but I'm sure the big man has everything under control. He has you. You've taken care of business in two or three days. You're the professional at this saving the universe game. You know what my game used to be. I'm a little lacking in the experience area of flexing authority as a supreme being."

"Experience is not needed. Remember, amateurs built the ark — professionals built the Titanic. What would you do if you were all-powerful, Esau?"

"If I were at the top, I would legalize prostitution. Prostitution would not be a sin."

Elijah exploded with laughter. When he finally calmed down, he said, "You are absolutely hilarious. I think that's the funniest thing I have ever heard. Out of all the things in the world, why would you morally legalize prostitution?"

"Because it's natural, so why make sexual pleasure a sin? Sexual desire is a completely natural and primal emotion in all of us. You're missing the point. Don't focus on the seller, focus on the product, baby. Pleasure is the treasure that the girl sells all day and night. Long after we're gone, dead presidents will still be getting their pump on. Prostitution was the first occupation in history. There was pimping going on in the Bible. And when all the buildings fall, pimping still gon' be tall. Pleasure is in man's heart. We want to be satisfied, we want to be fulfilled, we want to be embraced, we want to control. We want the primitive animal in us to come out. We want adventure, exploration, and excitement all at once. What do all the emotions equal? Nothing but the basics. Pleasure is all about fulfilling the two basic needs: power and sex. The rest is secondary."

"What about food?"

"I know many a man who's given me their last fifty, knowing that their next meal might be stolen. I could spin tales of old men who lay on their deathbed asking me to make their fantasy come alive. They didn't ask for a steak. I remember one cat who could pick a lock with his body. I mean, he was a walking skeleton. He looked like a pile of bones thrown together. Weighed about sixty pounds soaking wet holding an anchor. He walked right past the grocery store to one of my ladies. Pleasure is first, food is secondary. So if pleasure is in us anyway, why have us feel guilty about it? Pleasure is healthy. If there was no pleasure in the world, people would just walk around like robots. We know that's not what the creator intended, he just forgot to make prostitution a market segment in his style. Such a backwards society we live in. The people making the laws outlawing prostitution are my best clients. If I were on top, I would change all that. I would make pleasure a commodity and make the world a better place."

"Well if you let me cleanse you one final time, you can do just that. You can do whatever you want."

"I must be talking to a mannequin. The top of the system can't be a pimp. That doesn't make sense. That's like putting a cow at the top of the food chain. It just doesn't fit, baby. That just wasn't the way things were meant to be. Everything has its place. Everything has an environment. The world has to be in order for the continuum to endure its complex omnipotent cycle."

"That's sad. I guess I'll just have to find someone else for the job."

"Someone else?"

If one of your whores doesn't want to play right, you put her on the bench. Right, Esau?

"Hey, if the starters don't cooperate, you go to the bench," Elijah commented.

"Every man has to do what's in his nature. Who is the bench?"

"Sorry, team information is for players only. Why are you worried about it? I thought you weren't interested in the winning team."

"Let's be for real. How can you turn me into a supreme being? I really don't think I'm supreme being material."

"And why is that?"

"Because my actions are like iron and my words like silk. I'm the platinum passion and the copper stopper. I make the sun moonwalk and the moon sundance. I am ergonomically designed for success and nothing can contest. I can be the baby momma crusher or I can choose to finesse. I let my energy flow through your nerves via synergy and words, can you feel it? Everything in life has different roles. If the big man was a pimp, then that makes everyone else hoes. That's not the way things should go. The top has to care about everything he rules, but a pimp keeps his eyes on his money and his mind on making it."

"I'm going to explain something to you. I'm going to say this only once, so pay attention. All things are possible. If you want to become the most powerful being in the universe, it will happen. If you want to live your life as a two-bit pimp, that's your right."

"What about all that turning over a new leaf?"

"This is the newest leaf you can turn over. New rules, Esau. New rules. You are now subject to an entirely new set of rules. The things here on earth were put here for you to enjoy. Enjoy them as you desire. You have been given free will to whatever you please with from this day forward."

"Do you mean to tell me that I could stand out on the church steps and sell women and I still wouldn't end up in that place that's very hot?"

"Exactly."

"And why is that? Why am I not subject to the rules that everyone else is subject to?"

"In court I said you could possibly be granted a dispensation. An exemption from the rules for a specific purpose."

"And what is my purpose?"

"To rule. Unless you want to sit in the stands and watch the game, but you seem to me to be a man of action. Watching doesn't seem to be your style."

"How do I know that you're for real?"

"Are you scared of getting your feelings hurt? You're sounding like one of your whores now."

"What?"

"I said, you sound like a scared little bitch."

"You can't curse, you're a man of the Almighty. You're a prophet, how can you use such profane terminology?"

"Only man can taboo words. Words alone were never sin. Society made them sin. How can words be evil in themselves? They are words, just like everything else. What's the difference between the word fuck and the word luck? Nothing. They're both just words, made taboo by society alone. Where in any religious book does it say that certain words are bad, and certain words are good? Nowhere."

"So I can curse?"

"You're failing to see the big picture. Esau, you can do whatever you want. You have been granted a dispensation."

"Why did I get a break?"

"Because you're Esau Rontrez, damn it."

"Then it's all gravy, baby. I'll take that power with a side order of hot sex."

"That's what I like to hear."

As Elijah spoke, six naked women walked into the room. All six joined Elijah and Rontrez in the hot tub.

"Well this just gets better and better. I can find my own women but these look like they've been handmade," Rontrez admired.

"Not necessarily handmade, but hand picked. I know you can do things on your own. Actually, that's what I'm counting on. I just thought a little treat never hurt anyone."

"Nope, a little rest and relaxation is good for the soul," Rontrez replied.

"So tell me a little about things, Rontrez."

"What do you want to know? You seem to know everything about me anyway."

"Everything is not what it seems. Remember that. I only know what you did, not what you were thinking when you did it. For instance, why did you become a pimp?"

"Because I have pimp bones in my body."

"So what made you decide to sell pleasure for a living?"

"Because the stock market has always been a hundred percent when it comes to pussy. Like I said, it's the world's oldest occupation. Right up until the absolute end of all living things, the pursuit of pleasure and happiness shall remain in existence. Even though you just floated down from the sky, business is booming. No matter what the consequences, a trick will still buy it, marching day and night to the drummer's beat. Even during the recession, no birthday present, Christmas, or tuition for the little ones. Yup, daddy spent it up on his pleasure. Yup, they'll pay for pussy on Easter Sunday or greasy Monday. In a titty bar or out of the car. Not like Sam-I-am, Jake will eat brown eggs and ham. Yes, they want it in a boat, yes they want it in a moat, yes they want it like it's their right, and yes they need it morning, noon and night. It seems only right to me that a product that will never stop selling is a potential gold mine any way you look at it. Anything times infinity equals infinity. The money just keeps rolling in as long as you keep everything under control."

"How the hell do you get a dumb sex kitten to listen to you? How do you get them to go out and work, then come back and give you every penny?"

"Dedication, baby. Dedication is the reason she brings daddy her cash. On cold Washington nights, homage is the reason the girls didn't freeze up on me. Obedience is why I remained sovereign. I get in that broad's brain and that's where I remain. It's as simple as that. When you have the mind, the body will do anything I tell it to. There's two things I ain't never seen: a U.F.O, and a hoe that don't want dick."

"Your name on the street was the Sandman. How did you get that name?"

"Because I brought you a dream. I fulfilled untold fantasies of every variety."

"You don't miss it?"

"Once a pimp, always a pimp. It's not an occupation, it's a way of life. A way of thinking, a way of speaking, a way of getting things accomplished. I don't really miss being the Sandman anymore. I've moved on. I still like women, but I don't sell pleasure anymore. The game got violent after a while. I never was one for violence. There was no money in it. I've never started a conflict, but I can be the peacemaker or the peace-taker. It was the hater's decision. Pimps do what they want, haters do what they can. The game isn't really in my heart anymore."

"What's in your heart?"

"It depends on who's asking."

"Esau Rontrez is asking Esau Rontrez."

"Desire. I'm hungry for it."

"Hungry for what? It has to be more than this," Elijah said motioning around him. "It has to be more than this house, the cars, and the women. Is that all it takes to satisfy the great Esau Rontrez? Is mere materialistic garbage all you need in life?"

"I hunger for it all."

"You want the globe spinning on top of your finger like a basketball."

"No, but I want control of my environment."

"And control you shall have. I will grant you control of the most powerful organization on earth."

"And what is that?"

"Your army."

CHAPTER 19

Minzano stood in front of the Archknight and watched through his high-powered binoculars as the Pathem mansion went up in flames.

"Job well done, Dax. Well done indeed. How did you manage to get in there?" the Archknight asked.

"Like a thief in the night," Minzano replied. "Hired a man on the inside for the right price and it was all she wrote. I told him to place a bag under his bed, then I remote-detonated the explosive."

"What about the target from this morning?" the Archknight asked.

"Got him too. He was inside. How's Baxter?"

"He'll be fine. A few minor aches and pains. He'll survive," the Archknight replied.

"That's good to hear."

"Well, while we wait for confirmation on both of the bodies, I have another assignment for you."

"Really."

"Yes," the Archknight whispered. "An easy one. It shouldn't be a problem for you. That's why I'm choosing you."

"Who's causing problems?"

"Some nigger woman. The order came to me today. She needs to be taken care of immediately."

Minzano knew he couldn't question the orders, or ask what the target was guilty of, but one thing was for sure: he was expected to carry the orders out swiftly.

"She's a civilian?"

"Looks like it," the Archknight replied. "Not sure what the problem is, I just know it's urgent. Seems more urgent than what just happened. They want you to leave now and report back as soon as the job is finished."

"Got it."

"Another thing. You can do whatever you want with the body, but you need to cut out her heart."

"That takes time out of my escape. Is this absolutely necessary?" Minzano asked.

"It's ritualistic. For reasons you don't understand yet, it's a necessity."

"Where is she?"

"Here in Washington, DC. You are to depart immediately. The information you need is inside this envelope. You know that you saved Baxter's life."

"I guess you could say that."

"You know the punishment for dissatisfaction in this organization."

"I don't forget much." The punishment for failure was death.

"I'm sending three other knights with you, and another Archknight will be there to supervise the operation."

"I can do it myself. I don't need any help."

"This assignment is of vital importance. The orders come directly from the bottom."

"For a civilian? Who is she? Do we really need an army to go crashing in for one civilian woman?"

"We can take no chances with this."

"What, do I need a bunker too? I mean, why not paratroopers and a SWAT team? I don't need all these anchors tagging along."

"It's not optional."

"And one of you is coming?"

"Yes. Archknight Asmodeus will be with you."

The Archknights gave Minzano the creeps. They all reminded him of Count Dracula. The ones he had met were spooky-looking – pale and thin, but strong – and mostly came out at night. The people deeper down the Bloodline were even creepier. They had pale skin and would talk to each other in Latin or some other indecipherable language. Their eyes seemed to look straight through you, and when they spoke, if they wanted it to, their voice would sound deep and raspy one moment, then high pitched the next. The knights seemed like normal people. They at least looked and talked like human beings. But below the knights, things seemed to be unnaturally queer.

"Is something wrong?" the head Archknight asked.

"I'm just not used to having supervisors tag along."

"Don't think of him as a supervisor. Just think of him as a facilitator."

"He has to stay in the car, then."

"I doubt he'll want to have a part in the manual branch of the operation," the Archknight replied. "He'll want to extract the trophy, though."

"Why does he want the heart?"

The head Archknight did not respond to the question. "Bring the trophy here and we'll see if I can't pull you down another level."

"Really."

"I've heard and seen some good things about you, Dax. I could use a man like you among the ranks. Are you ready?"

"Yeah. I'm ready for whatever."

"Good. Your team is waiting."

CHAPTER 20

After hearing Bryant's report of what happened at the Pathem estates, Caviant stared at him blankly.

"It's for real," Bryant said. "At first I thought Minzano had some personal issues, but after talking with Pathem and Justes, I know that this is definitely happening. We need to put a stop to it."

"Do you understand how preposterous this sounds?" Caviant replied.

"I know, but you didn't see what I saw, and hear what I heard from those two men. Why would two clergymen lie? Why else would the Bloodline put a hit out on twelve ministers at one time?"

"I'll put this before the council. Where is Minzano?"

"He was summoned to another Bloodline meeting, he'll report in when he finishes."

"Hmph. Don't count on it," Caviant grumbled.

"Leo, we have to do something."

"Well what's the plan? Did the clergy come up with a plan?" Caviant asked.

"Not really."

"Tell them that before we bring down the Almighty's messenger, we need some evidence."

"I thought that was our job. We can at least get some wiretaps in his temples."

"Now you want illegal wiretaps in the church?" Caviant asked.

"Don't play the puritan role. We've done it before and we can do it again. We're not looking for evidence to present in court. The most prominent clergyman in this nation says Elijah is a fake. We could at least entertain his notion, considering that ten of his friends were just killed. They were murdered because they knew something, and they have the power to stop whatever is going on. I know it."

"Why don't you bring in Pathem? We'll see exactly what the situation is."

"Too risky. He's supposed to be dead. I have to leave him where he is. He's a celebrity. If someone recognized him, it could be disastrous."

"Where is he?"

"I gave my word to him that I wouldn't tell anyone."

"Let me know if you need anything," Caviant offered.

"I need those wiretaps. I need a surveillance team," Bryant said.

Caviant paused. "Okay. Do it. If you get caught, I don't know anything. I'll assemble a small team for you."

"Let me assemble the team," Bryant urged.

"Okay. I want a report daily. Code it at level Angel-zero."

"Thanks. I'm on it."

CHAPTER 21

Bryant looked around the small briefing room at his team. Three of the best agents he had ever had the pleasure of working with: Agent Thomas Cole, known as TC, Agent Eric Dino, and Agent Joshua Sesom. They had all been summoned separately and had no real idea why they were gathered together, but they did know that if Bryant had brought them together, it meant that things were about to get serious.

TC had what Bryant liked to call "kahunas." He had once been under investigation for illegal wiretaps in a drug cartel investigation. Though he was cleared of the incident, Bryant knew that the wiretaps were the only way for TC to have gotten his information. He followed his gut feeling to the very end, no matter the risk, and it rarely steered him wrong.

Sesom had been with the Bureau for over twenty years, and a close friend of Bryant's for almost as long. Agent Sesom was as experienced as it got in undercover surveillance, and he knew how to bend the rules without breaking them with perfection. Sesom. Sesom had also obtained Smicha from the Jewish Theological Seminary in New York. He once had aspirations of being a pulpit rabbi, but discovered he didn't have the stomach for synagogue politics. Given the situation, Bryant had a feeling that a religious perspective on the situation couldn't hurt.

Dino was young and hungry – for surveillance work and to prove his worth to the Bureau—and was often seen feeling his oats in his job. Sometimes Bryant thought that Dino believed he was in a movie. The way he would smart-mouth right back to the suspects and attempt outrageous stunts. Despite his arrogance, which Bryant fondly recognized as the same arrogance he himself had when he joined the force, Dino had received top marks in the training academy. Bryant had personally supervised Dino before – though he didn't look like much, he'd been impressed by his drive and intelligence.

All three men were ready for the briefing.

"Gentlemen," Bryant started, "I've assembled you to tackle a case of the most extraordinary kind. We're here to take down the leader of the world."

"Elijah?" TC asked.

"The one and only," Bryant replied. "We have reason to believe that things are not as they seem."

"Things are hardly ever as they seem," Sesom commented. "What reason do we have to believe that this immortal savior is counterfeit?"

"Several recent events have triggered this investigation: first, the murder of twelve clergymen; second, the reports of one of our finest undercover agents; and third, the testimony of two witnesses. This information has revealed compelling evidence we cannot ignore. Our assignment is to see if these accusations have any substance. If they do, we have to prove it."

"Are we free to use whatever we need?" TC grinned.

"Yes. But remember, if you get caught, I'm stupid and I don't know anything," Bryant replied.

"I didn't really count on the loyalty factor," TC said, chuckling to himself.

"So we're going to take down the king of the world," Dino stated. "I'm with you."

"Have we considered how we are going to apprehend him once the evidence is obtained?" Sesom asked. "His army is significantly bigger than ours. We don't run off of taxpayer money anymore. He now funds our operations."

"Leave it to him to spoil the party," Dino grumbled.

Bryant spoke up. "At this point, the apprehension has not been fully planned. Let's work on the evidence first. The first step is his temple in Washington, DC. It seems that he eats and sleeps there. I want it bugged – every room in it. If we can connect him to the Bloodline, it's enough to bring him down."

"Are there any agencies working with us on this one?" TC asked.

"The other agencies have been dismantled. Without any other countries to spy on, there's no need for the CIA anymore. We can't even get an Al Capone tax conviction here. There's no taxes, no IRS, no nothing. The other agencies have gone down the drain behind those two."

"Why hasn't our organization been taken off the map?" Sesom asked.

"It's about to be. Since there is no federal jurisdiction anymore, we're trying to convince Elijah's leaders that there is still a need for some sort of investigative organization that is separate from his army. We are losing the argument. Our funding is gone, as we have moved to the new world currency. It's only a matter of time before all four of us are standing in the unemployment line, receiving our smartchip allowance. We have to act now, before we look around and this man is charging us for air."

"I'll tell you this," Sesom started. "The bureau's welfare should be the least of your worries. If this man is who I think he is, we are really up against something that needs a little bit more than surveillance."

"What are you saying?" Bryant asked.

"You tell me," Sesom replied. "You summon us here together, and then tell us the man who has dropped out of the sky is not who everyone thinks he is. You wouldn't have been given permission to investigate if there weren't significant evidence proving your case. I've known Caviant longer than you have, and I know he doesn't trust anyone's hunches – evidence or witnesses only. What do you have? I can't work unless you tell me the whole story. I know about the assassination of the twelve clergymen. They were members of a sacred fraternal order. If you have an undercover agent in this order, congratulations, but I doubt it. Therefore, you must have an agent in the Bloodline. So tell me, why do you think Elijah is the deliverer of evil?"

Bryant was silent.

"Aaron Bryant, surely you didn't think that I would spearhead an investigation without knowing the story?" Sesom asked.

"You're right. I didn't tell you the whole story to protect some people."

"If you can't personally vouch for everyone in this room, then they shouldn't be part of this investigation," Sesom responded.

"I agree," nodded TC.

"Yeah. If you can't trust us, why'd you pick us?" Dino asked.

"You're right. But there is a lot at stake here. Leakage cannot occur. I picked you guys because you're the best. I'll tell you that two of the clergymen have survived."

"Bishop Dr. Bo Pathem – and who else?" Sesom asked.

Shocked, Bryant answered slowly. "A younger member, Chris Justes. Some say he has an uncanny ability to connect directly with God."

"Their Order holds cardinal secrets," Sesom said solemnly.

"Their brotherhood is so clandestine, we've never been able to infiltrate," Bryant admitted. "Sounds like you know something about them."

"Not much – just what I came across in my doctoral research. The Order of the Temple dates back to the 12th century. They were even more powerful back then, when they had the official blessing of the Catholic Church. You would know them by their more common name: the Knights Templar."

"*The* Knights Templar?" Dino asked. "As in the most skilled fighting units of the Crusades…White mantles, white robes… with big red crosses?" Dino made a cross on his chest with his index finger.

"Indeed," Sesom nodded. "They were a big part of the Crusades, but their story is much deeper. Originally, the Knights Templar was a Christian military order, founded to protect Christian pilgrims on unsafe journeys through the Holy Land. These men were famous and backed by church heavyweights, like Bernard of Clairvaux. With Saint Bernard's help, the Catholic Church officially endorsed the Knights Templar in the 12th century at the Council of Troyes. With this formal blessing, the Order became very popular, and grew rapidly in membership and power."

"Get to the interesting part," Dino said. "And how did Pathem get so rich?"

"The Knights Templar were far more than just elite soldiers. The brave men on horseback with red crosses on the front are certainly vivid imagery for the movies, but the Templars were far more than fighters. It's only a myth that the Templars were just cavalry. In a way, the Templars were the first multinational corporation."

"How did that happen?" Dino asked.

"After they received the blessing of the Church, people donated money, land, and their sons to the Templar cause, and the Order grew in money and power. To make them even more powerful, in the early twelfth century, Pope Innocent II issued a decree that exempted the Order from obedience to local laws. Not only were they a wealthy militia, they were subject only to the authority of the pope, not any specific country. They were exempt from any local laws and taxes. Noble families gave their wealth, land and businesses to the Templars to manage since they were so effective. Some would say they were untouchable. Their financial network spread through Christendom, and they even started a system where pilgrims to the Holy Land could deposit their valuables with the Templars so that they would not lose them to robbers along the road."

"They were bankers too?" Dino asked.

"And much more. Much of the Order was not trained for combat, but supported the combat positions and managed finances, land, and property. They were also rumored to be the keepers of sacred relics like the True Cross, and many other religious secrets and knowledge. In short, the Templars controlled the money, the best soldiers, and the deepest secrets. Templars were often the decisive force in key battles of the Crusades. A force to be reckoned with. One of their most famous victories was during the Battle of Montgisard, where 500 Templar soldiers helped a couple thousand infantry defeat Saladin's army of more than 26,000 soldiers."

"So what happened?" Bryant asked.

"When the Holy Land was lost, the Templars no longer had a central military mission, and support for the Order faded. There were arrests based on false rumors, a lot of them were encouraged by King Philip IV of France. You see, the king was in serious debt to the Order and saw an opportunity to avoid repayment. So he arrested and tortured the Templars in France. As far as anyone knew, the Templars were disbanded and their wealth seized. In secret, the Order reemerged underground under a different name. They held onto much of their wealth, and Bishop Pathem is their grandmaster."

"How do you know so much about the Order? Are you a member?" Dino asked.

"No," Sesom replied. "The Templars are a Christian organization. Since I'm Jewish and trained as a rabbi, I would be abruptly disqualified."

"Thanks for the history lesson, Sesom. Now, what did the Templars say about our new king?" Dino asked Bryant.

"The two clergymen – along with the undercover agent in the Bloodline – say that the hits were put out on them because the Templars were onto something. They knew who Elijah really was, so he sent the Bloodline to wipe them out."

"Is this a fact, or speculation?" TC asked.

"The Bloodline was definitely behind the murders, but we can't directly connect the Bloodline to Elijah. That's where we come in. Our agent in the Bloodline reports that the urgency of the attack on the ministers convinced him that the subject of the meeting was why they were to be killed."

"So who is Elijah?" Dino asked.

"No one knows for sure, but the clergy knows he is anything but good news," Bryant answered.

"Far from it. He is far from bad news and light years further from good news. He is the worst kind of news," Sesom answered.

"Who is he?" Bryant asked.

"I believe he is the evil in all of us," Sesom replied.

CHAPTER 22

Reclining in her bed, Oniva read her Bible by lamplight. She heard the door click open and bolted upright. It was about time Rontrez decided to come back.

"Esau, is that you?"

There was no answer from downstairs.

Oniva shouted louder. "Esau?"

No answer.

"Who's there?" Oniva yelled.

She heard someone coming up the steps. The steps were staccato and heavy, not smooth like Esau's movements.

Oniva, frozen with fear, heard the guest room door open. The heavy footsteps approached her own door, and she saw the doorknob to her room begin to turn. Oniva shrieked as the door swung open to reveal a masked man.

"Be quiet or I'll kill you," the man growled, raising a gun.

Oniva fell silent, realizing there was no escape.

"What do you want?" Oniva asked.

"I've come for you," the man replied.

"What?"

The man stepped forward with duct tape. "I'm going to tape your mouth shut because you screamed. If you try to fight me, I will kill you. If you cooperate, you will live. Do you understand?"

Oniva nodded.

The intruder stepped forward and reached for the tape he carried with him. When he leaned toward her, Oniva kicked him in the groin, and hit the man in the throat. She then dove to the foot of the bed and onto the floor, scrambling out of the room and down the steps as quickly as she could. She heard the intruder behind her, and before she could jump to the bottom of the stairwell, the intruder leapt at her from the top of the stairs. They tumbled down the steps, the intruder landing on top of her.

The man covered her mouth and whispered in her ear. "If you stop struggling, I won't hurt you. If you run, you'll die."

Oniva did not stop fighting.

"Oniva Mering, there are men outside waiting to kill you," Minzano brought his gun out for Oniva to see. "If I wanted to kill you, you would be dead already. I don't want to hurt you. Stop struggling."

Oniva stopped moving. Not necessarily because she believed him, but because she knew she couldn't overpower him.

"Thank you, Oniva. Now listen carefully. Is there anyone else in this house?" Minzano removed his gloved hand from her mouth.

"No," Oniva replied, picking fibers out of her mouth.

"Is there another way out of this house besides the front and back door? Any hidden entrance?"

"No."

"Then you need to hide in someplace you cannot be found. Do you have any ideas?"

"A couple. I can run pretty fast."

"The place is surrounded. You can't run, trust me on that. You're lucky you stayed in bed, or a sniper would have picked you off half an hour ago. They know you're in here. The lights have gone on and off in different rooms. If there's nobody in here, they're going to tear the place apart looking for you. You have to pick someplace they would never look."

Oniva thought for a moment. "I have some old trunks I could hide in. If you stack heavy stuff on top of it would they look there?"

"Yes."

"What if I call the cops before I hide so they won't have much time to look for me?"

"Your phone was tapped today. When they hear you calling the cops, they'll come in here and converge on you like locusts," Minzano replied.

"Okay, when they're all inside the house here, I'll kick a hole in the side of the attic. It would put me on the roof."

Minzano paused. It definitely sounded better than the trunk option. "There are snipers posted on both sides of your house. They'll see you on the roof. Is there a side window you can crawl out of?"

Oniva nodded quickly.

"Good. You can't look like a woman, either. Put on some baggy pants and a hooded sweatshirt. Then get on the phone. Where are some side windows that would work?"

"They're in the basement. But they're really tiny though, and they're high. You'll have to help me."

"Okay. We'll go down to the basement. Don't turn on any lights if you want to live."

Oniva felt her way down the basement stairs in the dark and groped around for the phone. "You have to promise me one thing," Minzano said.

"What?"

"When you get to safety, go to the church on Washington and Ninth, Holy of Holies. Sit there until I come. I'll remember what you look like. And take this." Minzano handed her his secondary gun.

"I don't like guns."

"I don't care what you like. If you knew what you were up against, you'd ask for a tank. Take it."

Oniva took the weapon and quickly grabbed a hooded sweatshirt and sweatpants from out of the dirty clothes pile in the laundry room. As soon as she was dressed, she dialed 911 on the cordless phone. Minzano hoisted Oniva up through the window as she started talking to the emergency operator. Almost on cue, he heard the other Bloodline Knights burst in the door and run up the stairs. It was only a matter of time before they came in the basement. How in the world would he explain why he was in the basement? He shut the window after

Oniva and turned around to see a television nestled in the corner of the basement. He quickly lunged for the power button and positioned himself near the bottom of the stairs.

Moments later, three knights came running downstairs.

"It's me, guys," Minzano said in the darkness.

"What the hell are you doing in the basement?" one of the knights asked.

"Looking. The TV was on, I thought she'd be down here. She's not in her bedroom or anywhere upstairs, either. She's hiding somewhere in here. I'll tell you what, we'll tear this place apart until we find her. Where is Asmodeus?"

"He's outside roaming around. He got out the van and wanted to walk around for some reason. I don't worry about that weirdo."

Minzano chuckled as he flicked on the light.

"It looked like she was in her room," one of the knights mentioned. "I'm trying to figure out where she called from if she wasn't in her room."

"She called someone? Who the hell did she call?" Minzano growled.

"She called the cops," one of the knights answered.

"She called the police?" Minzano asked.

"Yeah, she said someone was in her house or something."

"Then she still has to be here somewhere. Let's search the premises before the cops get here. I'm allergic to the law."

• • • — • • —

Oniva scrambled through her yard in the darkness, knowing the Bloodliners could be anywhere. She sprinted toward the small forest nearby. Surely, no sniper could shoot her in a forest. She would wait there until she could flag down some help. As she ran, she noticed an obstruction in her path. As she approached, she realized it was a massive, coiled serpent. She had never in her life seen a snake in Washington, DC, but the snake was as real as her fear. It glared at her with evil, cold, red eyes and it lapped the air angrily with its tongue. When she was a child, Oniva had seen green snakes at the zoo, but this serpent's twisted body glistened pitch black in the faint light from her house. She drew the pistol Minzano had given her, but by the time her eyes adjusted, the large serpent was gone. Without hesitation, she continued through the forest and into the late-night plaza nearby. There was a 24-hour Safeway inside the plaza, but as she made a beeline for shelter in the grocery store, the black snake slithered out of the darkness to block her path. In the middle of the parking lot, the serpent gazed directly into Oniva's eyes with its own red ones. The serpent opened its mouth and hissed:

"I want your soul."

Oniva's eyes widened and every nerve in her body screamed out in fear. The snake followed Oniva with its eyes as she ran into the Safeway, panting and sweating like she'd just run a marathon. She ran to the security guard on duty and yelled for him to call for help.

The people scanning their hands and foreheads at the grocery checkout paused, turning to stare at Oniva. As if in a nightmare, a man slowly walked through Safeway's sliding doors. The tall Caucasian man looked as if he had just walked out of a horror movie. His slender body was cloaked in a black tight fitting suit that seemed to strangely reflect light, as if his suit were metal. He seemed to shimmer as he walked. Oniva suddenly remembered him. He was the man she saw outside of the grocery store after she got knocked down by the ox-man. The thin man who was grinning before he disappeared. His skin was sickeningly pale, and he had on an ancient looking metal medallion with a symbol that she could not make out from a distance. She prayed that Rontrez would appear and save the day with his Glock or his smooth words. Knowing this was unlikely, she clung to the security guard, who appeared mystified by the situation.

Without a sound, the man seemed to glide toward them. As Oniva cowered behind the guard, he stepped forward and spoke to the pale visitor.

"May I help you, sir?"

"I have come for your soul," the man said to Oniva, looking through the guard as if he weren't there. He had a resonant, baritone, raspy voice. With one hand, the man tossed the guard across the room as if he were a rag doll and stepped toward Oniva. Oniva looked in his eyes and saw that his pupils were abnormally small and redness surrounded them. The man looked at the small crucifix pendant hanging from a thin gold chain around Oniva's neck with indifference. He placed his left hand over Oniva's heart, but quickly became frustrated. He hissed at Oniva while rapidly muttering words in a foreign tongue, his voice rising in pitch until it sounded as high and fast as a dentist's drill. As quickly and silently as he had entered the store, he withdrew, still staring at Oniva, then vanished into the darkness.

In a van, driving away from Oniva Mering's residence, the four knights passed the patrol cars speeding up to Oniva's house.

"Do you think they're going to kill us?" The fourth knight asked plaintively.

"Stop whining. They can't kill us. Asmodeus failed too. They're not going to kill an Archknight," Minzano answered.

"How did a civilian get away from us?" the second knight asked.

"Stranger things have happened. I mean, she didn't really get away from us. We never even saw her. At least I didn't see her. You guys see anything during your search?" Minzano asked.

The three men shook their heads.

"She probably heard me come in and freaked out. I mean, it wasn't the quietest entry I ever made. I thought she was upstairs. There are no exits for her to get to. Her files said she has no husband or kids. She probably got spooked and hid somewhere. We'll get her. She's a civilian. She'll go to a friend or relative's house."

Did you get her?
"No. I couldn't, master."
She escaped you?
"No, master. She was protected."
Does she bear the mark?
"No, master."
This displeases me. Break her.
"Yes, master."

CHAPTER 23

In the church of Holy of Holies on Washington and Ninth, Oniva sat, crying softly. She had no idea why anyone was after her life, much less why any spooky man would be after her heart.

The church was well kept and looked as if it was in regular use. It was not an enormous church, definitely not large enough for a televangelist, but enough space for a tight-knit community, looking to rejuvenate themselves spiritually, or perhaps learn something. Or perhaps not.

The sanctuary had magnificent stained glass windows, and a giant crucifix hung on the wall behind the preacher's pulpit. It was nothing like Oniva's small church back at home. The long, cushioned pews would ordinarily be welcoming, but tonight they were mere objects around her, feeling her fear. Oniva could feel her heartbeat, and it seemed to know that she had no clue what was going on. She tried to calm down, but it was harder than she told herself it was.

She had almost forgotten she had the pistol that the intruder had given her. She suddenly felt eyes upon her and looked up. A man was standing next to her. Without asking, she knew it was the man that set her free tonight.

"Hello, Oniva," Minzano muttered.

"What's going on?" Oniva asked the man.

"I was hoping you could tell me."

"I don't know anything."

"No one seems to know anything," Minzano grumbled.

"Who are you?" Oniva asked.

"Your only chance of living. Call me Agent Minzano."

"Agent, who were those men?"

"The Bloodline."

"Why is the Bloodline after me?"

"Because you know something. It seems to be a habit of theirs to kill people that know something. What do you know?"

"I don't know anything about the Bloodline."

"You sure?" It was obvious to Oniva he didn't believe her.

"I'm sure."

"You don't have the mark."

"No. It's in the Bible. 'If anyone worships the beast and its image and receives its mark on their forehead or on their hand, they, too, will drink the wine of God's fury,'" (Revelation 14:9-10).

"Are you a preacher or a preacher-ette?"

"No."

"Look, Oniva, you have to be someone of great importance. They sent four people after you, plus a boss. They sent an Archknight with us. That's unheard of for one person. That means you're a major pain in their operations. Don't tell me you don't know anything."

"I don't know anything, Agent Minzano," Oniva said, racking her brain for anything that might be of importance. "I did talk to Elijah, if that means anything."

"You met Elijah?" Minzano asked.

"Yes."

"Where did you meet him?"

"The day he came down from above, he knocked on my door."

"Really?"

"Yes. We dropped him off downtown and never saw him again."

"Did you say anything that would make him upset?"

"No."

"Have you spoken out against him anywhere?"

"No."

"Have you told anyone else not to get the mark?"

"No. Well, yes, I told one person."

"Just one?"

"Yes, just one person. My best friend Esau. The person who drove Elijah and me downtown to drop him off."

"Is Esau a preacher, or a clergyman or someone with great importance somewhere? Is he in opposition to Elijah?"

"No. We're not public people. We both met Elijah when he knocked on my door. That's it. Esau was staying over my house because I didn't want to be alone in all this chaos."

"Where is Esau?" Minzano asked.

"I wish I knew. I haven't seen him since he left with a friend of mine."

"We weren't sent to get him, we were sent to get you. You have done something to upset the Bloodline. Do you have any idea what it is?"

"No. But I want some answers. Where can I get them?" Oniva asked.

"Come on, let's go."

CHAPTER 24

Minzano led Oniva into a small room hidden beneath the pulpit of the Holy of Holies. The room had been used in the 19th century to conceal slaves fleeing to freedom, and it had been successfully kept a secret by the congregation ever since. Minzano helped Oniva down into the room and replaced the pulpit floor tile to conceal the entrance above them. Then, Minzano turned to the other two residents in the church's secret room.

"Pathem, she says she doesn't know anything. I thought you said Elijah just needs the keystone. Why would he want her dead?"

Pathem and Justes studied Oniva carefully. "She does not have the mark," Pathem noticed.

"So? Lots of people don't have the mark. The Bloodline isn't sending Archknights to wipe out every single person without the mark. Let me tell you this, they wanted this woman dead more than they wanted you and your friends gone. They didn't send anyone to make sure we did the job right with you until afterwards. With this one civilian woman, the bottom guys came up to help us kill her. I can't imagine what would be more important to them than wiping out twelve clergymen."

"Tell us what happened," Justes instructed Oniva.

Oniva began to describe her escape from the house and her arrival at the church.

"You said you saw a serpent?" Pathem asked.

"Yes. I saw it again when I went in the store. It was staring at me like it wanted to see me burn in Hell."

"As a matter of fact, I assume it did," Pathem answered.

"What?"

"The man in the grocery store, you said he put his hand over your heart, then pretty much vanished," Pathem asked.

"Yes. That's the way it happened," Oniva replied.

"Then the serpent wasn't a serpent at all. You're lucky it didn't catch you. Because it wanted you."

"Are you going to tell me the snake outside turned into a man and walked into the grocery store after me?" Oniva asked.

"I wish it were that simple. If it were, our problems would be quite less severe than they are now. The man in the store was of the deepest, darkest wretches of the Bloodline."

"Stop it," Minzano erupted. "I'm a knight, and I can't turn into a snake. We can't transform ourselves. What are you talking about?"

"You said there was someone from the bottom with you," Justes reminded Minzano.

"Yeah, an Archknight. So what? A man can't turn into—"

"It wasn't a man!" Pathem interrupted. "It wasn't an Archknight! They told *you* it was an Archknight. Archknights are still mostly flesh. They aren't completely demonic yet. Below the Archknight level is untold evil."

"I've met the Archknight I was with. He wasn't a demon, he was a man."

"The same man Oniva described?" Pathem asked.

"Yes."

"Then it wasn't an Archknight," Pathem replied.

"Are you telling me it was a ghost? A spook or something shape-shifting around town. I don't believe in ghosts. You're trying to tell us that me and Oniva met a demon tonight."

"Not a demon. A demon is a fallen angel. Though still extremely dangerous and to be avoided at all times, many are low-ranking. Tempters. What you met is an abysmal being of horror, pain, and malevolence. Much worse than a mere bad spirit or fallen angel. You might call him a warlock or sorcerer, or some other ill-fitting term. And you would be wrong. Inaccurately misguided, to say the least."

"The head Archknight called him Asmodeus," Minzano said.

Pathem eye's immediately widened. "Asmodeus?"

"Yeah. You know him?"

Pathem ignored the question and stared intently at Oniva. "You must be something special, child," he said to her.

"What do you mean? Who is Asmodeus?" Minzano interrupted. "How can he turn into a snake?"

"Do you remember in the garden of Eden?" Pathem asked. "Satan appeared to Eve as a snake."

"I missed Sunday school," Minzano mumbled.

"Yes. Are you telling me the man in the store was. . ." Oniva trailed off, waiting for an answer.

"Well, no. Asmodeus isn't Satan. But he is closer to Satan than he is to the average demon. We've met before. He goes by many names, depending on what language you select. Abaddon in Hebrew, Apollyon in Greek. The Bible speaks of him by name. If iniquity had a captain, Asmodeus would be it. The serpent was symbolic. Asmodeus can appear as certain animals and perform other supernatural feats with his demonic powers. So can many of the others. I'm telling you, the battle has not yet even begun."

"So if they want her this bad, she's the keystone," Minzano gathered.

"No," Pathem corrected. "I know the keystone is a man."

"How?" Minzano asked.

Pathem spoke. "Vincent, some things can not be explained, other things can not be taught. What you are asking now cannot be either."

"In the Bible, the serpent spoke to Eve, and Eve got to Adam," Justes added. "Oniva, are you married? Is there someone you're connected to who the Bloodline might want?"

"I'm not married. I don't have a boyfriend, either," Oniva replied.

"When I was in your house, there was another bedroom. Who sleeps in it?" Minzano asked. "You don't look like you have any children."

"I don't look like I have any children?"

"You don't look stressed enough," Minzano replied.

"Thank you, I guess," Oniva answered. "A friend of mine sleeps there. The one who drove Elijah downtown." Oniva told the story of the day Elijah knocked on her door the day he appeared to mankind. She then looked to Pathem and Justes before continuing. "I was worried about all the craziness going on here in DC and I wanted him to stay with me."

"You sleep in separate beds?" Minzano asked.

"Yes. We've known each other since junior high school. It's totally platonic."

"You sleep in separate beds?" Minzano asked again.

"Yes. I don't believe in pre-marital sex anyway, but we don't get down like that. We're just tight friends."

"Is he of the cloth?" Pathem asked.

"You sleep in separate beds?" Minzano mumbled again to himself in disbelief.

"Is he in the clergy?" Oniva involuntarily laughed. "Not at all. Not in any way, shape or form."

"I take it he doesn't believe in pre-marital sex either?" Justes asked.

"Actually, he does fornicate. Lots. I'm working with him on that."

"Would you say he was a good man?" Justes asked.

"Definitely. Anyone who knew him would love him. But someone who didn't know him might call him an arrogant rogue."

"Did you tell him anything against Elijah or the New Order?" Justes asked.

"Yes. I told him not to get the smartchip because of what I read in Revelation about the mark of the Beast. You know what I'm talking about."

"Yes, we do," Pathem replied. "Where is he now? What's his name again?"

"His name is Esau Rontrez. I don't know where he went. He left with a friend of mine a while ago and hasn't called since."

"Your friend is of great importance," Justes said, before he even realized he had spoken. Pathem looked at him for confirmation, and Justes nodded. He was certain that Esau was somehow of crucial importance to the crisis at hand.

"So the Bloodline wanted to kill me because I told Esau not to get the smartchip?"

"You are in the way of the plan, Oniva. That's pretty obvious," Minzano uttered.

"Why did they want my heart? Why did he put his hand over my heart? Someone please tell me what's going on. I'm scared to death." Oniva was frantic.

"First of all Oniva, you need to calm down," Justes started.

"Calm down? A half hour ago, men were in my house trying to kill me. A serpent told me he wanted my soul, and a sorcerer tried to steal it. I need some answers!"

"Oniva, fear gives the tempter confidence to destroy. Once you are afraid, the wicked one can convince you to do anything. The way you are feeling now is natural, and that is why the bad guys are winning. I need you to be brave. I need you to calm down and help us find Esau," Justes said soothingly.

"I told you, the last time I saw Esau he was with a friend of mine."

"Where did they go?"

"I have no idea. He's a grown man. He goes where he wants to. And why did that creepy man put his hand over my heart?"

Justes looked at Pathem. "He was searching for a gateway," Pathem answered.

"A gateway? A gateway to where?"

"A gateway to you."

"Well, what happened? I'm still me. Was it the cross I have on that protected me?" Oniva examined the sentimental crucifix charm on her necklace.

"Hardly," Pathem grinned. "Trinkets do not stop this kind of evil. The things we are dealing with are not out of movies or comic books. You did not see Count Dracula or a werewolf tonight. You saw a piece of the greatest evil imaginable. He could not enter you because you are a true believer. This is the only true weapon against what we are dealing with."

"He was really mad when he didn't get his way. Does that mean he'll come back for me?"

"Yes, but you won't see him coming. No more snakes and fakes. As long as you are in their way, they will attempt to break you. Your friend must really be something," Pathem explained.

"What do you mean?"

"They usually do not want true believers to die. Instead, they want them to suffer and lose faith. After they lose faith they are vulnerable, like a turtle without its shell. Evil loses a battle if you die a true believer, Oniva. But it seems they are willing to make an exception in this case. That's why I know that you are a key obstacle to the wicked plan."

"Why does evil lose a battle if someone dies a true believer?" Minzano asked.

"Your soul is immortal," Pathem answered. "When a Christian dies, their soul goes to the Kingdom of Heaven to live with God and his angels forever. This is exactly what the enemy *doesn't* want. Every soul in heaven is a victory for the Kingdom. When someone who is not a believer dies, their soul goes to Hell to suffer in the enemy's realm forever. This is the enemy's game plan. To collect as many souls in Hell as obtainable."

"How many souls does he want?" Minzano asked.

"All of them."

"Everyone in the world?"

"Everyone who is in the world and everyone who has ever been in the world."

"Then why did he take out your ten clergy friends? You were all these true believer people right?" Minzano asked.

"Yes, but we were definitely in the way. Evil made an exception, perhaps because we put the larger plan at risk. The ruler of demons has no patience for those that are a direct threat. He used one of his many instruments to clear a path for destruction."

"I'm as big a problem as ten clergymen?" Oniva asked.

"It seems you are even worse. Since you couldn't be taken by unearthly methods, I'm speculating he will now attempt to break you," Pathem said seriously.

"Break me. What exactly do you mean by that?"

"The same thing I suspect he is doing to the innocent men he has falsely imprisoned as members of the Bloodline."

"What do you mean?" Minzano asked.

"The supposed Bloodline members that are currently incarcerated are truly Christians – thousands of them. Some of them were my associates, and the most truly influential members of their community and their environment. He now holds them in a secret location and torments them, waiting for each one to renounce God. Once he renounces God, he is vulnerable to evil. He can not kill these individuals right away, or he loses. The tempter's greed will not usually allow him to kill a believer, because then their soul escapes his clutches. In Oniva's case, and in the case of my colleagues, there seems to be an extraordinary exception. We need to get to Esau before Elijah does, or this world will be plunged into chaos."

"So Elijah is also using despair as a weapon?" Minzano asked.

"Throughout history, it's been one of the enemy's most powerful systems. You're certainly familiar with the spiritual allurement of lust, vanity, and, in your case... pride. Even more powerful than those transgressions, the cardinal threat, is the temptation to despair. Despair is a primary spiritual concern, and it's the greatest danger to true believers, even ones who are not tempted by sin."

"Why is despair the biggest threat to true believers?"

"You can repent and be cleansed of your sins, but if you fall into despair, you won't believe there's anyone worth repenting *to*. The enemy will try anything to drive you to despair: attacking you mentally, emotionally, financially, and spiritually. Despair breaks you down from all sides and hits you at all levels to your very core. Are you familiar with Job?" Pathem asked.

"Who is Joe?" Minzano asked.

"Not Joe. Job. In the Bible, the enemy approached God and told Him that the only reason Job respected and feared God is because God had put a hedge of protection around Job, and blessed him. Job was remarkably wealthy. He had a large healthy family, a flock of more than ten thousand animals, and a legion of servants."

"Living the good life, was he? Reminds me of someone else I know." Minzano said, looking pointedly at Pathem.

"It seems Job and I have a bit in common. We both suddenly lost our estate because of an erratic suggestion," Pathem replied, returning

Minzano's glare, referencing Minzano's idea to burn his mansion. "In the book of Job, the enemy told God that if he took all of Job's possessions, then Job would curse God. The Lord then gave the enemy explicit permission to do whatever he wanted to Job's wealth and belongings, with a strict limitation not to harm Job himself. The enemy took Job's flock by way of bandits, attackers, and thieves, all on the same day. These same marauders murdered all of Job's servants as well, leaving a few alive just to tell Job the horror. On the same day, all Job's seven sons and three daughters were killed when a sudden mighty wind caused the house to collapse on them during a party."

"Took the kids too, huh. Did Job curse God?"

"No. Job remained faithful to God. But the enemy was not impressed, nor did he admit defeat. Instead, he doubled down. He said, 'Any man will give all he has for his own life. But now stretch out your hand and strike his flesh and bones, and he will surely curse you to your face,'" (Job 2:4-5).

"The Lord green-lit Job again?"

"Yes. The Lord gave the enemy permission to do whatever he wanted to Job, as long as he did not take Job's life. The enemy gave Job painful sores all over his body. Even Job's wife said to him 'curse God and die!'"

"Did Job take the advice?"

"No. He remained faithful. Even when his friends came to visit him with more wayward advice, he kept his trust in the Lord. As a reward for his faithfulness, God gave Job double the wealth he had before the tribulation. The Lord healed him completely, and gave him seven new sons and three new daughters. The point of that story is to learn how you can be tested by the enemy, and he is betting on you to lose."

"I guess today's lesson is that despair is a powerful weapon. Most are not as strong as Job was, and will collapse like that house. But some, like you and Job, are not going to fold," Minzano sneered.

"No, Agent Minzano. You simply stated the obvious. The lesson is that the enemy only wins if you die without faith. And the enemy will do whatever he can to take it from you, using absolutely any measure required."

CHAPTER 25

Bee-El and Egor walked down the dreary prison corridor. Progress was right on schedule – perhaps even ahead of schedule. Out of the comforts of home, each man was succumbing to pressure. The arrested members of the cloth had been without proper nourishment for days now. Their cells were freezing, they had not bathed in days, and there was no outside contact. Bee-El and Egor had seen worse circumstances, but they were informed that dire punishments were not needed to crack some of these men.

Bee-El walked to a cell he favored and looked at the man cowering inside of it: Deacon Blackwell. Bee-El remembered Deacon Blackwell as a man who preached down to people as if he were above them. It pleased Bee-El to see Blackwell begging for freedom.

"I have committed no crime," Blackwell pleaded.

"You have committed a crime against freedom, so yours has been usurped," Bee-El replied.

"What are you talking about? Do we not serve the same master?"

"Do you agree to follow Elijah and all he has to offer?"

"No, I serve the one and only true master."

"Then you shall stay here until you see the truth. I know you are angry. I know you want to lash out against me. I know you see me as the enemy, but in time you will see truth. Right now you see me as the enemy because your mind is in darkness. Soon you shall be bathed in righteousness. How long it takes depends only on you, my son."

CHAPTER 26

"Where are we going?" Rontrez asked Elijah from the limousine's luxurious interior. Rontrez was tired, and wanted a good night's rest. He had had enough sex to last any man a week, dined on the finest cuisine, and lived the life of a king. He had loved every minute of it, but now he wanted to rest and to speak to Oniva if she was still up. He had called several times, but she did not pick up her cell phone or house line. It was unlike her to be out late.

"To the beginning," Elijah replied.

"The beginning of what?"

"To the beginning of actuality."

"This looks like Fifth and Madison to me."

Elijah chuckled. "Outside is the Earth, Esau. Inside is the dawn of a new genesis."

"Inside of this car?"

"Inside of you, Esau. This is the beginning of opportunity, your chance to be the master of your own destiny."

"I feel a question coming on. What is it? What do you want, man?"

"I want to give you the power you want. I only want one thing from you in return."

"Here it is. Here we go with the favors. What is it?"

"I want you to be truly honest with yourself. That's all I ask."

"Okay, it's a deal."

"Esau, how do you know there is a supreme being?"

"There has to be a God. If there wasn't, I would be dead already. Plus, all those times my mother was praying, I know somebody had to doing something for her."

"You see that's what I'm talking about. You never got a chance to think for yourself."

"I think for myself every moment."

"No you don't. You never chose to go to church. You were just brought there by your mother. You didn't even want to go. You thought it was pretty boring, didn't you?"

"I sure did. I thought it was a waste of time."

"You never got a chance to choose what you wanted to believe in."

"So what are you saying?"

"I'm saying that if you had the chance, you would believe in Esau Rontrez."

"I do."

"I mean totally. I've never seen anything you haven't been able to do, Esau. You're even a spectacular athlete. Ever since you changed your ways, you don't have any enemies. You don't lie, cheat, kill, sell drugs, or commit any of the other dreadful wrongs you were exposed to as a child. That's why I was able to get you a second chance. This time, I want you to think for yourself. You can do anything. If you fall on your nose, then cry for help from whatever. But from the beginning, believe in yourself."

"Sounds easy enough."

Elijah started laughing out loud.

"What's so funny?"

"Esau, have you ever read the Bible?"

"Not really, but I remember most of the stories from Sunday school and stuff."

"Do you remember how that book says the Earth came about?"

"Yeah. God just created it. Then he created all the stuff in it."

Elijah started laughing again.

"What's so funny?"

"'Let there be light'? I mean give me a break. That doesn't even make sense. Everything was dark, and someone just flipped the switch and got the Earth rolling, huh? Does that make sense to you?"

"I must admit, it sounds pretty out there."

"You didn't answer my question."

"I guess I believe it, if it's in the Bible."

"You guess? That didn't sound too convincing to me, Esau. I think you were another victim."

"A victim of what?"

"Esau, do you believe in Santa Claus?"

"Hell no, there ain't no Santa Claus. If there was a Santa, how could he get his fat ass down all those chimneys, and get to every mall in the nation?"

"Exactly. But when you were little you believed in good ol' Santy Claus, didn't you?"

"Yeah. Everybody did, I guess."

"How did you figure out there was no Santa Claus?"

"My mom told me."

"Why did you believe in Santa Claus in the first place?"

"Because everyone else did, I guess. I just did. It was fun."

"Exactly my point. You are a victim of what I call orientational conformity. It's a clever type of socialization. Just because it was around you, and you were too young to think for yourself at the time, you went along for the ride. Involuntary indoctrination. Only when the truth was revealed to you did you then look back and see that the concept of Santa Claus made no sense. It's the same thing here with your little beliefs. You just go along for the ride. You don't truly believe any of that in your heart. You don't believe anyone walked on water then rose from the dead with holes in his body. You, of all people, *know* a virgin cannot have a child. You already knew this. You just didn't want to disappoint your family. And since you were little you were taught to sing, "Jesus loves me," and those other little ditties because you were too young to think for yourself. It was just orientational conformity. You never had a choice. If you had, you would have realized that it makes no sense. It's just Santa Claus on a larger scale! It's identical. If an alien came down here and saw how ridiculous the world was with this Supreme Being trivia, he would smack the life out of all of you!"

"I can't say some of the stuff isn't far fetched."

"Far fetched? Try ludicrous! What about the fantastic Ten Commandments? He gave them out and then all of them were broken by the end the book? Any true God would have enough sense not to keep a record of his mistakes, Esau. Wake up! If some crackhead walked up and smacked you in front of your women, what would you do?"

"I'd put some steel in him."

"Right! That's what any sensible man would do. If you listen to this magical sky fairy, you are to turn the other cheek and get smacked again. Then you are to love your enemy. Does this make sense to you?"

"No."

"That's all I want you to do. Think for yourself. Just as your mother took the blindfold off you with Santa Claus, I am taking the blindfold off of you with reality. Think for yourself! If it doesn't make sense, to hell with it! You're the man, Esau Rontrez. You are the most impressive young man I have ever seen, and I have been to the ends of the Earth. There is nothing that you have not been able to accomplish. Do you agree?"

"Pretty much."

"Of course you do. I just want you to start living life for *real*. You are born again. But this time, you will practice indulgence instead of abstinence. With the power invested in yourself, you will enjoy life's pleasantries to the fullest."

"This new beginning doesn't sound like the worst thing I ever heard."

"Anyone with sense would know it's the way life should be. Why should you hold back on the great things life has to offer, as long as you're not hurting anybody? You don't need anyone or anything to make your decisions for you. You are the true master of yourself. You are the man."

"Well if I am the master of myself, then I'm definitely not getting that microchip put in my head."

"So be it. Forget the microchip. I don't give a red cent whether you get it or not. It would just make things a lot more convenient for you."

"I'll be alright without it. As soon as this power thing comes into play."

CHAPTER 27

"What did you get on Elijah?" Sesom asked TC and Dino as they climbed back into the van.

"Some spooky stuff," TC replied. "It seems as if they tried to capture or kill a woman tonight, from what I gathered. They weren't able to because she was protected – whatever that means."

"Can you connect Elijah with the Bloodline?" Sesom asked.

"Well, not exactly. The Bloodline is putting statues of Elijah in all the thousands of churches that want one, but that's not criminal. Regarding the woman they went after tonight, we haven't positively identified the voice we have on tape. We believe it's Elijah, but we can't be sure. We put a transmitter in his vehicle. Wherever he goes, we'll know."

"Don't put too much faith in electronics," Sesom said. "They will not produce the evidence we need. I guarantee you, we are going to have to put our noses to the grindstone before this one is over."

"If the king of the world is a fake, then he's coming down," replied Dino. "The more time we waste, the stronger he gets."

"The bureau has been shut down," Sesom remarked. "Elijah's men have seized all funding and dissolved the FBI. We have all been reassigned to go after everyone in the United States that do not have the mark and investigate them."

"What?" Dino growled. "I don't care what Elijah's cronies have to say. I'm going to stay until this case comes to an end."

"Do you feel the same?" Sesom asked TC.

"Darn right I do," TC mumbled.

"Then it's official. We will continue our investigation until we have satisfied ourselves."

"Who will we report to?" Dino asked Sesom.

"No one," Sesom replied. "No one needs to know. That only increases our vulnerability to corruption. We can't get any funding, so the equipment we have here is all we can use."

"What do you think they want us to investigate all the non-chip citizens for?" TC asked. "Do you think Elijah is going to make them get the chip?"

"Probably," Dino said.

"No. He can't," Sesom demurred.

"Why not?" Dino asked.

"Because it's against the rules. Every person must get the chip of their own free will. Elijah can't *make* anyone do anything. It doesn't work like that. At most, he can control external factors to persuade you to get the chip of your own free will. Not having the chip now is very inconvenient, which makes many people chose to get the chip. But if I stuck a gun to your head and forced you to get the chip, or if I held you down and injected you with it, then it is not your free will. Has anyone else noticed that there are no laws requiring citizens to get the chips anymore? There is no organization enforcing their implementation either. Elijah is not physically forcing the chips upon anyone – he is just making life increasingly difficult for those without them. And if you get a chip, then you get an allowance. Additional allure. Aside from using positive stimulus, he's using negative impulses, such as inconvenience, displeasure and even embarrassment as those who don't have the chip increasingly become outsiders, as if they are not normal, or rebellious even. He's attacking people at every level, and now they're common enough that without one, it's almost impossible to access food or shelter. Personally, I would rather roll around on a bed of nails than be injected with a chip."

"So why does Elijah want us to find everyone without the chip?" Dino asked.

"So he may begin to break them."

"What do you mean break them?" Dino asked.

"Breaking could be considered the ultimate of all travesties. When you have nothing but despair or anger in your spirit, it becomes ripe for demons of all sorts to take or infest it."

"You mean like possession?" Dino asked.

"This is not *The Exorcist*. Yes, evil spirits can possess a person, but it is much simpler to use the human vessel as an instrument of evil. The process is actually quite complex, but yet simple. Better yet, the more you know, the more of a danger you become to yourself, so I will stop here."

"This religious stuff sounds spooky," TC interjected, sounding dismissive. "All we're missing is marshmallows and a campfire. On to reality: where can we find this cretin hustler and how can we connect him to the Bloodline?"

"I just spoke with Bryant," Sesom answered. "He suggests Elijah's main temple in Washington, DC. The same place we set the bugs."

"We haven't picked up anything on the bugs," TC reminded him. "Are you sure we should stick with this location?"

"Definitely. That's where the action is going down. We have it from a reliable source."

CHAPTER 28

Inside the temple in Washington, DC, Rontrez stood in the center of a colossal arena packed with clamoring bodies. Indecipherable designs were etched into the floor of the stage, but Rontrez didn't notice. Elijah stood by him, looking like the proud father of a newborn son.

Rontrez looked out at his audience. He felt like a celebrity. Every eye in the large chamber seemed fixed to him with admiration and respect. Rontrez had always wanted to be famous, just as most people did, whether they admitted it or not, but to stand in front of an assembly with hundreds of thousands of obedient eyes trained upon him felt surreal.

"Welcome to your destiny," Elijah smiled.

"Who are all these people?" Rontrez asked.

"Your army, Esau."

"All these people are my army. Who are they?"

"Your servants. Any powerful man needs servants. I'm sure it's in the rulebook somewhere. Any order you give, these men are here to carry it out expeditiously."

"Anything I say, these men can do?"

"No. Anything you say, these men *will* do."

"Where did you get them from? I mean, did you run an ad on the internet? I don't recognize any of these people."

"They were created to be your pillars of support, assistance and enforcement."

"I know they aren't doing this for free. What do they want in return?"

"You asked for power, now I am granting it. Among these men are lawyers, judges, doctors, police officers and every other profession you can imagine. I am presenting you with the means to accomplish anything. The circuitry to get any information you need, and the network to exact revenge on any enemy you want. Under your leadership, these men are the most powerful organization ever created. They are waiting."

"Waiting for what?"

"For your first instruction. Some of them have come a long way to see their leader. Don't disappoint them."

"Well, I said I would legalize prostitution if I ever came into power."

"And I also said that was the most asinine thing I'd ever heard of. Think bigger."

"Elijah, you are already the leader of the New Global Order, aren't you?"

"You asked for power, now you're asking me to take it back from you. I need you to make up your mind. Are you a follower or a leader? I need an answer."

"I'm a leader."

"Don't tell me, Mr. Almighty . . . tell them," Elijah said gesturing toward the crowd with a wry smile.

"I'll tell you what worries me."

"Please stop the wailing and moaning. You worry more than someone waiting for their HIV test results. I give you power, and you throw it back in my face. I might have been wrong about you. I might have been mistaken to think you could handle this responsibility and power that I have presented you with. You have climbed from man to emperor, now you want to run back down the mountain and hide in the valley. What in the hell are you worried about now?"

No pun intended.

"What do all these people want in return for their services?"

"Are we still on the price tag? Oh, spare me from the madness. Why don't you just bury me under a pile of bricks, because you're definitely not listening to me? I told you, that was your old life. On the new route, things have changed. We both agreed that change is good, didn't we?"

"As long as it's for the better."

"This change is unquestionably for the better."

"I know that these same people will be my downfall."

"You've got to be kidding me," Elijah replied dryly.

"Nope. It's just logic, really. I mean, I don't know these people."

"Who cares? Do you want the history of every person in this room? You're contradicting yourself. It seems like maybe you weren't ready for your wish to be granted."

"What I'm saying is I've never met any of these people, therefore, they have no reason not to betray me. I'm not paying them, I don't know them, and I have no idea what their wishes and needs are. There is obviously some benefit to serving me, or they wouldn't be doing it. Once the benefit runs out or is no longer satisfying to them, they will rebel against me. If I'm going to lead, my crew has to be thoroughbreds. People I know will be with me to the end."

"Well, they know you. Most have been waiting their entire lives to serve a man as intellectually powerful as you. A man that they are all prepared to die for – for the greater good. A man to lead this new world into true enlightenment, and conquer those who dare oppose him. They have already been trained, both mentally and physically, to serve you. Under your guidance they will ensure the peace and prosperity of the New Global Order."

"Are you somehow guaranteeing that they will not betray me?"

"No. I am guaranteeing that they cannot betray you. Now, are you a follower or a leader? The choice is yours to make, and the time to make it is now."

"I told you, I'm a leader."

"So, Emperor. Shall we begin?"

CHAPTER 29

Justes was exhausted. He had thought and prayed as he never had before. His wife had sustained his study with hot food for nourishment, back rubs, and words of encouragement. He was sure that somewhere in his reading lay the key to the plan of the "one of many." He pored over his Bible and even performed keyword searches on his computer, but still he came up with nothing. He reread the history of the Order, and reflected on how the Knights Templar members had been tortured into giving false confessions and burned at the stake for what they believed in – just like the Bloodliners persecuted Christians today. Mary's footsteps sounded on the stairs behind him, and he took a deep breath as she entered the room and placed a cold glass of orange juice on his desk. Justes thanked her with a soft touch on her arm.

"Why don't you give this a rest? You've been at this nonstop for hours," Mary said.

"Stopping is not an option. There is too much at stake," Justes replied.

"I'm sure there is, but sometimes it's better to let things run their natural course. There is a plan for everything. Just have faith."

"I have faith, but I will also do everything in my power to make sure the Lord's plan is carried out," Justes stated adamantly.

"If the Lord is as powerful as you believe Him to be, you couldn't truly affect the plan anyway. Just relax."

"Mary, I wish I could tell you everything, but I can't yet. What I can say is that things are not as they seem."

"Things are seldom ever as they seem."

"True enough," Justes agreed.

"I think you should let God carry out his plan, and everything will be alright. Did you ever think you might get in the way?"

"What do you mean?"

"Did you ever consider for a moment that your attempts to intervene might actually interfere with a plan that was built off of faith?"

"I don't think that's what's going to happen."

"Well the plan is built off of faith, correct?"

"Yes."

"All that studying and reading you're doing suggests that you don't trust in God or His plan. If God has a plan, let it take its course."

"I'm just trying to make sure everything is right."

"That's what I'm saying. *You're* trying to make sure everything is right. You're second-guessing God. That's not faith. You are trying to figure out the plan, are you not?"

"Not exactly."

"Then what are you going through all those books for? You're trying to figure out the plan, then I guess somehow try to assist it. Do you know how preposterous that sounds? Do you think God's plan cannot succeed without your help?"

"What are you trying to do here? Are you trying to discourage me? It seems as if you're trying to plant doubt in my head for some reason, or shift me towards despair."

Despair is the tormentor of Faith, Justes thought suddenly. Justes became aware that he and Mary were not alone in the room. They were the only people inside the small library, but something else alive was with them inside of the chambers.

"All spawned from the ungodly," Justes started, "I cast you out in the name—"

"All right, already," Mary said harshly. Her face and body twisted unnaturally, and in a moment Elijah stood before him in the cozy library.

Justes sat, stunned.

"Look, Chris," Elijah started, "I can't understand why you place so much doubt in me. Why don't you just let me do my thing, and all who are true believers will reign on high in my kingdom? You know that's how it's supposed to work."

"You are not of the Almighty, I command you to be gone."

"Look," Elijah said, unfazed. "The Jedi mind tricks don't work. What are you now, a wizard shaman? Let's be serious."

"What do you want?" Justes asked.

"That's not the question. The question is what do *you* want? I see you with all of these books and your computer, your technology – and look at this," Elijah grinned, holding up a compact disc, "The Holy Bible on CD. I see you are analyzing something. You are searching for something. Something that will give you, perhaps, a spark of divine insight to this great revelation. Or possibly some spectacular spiritual movement that will bring you all the answers in one glorious epiphany. I doubt you even know what you're looking for."

"I'm looking for a way to assist in God's plan, and make sure that your ways do not prevail."

"Well isn't that something. Tell me, Mr. Benevolent Soothsayer, why do you want to do this? Do you want to become a martyr? Is that it? Or do you have something to prove to yourself?"

"Whatever you're doing isn't working."

"The interesting part is that I'm not doing anything. It seems as if you're trying to figure out God's plan. Don't you find that pretty odd?"

"What's odd about it?"

"You're a mortal. You are beneath any kind of God, am I correct?"

"I am God's servant, and I am beneath Him."

"Well then how in the world do think you're going to figure out his plan? If you can figure out the plan, then obviously he is not above you. In your rigorous studies and vigorous attempts to figure out the formula, you have already proven to yourself that you do not believe."

"Satan, I cast you out!"

"I'm not Satan. More voodoo mind tricks and enchantment I see. Why do you want to throw me out, Chris? It's cold outside. Brrrr.

Chris, I'm not here to harm you. If I wanted to kill you, I could do it without exerting too much effort. All I want to do is talk. I am not evil. Those who are against me are evil. All I want to do is bring peace unto the world. Have you ever seen otherwise of me?"

"You sent men to kill me and my brothers."

"I didn't do that. I, for the life of me had nothing to do with what happened. You know as well as I do that was the Bloodliners. They have been brought to an end."

"Your tongue is as crooked as your ways. I cast you out of my sanctuary now. All that is not of Holy descent must leave now, in the name of God!"

Elijah crossed his arms and smirked. "I guess you expected me to melt or something. You want me to leave because you know I'm making a little too much sense. I'll be back to check on you. I'm not evil, Chris. You can believe that. All I want you to do is to see things for what they are and to realize that your actions contradict themselves. As a man of God, I do not want to be where I am not wanted. Therefore, I will gladly leave since you are so adamant. I love you in the name of the Father, my child."

With that, Elijah turned and left the library. Only a moment later, Mary raced into the room. Justes was surprised she did not run into Elijah, who should have been only a step outside the door.

"Chris, are you all right? I heard you screaming."

"Mary, things are as they have never been before. And part of me knows that before long, there is going to be a lot more screaming."

CHAPTER 30

Minzano climbed down into the hidden room in Holy of Holies and faced Pathem and Oniva. "Who is Captain Ario Samsere?"

Oniva shrugged.

"Think carefully, who is officer Ario Samsere to Esau Rontrez? Rontrez just sent some men to kill him."

"We have to stop it!" Pathem exclaimed.

"It's probably already been done. The Bloodline moves pretty fast at things like this."

"You saw Rontrez?" Oniva asked.

"Yea. Clear as I see you now. Elijah has just appointed him as the long-awaited leader of the Bloodline. The great one that they have been looking for all this time."

"What?" Oniva asked.

"No what about it. Your friend just put a hit out on a police officer."

"That's impossible. Rontrez doesn't kill people, he—"

"Yeah, yeah, yeah, lady. I just heard him send five men after a police captain."

Suddenly, Oniva remembered. "I know who he is," she said.

"Who?" Minzano grumbled.

"He was a crooked cop in our old neighborhood. He killed Rontrez's cousin three years ago. He would arrest innocent people to get promotions, and he would plant drugs on you if you drove a better car than he did. He killed people in the neighborhood, and with every murder he got higher in the police ranking. I remember he used to beat on members of my family too. He used to handcuff people, put them in the back of his squad car and drive them way out into the woods to beat on them or kill them. I never met him, but I remember who he is. He's an evil man."

"We have to stop them. With every murder, evil gains another victory," Pathem reminded Minzano.

"Are you kidding? We can't stop them now. That cop is a dead man," Minzano said.

"My goodness, aren't you a man of the law? You're going to leave a fellow officer to be slaughtered?"

"Tell me, oh holy one, what would you have me do? Put on a cape and go on out there in my pajamas and utility belt? Or do you want me to leave him a message? Dead men can't pick up the phone. Look, all your buddies got blasted less than a half hour after I got the phone call. It's been forty-five minutes since the hit was put out. If that man isn't dead right now, it's a miracle."

"Why didn't you stop it?"

"Stop it? Why didn't you stop the Holocaust, Pathem? You were here."

"Don't be ridiculous. I bet you didn't even attempt to contact him."

"Hey, don't preach to me. I don't see you running out the door to save the day."

"If he was a terrible person, how does evil win because he's gone?" Oniva asked Pathem.

"Oniva," Pathem started, "anytime a person dies who is not righteous, that person does not enter into the kingdom of heaven. They are forever in torment as the devil's slave. Evil becomes more powerful with that man's death, and again because whoever murdered him is also deep in sin – and throwing himself deeper into the abyss of iniquity."

"Agent Minzano, where is Rontrez? Can we get to him?" Oniva asked.

"No. There's an army guarding him. I couldn't even get near him."

"No," Pathem agreed, "A menial knight would not be able to get anywhere near the keystone."

Minzano cut his eyes at Pathem before turning to Oniva. "A funny thing, Oniva. The Bloodline has stopped looking for you. It's like you don't matter anymore. Why do you think that is?"

"I don't know," Oniva replied.

"It can be interpreted one of two ways," Pathem started, "It could be that you are no longer in the way of the plan, Oniva, and that evil already has everything it needs to casts its dark shadow upon this land."

"Why would she not matter all of a sudden?" Minzano cut in. "This has never happened before. When a hit is put out on someone – especially the way this one was, I mean, the Archknights came out from under the rocks and everything – we keep going until the target is dead. There is no time out. The Bloodline doesn't play tag."

"What's the second option?" Oniva asked Pathem.

"Perhaps, rather than being an obstacle, you have become an important part of evil's plan. This doesn't sound likely, but it's still possible."

"Why isn't it likely? Not that I want to be a part of anyone's plan except for His," Oniva said, touching the cross she wore around her neck.

"We have to be extremely careful not to underestimate the enemy. The Prince of Darkness is one of the most crafty and devious entities ever to exist. It doesn't really make sense that one minute you're an obstacle, and the next you're an asset."

"Why not?" Oniva asked.

"Because what would have happened if the Bloodline had managed to kill you? It doesn't check out that evil would now have to reroute its design. That sounds extremely sloppy and ill-planned. Not at all the grand scheme I predict the tempter to cast forth."

"Where is Justes?" Minzano asked, looking around.

"He said he had to go home and do some studying. We tried to stop him –"

"He did what! Does that idiot know he's on a hit list? What the hell is the matter with him? Where does he live? You have to call him. Get him to come back before they get to him."

"Justes is not a child lost in the wilderness, Agent Minzano," Pathem said firmly. "He is a very capable individual. I worry more about you than I do about him. Remember, evil will not kill the true believers unless is it absolutely necessary. Evil loses if a soul is delivered unto heaven. It is to our advantage that evil is greedy. This war against God is for the domain of *all* souls. The adversary wants *all* souls delivered unto Hell's gate, not just the bad ones. I've done some studying, and I have come to several conclusions."

"This is what you guys were doing when I was sent to kill you, right?" Minzano asked.

"I assume so, yes," Pathem replied.

"Well, what did you all find out?" Oniva asked.

"Unfortunately, the bad guys have the really easy part. You see, we are born with a tendency toward sin, so the wicked one wins from the beginning," (Psalm 51:5; 58:3).

"Sounds like the battle is already lost," Minzano said.

"Not lost. It just doesn't get any easier. The world is full of temptation, because the Devil himself has become the god of this age, and he devours whomever he can," (2 Corinthians 4:4; 1 Peter 5:8).

"The devil. You mean an orange guy with horns," Minzano muttered sarcastically.

"Be serious. The devil isn't a red, horned, lizard-man holding a pitchfork, as he is often portrayed. He is not just one physical entity – he can assume many forms and has done so throughout history. The only way we can overcome evil is by the true weapon: Faith. We identified at least five main ways in which the prince of this sinful world can attack. First, he keeps you out of places of worship and away from other people of faith. This prevents people from hearing God's word and being surrounded by the righteous – or, at the very least, people trying to do right. He has largely succeeded in this. Worldwide, church attendance is at an all-time low. People are scared to death of the Bloodlines church bombings, and kidnappings. The torture of Christians worldwide has caused people to go into hiding, doubt their faith, and even turn away from God. Unimaginable horrors committed by militias like ISIS and the Bloodline have plunged Christians worldwide into fear and despair. Those who were on the fence are now on the wrong side of it. Churches that have been community centers for years have closed due to bankruptcy and lack of attendance.

His second weapon is to cause trouble and division among brethren. Do you know that there are hundreds of different kinds of subsidiary religions and churches that say they serve the same God? The proliferation of different branches of Christianity creates division even among the faithful. This type of intrinsic division sets some of the groundwork for other means of separation and alienation, like racism, sexism, discrimination, and political polarization."

"What about churches that aren't worshiping the same God?" Minzano asked.

"That is the third weapon, which is technical. It corrupts doctrine, tainting the teachings and making it difficult to find the way. He has succeeded here as well. New types of churches with eclectic false doctrine are popping up all the time – it's impossible to even keep track. In many of them those who call themselves pastors are not even Christians. Some false teachings dabble in mysticism and occultism, and others are merely a front for taking money from their parishioners, and exploiting large financial markets."

"What's the fourth weapon?" Oniva asked.

"The fourth weapon is to get the righteous to backslide into secular activities through temptation. We all know how this goes. Evil already wins this battle, because we all carry the sin of Adam and Eve and are born with an inclination toward sin. We are born perhaps without the literal knowledge of good and evil, or right and wrong, but as soon as we do learn the difference, we often choose to go against God's will," (Romans 5:12).

"From what you're saying, it seems like we're doomed to fail from birth," Minzano spat. "None of this stuff even makes sense. You just said that we're born to be beastly. Cursed from birth. We're brought into this world just so we can screw up, and some spook god will punish us because we did wrong."

"What's the fifth weapon?" Oniva asked Pathem, seeing Minzano's palpable frustration.

"The fifth weapon is the most powerful – it's the devil's nuclear option."

"What is it?" Minzano asked.

"To render true believers obsolete."

"How would he do that?" Oniva asked.

"Contort religion. If everyone believes in Elijah, then they don't believe in God – because they think they already are. It's human nature. People are more likely to believe in what they see rather than what they do not."

"He's using all of the weapons now," Oniva observed.

"Yes, he has mastered the first four," Pathem replied. "He has created his masterpiece, and the fifth weapon is its impenetrable frame. If he is allowed to complete it, it will deliver all mankind into the hands of damnation."

"You said before you didn't have any solutions," Oniva started. "A lot has happened since. Do you have any ideas? I'm willing to help in any way I can, but I'm not sure what I can do. This all seems so far from reality."

"That is another sidearm that the adversary has. Most humans are not mentally prepared to deal with these events, which has rendered them useless. Most of us on earth now are mindless drones taking Elijah's orders like we were robots. It's too big a circumstance for us to comprehend, so we go along with the program. This makes his already elementary job even easier."

"But what do we do?" Oniva asked. "It seems like you have a grasp on the attack strategies, but what about our defenses? How do we fight evil, Bishop Pathem?"

"That's the part they forgot to figure out," Minzano scoffed.

"Bishop, is that true?" Oniva asked.

"Brother Justes was our greatest hope. At several points in his life it seemed as if he had the ability to connect directly with God."

"Well, I don't believe in God," Minzano stated. "I'm really not one for religion. If there was a God, why did he let the entire earth go to hell like this? No God I know of would do that."

"So you mean to tell me that after all this, you do not believe in the Lord?" Oniva asked.

"I saw a man come down from the sky like you did. Right now, I really don't know what's going on. The funny thing is that all the 'experts' – such as yourselves – don't know what in the world is going on either. If there is a God, why doesn't he come down and put in some work? Maybe help me pay some bills and take down the Bloodline."

They heard rushed footsteps, and Justes' feet suddenly appeared at the top of the stairs.

"And where have you been? Do you know that people want to kill you? Why would you walk out into the night like you're not on a hit list?" Minzano all but shouted.

"I had to leave. I was called to study," Justes replied.

"Called by whom?" Minzano asked.

"Called by my God."

"What? Called by your God? This is not New Mecca, will you use your head?"

Oniva stepped in. "Reverend Justes, Bishop Pathem says that you might be an important part of the solution. I don't think it was wise for you to go back home. They might have been looking for you there."

"I was very careful. I promise," Justes replied.

"I'm glad you are back safely. Any luck studying?" Oniva asked.

"Not the kind of luck I'd hoped for. I had a visitor."

"Who?" Minzano asked.

"The Father of Lies himself," Justes sighed.

"You spoke to the adversary?" Pathem asked.

"As clearly as I am speaking to you now."

"What did he want from you?" Pathem probed, looking concerned.

"I have no idea. I would say he just came to bug me, but I'm smarter than that. He had a reason for popping up like that. First he disguised himself as my wife. Then he just transformed into Elijah like he was made of play-dough. It was unreal."

"Do you remember what he said? Did he leave you anything or ask you anything?" Oniva asked.

"No. It just seemed that he took time out of his busy schedule to come spook the daylights out of me, then buzz around me like a horse-fly. I know his visit had a purpose, I just don't know what it was."

"What did he say to you?" Pathem asked.

"He just came to take some of my faith away, I guess. I don't remember what he said word for word, but had mentioned that because I was studying, that I must not trust God."

"Is that so," Pathem mumbled. "He came himself, he didn't send anyone after you, though he easily could have. You must be an important part of this."

"What part do you think I play in this? An ally or an obstacle?" Justes asked.

"I'm not quite sure," Pathem answered.

"Why doesn't that surprise me?" Minzano muttered to himself.

"There was another thing that shocked me," Justes continued, "He said he wasn't Satan."

"You called him the father of lies yourself," Pathem answered.

"Yes, but a strange part of me believes what he said," Justes replied.

"You said you went to study. Maybe you were close to a solution and he wanted to disturb your inner peace and throw you off track," Oniva offered. "When you're spooked, worried or confused, you don't think normally. Did you come to any solutions before he visited?"

"Unfortunately not. Just a bunch of theories and dead ends. The one of many isn't mentioned anywhere I could find."

"Of those theories, do any of them strike you as plausible?" Oniva asked.

"They all do. And then again, they all don't. There is no reference to exactly what is happening right now. Everything seems to be in place, but with certain strange exceptions. These exceptions are what is throwing me off."

"Exceptions like what?" Oniva asked.

"Idiosyncrasies in the prophecy itself. Several strange things that are happening now that contradict the way the Lord usually works. God does usually not allow evil to deliver this magnitude of miracles so consistently. I'm thinking this would be for four reasons. One, if evil routinely performed miracles, too many people would be looking for the benefits of miracles, and would not try to resist evil's ways. Two, God performs miracles on the basis of faith. Most people can't get God to perform a miracle because they don't have enough faith. If anything routinely performed miracles, most people would have faith in that being automatically, which is why God doesn't routinely perform miracles in the public eye, yet performs miracles in individual lives every day. The third reason I found is that God generally has used miracles as a 'seal of approval' to show that a prophet, or pastor or whomever has His approval. It would be very confusing for the righteous if evil people could frequently do the same things. The fourth motive is by far the most important. If the devil routinely performed miracles, many people who sincerely want to follow God would be misled. Evil has always been able to perform miracles. I didn't expect this level of a performance."

"Where did you come up with these four considerations?" Pathem asked.

"By studying numerous reliable sources."

"What sources?" Pathem asked.

"I've gone through other books outside of the Christian religion."

Oniva hesitated. "Maybe that's what they want you to do," she said. "Maybe they want to draw you outside of your boundaries, weakening your faith. Maybe this is why these idiosyncrasies were planted."

Pathem grinned.

"So you think I should stop trying to figure things out?" Justes asked.

"Honestly, I'm not sure what we should do," Oniva answered. "For now, we just have to stay planted."

CHAPTER 31

Captain Ario Samsere was parked in an alley off of Georgia Avenue, the bobbing head of a hooker in his lap. Slowly, a windowless van pulled into the alley, blocking its only exit. His eyes followed the van in his rearview mirror with indifference. He really didn't care who saw him with the whore now. He wasn't a police officer anymore, but part of Elijah's army. And although the world was seemingly at peace, Ario knew only too well that he would still live the pleasures of life to the fullest. He relaxed as he felt his orgasm come, and the girl began to sit up.

Suddenly, a deafening crash cut through the silence of the night as his car window shattered. Muffled by a silencer, the Ruger belonging to Bloodline Knight Manson emitted only a series of dull thuds as Manson emptied his clip into Ario's stomach. Ario had begun to reach for his gun, but did not even get a shot off. The girl sat frozen in fear. Manson reached through the shattered window and let himself into the car. Two men emerged from the shadows, grabbed Ario's body, and roughly shoved it into the back of the waiting van.

Manson eyed the girl for a moment, loading another clip into his Ruger. He looked at her youthful face and realized she was paralyzed with fear. This excited him. He looked her up and down without saying a word.

The young girl saw that Manson had wild eyes, and she knew instinctively that she was in mortal danger. The alley was blocked and there was no escape. She felt as if she were trapped in a nightmare, and she heard only her own panicked breathing as she glanced between Manson and the two men leaning against the doors of the van.

Manson made his decision. "Get out," he muttered.

The girl crawled reluctantly out of the passenger seat out and stood before Manson, fear in her eyes.

"Walk," Manson barked, shoving her towards the van with the barrel of his gun.

As she approached, the men watched with newly piqued interest. Manson opened the back of the van and motioned her in with his gun. She crawled obediently into the back of the van, the men grabbing roughly at her soft skin. Manson shoved her off balance, and the van door slammed shut.

• • • • • • •

"Whoa, look what we have here," TC reported through his radio. "It looks like they're dragging a dead body up into the temple. And they have someone else with them."

"What?" Dino asked grabbing his binoculars, "Let me see."

Sure enough, he saw the figures of two men dragging a barely conscious woman, her clothes torn, up the steps to the temple. Beside them, three men hauled the bloodied, bloated corpse of a man in a police uniform.

"Let's go investigate," TC muttered.

"I'll go. You stay here and monitor everything those bastards are saying. This will give me a great chance to see some faces, too," Dino grinned.

"Dino, don't be a cowboy. You'll come up missing in there," Sesom warned.

"I'm coming with you," TC said. "There are five of them. You couldn't take five armed criminals on a *good* day."

"Do we really have a choice? We don't have any backup. If we both went in and got killed, there would be no one to report all this great intelligence I'm about to gather," Dino replied, winking.

Before TC had a chance to respond, Dino disappeared into the night.

• • • • • • •

Dino swiftly approached the men, thinking quickly as he walked. Dino remembered that since Elijah had taken over, there was no legal jurisdiction he could confront these men with, though they were obviously breaking the peace.

"Need some help?" he asked, gesturing toward the young woman.

"Thanks," one of the men replied. "Where art thou delivered?"

Dino paused, unsure how to answer. Sesom's voice crackled in Dino's head through his microscopic earpiece. "He just asked what Bloodline chapter you're from. Tell him you're spawned from the 66th."

"Spawned from the 66th," Dino replied. "And you?"

"24th precinct, Serpents of Eden," Manson replied, turning back towards the temple. Dino grabbed the woman's ankles and followed them up the steps. Although the façade of the building lacked any security, there were several armed guards waiting immediately inside the doors. Dino wanted to ask where they were taking the bodies, but did not want to arouse suspicion. Bryant had briefed them carefully on the organization, and Dino remembered that usually questions were not tolerated. As they carried the bodies to an elevator, Dino heard the young woman weakly pleading for help, but there was nothing he could do. All that he needed now was to connect this to Elijah.

As the elevator began to rise, one of the men spoke. "66th, huh?" Manson clarified. "Angels of Descent, right?"

Dino nodded.

"Where are you in your journey?" Manson asked.

Dino still could not interpret the phrases. He listened for help from Sesom or TC.

Back in the van, TC shrugged. "I'm clueless," he said.

"You're on your own," Sesom informed Dino.

"The beginning," Dino said confidently, hoping he was somewhere near faking it.

"Congratulations," Manson replied, "but you really shouldn't be here."

"I know, but something inside me wants to meet the Great One," Dino replied.

Manson nodded and fell silent, staring intently at a spot on the floor as if waiting for it to come to life. "He is here. We're taking the girl to him," Manson replied.

Dino wanted to ask why, but knew better than to draw unneeded attention to himself. He discreetly glanced at the spot that Manson had seemed to concentrate on, but there was nothing of interest there.

The elevator door slid open, and before Dino's eyes lay a vast labyrinth unlike anything he had ever seen, either in life or in his dreams. Everything was shiny white and branded with indecipherable letters and symbols. Through an open door, Dino caught a glimpse of what looked like a command center, filled with an army of men busy with satellite consoles that Dino recognized from his time in the military. The walls were covered with hundreds of flat screen monitors, each displaying a bird's eye view of a different city. He noticed the colored dots on the screen, each attached to a citizen. Most of the dots were green, but a few scattered dots flashed red. Green he gathered was someone in compliance. Red it seemed was someone without a smartchip. It looked as if they were tracking individuals through the smart chips, and watching citizens' every move.

There is no way these people can watch everyone in the world, Dino thought to himself. That couldn't be possible. He and his newfound associates walked past the open door into a large corridor that felt endless. Dino noticed another command center, supported by younger operators looking at large screens, exploiting social media. The young men and women seemed to be manipulating social media platforms to influence public opinion and actions. Within seconds, one woman had created a hashtag #TheComing with a flattering picture of Elijah. With a motion on her touchscreen tablet, she added 500,000 likes and shares. Their digital world map displayed how quickly the message disseminated across the world.

On the outside, the building was the size of a cozy neighborhood church. But on the inside, it felt more expansive than a major airport. Dino was also mesmerized by the paintings in the corridor, which seemed to writhe inside of the wall in his periphery. The eyes of the people in the paintings seemed soulless and blackened by evil.

Dino couldn't help himself, and he stared at one of the people in the paintings. Though it resembled a human being, it was something else entirely. It looked as if it wanted to hop out of the wall and let loose its fury. Dino shuddered. The entire place gave him the creeps. Though it called itself a temple, it looked more like a space station – and the people inside definitely didn't strike him as the moral type.

Dino and the Bloodline members dragged the two bodies further, then stopped abruptly, causing Dino to drop the woman's legs and stumble. He looked around, looking for the cause of their sudden change of plans. When he saw nothing, Dino turned to face the other men.

They stood shoulder to shoulder, looking at him with hard looks on their faces. Though he felt the tension mounting around him, Dino held his cool.

"Where did you say you were from?" Manson asked.

"66th," Dino replied.

They remained silent. Fear crept up Dino's neck as their icy silence continued, but he had no option other than to stand his ground.

Manson looked at Dino when he spoke. "Gentlemen, we have an infiltrator."

As if on cue, one of the Bloodliners pulled out his handgun and shot Dino through the heart. Dino collapsed, the life seeping from his body. His vision blurred, and his foes were replaced by a man dressed in white. As the man approached, Dino recognized the man as Elijah.

"Rise, my son," Elijah instructed.

Dino rose up without effort, suddenly without pain. The blood on his clothes was gone. He looked behind him to see his own body, lifeless and bleeding on the ground. As he turned, the corridor twisted around him into a fiery furnace. There was nothing around them but heat and flames, but Elijah remained calm.

"My son, I know you to be good at heart, but the good must suffer to find meaning in their path."

Dino shouted above the leaping flames, fear in his heart. As a child he had heard stories about burning in Hell for eternity. He had ignored them, but tears now came to his eyes as he asked, "Is this is Hell?"

Elijah was silent, and Dino started to cry.

"I know you fought for prestige in your organization. You were hungry for power, authority, and recognition. These earthly desires cannot help you now. You had no faith in your Lord. All that is not within you is left behind."

Dino looked around him to see angry souls in torment, waiting for him to be cast down with them. Elijah's image began to fade away.

"No!" Dino cried. "Lord, please don't leave me here!"

Elijah had faded away but his voice was still clear. "You do have one option. I still know you to be a kind individual. You may return to your past to do my work."

"What do you want me to do?"

"The fear of the Lord is the beginning of wisdom, and knowledge of the Holy One is understanding. There is much evil still upon this earth. You have the option of making this earth as I intended. The decision is yours."

CHAPTER 32

After a minute of radio silence, Sesom spoke. "What happened to Dino?"

"I don't know," TC answered. "There was no sound after he got off of the elevator. Like he's on another planet. There's no static, no nothing. I'm checking my equipment now."

"Don't bother," Sesom replied.

"What do you mean?"

"As I expected, Elijah's temples are far more than they appear."

"Well what are they?"

"Gateways to the worst kind of evil."

"What?"

"Gateways, strategically set up around the globe. The devil's fortresses. Though this sinful world is the enemy's domain, the destroyer of souls is bound. He's bound like a pit bull chained to a pole – powerless unless we chose to enter his radius. He cannot force us to follow him against our will, but he can make it very tempting not to. He rules over the sinful world as well as his unearthly region for the afterlife, and he is now attempting to bring the two together."

"Can he do that? I'm not much for religion. Never got plunged under water or ate bread crumbs at church, but I always try to do the right thing. Can what you're saying really happen? Yes or no," TC asked.

"It's not that simple. You're looking for cut-and-dry answers in an ocean of theology and unrevealed history. There are very few yes and no answers in this battle, but without a doubt, our enemy is winning. With every passing second we are closer to checkmate."

"Well the devil, or whatever he is, is powerful. I mean look around you. He has the world in the palm of his hand. Your enemy is running the world. In the literal sense too."

"Evil rules the world through deception and sin, not legitimately by God. Yes, evil has power, but it is limited. Resist the devil, and he will flee from you."

· · · · · · · · · ● ● ● · · · · · · · · · · · · · · ● · · · · · · · · · · ·

Manson and the other two Bloodline members stopped before Rontrez's throne in the grandiose sanctuary, dragging two bodies: a dead man and a breathing woman. Rontrez recognized the man immediately as the corrupt cop who had murdered over a dozen innocent men, including his cousin. He recognized the woman as an associate, Samaria, who used to walk around the neighborhood like she was a goddess. Rontrez remembered how Samaria would only be seen with the richest men in the city, who made their money squelching the last dimes out of the poor, or the cutthroat drug dealers who killed for a dollar and infested the neighborhood with poison. Samaria was once pretty and Rontrez once tried to recruit her for his stable, but she had embarrassed him and spat in his face. At one point in time Rontrez did not like to see individuals at rock bottom, but his years on the streets had hardened him. Rontrez looked with pleasure at the sight before him. The same woman that wouldn't give him the time of day, who would spit on a man when he was down – lay before him now, dirty, sobbing and obviously pregnant. Instead of having sympathy for the woman, Rontrez's mouth curled into a smile.

"As the sweet nectar of summertime transforms into the icy bitterness of winter's kind, so the tide turns," Rontrez said, smirking.

Samaria stared up at Rontrez from the floor before him. For a moment she didn't recognize him, but she knew only one man who spoke in fortune cookie half-rhymes. The Sandman.

"Just as day becomes night, you have faded from a self-proclaimed goddess to a nasty, trembling blight that offends my eyesight," Rontrez continued.

She was afraid, but anger rose to mask it. "Sandman, what the hell have you got me in here for? Tell these goons to turn me loose before-"

She couldn't even finish the sentence before Rontrez's backhand collided with her mouth, and she dropped to her knees shaking. Rontrez stooped to look at her closely.

"Yes, indeed. Bow down to your new god. You think you are a goddess, so I guess now we are a perfect match. Except there's one problem. You aren't worth a place in my stable. Look at yourself. You disgust me with your very presence. You're bloated, you're nasty, you smell like gunk, funk, and skunk. You look like you ain't bathed good in twelve pecan seasons, and now your goddess throat is wrapped around men all night. I don't want you in my sight. You make me want to vomit, you wretch. You used to walk the streets like the sun didn't shine until you walked outside. Now the sun doesn't shine until you walk inside. Look at yourself. You're a vile disgrace to any animal walking this earth. I see you're also carrying an unborn life with you. And his life is probably as doomed as yours. And hell knows I wouldn't drink out that chest if I was in the Mojave Desert."

Though she was angry, Sandman's words cut her to the bone. She had had a hard time finding a trick in the new cashless society. A street prostitute couldn't collect payment with the chip, and many wouldn't pay a hooker where their actions could be traced. Samaria knew that, as a pimp, Rontrez understood the hardship she faced. Even the pawnshops where she used to exchange the jewelry and valuables she received were now on the smartchip system. She wasn't sure exactly who Rontrez was now, but she did know she wanted to be a part of it. She looked around at the labyrinth she was in. To her, it looked like the inside of an exotic mansion. She was kneeling in lavish surroundings, and Rontrez's immaculate white suit looked so clean that the material seemed to glow with a magical radiance. Samaria looked around again and saw Rontrez's faithful army surrounding him as well as the men that still held her. Even in this time of peace, she saw that the Sandman still had some authority.

Her tone went from furious to humble in less than a second. "Sandman, we can help each other," Samaria offered.

"Help each other how, tramp?"

"Sandman, I can work for you. I just can't go back out there on them streets. Not when I got this baby." Samaria outstretched her arms to Rontrez, so vulnerable she seemed to be offering her soul. Rontrez saw the telltale needle marks in her arms.

"You on that white, ain't you, girl," Rontrez said nodding towards her track marks. He guessed it was heroin, but it could have been something else.

"I ain't no dopehead, Sandman, I swear. Times just got hard for me. I'm all alone," Samaria cried in desperation. "I'm just trying to make it!"

"Save the tears for somebody who cares. I would rather trust a squirrel with both of my nuts than trust a dope fiend whore."

Samaria started to cry. "Please don't kick me out, I can't make it out there by myself! I can't do it!"

"Get this piece of trash out of my face," Rontrez said, turning around.

As Samaria pleaded for Rontrez to change his mind, Manson and the other men dragged her out of the sanctuary and back into the elevator, where Asmodeus was waiting. The Bloodline soldiers tossed the woman into the elevator and exited swiftly, leaving her crumpled and sobbing on the floor.

All three men did not hesitate to leave any room with Asmodeus in it. Like his body, his face was long, thin, and sallow; not young, but without wrinkle or blemish. His downward-sloping eyes and eyebrows were unusually large, and they shone menacingly out of his gaunt face. Since he was tall, this feature also made him appear as if he was always looking down in disgust at everyone around him. He wore a circular gold medallion with a brilliant red gemstone surrounded by four arrows set in diamonds. The black rim of the medallion matched his jet black hair, which he kept tied back in a ponytail, exposing his paper-thin white skin. It wasn't even his appearance that bothered them most, but the overwhelming sense of unease they felt in his presence. It didn't help that Asmodeus didn't speak, except to the Archknights in an indecipherable tongue. Usually, you just knew what he was thinking when he looked at you, just as he had told each of the three men who had dragged the woman into the elevator to get off, without opening his mouth or using a gesture.

Elijah stepped out from behind Rontrez and smiled. "Bravo, emperor. Bravo. A job well done indeed. A decisive man. A man that no one can push over. It's good that your soldiers were witness to it. That's just the kind of man these people need to follow. They now know you are a force to be reckoned with. That's the way it needs to be. Lead by example, and these men will stumble into victory. You were born to do this."

Despite his emaciated appearance, Asmodeus lifted the sobbing woman off the floor with one hand. Samaria caught her footing, but just as quickly as the elevator had begun to move, it stopped. The doors had not opened, but the man was gone when Samaria turned to face him. All that remained were the human-like hieroglyphs patterning the walls. She leaned in to look more closely. Samaria used to draw when she was little. She was into different kinds of art, but could not quite place this – it was like nothing she had ever seen before. As she looked one of the creatures in the eye, the elevator door opened.

Beyond the door, there was only a vast field of darkness in all directions. Samaria retreated into the relative safety of the elevator, hoping the doors would close, but they did not. Instead, a comforting voice came from beyond the darkness.

"Samaria," a soft, soothing voice whispered.

"Samaria Ohola," the voice whispered again. "Look at what you see before you: nothing but a void of darkness. This is truly how the world has treated you. They have turned the lights out on you. My child, observe your surroundings now. You are cornered, just as the world has trapped you. Beyond this box is nothing but cruelty and hatred, as mankind has left you alone to suffer without mercy. I am here to change all this."

In the distance, Samaria saw an orb of light from which the soothing voice emanated. The light radiated comfort. "Poor sweet Samaria. I am here to rescue you. Misunderstood and abused, forgotten and mistreated. . . I understand. Only I understand what you truly need."

"Who are you?"

"I am your salvation, child."

"You are God?"

"Call me whatever you wish, but I am here to save you, and to protect you. You will suffer this cruel earth no more."

The orb of light stretched into the shape of a man until Elijah stood before her, floating, emanating radiance and comfort. Samaria humbled herself at the sight of her new savior. She dropped to her knees and reached for him. As Elijah placed his hand on her shoulder, her problems seemed to fade away.

"I will appreciate you as the goddess you are. I know what you truly are, and that is a miracle. I have seen your spirit for what it truly is. You are a princess, and your palace will be laid before you."

"What do I have to do?" Samaria asked humbly. Before she heard the answer, she knew she would do anything he requested of her. As she waited eagerly, Elijah paused deliberately, finding her subservience amusing.

Samaria trembled with anticipation until Elijah finally spoke.

"All I need is your cooperation, and undivided loyalty. Can you do this?"

"Yes, I can, lord."

"Then rise, my child. Rise as a new goddess. Rise as my powerful companion."

CHAPTER 33

Rontrez leaned back and watched the bubbles swirl around him as he relaxed in his hot tub. That's what the world was to him now. A hot tub. He was the big daddy among all the bubbles of regular people. He ruled on high, and everyone else swirled around him. With him in the hot tub were some of the most beautiful women he had ever seen – curvy and intelligent, just as he liked them. He could talk with them about any issue he wished, but, most importantly, about himself.

He spoke to one of his favorites, a woman named Mystery. Rontrez had seen many gorgeous women in his lifetime, but few truly mesmerized him the way Mystery did. Usually Rontrez took what women said to him with a grain of salt, with very few exceptions. These exceptions were usually women he was related to, and even some of those weren't worth excepting. He had talked with Mystery for long periods of time about topics that ranged from sex, intimacy, and relationships, to love, life, and God. She now sat with him smiling, comfortably discussing Rontrez's past affiliations.

"You know, it takes a man to make the changes you're making."

"It takes a man to do a whole lot of things," Rontrez agreed. "And it takes a soldier to come in to make some changes and flex authority."

"I like what I see," Mystery cooed. "Though I haven't known you that long, I think you have what it takes."

"As do I."

"But there is something you're missing to make things go smoothly."

"Oh really," Rontrez replied, a little amused. "I suppose you are going to tell me what that is."

"You have money, you have the authority, but you don't have the respect."

"What?"

"You don't have the respect you need to be a true leader."

"You have some nerve," Rontrez started, his expression hardening.

"Oops, I must have hit a weak spot. I didn't know you were so sensitive, Esau. I didn't mean to hurt your feelings. But Trez, we're too real with each other for me not to come direct like this. I need you to hear me out."

"I'm listening."

"Of course all of us around you respect you, baby. I'm talking about those on the outside. Look at how that tramp came at you today." Mystery gave Rontrez a split second to think. "Yes, you handled it perfectly, but things like that shouldn't even happen if the respect factor was proper."

"When you're on top, you always have people trying to take you down. It's all in the game. If it wasn't, then everybody would be on top. Do you feel me?" Rontrez replied.

"Yes, but only those who have the desire to be on top would oppose you, not those who just think they can get away with it. That tramp came in here and talked to you like you were a roach. Things like that can't happen in this type of game. If they do, people will know they can try you. And she did try you."

"So I checked her into the smackdown hotel and gave her room service."

"You can call it what you want. The fact is, she came at you wrong, period. There are a thousand more like her that are going to do the same thing if we don't get right, baby. Players plot and strategize."

"And just how do you suppose we take care of this? I expect most people to come at me with a problem. But from you, Mystery, I expect a problem and a solution."

"And a solution I have. There are two things that can instill cooperation. One of them clearly works better. The first is positive reinforcement, the second is fear. You know which one we need to use."

"Yes. Fear works better. But how do you suppose we should instill fear in these times of peace?"

"It is your world, Esau Rontrez. You do it however you see fit. However, I do have some suggestions."

"Run them down for me."

"First, any who oppose you must be dealt with. I mean dealt with quickly and mercilessly. I ain't with no play-play foolishness. If you don't want to do this, I can shut my mouth right now. I don't talk to hear myself speak, I talk to spread knowledge to those who desire it. Other times to those that need it."

"I like where you're coming from – and I like you, Mystery."

"You don't like me, you like my style."

"I like you and your style. Together, you and your style make a dynamic couple."

"Why is that?"

"Because you're finer than a glass of wine, sweeter than honey, and softer than a down-feather pillow. You walk like a Mercedes, and you talk like a writer. You're hot enough to make Tex Mex cough, but sweeter than apple cider."

Mystery grinned enigmatically. With many individuals, Rontrez could tell what they were thinking, but for some reason Rontrez could never quite tell with Mystery.

"I would tell you I like you too, but you already know it," she replied. "But I can tell you that it's only going to be a matter of time before someone tries to take you down, baby. All these nice things you have can only last for so long. Let me show you why."

Mystery reached from the hot tub to her bag and brought out a hundred-dollar bill. Mystery held it vertically between her middle and index fingers and stretched out her hand to Rontrez.

"Now, baby. You can have this bill. All you have to do is stop it from hitting the water when I let it go. If it hits the water, it belongs to me. You got it?"

Rontrez nodded. He had no clue what point this trick served.

"Okay," Mystery continued, "When I say 'go', you try and grab this bill."

Rontrez positioned his hand right by the bill and held his thumb and index fingers on either side of the bill. Mystery grinned and let out a slight chuckle. For the thousandth time, Rontrez realized that Mystery was exquisitely alluring. Rontrez pinched his fingers even closer to the bill, until he was almost touching it. Mystery's grin became an amused smirk.

"Ready?" she asked.

Rontrez nodded.

"Go," she mumbled, and released the bill.

Before Rontrez had a chance to grab the bill, it was past his fingers and headed into the water. He lunged at it with his other hand, but it was too late – the bill was already being buffeted around the hot tub by the bubbles like an abandoned raft.

"Mm," Mystery mumbled. "Maybe next time."

"You got voodoo in you, woman," Rontrez grumbled.

"Shall we try it again?" she asked, reaching in her diamond-studded purse for another hundred-dollar bill.

"It's on," Rontrez mumbled back, baffled by the fact that he hadn't even come close.

"This time it's double or nothing. If you get this one, you get to keep the one in the water, plus this one. If you miss it again, you have to follow my agenda – because you know it works."

Rontrez ignored Mystery's words as he positioned his hand around the bill.

"Go," Mystery said, dropping the bill.

Again, the dollar bill slipped past Rontrez's outstretched fingers into the hot tub. Rontrez was flabbergasted. He watched, astonished, as the bubbles carried the bill in circles.

"And what is the moral of this little charade?" Mystery asked. "I wonder." She paused for dramatic effect. "I have just proven to you that we need to shape up. Everything looks good now, but this is just the beginning."

"How in the world have you proven to me that I need to shape up?"

"I just showed you that no matter how hard you try, the reactor loses. The actor wins every time. We have to be proactive instead of reactive.

We can't possibly stay on top if we only react. When that whore slick-talked you, you reacted. When Elijah comes to you with circumstances, you react. When situations come upon us, baby, you react. You can't win when you react. You can never win that way. You have to be proactive, and make everyone else react. Look at what we have now. People going against your right-hand man. Problems like this should be taken care of in the first place. We shouldn't have to deal with this kind of foolishness."

"Well what do you suppose we do?" Rontrez asked.

"Do you want to know the truth?"

"The news is my hooker and the truth is her pimp," Rontrez replied. "All I want to hear is truth. All the rest gets deferred like a bad dream — it rots and festers."

"Elijah has to go. He's too soft."

"The man is. . ." Rontrez trailed off, shocked.

"See, look at that. Do you mean to tell me that you're intimidated by a man? Maybe you're not the man I thought you were. Do you think Elijah is running the show better than you ever could?"

"Nobody could run the show like I could," Rontrez said, feeling his confidence in every word he spoke.

"You told me he has offered you ultimate power. You need to take it," Mystery advised.

"Isn't he some sort of angel? I mean, the man dropped down from the sky. I can't deal with him like I can deal with the next man."

"Do you believe he is all-powerful?"

Rontrez paused.

"You did not answer. That means it's a yes, but you don't want to admit it to yourself. I read individuals pretty well. You told me that Elijah asked you if you wanted to be a god, and you said no. Why? Beats the hell out of me."

Does it really?

"A man can't be a god. That doesn't make sense. I've explained this to both of you already, and I don't like repeating myself. You know where I stand."

"What if I told you that you were more than a man?" Mystery hissed in a low voice. "You are capable of taking command. But you're scared."

"I'm not scared of anything."

"You're scared of yourself. You think you might not be able to handle it. You think this might just be out of your arena. But I'll tell you what. Right now you are reacting. You're not acting. Neither is Elijah. You told me about your past – you can be proactive. You anticipate that man's next move, then you act before he does. It's like a big game of chess, but this here ain't no game. Right now, I see a whole lot of problems brewing. First, jealousy. People are going to want to take your throne. You have to act now and let everybody know that you have this spot on lockdown. You have to step up."

"I see where you are coming from."

"No you don't. You don't hear me. You're just listening to me talk. Elijah knows you are the man for the job. So as soon as you move that man out of position, you can take what belongs to you. It's yours. It was yours from the beginning. You know that power isn't asked for, it's taken."

"No man can be a god. I came from the womb, not from the skies."

"You have to be kidding me! The man asks if want to be a god and you turn him down like he was offering cab fare. What's wrong with you?"

Rontrez was aware that the woman had now stepped out of her bounds, and felt it his personal duty to inform her of this.

"Look, Mystery, I don't know what the hell you been eating or drinking, but it is affecting your judgment for the worse. You need to bring your voice back down and stop hollering like you have lost your damn mind. Ain't no children in here. Do you read me?"

"Yeah, but you're acting like a whore."

"I believe I need to smack your mind back in place," Rontrez warned, anger bubbling up within him.

"Maybe you are not acting," Mystery yawned.

Rontrez clenched his fists and his blood began to boil.

"If I could reach you I would smack you," Rontrez growled.

"I've already won the battle," Mystery grinned

"Woman, stop playing with fire before it burns you."

"It was that easy to get inside your head, Rontrez? I've got you all upset without even putting any effort into it. I just shook you out your game in a matter of seconds because you reacted. Do you see the point a little more clearly now? You can't let someone else force you into the position of a reactor. If you don't take the bait, if you don't jump when the enemy says 'boo', you don't turn yourself into a reactor. I would like sex about now. What about you?" Mystery eased herself off the wall and floated seductively toward Rontrez.

"It's on."

Dino slowly stood up, feeling like a newborn uncurling itself. He now existed for only one purpose, to serve his lord. Just as in his first life, he hungered for recognition within his department – but now, his department was his quest to serve his master. He walked down the temple steps and back to the van, opening the door slowly and deliberately. As soon as he stepped inside, TC looked at him and sensed that something was wrong. Usually, Dino would have some cocky remark about a job well done, but now his face showed only grim determination.

"What happened in there, Dino? I thought we lost you."

"Everything went cool. The place looks small, but it's as big as a city inside."

TC watched the life slowly return to Dino's eyes, and noticed Dino looking around the room like he had lost something.

"The bugs on you quit. Could you connect Elijah with anything inside?"

"Yeah, he was in there. He's got a smooth operation going on in there. I got some pictures," Dino said, removing the audio recorder from his shirt button. He carelessly tossed it on the equipment desk, where it fell from the edge and rattled to the floor. TC eagerly bent down and picked up the card. In his thirty-six years, this was the last conscious move TC would ever make.

Dino switched the transmission device off. Over thirty miles away, Sesom was now cut off from anything happening outside of his range of vision. Dino reached for an electric pulse stunner on the edge of the weapons counter that he had spotted seconds earlier when he was looking around. He activated the weapon, and blue sparks emitted from the teeth of the weapon before the metal edges of the weapon entered the back of TC's neck. TC heard a low buzz behind him, but he felt the jolt of electricity before he could remember what the sound was. His body seized with the energy from the weapon before crumpling to the floor. Dino stepped over him and pulled out the weapons drawer, aware that TC was still breathing. He selected a few small hand grenades and headed toward the van's front seat with them in his hand, stooping momentarily to take the keys to the van out of TC's jacket. He started the van, and pulled onto the street.

He drove out of the city until he was surrounded only by trees and darkness. As if he knew where he was going, he turned onto an unmarked side road, which opened up to reveal a magnificent brick building. On the front, the three door entrance was encased in a large elegant semi-circle of glass, surrounded by a gold border. Dino pressed the accelerator to the floor, racing toward the building. Steadying the wheel with his knee, he pulled the pins out of the grenades, opened the door to the van, and dove out of the vehicle onto the concrete. He sat up in time to see the van crash through the entrance of the building. Accompanied by the unnatural crash of hard steel against wood and glass, Dino turned and walked away. Moments later, the building was consumed by a raging inferno.

Dino strode confidently into the darkness.

CHAPTER 34

Rontrez walked quickly down the corridor, barely noticing the paintings that lined the walls. Some of the distorted figures seemed to admonish him; others seemed almost indifferent, their faces contorted in a snarl. Rontrez opened the doors with his mental signal, enjoying each power he had seemed to gain with his newfound position as a semi-god. As he strode toward Elijah's chambers, the doors opened to reveal his conversation with a thin, pale man dressed in black. The thin man wore an ancient looking medallion. With him were three other men Rontrez did not recognize. The thin man seemed to smirk at Rontrez briefly, as if he knew something that Rontrez didn't. Rontrez eyed the thin man's spooky, solemn face, unable to discern why he was so unsettled by the play of the sinewy muscles under his skin. Perhaps he didn't see a smirk after all, just an indescribable, discomforting oddness.

"The man of the hour," Elijah greeted him. "My instrument of transformation."

"I think you know why I am here," Rontrez replied.

Rontrez noticed a brief change in the thin man's demeanor, as if he were thinking about showing some sort of emotion, but then decided against it.

"It is true. At no time in eternity could you label a true master clueless to his environment. What is it that you seek, son? Is it questions, or it answers?"

"I seek nothing. I have come to grant."

"Well be seated, and indulge us in your gift."

"This conversation is between two soldiers of fortune," Rontrez replied.

"Oh, forgive my discourtesy. Allow me to introduce some trusted associates of mine." The men did not rise from the large shiny, black, rectangular marble table. Each man nodded indifferently as Elijah introduced him. There was Mammon, a short man in a gray power suit. He looked like some sort of crude rat. He had a pointy nose, and if Rontrez could pick a man out the group who would have a million dollars stashed under his mattress, it was Mammon. His greedy eyes darted around the room, resting briefly on Rontrez with contempt.

Next was Egor, a man who made no attempt to hide the fact that he didn't care how he looked: his hair was uncombed, his clothes were covered in a thick layer of grime, and he looked devoid of all energy. He sat unmoving, staring blankly ahead, looking like a soulless vessel of flesh.

Next to Egor sat a fat man who hardly looked up from his gourmet meal when Elijah introduced him as Bee-El. Rontrez admired a person who could accessorize, but Bee-El had clearly overindulged himself. As Bee-El cloaked himself with expensive clothes, Rontrez noticed he coated himself just as well with food. His suit was sharp from his ten thousand dollar hat to his six thousand dollar imported zebra skin shoes. They perfectly matched his black suit with a designer white accent. Though he was extremely large, it looked like he did not have a problem covering himself with money. In front of him was a plate of gourmet food, prepared by a chef that seemed to be nowhere in sight. Rontrez smelled the aromas, and instantly wondered what the man was eating. His food dripped from his chin onto the table and his clothes. He had no napkin to wipe has hands or face that was covered in what resembled sauce, and he chewed loudly with his mouth wide open. The diamond and platinum watch he wore shone brilliantly under the chandelier, as did the rings he wore on each finger, all of them studded with large jewels and dripping with grease.

Though all of the men seemed thoroughly different, Rontrez could tell that they were close. Elijah saved the thin man in black for last.

"You may call him Asmodeus," Elijah explained. "These men have stood by my side longer than you would care to believe. As you are the key to the inevitable evolution into a new epoch, they are the critical enzymes of this transition. They are the men behind the curtain, if you will pardon the expression. Have you come to grant ability or conversation, Rontrez?"

"I have come to rule."

"Indeed, you have finally risen to the spectacular occasion that has been presented to you. Tell me Esau Rontrez, what do you request of me in your rule? I am here to serve you, as are my dedicated associates."

"First, I would like what cannot be given," Rontrez replied.

"You desire the first slice of narcissism," Elijah grinned. "You fool yourself, though. You do not only want power, you also want respect equally dispersed about your place in this uncharted future."

"There was a time you told me you didn't know what I was thinking. I see this has changed," Rontrez replied.

"No, it has not changed, but a master of self looks with more than his eyes. He uses the instruments that cannot as easily be manipulated."

Rontrez was silent.

"Are you ready to take this universe into a new era of peace and prosperity?" Elijah asked.

"Yes."

"So shall it be etched in the corridors of eternity. So shall it be written," Elijah's entourage joined in as he spoke the last sentence: ". . .so shall it be done."

"Shall we make it official, brethren?" Elijah smiled.

The men started to stand up from the large table. Even Bee-El stopped stuffing his face, groaning with effort as he pushed back his chair. Rontrez noticed he did not even wipe the food off his chin before standing up. The five men gathered around Rontrez in a rough circle.

As Rontrez looked up at the mirrored ceiling, he noticed that each man was standing stiffly, as if he were guarding an unmarked spot on the black tile. The lights suddenly dimmed and the candles in the room grew into wild flames, as if they had a life of their own. At any time Rontrez believed the flames would hop off of the candles and start to race about the room. He looked at the men again and saw that they were not standing in a circle at all, but a perfect pentagon. With a look of pride and hunger mixed in his eyes, Elijah stretched out his arms. His colleagues joined hands, linking the pentagon surrounding Rontrez. After the first moments of anxiety had passed, he no longer felt intimidated by Elijah and his men, but protected. Invincible.

The flames leaped higher, and Rontrez heard thunder as loud as if it was inside the building, but he didn't flinch. He felt a wetness on his forehead, and he touched his hand to his head. There was blood on his hands. He looked up again to see that the mirror had been replaced by a window – and through this window was the most horrific sight Rontrez had ever beheld.

A terrible abyss of living flames leapt up further than the eye could see. Inhuman screams and roars of demonic laughter filled the air. Fire lashed angrily into the air, each flame seeking oxygen from the depths of the pit. As his eyes adjusted, Rontrez saw with clarity into the heart of the fire: within the red flames were burning souls. The room seemed to shatter into splinters around him, and Rontrez found himself within the frightful inferno. Though he was among the scorching flames, but did not feel one degree of heat that they cast forth.

He calmly gazed around into the bowels of the horrific burning abyss and saw worse than death – only a glimpse of what the world was to become. He watched the tall infernal flames engulf shrieking black silhouettes.

He glanced at his companions and felt that he was completely protected. A thin, bright trail of fire raced up around him, and he saw that a pentagram of fire had become visible in the flames beneath their feet, encircled by the men's joined hands.

Rontrez looked at the faces of his protectors as Asmodeus spoke.

"Esau Rontrez, do you believe in fate?"

"No," Rontrez replied, blood dripping from his forehead.

"A master of self cannot believe in fate," Elijah explained, "You have now seen what the world is to become if change is not. You must learn to truly master yourself, before it masters you. Esau Rontrez, are you a true master of self?"

"Yes."

Mammon then spoke. "Will you take from the less deserving and deliver unto the righteous?"

"Yes," Rontrez answered.

"For into a malicious soul wisdom shall not enter; nor dwell in the body that is subject unto sin," Mammon replied.

Bee-El spoke next, "Are you willing to rule, knowing death and providence will exist inevitably?"

"Yes."

"What must be shall be, and that which is necessity to he that strives is little more than chance to he that is willing," Bee-El replied.

Elijah spoke again, "I offer you all the pleasantries of the flesh, and all the benefits from beyond. You will separate the light from the darkness, you will make weal and create woe, you are the lord! I offer you the tidings of an eternal rule. I offer you what has not even been imagined, and I grant the possession of omnipotence. You will know all, be all, have all and deliver all, and the glory and honor of nations will be delivered unto you. Let your strength be the law of justice, for that which is feeble is found to be worth nothing. Esau Rontrez, do you accept?"

"What is the cost?"

"There is no price, there is only conviction. You must pledge allegiance to Esau Rontrez and rebuke all else. Do you accept?"

"I accept."

"Then all living things shall comply. So it is written," Rontrez spoke along with them: "So shall it be done!"

"Fall into your place at our side, as ruler of all things in existence," Elijah continued. "All shall bend to your whim."

Elijah and Bee-El broke their hands and let Rontrez fall into place, making the pentagram a perfect hexagram. The men shifted their feet with minimal effort, creating the hexagram. Six points, six angles, six sides.

"Rontrez, you have been given a new birth unto a new world. Spawned from the land of the unrighteous, you have now become an immortal divinity with powers beyond imagination. You have been granted a new name. A name befitting a true master. A name so powerful it can only be uttered in hex. We are joined together in blood, in the sacred bond of eternal brotherhood and salvation. We renounce all that is not of our master, and submit our spirit unto the everlasting. We offer our eternal existence into the plane of divinity. We know and acknowledge no other master. As we utter his name, we shall be granted boundless powers, and omnipotent knowledge of all things across time, being, and actuality."

Elijah opened his mouth and gave the first syllable of Esau Rontrez's new name, "Az."

Asmodeus went next, "Hee."

Mammon spoke after Asmodeus, "Dah."

Egor uttered the fourth syllable, "Ah."

Bee-El spoke the fifth hex, "Ha."

Without knowing how, Rontrez spoke the last syllable of his name: "Kuh." Asmodeus started again, "Az," and the hex continued to repeat in rotation, each person mumbling a different syllable than the last round. With each repetition Rontrez felt himself growing stronger. By the sixth and final revolution, he knew he was truly invincible. His new name gave him a new being: Azhidaahaka.

CHAPTER 35

The next morning, Bryant went downstairs for the closest thing he had to breakfast – lukewarm coffee. He was worried about Minzano, who he hadn't heard from in days. This was not the first time this had happened, but it didn't take Bryant long to hear about Minzano's outburst in Caviant's office. Minzano hadn't been seen or heard from since.

His cell phone rang, and Bryant did not want to answer. He was enjoying his breakfast. Actually, he wasn't, but he was pretending to.

"Go ahead," he grumbled.

"This is Agent Sesom."

"Joshua, this line is not secure," Bryant warned.

"I know that. This is about to be public knowledge."

"What is it?"

"Someone bombed York."

"What?" Bryant said in disbelief.

"Someone bombed York Temple last night."

"Was anyone hurt?"

"No."

"Who did it?"

Sesom remained silent.

"Who was it?" Bryant barked at Sesom, rage overtaking his initial shock. In the back of his mind, Bryant knew that Sesom was just as upset that his synagogue had been destroyed. Sesom had been a member of York Temple for over 17 years, Bryant for longer.

"We're not sure. Remains of our van were found on the premises. Someone activated all of the hand grenades and drove the van into the temple."

"Who had the van last?" Bryant asked.

"Our team."

"What?"

"Yes. Our team. TC and Dino were watching Elijah's headquarters, and I was listening remotely. TC spotted men bringing two bodies into the temple. Dino went inside the headquarters and fooled the Bloodline into thinking he was one of them. A few minutes later, we lost the signal. Then I heard Dino come back out, mumbling. I have it recorded, but it's nothing useful."

"Get a meeting together now."

"This is the meeting. I haven't seen or heard from Dino, and I know TC was in the truck when it blew."

"Are you sure?"

"I heard it on the equipment. Dino might have been in there too, but I'm not sure."

"Is there anything left of the temple?" Bryant asked.

"No."

Bryant's heart sank. He thought for a minute. "Josh, you said that Dino fooled the Bloodline into thinking he was one of them. That's not easy to do. How in the world did Dino get inside?"

"We talked him through. You taught us some of the signs –"

"But there are so many. So many signals, words, gestures, warnings, looks. Can you bring me the surveillance data?"

"I'm on my way."

••••••••••• • • •••••••••• • • ••••••••••

In less than an hour, Sesom and Bryant were listening to the audio recording on Sesom's laptop.

"Where art thou delivered?" Bryant heard a Bloodline member ask Dino. Bryant understood that the man had asked what Bloodline chapter Dino was from. Minzano's intelligence had given Bryant superior insight to the inner workings of the Bloodline. They were the most complex organization he had ever encountered, and their impenetrability was breathtaking. Impenetrable, until Vincent Minzano. The more Bryant thought about it, the more spectacular his agent became.

On the audio file, he heard Dino tell the men he was spawned from the 66th – Minzano's chapter. Bryant paused the audio.

"Here is mistake number one," Bryant pointed out, "but it's not too bad. When asked, a Bloodline member gives a precinct number and then the precinct's name. Dino just gave the number," Bryant restarted the audio.

"24th precinct, Serpents of Eden," the man replied.

The audio was quiet but for the even rhythm of footsteps as the men proceeded into the building. After a moment passed, Bryant heard the elevator chime and its doors slide shut. As the elevator began to rise, one of the men spoke.

"66th, huh?" someone spoke up, "Angels of Descent, right?"

Dino did not respond audibly, and Sesom and Bryant assumed he had nodded.

Bryant stopped the audio once again. "The 66th is not the Angels of Descent. They are the Blood Brethren. But we can't assume that the other knights knew that. There are thousands of chapters across the world – it's possible that they really don't know the 66th." Bryant started the audio again.

"Where are you on your journey?"

Pausing the audio, Sesom sighed. "That's where we got stuck. What's he asking, exactly?"

"He's not asking anything. It just sounds like he is to an outsider. He's *saying* something."

"What's he saying?" Sesom asked.

Bryant rewound the audio and listened carefully, his brow furrowed.

"I don't know. I would have had to be there. His hand gestures, his position in the room, and his stance are all part of the message. Their codes are almost indecipherable. Do we have a camera in there?"

"No, not on the elevator. Dino wasn't wearing a video camera. We had no idea he would actually get inside of the building. He did have a micro-camera that captured still photos hidden in a button on his shirt, but I believe it was destroyed in the explosion. Near the end of the audio you can hear him give it TC."

"Do we have any clue where Dino is?" Bryant asked.

Sesom shook his head. "Remember, it was your call not to have tracking devices on the agents. We didn't want the Bloodline to be able to track us either."

Bryant now wanted to take back his decision.

"What do you think the man on the elevator was telling Dino?" Sesom asked.

"I can't be sure without seeing him, but I believe it was a warning."

"A warning?"

"Yes. He's telling Dino that he needs to be a certain rank to progress any further."

"What rank? How deep down the Bloodline is Dino supposed to be?"

"That I don't know. The soldiers' signals would have given us that information. Notice there is only one person talking to Dino. He is the highest ranking among them, likely a knight. The most important thing to acknowledge is this: at this time, they have definitely not accepted Dino as one of their own."

"What makes you say that?" Sesom asked. "They haven't killed him yet."

"They only communicate in code when they do not want outsiders to understand the true meaning of the messages. They're not speaking normally, meaning they do not take Dino as a brother yet. The Bloodline handshake and precinct were not enough. They are testing him now. If they were not, they would speak so we could understand."

Sesom nodded as Bryant started the audio.

"You're on your own," Bryant heard Sesom inform Dino.

"The beginning," Dino replied. His response was confident, but Bryant let out a sharp breath and lowered his head.

"That's where he screwed up big time," Bryant regretfully mumbled, stopping the audio. He paused for a long moment, gazing blankly ahead, as if he blamed himself for Dino's mistake. "There is no 'beginning.' The answer is 'in darkness.'"

"'In darkness.' Do we even know what that means?" Sesom asked.

"Minzano explained it as an extrapolation from the beginning of Genesis. Chapter 1 verse 2, to be exact. It states that in the beginning the earth was formless and empty, and darkness was over the surface of the deep. Hence the phrase 'In darkness.'"

Bryant sighed, hesitant to continue. Whatever had happened to Dino, it wasn't good.

"'Well, congratulations," the Bloodline soldier replied, "but you really shouldn't be here."

"I know, but something inside me wants to meet the great one," Dino said.

There was a pause, then the soldier replied. "He is here. We're taking the girl to him."

Bryant stopped the audio and spoke. "And that's the death sentence. They know he is not one of them."

"What did they say? I didn't hear anything," Sesom replied.

"Exactly. The Bloodline not only uses words, but silence as well. They have the most advanced forms of non-verbal of communication I've ever seen. Dino was being put through a trial. Notice that no one but the trial administrator speaks to Dino. No one else can talk to Dino, and luckily, Dino did not try to talk to anyone else, or he would have been exposed even sooner. A trial is a series of rituals, questions or signals for Dino to interpret. If the trial administrator pauses for more than six seconds, then the man on trial has failed. After the six seconds is up, the trial administrator glances at the floor, which begins the appeal process. If you didn't already know what he was doing, you wouldn't even notice it. The administrator of the trial was waiting for one of the other men to speak up while he looked down at the floor. If one of the other men believed he was truly of the Bloodline, he could have spoken in Dino's defense by asking him a different set of questions. But it looks as if Dino's act fooled no one. The soldier must have looked up, then down, then back at Dino, which confirmed that Dino was an outsider. A trial is a serious event, and Dino failed."

"The punishment for this is death, am I correct?"

"Yes," Bryant replied.

"But I heard Dino come back into the van. It's on the audio – listen for yourself."

On the recording, Bryant heard Dino open the van door and climb back into the van, but he was unusually silent for a man who always had to have the last word. The Dino Bryant and Sesom knew would have said something like, "somebody go in there and tell the Bloodline that they can kiss my entire ass, because I have the buzzards on tape."

"What happened in there? I thought we lost you," TC asked.

"Everything went cool. The place looks small, but it's as big as a city inside."

"The bugs on you quit. Could you connect Elijah with anything going on inside?" TC asked.

"Yeah, he was in there. He's got a smooth operation going on in there. I got some pictures," Dino said flatly.

Bryant heard something light fall to the floor before the recording ended abruptly. The audio file continued to play, but they could hear nothing but static.

"That's it?" Bryant asked.

Sesom nodded.

"Why did they stop transmitting?"

"I have no idea. It seems like somebody just flipped the switch."

"Could it have been an accident?"

"No. TC has been doing surveillance for more than fifteen years, and Dino would have had to reach over TC to do it if he'd just gotten into the van."

"It seems like someone had something to hide. Since TC is dead and Dino is missing, it seems like the only man with an answer is you."

"What do you mean?" Sesom asked.

"Josh, did you cut off the transmission?"

"No, I did not," Sesom replied firmly.

Bryant believed him, but had to ask. Bryant did not think Sesom would bomb his own place of worship.

"Sesom, I have a serious question," Bryant stated.

"What is it, friend? I have no secrets from you."

"Why weren't you there with them?"

"Aaron, I was trying to make sense of this chaos. I was trying. I was studying, thinking, and praying."

"What did you find?"

Sesom fell silent for a moment, and Bryant felt his chest tighten with fear as he studied his mentor's grave expression.

"I believe Olam Haba is upon us."

Olam Haba, Bryant thought. The world to come.

CHAPTER 36

It looks like I've got a bad reputation. I've been called names from devil to Satan to everything in between. I could claim to be misunderstood or to be righteous, but I am neither. I am Absolute.

I am indeed the Truth, the Light, and the Everlasting. Man can not exist without absolute truth, absolute knowledge, and absolute boundaries. Not the ways of fabricated religions, orientational conformity, or programmed morality, but the absolute truth of self-actualization. It's quite humorous how man wishes to characterize me as a devil. . . some red, horned, misshapen figure with a pitchfork, as if there were a haystack nearby. Ugly indeed. But the Truth is ugly at times. For eons I have been blamed and labeled, but for all beings, a time comes when the stage is set. The final battle begins.

Still hidden underneath the Holy of Holies, Minzano grew angry and restless.

"Forget this. I'm sitting here growing old while the enemy becomes stronger. I haven't ate good, slept good or sexed good since I've been down here. If one of you so-called holy men can't come up with a plan to fight, then I will. And I don't turn the other cheek, Bishop."

"So, Agent Minzano, you are going to take down Elijah's entire army by yourself?" Pathem asked.

"I don't see anyone else doing anything but talking. I'm not really a talker."

"There have got to be others who know the truth, we just have to find them," Oniva suggested.

"That's half an idea," Minzano grinned. "But how would we find the people that are on our side? Do you have the other half of the idea, or do I need to rent a blimp and advertise?"

"I don't know exactly how to find them," Oniva confessed. "Pathem, do you have any ideas for finding others?"

"There might be some, but Elijah has imprisoned them as Bloodline members. I do not know where they are kept," Pathem replied.

"Do you think he's killed them?" Oniva asked.

"Maybe some, but definitely not all of them. As I said before, he will only kill them when they lose faith. Some of the weaker ones probably have lost faith and cursed God, as has been foretold," (1 Timothy 4:1).

"What happens then?" Oniva asked.

"When they lose faith, Elijah will kill them immediately. But as long as they keep faith, they are protected."

"Faith?" Minzano spat. "The word should be taken out of the dictionary. Man isn't worthy."

"Don't put your faith in man, put your faith in God," Justes answered calmly.

"There is no God. Elijah's not a god, he's a hoax," Minzano growled. Pointing to Oniva, he continued, "Your friend Esau is a hoax too. He's a man pretending to be something else. Elijah and company has got your friend's head all pumped up like a hot air balloon. This is crazy. I don't know what hocus pocus Elijah used to drop himself from the sky like a paratrooper, but I don't buy it. Where's my piece?" Minzano snarled, looking around for his gun.

No one spoke.

"Cute. Real cute. Whoever has my gun will give it back before I start collecting dues from the church," Minzano snarled, eyeing Justes and Pathem, infuriated.

"I have it," Justes admitted. "Minzano, this thing is going to cause nothing but trouble. I think it is best if I keep this."

"I think it's best if you give it back before *I* cause trouble. Avoid the rumble," Minzano said, clenching his fists. It looked as if he was about to snap.

To avoid further chaos, Justes pulled the gun from the small of his back and hesitated.

"Agent Minzano, what are you going to do with this?" Justes asked.

"The only thing that makes sense," Minzano barked, snatching his pistol from Justes.

"What is that? Share your plan with us, Vincent," Pathem said.

"Obviously the Rontrez guy has a lot to do with the wrong side of things. So, as we say in the business, he needs to be neutralized. The 'one of many' is about to become one of many deceased individuals."

"You're going to kill Esau?" Oniva gasped.

"Lady, in case you're missing something, Rontrez just ordered a hit, so he loses his status as a righteous lamb. More importantly, it's obvious he is the root of the Bloodline's plot. I don't know what the plot is, but I know it's not good. With Rontrez gone, things get bad for the bad guys. Pull out the root, and the plant dies."

"That might make things worse," Justes said.

"It might make things a lot worse for him when I put his head through a meat grinder," Minzano replied.

Pathem stepped forward. "Vincent Minzano, you are familiar with this organization. The first time you saw Esau, you reported that you could not get near him. What makes you think that you could even get in the same room with him? What makes you think that you could get close enough to kill him? Do you think it's going to be that easy to wipe out their messiah? Do you think they would just let you blast his head off? If you are indeed planning to go through this foolish mission, you'd better dig a grave before you leave. And believe me, Esau Rontrez will not be in it."

Ignoring Pathem, Minzano climbed up the ladder into the sanctuary of the church, the heavy wooden door of the church creaking shut behind him as he walked out into the night.

"Do you think we should go with him?" Justes asked.

"No," Pathem instructed gravely, "His fate is already sealed."

"Chris," Oniva asked Justes, "what is Elijah doing to Esau?"

"It seems as if your friend has been broken," Pathem noted.

"What do you mean, broken? I don't understand."

"That's a blessing," Justes replied.

"I need to know what's happened to Esau. I've known him for a long time. Maybe I could see him and help him."

"I wish it were that simple. Esau has been transformed, both mentally and spiritually. Physically, he remains intact. He's probably in better condition than any of us," Pathem said.

"He's been brainwashed or something?" Oniva asked.

Justes shook his head. "Brainwashing is nothing. Sessions with a psychologist can repair those damages. This is a thousand times worse. A more accurate term for what is happening to Rontrez would be soul-cracking."

"What is that?"

"It's like cracking open the soul, which then opens various doors to the powers that exist, including the malicious and demonic powers. Put simply, it's like creating a tunnel or a doorway. Pulling that power into yourself through another person. In this case of Esau's doorway, Elijah is pulling power into himself. To him, Esau is only a vessel. Every soul that is lost to demonic powers only strengthens Elijah. What's incredibly insidious is the process."

"What's happened? What did Elijah do to Rontrez?"

"First, he drives you to your lowest point, into a state of spiritual bankruptcy. Your lowest point in life. For the rich, they'll be broke. A loving man will lose his family with a newborn baby to a drunk driver. Whatever your weaknesses, the enemy will use them to attack you where it hurts the most. Your spirit. It's far more than physical — those kind of wounds can easily be healed. Once you are in despair, and spiritual bankruptcy, he will build you back up, but in a different image. He promises the world to those who will obey him. Soul cracking is a supreme spiritual extraction, the ultimate mind screw. Instead of going after blood, he's going for their soul. Their very essence. It's quite literally like a psychic hammer. Break their soul, and pull the power through the doorway. It's part of what happens to every soldier that enters the Bloodline during initiation. With each soul cracked, the Bloodline grows stronger not just in sheer human numbers, but also on the spiritual battlefield. In spiritual warfare, as each Bloodline member opens themselves they become a doorway, a beacon for more unearthly evil to enter this domain. Elijah is also trying to torment the true believers into divorcing reality, then they will become ripe for the taking. Even true believers can be tormented into losing faith. Once they have abandoned morality, they can be built back up in the devil's image."

"I've seen this happen. This is how even smart people get sucked into cults and things like that," Oniva replied.

"Exactly. A cult member will exploit your weakness, but you won't realize it. As a matter of fact, you will thank them for it."

Oniva nodded. "What is Elijah's next move? If we know where he's headed, we know how to cut him off," she said.

"Now you're thinking. Simply put, Elijah's master plan is this: to get all non-believers to believe in him. This is almost complete. Most people who believed in nothing before now believe in Elijah. He has also pulled the borderline believers to him."

"Borderline believers?" Oniva asked.

"Yes. Borderline believers can be newcomers to Christianity that have not transitioned from their previous ways. Some would be backsliders, people who were committed at one point, but have fallen back to their old habits. Some are folks who claim to believe in Jesus Christ, but don't really practice the virtues or teachings of Christianity. Basically, anyone who is not committed to Christ, but would still classify themselves as a Christian. The borderlines have been pulled off the fence, and pulled in the wrong direction, toward Elijah. His final task is to get true believers to curse God. I'm not sure how he is going to get us to do that. That's where we're stuck," (1 Timothy 4:1).

"The enemy will show his true self as it states in Revelation," Oniva reminded him (Revelation 6). "If everyone thinks Elijah is God when the plagues come, people will curse him, and thereby curse God."

"Yes, I thought of that too. But that won't stop our enemy. We would have to curse the Almighty himself, not Elijah. Elijah is very far from the righteous God we believe in. If we deny Elijah, we are still on the right path."

"I follow you," Oniva replied. "I can't think of anything that would make me curse my Lord and savior."

"Me either. And the interesting thing is, he can't *make* us do it. He can't force us against our will," Justes responded (1 Corinthians 10:13). "Elijah sets hidden snares for those who do not stray down his path, but I don't see how he plans to do this. It seems his other phases of the plan are airtight, but this critical part is lacking."

"Chris, I know that Elijah is not God, so how can he perform such powerful wonders? How was he able to drop down from the sky and do all these things?" Oniva asked.

"Oniva, nowhere is it written that evil is weak, powerless, unconvincing, or ineffectual. The heathen is indeed strong, as are his armies. In the Bible, we are actually warned against these kinds of powers," Justes answered (Revelation 19:20, Matthew 24:23-25). "The author of evil and its demons are *supernatural beings*. Supernatural beings are not bound by the laws of nature. They do not have the same powers as God, but they do still have abilities far beyond our comprehension," Justes replied.

"We need to act, Chris. How can we make sure that the saved ones don't curse the Lord Almighty?" Oniva asked.

"We can't," Pathem answered. "And there are not too many times that I will say 'can't,' but we don't have access to the world."

"Only Elijah has access to the world," Oniva grumbled.

"No, there is one other person," Justes said thoughtfully.

CHAPTER 37

Justes walked along the street back toward his house. He was unarmed, but he had no fear. He was absolutely famished. He snuck into a buffet restaurant and pulled the microchip out of his pocket, thankful Pathem had thought to give it to him. After he fixed his meal, he squeezed the chip tightly between his fingers and passed his hand through the scanner as if the chip were implanted. The microchip worked, and Justes walked toward the main area with his tray. All the tables were full, except for one old man sitting by himself at a four-person table. Justes walked toward the old gentleman and smiled politely.

"May I sit down?" Justes asked.

"Go right ahead. A man has free will, hasn't he?" the old man replied.

"Within boundaries, of course," Justes responded.

"The mind knows no boundaries," the old gentleman replied. "Knowledge is infinite. Certain rules and systems just poison it."

Justes sat and bowed his head over his food. He glanced across the table at the old gentleman and silently included his plate in his blessing. The old man looked like a poor soul indeed, but filled with the knowledge of ages.

"Where are you from, sir?" Justes asked.

"Back and forth. Roaming throughout the earth," the old gentleman answered, the corner of his mouth curling into a wry grin.

Justes became uneasy. He knew he'd heard that phrase before, but, exhausted and hungry, he could not place it. One thing he did know is that he didn't like the way it sounded. His mind raced frantically.

"Who are you?" Justes asked.

"Though your mind is tainted, I want you to use it briefly," the old man said.

Justes froze, his heart racing, as the phrase sunk in.

The Lord said to Satan, "Where have you come from?"
Satan answered the Lord, "From roaming throughout the earth, going back and forth on it," (Job 1:7).

"You're quick, Chris," the old gentleman replied with a sardonic smile.

"Why are you here?" Justes asked.

"I can be where I please. This world is my domain."

"What's your big plan?" Justes retorted. "What plan could you have to win a war that you are destined to lose? Who are you really? I could call you Satan, or devil, or Prince of iniquity, but I prefer to address you as your persona dictates."

"You have piqued my curiosity."

"I name you Evil."

"Not too sophisticated, are you? A high schooler could have at least given me 'Malevolence'. I didn't expect you to give a well thought-out answer anyway. Everyone wants to personify evil—because no one wants to take responsibility for their own actions. Everyone has to place the blame somewhere. They'll never be intelligent enough to point the finger at themselves, so what do they do? You create a fictitious entity and blame it. You blame this devil, or this 'Satan' for every bit of evil that goes on in this world we live in. If a tropical cyclone or a tsunami takes out a city, it wasn't a rapidly rotating storm system or displacement of water that caused the damage – it was Satan. If a white collar worker sniffs up a quarter pound of cocaine and shoots up a movie theater, a church, a nightclub, or a high school it wasn't the cocaine, the bad parenting, or the mental illness that did it – it was the devil. Let's be real. People don't need any imaginary entity to screw up royally. They do that all by themselves. And, I might add, they do quite a marvelous job at it. If I wasn't so disgusted, I would applaud. Chris, you are quite mistaken. I am *not* Satan, I am *not* the devil, and I am *not* evil."

"What are you?"

"I am the deliverer. Now that you have asked your question, let me ask mine. What is the meaning of your essence?"

"What?"

"What's the meaning of this?" he said, gesturing broadly around them.

"I don't follow."

"Why are we here? Why is your spirit in existence…what exactly is the point?"

"We're here to serve God."

"Then we've all messed up, haven't we?" the old man smirked.

"What are you saying?"

"You were created in some divine image, correct?"

"Yes. God created man in his own image," Justes replied (Genesis 1:26).

"Well, then something's wrong, son. Romans 3:23: 'For all have sinned and fall short of the glory of God', remember? So either whatever God you're talking about screwed up, or every being that has ever been in existence has screwed up. Which one is it?"

"Man is imperfect."

"I thought you'd say that. Which is why I have to ask again: if every one of you are put on Earth to fail, than why are we here?"

"Are you trying to confuse me? It's not working."

"Not at all – just the opposite, Chris. I want to free you. I want your mind as free as a bird. I want you to do everything you've ever wanted to do but had to deny yourself. If you're destined to fail, why must you deny yourself? Why not live freely? What about the woman in the front row of your congregation that you've lusted after from day one? She wants you bad, ole boy. You know her husband is overseas in a brothel somewhere, and she is ripe for the taking. Live life!

If I were you, I would bang her in 16 different positions until the sun came up. But you? Nope. Gotta stay clean for your spooky ghost in the sky. Get real, Chris. Live. You've been on earth for 32 years, and you haven't lived for one day. You haven't gotten high with a beautiful woman then banged her brains out. You haven't driven a car down the open highway at 110 miles an hour. You haven't run off to the beach for a fling, you haven't slept until two in the afternoon. You haven't hit a jackass who really deserved it. You've never gotten drunk and partied like there was no tomorrow. You haven't stuffed your face with the best of foods until you couldn't eat another bite. You haven't lived."

"I have lived to the fullest."

"What? You must think someone can hear you, because you sure don't believe what the hell you just told me. You've lived to the fullest? You can tell me you've lived to the fullest when you've banged that cutie who is undressing you with her eyes every Sunday morning while you're behind that pulpit."

"Most men have no problem feeling disdain for some other woman's husband."

"Whatever you say. Life is a beautiful thing if you learn to enjoy it. I'll tell you what, I'll make you an offer."

"The answer is no."

"You haven't heard the offer yet. How can the answer be no?"

"This is that free will thing you were talking about. The answer is no."

"All I want to offer is wisdom, Chris."

"I have wisdom already."

"Chris, there is no wise man that does not realize he is ignorant."

"If I want more knowledge, I'll read a book."

"Reading is good. Living is better."

"This conversation is over. If you'll excuse me, I'm very hungry."

"There is food for the body, food for the mind, and food for the soul. You hunger for all three, Chris." With that, the man pushed his chair back and left the table, his plate of food still untouched. Justes wondered if it was because he'd said a prayer for it earlier.

With every passing moment of time I realize that I am needed not only as the profound antagonist in their warped view of existence, but as a crutch to blame for their own iniquity. They need me so they can point the finger at something. They need me so that they can shift the blame away from themselves, toward a self-created threat that is supernatural, and that can not be directly refuted.

They want someone to call the bad guy. Everybody wants to be a hero — and every hero has a villain.

This villain has been created from nothingness. This villain has been manufactured by the minds of the weak as an excuse for all who cannot assume responsibility for themselves or their environment. What this villain needs is justice.

Azhidaahaka felt as it never had before. Its flesh looked the same, but the innards seemed to operate as an entirely new kind of being. The being remembered a now-distant childhood when it had played Pac-Man, chomping up the power pellets that rendered him able to destroy his enemies. It now felt as if it had swallowed a hundred power-pellets, all of them with permanent effects. It did not desire to eat, it did not crave sleep, it did not hunger for recognition . . . only for destruction.

Azhidaahaka was aware of its awesome power. It had flashes of its former life, but none that it cared to remember.

Azhidaahaka was aware of itself and that it existed to rule. It sat at the head of the table, Mammon to his left, and Egor at his right. Facing Azhidaahaka at the other end of the table was Elijah, with Asmodeus to his left and Bee-El to his right.

Azhidaahaka was perfectly capable of talking to anyone in the room without moving its mouth, but it choose to use its mouth because it could. Armed with the vastness of its newfound knowledge, Azhidaahaka knew that the men before it were also of supernatural origin. How much more powerful was Azhidaahaka than they? That was one thing Azhidaahaka could not ascertain, and this frustrated it somewhat. How could they block its knowledge? Its attention was drawn elsewhere as it felt someone trying to enter its temple – but it wasn't sure who, or how. It sat back for a minute and did not think. For a moment it merely existed, and bathed in its own magnificence.

The five beings looked at Azhidaahaka as they would a child. With its eyes closed, Azhidaahaka felt their gaze, but did not acknowledge it. After all, it was all powerful. Bee-El was eating again, and Azhidaahaka wondered why. It did not desire food at all, but its cohort was eating enough for a small country.

In its oasis of omnipotence, Azhidaahaka did not realize there was one large blind spot: it had no idea why it truly existed. It had desires just as any being, but no concrete objective for continuation.

It opened its eyes and looked across the table at Elijah. Across from itself it saw determination, persistence and a sense of purpose.

For an unknown reason, Azhidaahaka granted a long silence in the room. It did not speak with its mind, body, or tongue. To an outsider observing the six men, the assembly would have seemed like a board meeting or an executive council, but to the insiders, it was anything but. Elijah finally broke the silence.

"Master, there are many who still oppose you."

Azhidaahaka's answer came as if it had been ruling for an eon. "Then they shall taste vengeance. All who dare oppose me shall feel my wrath. For those wretched souls, only oblivion awaits."

Mammon spoke. "Master, the reports are in. There are still over a hundred thousand people in your domain who do not have the chip."

"Call your soldiers. All will grovel to their true master."

Bee-El briefly stopped gorging himself and shouted around a mass of chewed food.

"What are we going to do with the bastards in lock-up?"

"Are they broken?" Elijah asked.

Egor yawned as if he hadn't slept in days and replied silently, seemingly unwilling to expend any physical effort. Some of those framed as Bloodline members were indeed broken, but many still held tenaciously to their faith.

"They *will* be broken," Azhidaahaka snarled, turning its gaze to Bee-El. "It seems as if someone isn't doing their job. Perhaps you need some assistance."

"No assistance is needed, master," Bee-El said defensively. Asmodeus let out the closest thing he had to emotion by a quick smirk. Though Asmodeus had no sense of humor, he did find the present situation amusing. Some of his most ancient associates just got chewed out by the new guy. Asmodeus was unconcerned, for he bore no responsibility for their failure. He just enforced the laws of darkness. Everything else was everyone else's job.

Asmodeus looked around the table with indifference. He wanted to leave – there were tasks to complete. There were still many cloaked under the protective aegis, shielded safely away from the wrath that he could wreak upon the universe. Asmodeus knew that many innocents would be slaughtered when the war truly began, and this excited him. Fear would sweeten their blood. He had yet to crack Chris Justes, but the game had just begun. Asmodeus knew that Justes was just a cornered animal. He could perhaps claw and scratch to protect himself, but there was no running and no hiding. A man could only win so many battles. A man could only resist temptation for so long before he gave in. For the past 32 years they had tried sex, money, power, drugs, trickery, and most recently, logic – but they had failed.

Elijah liked to be polished, and plan every element of his endeavors. Because of his attention to detail, he was very successful in his undertakings, and Elijah did not fail to let the others know how triumphant he truly was. Asmodeus preferred to utilize brute force. When a spirit was not already ripe for the taking, Asmodeus was the kind of creature to launch a blitz and attack without mercy, beating his opponent into spiritual submission. Other times, he would enter a spirit that was ripe for the taking. However, overcoming his true enemies always took work. With some it took much work, others little. Sometimes a loss of money was all it took.

Asmodeus was well respected among the council, but not well liked. He could taste the others' fear and it inspired him, but not as much as to become drunk off the blood of saints. In his countless years of walking the earth and beyond, Asmodeus had grinned upon the death of hundreds of millions worldwide. He had seen millions mercilessly butchered, starved, raped, tortured, and eaten. He had witnessed genocide so many times that it no longer stimulated him. He would not be satisfied until the entire war was won.

Asmodeus looked silently at Elijah. *Let me handle Chris Justes.*

Elijah answered with a harsh glare.

No.

Asmodeus growled with dissatisfaction.

Azhidaahaka was unaware of the exchange as it spoke to Mammon about his role in the new reign, to oversee the new economic system. Elijah was amused that it had chosen the greediest entity in existence to handle the money. Then again, the new guy didn't know anything. Elijah was well aware of the learning curve, and in many ways it was to his advantage.

Master, let me handle Justes.

Without turning his gaze back to Asmodeus, Elijah responded. No.

Visibly agitated, Asmodeus was unable to contain himself. *Your pride will be your downfall. Worry about the woman.*

The girl is nothing.

Then why hasn't she been broken?

She is protected on all sides. There is no gateway — not yet. When I take Chris Justes, the girl will follow. Justes reinforces her faith, hope, strength, and love. Without him, she will be vulnerable.

Your most recent failure complicates things considerably.

"Silence!" Elijah erupted aloud.

Its attention drawn to their conversation, Azhidaahaka realized that someone had dared speak without its permission. Enraged, its voice grew hoarse and guttural.

"Silence, or I will provide you only with permanent stillness upon my domain," he roared.

If Asmodeus had been an emotional creature, he would have rolled his eyes. Instead, he kept his gaze fixed on Elijah. Asmodeus would not underestimate Justes. He would find a gateway yet. Chris Justes and those like him *would* be broken.

CHAPTER 38

As Justes circled back to the church to get Oniva, he felt uneasy, as if the old man from the restaurant was grinning in every shadow with his sick smile. Though Oniva was already wanted by the Bloodline, Justes now truly understood the adversary's power. Though he couldn't quite place it, there was something special about Oniva, and he knew he would have a better chance of saving Rontrez if she were with him. Justes climbed down into the chamber to see Pathem and Oniva talking softly. She smiled at him as he approached.

"Back so soon," Oniva said worriedly. "What happened?"

"I had another visit," Justes replied.

"By the wicked one?" Pathem asked.

Justes nodded.

"What did he have to report this time?"

"The usual."

"There is no usual for evil. He has presented himself to you twice. There is a reason for this, Chris. You must think about what he wants from you."

"Bishop Pathem," Oniva asked. "Do you know why Elijah is breaking Esau? Why is Esau in the plan?"

"I don't know." Pathem answered. "I do know that if Vincent Minzano kills him, it will make things a hell of a lot worse. Literally."

"We've got to find Rontrez," Justes murmured. "But we can't get into that building. He has to come out."

Captain Ario Samsere regained consciousness in a vast field of white, dressed in the same clothes he had been wearing in the police car. Though his shirt appeared to be soaked in blood, he felt no pain. A blinding light emerged from the haze, and he shielded his eyes with his hand. The light drew closer, and without knowing why, he dropped to his knees.

"Where am I?" Ario asked.

"Fear me not," came the soft reply, in a voice he recognized as Elijah's.

"Elijah, is that you?" Ario asked, squinting into the light from between his fingers.

"It is I," Elijah said gently. "Why do you doubt me, my child? All your life, you have denied me. Denied the existence of any being or design greater than yourself."

"Am I dead?" Ario asked. "What is this place? Is this heaven?"

The voice started off gentle and loving. "How can this be heaven," he said, his voice contorting, deepening and dripping with rage, "when you do not believe in it?"

What Ario thought was his heart shuddered. The light darkened before him and the whiteness surrounding him turned a dark, burnt red.

"Do you believe now?" the light laughed. "Do you believe in the forces now?" The being continued to laugh as the last of the whiteness gave way to the fiery, sizzling redness that now surrounded him. As he looked, he saw he was at the bottom of a blazing abyss, with flames leaping up as tall as skyscrapers. The outline of the light solidified and sharpened, now a human silhouette backlit by the scorching flames.

"You have but one purpose now, damned one," the figure howled with laughter. "You will serve me for eternity."

"I will serve no one!" Ario cried desperately, trying to focus on the being: Azhidaahaka.

"Fool," Azhidaahaka growled, stepping out of the shadows. "As if you knew what eternity truly was."

Ario tore his gaze from the man who looked like Rontrez and looked around frantically, but he saw nothing but flames.

"There is no escape for the souls of the condemned," Azhidaahaka cackled. "You shall suffer as no man on earth has suffered."

Ario suddenly felt agonizing bites all over his body and realized he was naked. He looked down and saw hideous worms covering his body and eating his flesh. He screamed in fear and pain and swatted at them, but it did no good – the gruesome beasts held fast to his body and continued gnawing. Occasionally he would knock one loose, and each one tore off a chunk of his flesh in its mouth as they fell back to the burning ground. But as soon as he knocked one off, he spotted more munching their way up his leg faster and more aggressively, seemingly to avenge their brethren.

He was overcome with nausea as he smelled his own flesh cooking in the flames around him. He saw his skin blacken and he shrieked with horror, but his screams did nothing to ease his suffering. He felt a newly acute pain and looked down to see one of the worms gnawing furiously at his testicles.

Ario bellowed into the air, hoping to wake himself from what could only be a nightmare. But however loudly he screamed, his wailing was no louder than the other tormented souls who suffered in inferno alongside him.

Fluid poured down from out of the endless black sky, but instead of putting out the flames, it ignited them further. As the fluid hit Ario, he realized it was blood. The blood of the innocent men he had killed.

"Drink deep and indulge your fate," Azhidaahaka growled. "Welcome home."

CHAPTER 39

As we approach the current aeon, a major episode of cataclysmic devastation will strike all levels of existence. The occurrence will approach in legions, destroying everything in a 360 degree radius.

The people of the kingdom have been corrupted by wickedness, and that of the unrighteous. The devils of the underworld shall break through the gates of inevitability, and on this day, the creatures of darkness will enter the lands, and they shall rule them as their own. God has been elected. Now souls will be recollected, thoughts will be redirected, as believers die disrespected.

Justes and Oniva drove through the cool night toward Elijah's temple. Neither knew what to expect, but they both understood that if they did nothing, then the unthinkable would happen. Oniva smiled wryly to herself as she thought about how much of the present seemed unreal – they were both wanted by the government and the Bloodline, but entirely preoccupied by other questions.

"What are we going to do once we get there?" Oniva asked.

"The plan isn't necessarily concrete. Minzano says that Rontrez is calling the shots for the Bloodline. I'm hoping there's a way to show him what's right. You know him. He'll listen to you. I hope."

"How are we going to get in contact with him? The place is crawling with Bloodliners, and we're both on a list of people they want to kill. I don't know how we'd get inside the building or get Rontrez out. Do you?"

"Nothing foolproof just yet. Do you have any method of contacting him? Maybe a cell phone?" Justes asked.

"He had a cell phone, but he didn't give out the number to anyone but family and close friends. He always said he didn't like being accessible."

"Does he have the phone with him?"

"I don't know."

"Let's call him," Justes shrugged. "I know it sounds simplistic, but we have nothing to lose and everything to gain. If we get a hold of him, maybe we can get him to meet us. I just hope the Bloodline will let him out of their sight."

"Speaking of the Bloodline, Chris, how come you and Pathem seem to know a bit more than everyone else about what's going on? What kind of brotherhood are you in?"

"An old one."

Oniva looked at him searchingly. "You're going to have to come stronger than that. You've been exposed to some knowledge."

Justes was bound by oath, and Grandmaster Pathem was not here to grant an allowance. He had to be careful.

"Are you familiar with the Poor Fellow-Soldiers of Christ and of the Temple of Solomon?" Justes asked, attempting to be vague.

"Yes. The Knights Templar. What about them?"

Justes let out a short laugh, impressed. "Pathem and I are the last ones."

"Descendants of the Knights Templar?" Oniva asked, staring at him quizzically.

"Don't believe me?"

"I didn't say that. The Templars were quite unceremoniously disbanded in the 14th century. A lot of influential people had serious concerns about an army that did not report to any government. A cavalry regiment that was able to move freely throughout all borders and was immune to all taxes and local laws might cause some tension."

"Yes. The Templars were getting too powerful. At dawn on Friday, October 13, 1307, agents of King Philip IV arrested most of the French Templars – because he owed them sizeable debts that he didn't want to pay. The captured Templars were tortured to extract false confessions, which Philip used as evidence to dismantle the Order and burn the brothers alive."

Oniva nodded sadly. "The inquisition of the Templars is a tragic chapter of history. Some historians have speculated that it is the origin of the superstition surrounding Friday the 13th."

"I see you are a quite a history scholar," Justes said, raising his eyebrows.

"Just a student of history. Christian history fascinates me, but now I'd rather discuss the Christian present. Specifically, what would the Knights Templar know about what's going on right now."

"The Order guards many secrets and relics. We study the Bible in a way most people cannot."

"For example?"

"You've heard that history repeats itself. Sometimes, the enemy works in patterns. Just as the Templars were persecuted and burned alive years ago, the Bloodline persecutes Christians today in a similar way. When you study –"

Justes's speech stopped short as they rounded a turn and saw a vehicle on the road's shoulder, its hood up and lights flashing. He slowed to see a beautiful woman waving them down. Justes pulled his Camry behind the disabled vehicle and got out of the car.

"What's the problem, miss?" Justes asked. As he looked into her eyes, Justes felt the demon of lust attempt to settle upon him with such force that he shuddered, banishing it with a silent prayer. Almost imperceptibly, Justes thought he saw the woman flinch.

"It just stopped. I don't know what happened, I have plenty of gas."

"Let me take a look," Justes offered, eager to look anywhere other than at her. Oniva got out of the Camry to see if she could help – she wasn't a car expert by any stretch of the imagination, but she wasn't one to sit on the sidelines when she might be able to be of any help or comfort.

Justes glanced under the hood, but it was too dark to see. As he walked past Oniva to get a flashlight from his glove compartment, he seemed flustered, and Oniva sensed that something was wrong. She walked to the hood of the car to greet the woman and felt herself stiffen defensively as she met the statuesque blonde woman's smoldering gaze.

"Hi," the woman said cheerfully. "I can't thank you enough for stopping."

"Good evening," Oniva replied, offering a hand more out of habit than desire as she silently envied the woman's figure. "My name is Oniva."

"Some people call me Mystery," the woman grinned, taking Oniva's hand with her own soft one. Oniva never lied, so she could not bring herself to say it was a pleasure.

Mystery broke the awkward silence.

"Is that your husband?" Mystery asked, gesturing toward Justes.

"No," Oniva shook her head. "He's just a friend of mine."

"Well, it's always good to have friends. Especially such sexy ones," Mystery grinned.

"We're not like that. He's a minister."

"Reverends need a little love too. He could have you speaking in tongues, girlfriend."

"No, Mystery. Our relationship is platonic."

"You're not serious," Mystery said authoritatively. Perhaps because she was much taller, or because she was used to giving commands, Oniva felt that Mystery was beginning to talk down to her. Whichever it was, Mystery made Oniva feel insecure. She was indeed intimidating. She was beautiful enough to make the Pope himself turn his head, Oniva thought, and would almost certainly arouse lust in any man – and some women, for that matter. Oniva glanced away from Mystery's knowing smirk to examine her sleek black sports car. Oniva registered with surprise that it was a Lamborghini, which she had never seen before – and certainly didn't expect to see on the side of the road.

"Would you like a drink?" Mystery winked. "I have a cooler in the back with all the good stuff in it."

"No thank you," Oniva declined. "I don't drink."

"No sex – and no drinking, either? What are you, a nun? Can't get nun' or never had nun'." Mystery smirked, sounding almost as if she were chastising her.

"No. I choose not to partake in alcohol. I try to stay on the right side of things. If I don't take the first drink, I can't become an alcoholic."

"Nothing wrong with that," Mystery replied. "I have some apple juice in the back if you want some of that."

Oniva couldn't tell whether Mystery was joking. She felt that Mystery was being sarcastic, but she was determined not to give in to the insecurity she felt but could not place.

"Apple juice sounds nice," Oniva replied.

"Cool, follow me."

As Oniva and Mystery headed toward the back of the Lamborghini, Justes passed with the flashlight. Oniva turned sideways to avoid pushing him into the street, and Mystery followed, slowly twisting her pelvis against his. Justes almost dropped his flashlight with shock, but before he had time to react, the moment was gone. With another swish of her hips, Mystery was on her way to the trunk. Shaken, Justes continued to the front of the car.

Mystery opened the trunk to reveal a cooler. Oniva admired Mystery's outfit in the light from the trunk. She wore an impeccable linen suit with a matching blouse. Oniva couldn't resist looking at her shoes, and she recognized her pumps as the pair she had always wanted from Nóir's, the expensive clothing outlet. The price tag on the shoes had been $450, and on Mystery, they looked worth every penny. She remembered when Rontrez had offered to buy her the shoes and now, for a moment, she regretted not having taken him up on his offer.

Mystery flipped open the lid of the cooler to reveal the most extravagant arrangement of wine, champagne, and liquor that Oniva had ever seen. Strangely enough, nestled amongst the wine was a single glass bottle of apple juice.

"Sure you don't want anything stronger?" Mystery asked.

"I'm cool," Oniva replied.

"Here – take some of this communion wine for your reverend friend," she said dryly, winking as she offered Oniva a bottle of wine. Without knowing why, Mystery's wink made Oniva's heart thump.

"He doesn't drink either. Only during the actual communion ceremony," Oniva replied.

"Tell him that this is rehearsal," Mystery said, still sarcastic and casually authoritative. Mystery was indeed a domineering woman with a unique appeal.

"What do you do for a living, if you don't mind me asking?"

"It depends on what day of the week it is, sweetheart. I'm a woman of many talents." That much Oniva had already assumed. "I used to be into learning the ropes to skip and the ropes to know. Now I am into teaching those who desire wisdom. Ropes and otherwise," Mystery finished enigmatically. Oniva noticed Mystery eyeing the crucifix that hung around her neck.

"That's nice," Mystery complimented. "Where did you get it?"

"It was gift from my grandmother. She died when I was very young. I hardly ever take it off."

"May I see it?" Mystery asked.

Oniva did not want to take the charm off, but something about Mystery's tone almost forced her to.

"Come on, it's beautiful. I just want to see how it looks around my neck. I saw you looking at my shoes earlier. Why don't we swap for a minute, it looks like we both wear the same size. We both don't know anything about cars, why don't we have a ladies session?"

Before Oniva could respond, Mystery began taking off her shoes. Oniva wanted to try on the shoes, but did not want to take off her sentimental necklace.

She looked at the shoes and saw they were really her size. It was odd to Oniva that as tall as Mystery was, they wore the same size shoes. As if in a dream, Oniva began to remove her shoes and socks, feeling the cold asphalt under her bare feet. She slid into the shoes, feeling like Cinderella sliding into her glass slippers. They felt like they were created for her. Not wanting to break her end of the arrangement, she reluctantly unhooked the chain from her neck and handed it to Mystery. Mystery slipped it on and looked into a compact mirror she pulled from her suit pocket.

"It's beautiful," she admired. "I have to have it. Name your price."

"I'm sorry, Mystery. I can't sell it. It means the world to me."

"How about those shoes?" Mystery said, raising her eyebrows in suggest. "They fit perfectly. They were made for you."

Oniva looked down at the shoes. They looked beautiful, just as they had in Nóir.

"Oniva, those shoes look dynamite on you. Go ahead and treat yourself."

"I found the problem," Justes called to them. "Try it now, miss."

Without taking the charm off, Mystery mumbled a 'hold on' and stepped around to the drivers seat. Sure enough, when she turned the key the Lamborghini roared to life.

Justes slammed the hood shut and Oniva went to join him, not wanting to leave him alone with the compelling stranger. "Thanks, sweetheart," Mystery cooed seductively as she climbed out of the car. "Is there anything I can do for you in return?"

"That's quite all right, miss," Justes replied.

"We were never formally introduced. The name is Mystery."

"Chris Justes," Justes greeted.

"Oniva tells me you're a priest or something," Mystery said, gazing at Justes.

"Yes, I'm a minister," Justes replied.

"Look, Rev, I won't lie to you. I had a little too much to drink while I was waiting for some good people like you to stop. I don't think I should drive. Can you drive me to the nearest hotel while your friend follows?"

Justes searched his mind for a solution. He did not want to leave the woman to drive home intoxicated, but he knew he could not be alone with her while the demon of lust intensified its assault, attempting to break him with every passing second. He had no idea where the nearest hotel was in this part of town.

"Oniva, do you mind driving Mystery?" Justes asked. "I'm not too good at whipping those exotic cars. I'm a four-door man, myself."

Oniva hesitated, then agreed. Mystery got into the passenger seat of the Lamborghini, still wearing Oniva's crucifix. Oniva reached to start the car, but stopped as soon she saw the light glint off the charm around Mystery's neck.

"Mystery, I need my necklace back."

"I thought we had an arrangement," Mystery replied innocently.

"No. You must have misunderstood me. As a matter of fact, you couldn't have. I said it is not for sale." Oniva reached down and began to remove the pumps.

"Your necklace has made quite a home on my neck, Oniva. Why spoil a beautiful relationship?"

"Sorry, I can't do it. I'm not going to say it again."

"I don't like repeating things myself," Mystery replied, making no motion toward the necklace. "How do you like this car?"

"It's a beautiful car, you keep it well cleaned and in good order. My necklace, please."

"Would you like it?"

"Yes, I would like my necklace back."

"No, baby, the car."

"What?"

"Most people tell me I speak clearly, Oniva."

"You're going to donate this car, huh? Mystery, give me my necklace. You're getting on my nerves."

"Listen, I've had this car for a minute. It's paid off, and it attracts too much attention. I want something a little different now. Money is not a problem for me, Oniva. I have never seen anything this beautiful in my life. I have to have it. This automobile is a small price to pay. We can make the transaction right now. You have a chip, don't you?"

"No. I don't have one."

"Let me give you one. It only takes a few seconds. Then I can give you this car in two more seconds," Mystery offered.

"I don't want it. The Bible speaks of the mark, and the consequences to those who wear it," Oniva said adamantly (Revelation 14:9-11). "And if you don't give my necklace back, we are going to have a problem. Here are your shoes."

"You're not going to do anything to me but love thy enemy, Oniva. I could slap you across the face and you would do nothing. I am going to get out of this car, and leave you with it. It's yours. I'll just keep the necklace. You just turn the other cheek like a good little Christian."

Oniva locked the doors of the Lamborghini, hoping to at least slow Mystery down. Oniva wanted to scream with frustration and throw punches at Mystery, but she kept her temper.

Mystery paused for a moment before she burst out in laughter, unlatching the necklace and handing it to Oniva. "I was just teasing. Will you forgive thy neighbor?"

Oniva nodded tersely.

Mystery decided to take her failure as success. She would now flip the script. "There was no way I was going to take your necklace without your approval," Mystery assured. "I still want to trade you the car for it, though. Take it, it's yours."

"I don't want the car. I'll keep this necklace."

"That's not the best business deal I've ever heard," Mystery grinned.

"Some things aren't for sale," Oniva replied.

"Everything is for sale. Some things just have a higher price tag than others. Everything can be bought – not just with money. Some things must be bought with blood and suffering."

"You're wrong. Some things cannot be bought, period."

"Like what?" Mystery asked, her voice dripping with condescension.

"Like my soul."

"Your soul has already been purchased."

"I'm not even going to entertain that suggestion," Oniva blurted out.

"Look at your necklace that you held onto for dear life. According to your religion, your soul was purchased by some moron from Nazareth. He was nailed to that cross like a picture frame. He purchased your soul with his blood, right?"

"There a little more to it than that, but–"

"But you just told me that your soul can't be bought."

Oniva was becoming more frustrated by the second. Mystery felt herself breaking through Oniva's cool exterior.

Mystery waved, and Oniva turned to see Justes staring at her through the window of the vehicle.

"Is something wrong?" he asked.

"Everything is alright, Chris. I just had to get something straight, that's all. Let's go."

Justes knew something had shaken Oniva, but he wasn't sure what. As soon he was safely in his car, Oniva pulled onto the road.

As soon as they had accelerated, Mystery broke the silence. "Boy, it's good to be a woman," she exclaimed.

All Oniva wanted was to drop Mystery off at the nearest hotel, but she couldn't resist asking for Mystery's rationale.

"What makes being a woman so great?" Oniva asked.

"Because pussy makes the world go round. It's an undeniable fact."

"Can you please refrain from using that word? I hate it."

"Oh, you mean *pussy?*"

"Yes, that word."

"Okay, sorry about that. Now what did you ask me?"

"Why is being a woman so great?"

"Because we run the world."

"We do? Someone forgot to tell me. In most countries there has never even been a woman president. . .when there were countries to be president of."

"Forget all that. That's bureaucratic stuff. Men need to run bureaucracies because they are experts at lying, deceiving, and running weak game."

Oniva couldn't help but chuckle.

"We have absolute power over men – when we chose to exert it," Mystery continued.

"Men tend to think with the wrong head," Oniva admitted, "but some of us don't want to sleaze our way through life. We'd rather earn it. It's a lot more fulfilling."

"Of course it is," Mystery agreed. "Just because I look good doesn't mean I slept my way to the top. That's only what ugly people think. When you first saw me, is that what you thought?" Mystery gleefully anticipated Oniva's first solid lie.

"When I first saw you I thought a lot of things. None of which will be said," Oniva replied, much to Mystery's dismay.

"What I'm saying is, you don't have to sleep your way to the top. For instance, did you ever wonder why powerful executives don't have good-looking secretaries? They're always average looking or some old lady. You have never seen a perfect ten secretary for a truly powerful person. It doesn't happen. Some lowlife, mid-level executive, or some small business might have one, especially politicians, but not in a large company or organization. That's only in the movies."

"Okay, so why is that?"

"Because a gorgeous woman in the equation changes everything. It throws the whole chemistry in another direction. If there is a gorgeous woman around, suddenly all the fragile male egos are multiplied by a hundred. They dress a notch up, they act a notch up. The man that has never ironed a dress shirt in his life will now iron it. A man with low self-esteem will now go out of his way to impress the dang secretary. The head guy will make sure he gives all the orders he can in front of the new secretary. Negotiation meetings would last ten hours because no one wants to be the small guy in front of the beautiful secretary. When there was the old lady secretary no one cared about getting chewed out, but now they do. Even aside from this, now there's a contest to see who can get the most attention from her, and who can get her in bed the quickest. It's hilarious, when you think about it. Anyone with that much power in their presence was destined to rule."

"All this is interesting."

"You haven't even heard the beginning. Do you know that everything men do revolves around us?"

"How so?"

"Think of the cars they drive. Why does a man need an $80,000 automobile?"

"As a status symbol."

"For whom?"

"For society."

"Think harder. Men will fart in front of each other, scratch their nuts in front of each other, curse, fight, watch porn, belch, even walk around in their dirty underwear in front of each other. Do you really think they are concerned with what other men think about them? On a professional level, perhaps, but not on a social level. On a social level, it's all about us. If there was a city with no women, how would the men dress in this city?"

"If there was a city with no women, I don't think there would be any men in it. They would leave to find us," Oniva replied.

"Exactly my point. Now reverse the roles, how long could a city of only women last?"

"For quite some time, I imagine."

"Correct again, my friend. That is, until we couldn't find a way to stop all of the men from scaling the walls. Every man in the world would be trying to figure out a way to get in that city. They would be knocking each other down trying to get into that city. Anything it took, bribery, firstborn child, anything. An electric fence wouldn't stop them. The funny thing is that we could care less if there was a city of just men. We would never visit. If anything interesting ever happened there, we'd just watch it on the news. It's important you know that you are stronger than a man. Once you realize this, you can act accordingly. Oniva, do you think you need a man to survive?"

"A man, no. A good man would be very nice to have around. The Bible says a woman is to be the man's helpmate. A husband is the head of the household, just like Christ is the head of the church. I would help a good man to the ends of the earth if he was mine and only mine," (Genesis 2:18-22, Ephesians 5:22-30).

"Wrong, genius," Mystery disagreed, her voice rising. "You are the master. He can't live without you. You make the decisions, he follows. That's the way it goes. Sometimes it's all right to let him think he is making the decisions, but always know you are the true master. Oniva, you make your own decisions. Don't worry about what some man tells you. That's sickening!" Mystery was almost yelling now. "I hate to see strong women like you play that passive role. It wasn't meant to be. Men were given brawn because they are doers, women were blessed with brains because we are thinkers. You tell me, who should be the master, the doer or the thinker?"

Mystery awaited an answer.

"I don't have an opinion on this," Oniva answered.

"It's a common sense question," Mystery countered.

"Should we call manholes personholes? Is that what you want?"

"You're trying to be funny and this is serious," Mystery shouted. "I'm not a feminist, I'm a realist. I study truth and deal in reality. I just want a strong woman to stand up and make her own decisions. When we met, all I saw in you is strength. I just want you to use it. Right now you are a follower, I don't like that for you. You are a leader. Do you have a man in your life?"

"No, not like that. Chris and I are just friends."

"Someone else, maybe?"

"No boyfriend. Just a good friend."

"What's his name?"

"Esau."

"Esau Rontrez?" Mystery answered.

"Yes, do you know him?" Oniva asked.

"Yes."

"Do you know where he is?"

"Yes. He is in the temple downtown."

"Are you a member of the Bloodline?" Oniva asked seriously.

Mystery laughed. "Be serious. I said I study truth, not occultism."

"How can we get in the temple to get him out?" Oniva asked.

"We won't. I'll have him come out."

"How are you going to get him to come out? I can't get a hold of him."

"For a Christian, you sure don't have any faith," Mystery grinned.

"Man fails at times," Oniva responded.

"I'm not a man, I'm all woman," Mystery smiled.

"But you are from a man's seed and a man's origin, right?"

"Do you want to see Esau?" Mystery asked.

"Yes, where is he?"

"Ditch old faithful back there and we'll roll."

"No, Chris comes with us. This is important," Oniva insisted.

"No deal. Consider this a private affair."

"Why don't you let Rontrez decide who he wants to see?" Oniva offered.

"If you know Rontrez, you know he doesn't want any interference when it comes to his ladies."

"If you knew me, or Rontrez, you would know that we don't get down like that," Oniva informed Mystery, growing frustrated.

"You've got to be kidding me," Mystery fussed.

"We are just good friends. No sex."

"Oniva, let me ask you a question, and I want an honest answer."

"Okay," Oniva replied.

"Do you find me attractive?" Mystery asked.

Oniva was simultaneously frustrated and awestruck. Oniva wasn't sure if Mystery was hitting on her, or trying to be cute.

"You're a very pretty woman. I don't know if I find you attractive. I'm not a lesbian."

"Don't act like that," Mystery snapped. "Just because you find me attractive doesn't mean you are homosexual. Don't be insecure about your sexuality! You're too strong for that. I just asked you a simple question."

In a strange way, Oniva did find Mystery attractive. The woman was undeniably dazzling. Everything from her immaculate facial structure, to her commanding demeanor and her magnificent attire made her irresistibly magnetic. Her styled hair, manicured hands and feet, and toned body were as if she had walked out of a super-model magazine.

"I just told you were a pretty woman, but I'm sure you knew that before today. What else do you want?"

"I want the truth you promised me. I didn't ask if I was pretty, I asked if you were attracted to me."

Oniva was silent. "I'm not sure I could find any woman truly attractive like you seem to mean. I don't appreciate that question, either. Don't ask me anything like that again."

"Look at that. You are denying yourself. Right now you are shutting down your mind because you want to deny the truth. Truth is so relative to you. I thought Christians were supposed to tell the truth."

"What is your faith? Do you believe in anything? Besides money, I mean."

"I don't believe in money. Money comes and goes. I've been rich, I've been poor. I believe in nothing but truth. Elijah is the truth. Any man that can come down from the sky and change utter chaos into everlasting peace gets my vote any day."

"Everything is not what it seems, Mystery. This world is in danger. Take me to Esau."

"No problem. Ditch preacher man back there. Esau doesn't like people he doesn't know."

"He'll love Chris," Oniva replied, becoming more irked by the moment.

"Okay," Mystery started. "I'll give you your options. One, answer my question. Two, ditch the square, and I'll take you to Esau. Or three, you could let me keep the necklace."

"Okay, I don't find you attractive."

"You're lying!" Mystery exclaimed.

"Are your feelings hurt?" Oniva asked.

"I saw the way you looked at me. You wanted me. You wanted to know what it would feel like to be touched by someone who could understand your needs as a woman, and not someone who is going to get his eight minutes in and roll over and start snoring."

"Are you sure that's what I was thinking?" Oniva asked.

"Yes, and I want you to stop denying yourself. Self-denial is the most unintelligent concept I have ever witnessed. As long as you're not hurting anyone, live life."

"Great sermon. Where is Esau?"

"You don't get to see him, because you lied."

Oniva snapped. "Woman, do not play with my emotions! If you know where Esau is, tell me. I don't know what kind of sick fucking game you're playing!"

Oniva snapped to her senses when she heard herself curse. She could not remember the last time she had used profanity. It had been at least fifteen years.

Oniva looked at Mystery, who was grinning with satisfaction.

Yes. She was beginning to break down.

"I'm sorry for cursing at you," Oniva apologized.

"No apology needed. But you feel better, don't you? Expressing yourself can do a world of wonder, don't you agree?"

Oniva shrugged tersely. "So where is Esau?"

"Keep going straight from here," Mystery said. It was seemingly a response, but Oniva knew that Mystery was not talking about any kind of street.

Oniva glanced in her rearview mirror and breathed a sigh of relief as she saw that Justes was still close behind her.

"Your reverend is safe," Mystery said. "So I would like you to tell the truth. I don't think I've heard it."

"You've heard everything I have to tell you until I see Esau Rontrez," Oniva replied adamantly.

"Stop the car," Mystery barked as they approached an intersection. Oniva complied.

"Unlock the door, please," Mystery said harshly. She opened the door and turned to Oniva. "Are you going to tell the truth?"

"I've said all I have to say until I see Esau," Oniva growled.

Mystery smiled and gracefully exited onto the sidewalk. She strode into a late-night pizzeria packed with patrons having their chips scanned.

Justes pulled up behind the Lamborghini and got out.

"What happened? Was she hungry?" Justes asked.

"We had irreconcilable differences," Oniva stated.

"Are we still taking her to the hotel?"

"No."

"Why not? Do you think we should let her drive home drunk?" Justes asked.

"She wasn't drunk. Believe me, she'll make it home just fine."

"She must be really drunk, she didn't even take her keys," Justes said, noticing that the engine was still running.

"I've never met a drunk person to articulate her words, piss me off, walk straight, and hit on me in the same minute."

"She hit on you?" Justes asked.

"Are you jealous?" Oniva replied, still looking straight ahead.

"Yes and no," Justes replied. "Oniva, I'm sure you know why I had you ride with her. She was something out of this world. When I saw her, I committed adultery in my heart. The last place I needed to be was alone with her in a Lamborghini. It seemed that your time wasn't much easier."

"Oh, Chris. I'm sorry for snapping. She just really got under my skin. She said she knew Esau and where he was."

"What? What did she say — did she tell you where he was? Why didn't you ask her to take us to him?"

"Long, ugly story, Chris. She did know Esau, but she wanted to leave you behind."

"Why?"

"I don't know."

"Hey, where is your necklace?" Justes asked.

Oniva clutched at her neck and screamed. She pushed past Chris and raced toward the pizzeria. Anger swelled in her heart and fury raced through her veins. She grabbed a glass parmesan container off of the counter, confident that if she saw Mystery, she would smash it over her attractive head and get her property back.

Justes ran in the pizzeria after Oniva. "Oniva, put the cheese back down. Please. . . put the jar of parmesan cheese back down."

The people in the pizzeria could sense Oniva's anger, and it had drawn attention. Even the rough-looking characters seeking temporary refuge inside of the pizzeria had backed up to clear a space for her. It was an unusual sight: a small, angry, young woman armed with a canister of Parmesan cheese, followed by a suburban minister who oddly looked as if he was the only one with a chance of talking her out of doing whatever she came to do.

Oniva didn't see Mystery anywhere, and a six-foot woman dressed in an elegant white suit would have been hard to miss. She scanned the small room, packed with patrons dressed casually and in dark colors, and decided that Mystery must be in the restroom. She stalked toward the back of the restaurant and Justes followed, urging her to stop. When she reached the ladies room, Justes grabbed her arm.

"Oniva, you're acting like a madwoman. What are you doing? Are you going to assault her with a glass can of cheese? Please, calm down." As Oniva moved to snatch her arm away, Justes saw the glimmer of a chain peek at her neckline.

"Your necklace is on. It's tucked under your shirt, Oniva."

Oniva pushed open the door to see Mystery leaning against the sink with her arms crossed, grinning as if she were expecting them.

Oniva and Justes stood speechlessly in the doorway—Justes once again taken aback by the woman's unnatural beauty, and Oniva still astounded by the realization that her necklace was on.

"Good to see you again, Chris," Mystery smiled slyly.

"Sorry to bother you, Mystery," Justes started. "You left your keys in the car. And the engine running."

"How thoughtful of you, sweetheart. You ran after me just to give me my car keys?"

"Don't mention it," Justes replied, averting his gaze. "Do you know where we can find Esau? That would return the favor. We urgently need to speak with him."

"Esau who?" Mystery asked.

Oniva fought the urge to smash the cheese can upside Mystery's head. Instead, she rolled her eyes and headed back into the restaurant. Justes held the door open, not wanting to go into the ladies room to return Mystery's keys. He held the keys in his outstretched arm, signaling her to come get them. Mystery grinned slowly and shook her head, and, using her index finger, beckoned Justes to come in.

Justes shook his head. He jingled the keys, but she made no movement toward the door.

"Why don't you take it for a spin, Chris?" she offered.

Not wanting to play the game and afraid he might lose, Justes tossed the Lamborghini keys onto the floor at her feet and left without a word.

When the bathroom door closed, Mystery folded her arms and mumbled into the air. "The reverend threw my keys at me."

Outside the restaurant, Oniva sat on a bench. Moments later, Justes stood beside her.

"I'm not going to ask what's wrong, because you might not know either. But I do know you can't let people make you crazy like that. Do you remember why she got out of the car in the first place?"

"No," Oniva replied. "She just got out. She told me to pull over and—"

"Did she tell you, or did she ask you?" there was urgency in Justes's voice.

"She told me. She told me to stop the car."

"When?"

"Just before I stopped the car."

"What did she say? Did she say she was hungry or had to go to the bathroom?"

"No. She just told me to stop the car all of a sudden. I had to stop anyway, because the light was red. Then she asked me to unlock the door–"

"She asked you. . . are you sure she asked you, she didn't tell you?"

"Well she told me, but she said please."

"And then she just got out, right?"

"Yes. What's going on? What's wrong?"

"There's a reason she got out of the car so fast."

"Why?"

"Because she had to. Behind you, right before you stopped, I said a prayer for you. I was trying to get myself together and I asked God for the demon of lust to be sent away from me and for anything unholy to be cast from your reach. Right then, you stopped the car and she got out. I –I don't think that was a coincidence. You still had an encounter in the pizza place because you chased *her*. When I asked her to come get her keys, she wouldn't, but motioned me to come to her. Since I didn't, she just told me to take the car."

"Chris, she wanted my necklace badly. Why? What's so special about it?"

"Nothing. Nothing at all. It's a trinket to her. Trinkets can't stop anything from happening. It's what it meant to you. It has even more than the religious significance for you. She tried to bribe you for it, didn't she?"

"Yes, she even offered the car for it."

"Exactly. She wanted you to trade something you care about – something that is important to you both personally and spiritually – for material goods. After you trade what you believe in and sell a piece of yourself, you are ripe for the taking. It's all downhill from there. I see you still have it. That's a good thing."

Oniva didn't want to ask why Mystery had hit on her. Oniva just wanted to forget it.

"You see, it was trying to break you. It was trying to crack you. It just needed a point of entry. It tried greed, then it played on your anger, seeking some kind of gateway to penetrate. It probably played on your pride and lust desires and anything else it could think of. You said she was flirting with you, right?"

"Yes."

"Well, she sure played on my lust as well," Justes muttered, looking abashed. "You have to be careful, Oniva. Do you see how you were ready to bash her with the glass can of shredded cheese? If you had, she would have won, that's how it works. The gateway would have opened. That one action alone would have brought about others. You see, she would have fought back, and you would have defended yourself, and you might have killed her in your rage. She would not have really been dead, but she would have been to you and the cops. And then you go to prison, where you have to kill again to defend yourself, until that becomes your way of life. Do you see what I mean? Did she tell you where Esau was?" Justes asked.

"She didn't tell us anything we didn't know already. She told me he was in the temple."

"Did she say anything else?"

"Oh, she said plenty. She didn't say anything that I was interested in though."

"Well let's head over there," Justes suggested.

"The Lamborghini would get us there faster," Oniva winked.

"What did I just tell you? Leave—"

"I was just playing, Chris. Take a chill pill."

Justes and Oniva headed toward the Camry.

"Have you thought of how we're going to get into the temple?" Oniva asked.

"Me? I was busy praying. What were you doing the whole time, Miss Parmesan?" Justes responded.

"I was chatting with the demon of lust. That's a pretty original justification, if I do say so myself. Come on, we need to put our heads together."

"Indeed," Justes replied.

"Chris, I sure miss Esau. He is always around making everything alright. Anything that happens to me, he seems to have the cure."

"You love him, huh."

"Yes. It's not a lustful or physical love. It's the kind of love you have for family. One thing annoys me. Why was the lust monster a woman? I've never even had sex with a man, why would she or it or whatever it was try me with lady bait?"

"Don't worry, a man might be next. If you think the Lord works in mysterious ways, you should try studying his enemies."

Mystery walked into the large room where Asmodeus stood with his back to the entrance, looking out of the large window over the former Washington, DC. Azhidaahaka sat on its throne, seemingly deep in thought. Its eyes were closed, but Azhidaahaka did not see with its eyes anymore. It saw with its existence.

Mystery did not appear tall and blonde as she had been only moments before, but as an equally beautiful but entirely different woman with brown skin and voluptuous curves. It was the same form she had taken when she had first seduced Esau Rontrez, poisoned his mind, and brought him into the waiting arms of the circle.

Outside of the circle, she was called any name she saw fit. Inside the circle, she was Mystery, daughter of Asmodeus.

Mystery approached her father and whispered in his ear.

Asmodeus remained still for a moment, then exploded with anger, replying to her report with a backhand. Asmodeus had been correct – the woman was trouble. She was as powerful as Justes, but it was to their advantage that she didn't know it. The master had overlooked this.

CHAPTER 40

Vincent Minzano strode up the marble steps of the temple and double-checked his two Special Operations command pistols. They were loaded and ready, and he kept the extra clips at his waist. He noticed there was no guard at the door, but dismissed the notion as he walked up the steps. The first time he had been to the temple to see Rontrez, the door had been open. Now he wondered what his entrance strategy would be. As he reached the threshold, the door opened of its own accord, as if the temple offered itself to him. He stepped into the pitch-black interior of the temple, and the heavy door creaked shut behind him, enclosing him in a thick blanket of obscurity, and blackness. He felt like Luke Skywalker walking into Jabba's palace. Minzano walked further into Jabba's palace and it gave him an uncomfortable feeling. His position as a Bloodline Knight comforted him somewhat, but he still wished he could see.

He could sense no sound or sign of life, but he didn't mind being alone – and at present, it was probably safer. He was used to working unaccompanied, but he now thought of Mona, recalling his plan to propose to her until she announced that she had been cheating on him for the last eight months. Minzano left bad enough alone, but not before Mona cleaned out their bank account and took his car. He eventually found his car, but he never really understood what had happened. Since he was a magnet to bad men, it was no surprise he attracted Mona. On his undercover assignments, there were times when he thought of nothing but her. She was the reason he would come home. She couldn't cook and never really tried, but they were oddly compatible, and they complemented each other.

Now he had no one, and it had been that way for years. Sex was no problem – it seemed that every woman in America wanted a bad boy, and his undercover persona almost always met the qualifications. Minzano had gotten over Mona, but did miss the warm thought of coming home to someone.

He groped along the walls, but he could find no exit. The chamber was like solitary confinement: pitch black, with no source of life or energy. Minzano circled the room again, but there was nothing. He could not even feel the door through which he had entered.

In Azhidaahaka's chambers, Bee-el, Mammon, Mystery, and Egor now sought an audience with it. Azhidaahaka remained seated on its throne as they entered. It did not rise as they walked into its sanctuary, nor did it acknowledge them as they walked into its presence.

"The time has come, my lord," Mystery stated.

Azhidaahaka rose and walked to the edge of its sanctuary, the glass doors sliding open at its thought. Azhidaahaka, now wearing a sharp black suit and a billowing cape, walked onto the luxurious balcony and looked out over the city, lights sparkling in the distance. In other circumstances, the view might be considered romantic, but it had no concern for romance. In essence, it was a foreign concept.

The four other beings followed Azhidaahaka out into the night. Azhidaahaka thrust its open hands in the air and let forth a sickening yell. A peal of thunder sounded and the night sky blackened as furious red lightning streaked across the sky. Azhidaahaka rose into the air and drifted over the ledge, floating downwards toward the city concrete. Tonight, all who opposed him would bathe in blood. Azhidaahaka – the dragon of death – was now prepared to enslave its enemies as it displaced their souls and replaced them with its own. Tonight was a different kind of Passover: the Bloodline Passover. All whose doorways did not bear the sign of the master would perish.

<hr>

"What is that?" Justes asked, squinting up at the temple. There was a descending object seeming to defy gravity. "My eyesight isn't so good, but it looks like a man."

"That's Esau!" Oniva exclaimed.

"In the sky?" Justes asked.

"Yes, that's him!" Oniva leapt out of the Camry and waved frantically to catch his attention. As he watched the figure descend to the concrete ahead of them, Justes was overcome by a sense of foreboding.

"Let's go, Oniva. I think we really need to go."

Oniva continued to wave at her long-lost friend, tears in her eyes.

Even from this distance, Oniva could tell there was definitely something different about him. As crazy as he was, Oniva didn't think Rontrez would ever wear a cape in public – and how could he possibly float?

Azhidaahaka stood, examining the lost soul in its presence. It found the figure strangely intriguing, as if the woman was a toy from a now-distant childhood. She spoke enthusiastically to Azhidaahaka, but it was not concerned with the content of her speech. Instead, one thing was clear: she did not fear Azhidaahaka. This angered it.

"Esau, I was so worried about you," Oniva cried, running toward the creature that looked like Rontrez. "Are you okay?" she gasped, ignoring Justes's shouts behind her. As she drew closer, she saw the red glow in his eyes and stopped dead in her tracks.

Azhidaahaka sensed the fear in its target, and this amused it. The woman did not bear the mark, and would be slain according to the law.

"Esau, what's happened to you?" Oniva asked, frozen with fear. "What's going on?"

The dragon of death strode steadily towards Oniva, its icy gaze fixed upon her.

Oniva's eyes widened, and she turned on her heel and ran. She sprinted back to the car and to Justes, who had been screaming for her to come back since she had started toward Esau. Justes threw himself behind the steering wheel just as Oniva reached the car, and she jumped in as quickly as she had jumped out. The smell of burning rubber filled the air as Justes banked the wheel as hard as he could to the left and slammed on the gas pedal.

As the car sped away, Azhidaahaka allowed itself to grin. All could run, but none would escape.

• • •

"What was that?" Oniva gasped, every hair standing on end. "Was he a man?"

Justes sighed solemnly. "A man totally energized by demons," he replied.

CHAPTER 41

Elijah looked out over his new kingdom and smiled. The sky was black and filled with screams. The untold horror had begun. Asmodeus stood silently beside him. The last piece of the puzzle was not yet in place, but it was only a matter of time. With the master, it was always only a matter of time. Flawless planning was his strength, but greed and pride were his downfall. Though greed was Mammon's game to win, Elijah played it exceptionally. Everything had come to pass just as Elijah had planned it, and Asmodeus knew that his master's cup runneth over with arrogance.

"You still do not have Chris Justes, nor Oniva Mering," Asmodeus reminded him.

"They are nothing," Elijah said flatly.

I beg to differ.

"Who are they, then?" Asmodeus asked. "Why are they part of the grand scheme?"

And grand it is.

"They hold the weapon," Elijah answered, "and they have not yet turned it against themselves."

"Are you going to wait?" Asmodeus asked sarcastically.

"There will be no more waiting. All will be mine when it is time," Elijah snarled. "Do you doubt me?"

"You underestimate much," Asmodeus warned. "A few strong links in the chain can be enough to choke you."

"They are clueless, they are scared, and they are hiding. When the final battle has taken place, all actuality, essence, and fundamental reality will fall unto me."

"There are several variables we have not yet considered," Asmodeus continued.

"Asmodeus, you do not plan," Elijah said. "You beat your adversaries to a pulp and return for the kill. Why are you planning now? You are a powerful aggressor and a dynamic deputy, but planning isn't one of your strengths. But that doesn't matter – I need a barbarian on my team any day."

"Truly spoken. So let this barbarian loose to break those who oppose us."

"What exactly do you plan to do? Usurping Faith is not a matter of brute force. Describe your plan, Asmodeus."

"Fear," came his growled response.

"Sounds a little primitive," Elijah replied.

"But effective. As you know, this is a different kind of pain. Every being has a weak point. Every mortal *will* bend, and every individual has their price. We must find the proper weakness and exploit it. When the target seems indifferent to incentive, all can be shattered through fear."

"How do you plan to instill this fear? Azhidaahaka seems to be doing a magnificent job – and the fun is just beginning."

"I will instill fear with a vision of the inevitable," Asmodeus said simply.

Elijah scoffed. "As wonderful as that sounds, I'm very disappointed in you."

"I imagine you are dissatisfied with many things. But as I'm sure you wish me to ask, why are you now discontented?"

"While you are busy trying not to underestimate those insignificant souls who are temporarily out of place in the plan, you underestimate *me*."

"Is that so?"

"Unquestionably so. Do you think I started planning yesterday? Or even an eon ago? No. This has been in the making since before the beginning of time. The chessboard is set, and the opponent is nearly checkmated."

"Nearly. Nearly is the operative word at this turn of events."

"Yes, it is. However, the pawns that are still wandering around protecting the prize are both weak and clueless to what is at hand."

"As in chess, when a pawn reaches the end of the board, it becomes powerful."

Elijah whipped his head to face Asmodeus, hissing with rage. "As I have recognized, Asmodeus. Do you think for one minute there has not been a plan for them? Do you believe for a second that I will let two whelps interfere with inevitability? Do you think for one instant that there is not already a plan in place to contain them, to mislead them, and to break them? Do not take this as a personal challenge. Do not waste your time trying not to miscalculate those temporarily outside of the final chart of inevitability. My planning is flawless, my timing is immaculate, and everything is in place."

"Really."

"I have watched and studied Chris Justes since his entrance into this world of iniquity. He is a mere 32 years of age, friend. From the moment of his birth, he was etched into the plan. There are certain ways you get him to bend. The usual order of business won't work. Money, sex, power, and the like mean nothing to him. Absolutely nothing. But he is merely a man. And all men have weaknesses. Let me bestow upon you some insight. Since day one, I have had to protect him."

"Protect him from whom?" Asmodeus asked. "Is there a reason you let his sword become so razor sharp?"

"I had to shield him from himself. His sword of Faith is razor sharp, because he will slay himself with it. If Chris had found me any sooner, it would have been a disaster. Asmodeus, his faith was only way he would deny himself completely for 32 years. The man has denied himself for so long, he has no idea what his weaknesses are. . .but I do. He has no idea how vulnerable he is. But I have taken careful notes. The plan is already in progress. It has been in place for some time now, ready to launch. It's quite amusing, really. You would probably smile if you knew how."

"I will smile when the war is won. Maybe."

"Just a matter of time. Everything is falling into place, like the leaves of autumn."

"What is the weakness?"

"A common one, actually. An awfully typical inclination. When the sword grows too sharp, sometimes it cuts the owner. Worry not. Everything is under control."

Smirking, Elijah laid out the plot without saying a word. Asmodeus stood in silence, taking a moment to absorb its complexity.

"Ingenious. Absolutely astounding tactical intellect. I see that we don't have much too worry about after all."

"You can still try fear, if you'd like."

"No. I don't think that will be necessary."

Asmodeus knew that Elijah had just wanted to hear him say it. Asmodeus signaled, and Bee-El, Mystery, Mammon, and Egor joined them. Without speaking, they knew it was time – time to oppose Azhidaahaka.

Elijah transformed into a being of great light, and the others morphed into beings of great darkness. They rose into the air, ready for their own deliverance.

Legions of other beings of light followed Elijah as the beings of darkness gathered their thousands of numbers as well to follow Azhidaahaka's path of destruction.

Azhidaahaka knew what was upon it before anything happened. It was being attacked. Why? It did not know, nor did it care, but Azhidaahaka's reinforcements would soon come to annihilate all who dared oppose it. It opened its mouth and let out a frightful roar, one hundred times more beastly than any lion, and watched shapes of darkness hover above him. These were Azhidaahaka's servants and soldiers, gathered for battle. Azhidaahaka was not a being of patience, and did not wait for the enemy to settle upon it. It rose into the air, and the world watched as its soldiers of darkness followed.

Trumpets sounded from the beings of light as Azhidaahaka and its minions approached them. Every living individual watched. The trumpets blared as loud as the day Elijah descended from the sky, and

Azhidaahaka and its dark army set upon the beings of light. There was then a voice for all to hear:

"Behold, the lord thy God has returned to devour darkness. Let the final battle begin."

The dark shapes shrieked hideously as they furiously attacked the beings of light. When they collided, it violently created an ugly gray substance that spewed sulfurous clouds into the atmosphere.

The shapes had no concrete form, faces or limbs. Shapes that seemingly lived in themselves, thriving off of their companions' energy and essence, making themselves more powerful. All upon the earth somehow knew the great forces of good and evil had irrevocably come together for the final battle. The battle for all things within existence and without. All understood the victor of this war would be the owner of all souls.

The earth filled with noise as Azhidaahaka directed its army of evil into the territory of light. Red lightning streaked across the black skies with thunderous clamor and the beings of light emitted majestically mystifying but authoritative trumpet blasts, even though no musical instruments were visible.

The beings fought each other with great vengeance and anger, battling not with guns, and armor, but warring with will.

It was an intense combat beyond the most radical of any potential dream or thought. The two forces clashed together in extreme aggression, focused only on the elimination of its opposite. The ghastly screeching of the shapes of darkness attempted to drown out the ear-shattering trumpets, as each side assaulted the other side with furious rage.

There were no rules of battle, no visible attack strategy, no territory to overtake, and no option for either side to retreat or withdraw itself. It was clear: only one side would exist. And each force fought, acknowledging this undeniable law.

Each side attacked its enemy with unmistakable precision and acrimony. The antagonism almost took physical form as each squadron willed itself against the other one.

The black sky, split by the red lighting streaks, favored no one, and piercing thunder could still be heard above the sounds of the mystical combat.

It seemed that the beings of light were easily overtaking Azhidaahaka and its armies, but the tide quickly turned. Flames leapt out of the ground like giant geysers as Azhidaahaka itself began to take part in the battle, willing enemy after enemy into oblivion. The creatures of light began to disappear, and with each victory, Azhidaahaka felt itself grow stronger. Soon the blaring trumpets had dissipated into an almost comical whimper, before they finally silenced.

The hideous shapes of darkness howled their victory to the skies, and swam through the air shrieking in glory.

Azhidaahaka stood among the wreckage, victorious.

• • • • •

"I don't believe it," Justes said to Pathem back in the church. "How could this be happening? This isn't in the Bible. Bishop, what is going on?"

"I must reveal myself to you now, Chris. Things have become worse than you could imagine."

Pathem's voice was different. Kinder and gentler than before, but laced with a note of severity.

"I am the Archangel Michael of the Seraphim."

Justes fell silent, his eyes wide. He knew the Seraphim was the highest sphere of Archangels. Oniva studied Pathem as if she expected gigantic wings to burst from his skin at any moment.

"What do we do now, Michael?" Despite her best efforts, Oniva could not help but sound bewildered. "What's going on? And I don't mean to be bothersome, but why have you waited until now to reveal yourself? The situation has seemed critical for some time."

Justes still did not say a word.

"What is happening now has not been written. This is a new devil," Pathem replied.

Finally overcoming his initial shock, Justes managed to speak. "How do we fight it?"

"We must use the only weapon we have: Faith. That is why I did not reveal myself to you. Believing concrete evidence is not faith. Faith is confidence in what we hope for and assurance about what we do not see. If an Angel appears to you and instructs you, you do not obey out of faith. You obey because you have seen a miracle with your own eyes. There's a difference."

"What was the battle we just saw? What just happened?" Justes asked.

Pathem looked at Justes solemnly. "Chris, I believe you know."

"What do we do? What next?" Oniva stuttered, unsure which question to ask.

"We must destroy our new adversary, thus defeating the old one. I will lead us. We must go to the temple."

"We've been there already. We can't get in, and Rontrez doesn't even recognize me for us to talk to him," Oniva answered.

"There will be no talking this round, Oniva. There is no need for recognition. I am a warring angel. We will depart for the temple and put an end to this."

Pathem then began to glow with warm radiance, and his clergy robe suddenly appeared spotless and white as three pairs of wings emerged from his radiant aura. "I will set forth to destroy our enemy for good. Meet me at the temple. Oniva, I am truly sorry, but your friend has accepted evil into his being. There is nothing I can do to save him now. I will gather the others. You will know what to do when the time is right."

"Michael," Justes asked, "What is the one of many? Why is Esau so special?"

Pathem turned slowly. "Chris, do you know where civilization originated?"

"Yes, in the Garden of Eden. And it's been definitively and scientifically proven that the first humans originated in Africa. Personally, I believe the Garden of Eden was near the Nile. Even if they don't believe in Christianity or its principles, any legitimate historian will tell you that civilization began in Africa. But what does this mean?"

"One of many descendants. One out of many direct lines to the original man. The Edenic Man."

With that, Pathem was gone.

As they walked outside the Holy of Holies and got into the car, Oniva noticed Justes's furrowed brow.

"Chris, what's wrong? I know everything is not all right, but it seemed like the angel scared you?"

Justes remained silent until after they had pulled out onto the road. "Oniva, do you know what a Seraphim is?"

"It's a kind of angel, isn't it? For a while, I didn't even realize angels had levels."

"Yes, they certainly do. In Christian angelology, the Seraphim are the highest-ranking celestial beings in the hierarchy of angels."

"So what are the regular angels called?"

"It would depend on which class of angels you were referring to. In the highest sphere, but still lower ranking than the Seraphim, you would have Cherubim or Ophanim, and that is what worries me."

"Why does an angel worry you?"

"Oniva, I have studied religion all my life, even when I was a boy. In Jewish, Christian, and Islamic literature, Michael is indeed a warring angel. In the Bible, he is depicted as the leader of the heavenly hosts, the great prince who protects the people. And in the book of Revelation, it is Michael who leads his heavenly armies against those of the dragon and his heathens," (Daniel 12:1, Revelation 12:7).

"So what worries you?"

"Several things. Several things are wrong."

"Start with number one."

"First, as I said, Michael is a warrior, a mighty battle general for the Lord. Why in the world would he be watching us all day long locked in a church cellar? Why would he be hiding in the basement with us while evil conquered all? A Virtues angel or a lower-ranking angel would do that, not a Seraphim. As a midlevel angel, a Virtues angel would even provide a stronghold and inspiration, but since things have gotten worse, there has been no leadership or direction from Pathem. Second, Pathem is a prominent man. People know of him around the globe. It's not written anywhere, but it seems to me personally that it is pretty much in an angel's protocol to keep a low profile. An angel would never be anyone famous, let alone the notably rich celebrity grandmaster of the Knights Templar. Angels help people in everyday lives anonymously, receiving absolutely no fame, credit, or monetary reward for their actions. They just help when it's time to help. Pathem has written books, been on TV, and he is the head of a serious fraternal organization. Angels don't do that."

"Are you saying he's a fake?"

"I'm not saying that. I'm just saying everything doesn't seem right. For Michael to be a warring archangel who has gone against evil before, why would he stay out of this one for so long?"

"Maybe there is a reason," Oniva replied. "Our only weapon now is Faith. If we lose that, then we have nothing. But I will admit, it is mighty hard to keep faith with the walls of reality collapsing all around us."

"I agree," Justes replied. "But it seems almost cowardly that Michael would not be fighting along with everyone else."

"Chris. Are you are beginning to break? You are doubting an Archangel."

Justes realized that she was right. He was losing faith – the only weapon he had. Thankfully, he had Oniva, who was smart enough to realize it.

"I have something to add to your theory – and you probably won't like it," Oniva said.

"Speak on it."

"How did you join the Order?"

"The Order of the Temple is invite only. You are selected."

"Who was the first person to be selected that you know of?" Oniva asked.

"Grandmaster Hall, sometime in the 18th century."

"That's interesting, if you look at the history of the Templars. There is no clear historical connection between the original Knights Templar, which were dismantled in the 14th century, and your organization, which, as far as you know, emerged in the 18th century. Amidst the complex history of the Templars, you are overlooking one thing: the four hundred year gap. Also, the original Templars were members of a monastic order and most were *required* to take vows of celibacy and avoid all contact with women, even members of their own family sometimes. Therefore it was not possible, in most cases, for Templars to have any descendants. So, if the Templars by definition didn't have any descendants, neither you nor Pathem could be a descendant."

Justes thought for a moment. "The Templars were great men."

"I don't dispute that. The Templars fought and died for what they believed in. But if you all are direct descendants, or even selected by descendants of the Knights Templar, every single one of them must have broken their oaths."

"Your point?"

"My point is that the 'Holy War' the Knights Templar fought was for political power, religious sovereignty, money, and land, among other things. Not about God. The Crusades didn't even work. The Holy Land was never captured and held for any meaningful amount of time, even by the elite Templars. To this day, the Muslim world still controls the Holy Land. If the Crusades were divinely ordained by God, don't you think they would have been successful? The Crusades were about power – the kind of power Elijah has now."

"Are you saying the brotherhood wasn't great because we didn't win?"

"I'm not saying that the Knights Templar weren't great men. I'm saying that the whole thing was wrong. It was about an agenda. The historical Knights Templar were men of renowned skill, faith, and bravery who got caught up in an agenda. You are a man of great skill, faith, and bravery. I don't want to see it happen to you. It's the pattern you were referring to before we ran into your lust monster."

Justes drew a sharp breath and gritted his teeth. "We're almost there. I have a feeling trouble will be waiting for us."

"Speak of the...." Oniva's voice trailed off as they rounded the final turn to see Rontrez outside the temple. She got out of the car and approached him cautiously, Justes a step behind her.

Azhidaahaka didn't know why a mere mortal would dare approach it, but it did smell her terror. The fear would sweeten the taste of her spirit. It stood menacingly, savoring her brazen approach.

Oniva shook her head as she approached. "Oh, no, Esau. That's not even you."

Impulsively, she grabbed her friend's hands with her own and suddenly felt as though she were sucked into a void, racing through darkness, her own name and Esau's echoing around her. Bracing herself for impact, she squeezed her eyes shut and curled into a ball to protect herself.

Suddenly, the cavernous air around her became muffled and warm, as if she had been plunged into a vat of viscous liquid. She tentatively opened one eye, trying to make out her surroundings. Oniva was suspended in a world of formless color, unable to make out the foggy shapes around her because they had no clear boundaries. Intent on checking herself for injury, she instead discovered that she herself had become such a mass, her senses both muffled and heightened by her surroundings. She felt as if she were in another world. There was no ground and no sky, but a vibrant landscape like an endless galaxy, filled with other shapeless masses of color. Oniva floated past the matrices of light, bewildered.

A strange notion occurred to Azhidaahaka. It knew its invincibility had been compromised, but it wasn't sure how. Something was not right.

Pathem stepped out of the darkness and placed his palms, dripping with oil, on Azhidaahaka's brow. Oil proceeded to drip down Azhidaahaka's forehead from Pathems hands. Justes stepped up and placed his hands upon Azhidaahaka as well, praying silently. Pathem stepped back and removed his hands from Azhidaahaka.

Against her will, Oniva began to move backwards as if a giant vacuum or whirlpool was trying to grab her to its unknown depths. After moments of fighting the pull, its grasp was released, but Oniva knew she still only had a little bit of time. A little bit of time for what task, she wasn't sure. It became harder to move, as if invisible strings were attached to her body, pulled by a hidden source.

In the distance, Oniva heard a woman cry for help. She looked around, but did not see where the screams were coming from. The new world was confusing as Oniva did not even feel real. Her movements though self-induced seemed sporadic and effortless. The screams for assistance seemed to be coming from all sides of her, and Oniva could not figure out which way to go. And time was running out.

The color drained from the scene around her, and her surroundings faded to black. She rushed among the dark, searching for the voice. She had no voice of her own to shout, but she hoped that the voice knew to keep yelling until she could find it. Oniva quickly floated through the darkness and found herself in the woods by her house. The ones Rontrez always used to say a bear would come out of and gobble her up. Following the sound of the cries, Oniva ventured deeper into the woods until she came upon a small clearing.

In the center of the clearing, a group of monstrous humanoid figures danced in a circle, taunting a small figure. As she approached the edge of the clearing, Oniva saw that in the center of the circle was the source of the scream: the huddled body of a terrified young boy. Although the boy already lay in a fetal position on the mossy ground, the ghastly demonic figures continued to laugh and torment at the boy as he screamed.

Instantly, they saw her.

Every nerve in her body screamed at her to run, but she kept her gaze trained on the boy. He raised his head, tears streaming from his eyes, and looked at Oniva – and she saw that it was Esau, at about age six.

The five red figures lurched toward Oniva as if to attack, but she stood firm, as if they were not there at all. Alarmed, the beings howled at Oniva, but she did not run. The red beings rushed toward Oniva again in a furious assault, but stopped short in their tracks. Each of the five beings ran back to Esau, as if to protect him was to protect themselves. Unperturbed, Oniva stopped at a short distance from the grotesque creatures, and the beings became wary, but Oniva did not communicate with them. Without physical speech, she communicated to the boy in what seemed to be energy. She had no hands with which to reach out, but the shining blue light of her body extended itself towards the boy.

Esau, what have they done to you?

The boy's screams ceased, but he remained on the ground.

Esau, come here. Come to me. The little boy suddenly stopped screaming and looked up at Oniva.

Esau, come here, you have to come to me.

The little boy shook his head furiously, paralyzed with terror.

Esau, please. You have to come to me.

Again, the boy shook his head adamantly.

Oniva took a small step toward the circle of demons guarding Esau, and they let forth a chorus of high-pitched, horrific screams.

"Stay back, or we will kill him!" one of the demons shrieked.

Oniva did not respond. She knew she was not here to talk to them, and that she would gain nothing from communicating with evil.

Esau, do you know who I am?

The boy nodded, sniffing and wiping his eyes.

Do you know that I love you?

He nodded again.

Then please, come to me. I will not hurt you. I love you. Oniva had no hands with which to reach out, but she reached out again with her energy.

The small boy began to stand, but the demons began to shriek and wail at an immeasurable volume, scaring the boy back to the ground.

They can't hurt you, Esau. Do you want to come to me?

He nodded.

Then come. As long as you want to come, they can not harm you.

The demons howled loudly in protest, their screams almost unbearable.

"We will devour your rotting flesh and feast upon your damned soul," one growled.

Esau, please. Come to me. I want to help you. As long as you want to come to me, those mean things can not hurt you. Please!

Esau remained where he was, petrified.

Oniva began to sing, quietly at first, her voice piercing the dissonant howls that filled the air.

"You gotta believe. . .You gotta believe . . .gotta believe in Him. . ." Oniva's voice soared above the dark woods, echoing from every corner. It was almost magical, beautifully spreading the song around her intimidating environment.

Staying close to the ground, the boy began to inch toward Oniva. The demonic shrieking escalated, but Esau was drawn to the loving voice, singing the irresistible melody he knew so well.

Suddenly, the boy leapt up and ran toward Oniva as quickly as he could. In a fit of rage and frenzy, the demonic beings flew after the boy, screaming what they would to do him if he didn't stop. The boy sprinted toward the voice and kept his eyes fixed on the singing blue light. As the boy reached the blue light, he stretched out his hands and—

As suddenly as Oniva had arrived in the transcendental dimension, she now found herself standing before the temple, still clutching at the air where Esau's hand had been.

Rontrez lay on the street, barely conscious and breathing heavily. His eyes were glazed, but bore no traces of red. He regained consciousness and slowly sat up, like a man who had just awoken from a hundred-year slumber. He looked up at Oniva and the two holy men. Rontrez shook himself, and remaining seated on the ground, he stretched as best he could. His jaw cracked loudly, and he let out a long cool sigh.

"What in the world happened to me?" he mumbled. "I feel like I got run over by a truck."

"Do you remember anything?" Oniva asked.

"Last thing I remember is that Elijah dude giving me the VIP treatment, moving me up into the castle, introducing me to all these people. Then I was in a hot tub with this lady named Mystery. Everything after that is foggy."

"Did you have sex with Mystery?" Oniva asked.

Rontrez laughed. "That's affirmative. That's affirmative about twenty or thirty times. Taxed her like the IRS."

"She was a tall, well-dressed white woman, right?"

"No. She was brown. With some curves." Rontrez grinned slyly. "And most of the time, I didn't see what she looked like with her clothes on."

"Evil appears to each in its own way," Pathem said.

"You mentioned Elijah introduced you to others. Who?" Justes asked.

"Yeah. I met his whole crew. There was. . .a roly poly rich fellow in there. His name was Bee-El or something. He ate about twenty steaks between now and later."

"Archdemon Beelzeebub," Pathem informed them. "His favorite weapon is gluttony."

"There was a shady-looking cat in a suit. He looked like he'd walk off with a skyscraper in his pocket if you let him. Mammon?"

"Mammon, the duke of greed," Pathem responded.

"There were a few more. There was a dirty fellow in there. Looked like he hadn't moved in ages, and he cut some corners on hygiene."

"Belial, prince of sloth and laziness."

"What about Mystery? Who was she?" Rontrez asked.

"Lust," Oniva answered.

"What a news bulletin," Rontrez answered, groaning as he got to his feet. "There was one other man – a guy that looked like a walking skeleton. Thin as paper. He might have been mute."

"That was the Archlord demon, Asmodeus," Pathem said. "Oniva, he was the same one that came for you when you were with Agent Minzano."

"How are you such an expert?" Rontrez asked, squinting at Pathem. "I've seen you on TV but this stuff ain't in the Bible or the Koran or the Buddha book."

"Everything is not as it seems, Esau," Pathem answered.

"Amen to that," Rontrez agreed, shaking his head in disbelief.

"Michael, what happens with the one of many now?" Justes asked Pathem.

"Nothing we have to worry about. Our prophecy is written, and it is different from any scheme any being could concoct," Pathem replied.

"So what happens now?" Oniva asked.

"It's over," Pathem answered.

"It ain't over," Rontrez growled. "Not yet. Not until I put something to Elijah for running over me. Niva, if you can find a place that's open, go pick Elijah out a nice casket. Now, I know a shotgun won't exactly do the trick. So what will, Reverend, a missile? 'Cause I'm about to go in there and wage my own holy war. I ain't scared of Elijah. Someone give me a blowtorch or something so I can flame his crusty kingdom into ashes. Are you ready? Because I'm ready to get at him for rudely throwing my whole chemistry off. A power move is in play here. No spectators allowed. Either lead or get the hell of the way. Literally."

"Rontrez, calm down," Justes urged, gently placing his hand on Rontrez's shoulder. "You're angry, and the spirit of wrath is upon you. You're not thinking straight. We should go home, rest, and plan our next move. We have recovered you – let's not ruin this victory with anger."

"Get your hands off me," Rontrez fumed. "You mean to tell me no one is with me?"

"This must be taken care of," Pathem said. "Come."

Justes was shocked. "I'm not going to argue with an Archangel."

"Archangel?" Rontrez asked, eyeing Pathem skeptically.

"I'll know where to find you," Pathem said shortly to Justes. "It's not too safe out here right now."

Justes and Oniva watched as Pathem and Rontrez made their way to the door of the temple.

"Here, take this," Pathem said, handing Rontrez a pistol.

"That's what I'm talking about," Rontrez grinned. "You're my kind of reverend. This week we don't turn the other cheek. I don't think this will work, though. I need something on that ghost level."

They reached the top of the stairs, and the temple doors opened for Rontrez as if they anticipated his arrival. They entered, and the heavy door slammed shut behind them.

They stood in absolute darkness for several moments before a faint light flickered on at the other end of the corridor, dimly illuminating the hallway before them.

Rontrez strode purposefully down the hallway and Pathem followed close behind him. As Rontrez reached the end of the long corridor, he saw a shadowy figure in the doorway. It stood motionless, somehow beckoning or daring Rontrez to come closer. The figure in the light seemed to know that Rontrez was angry, and coming to avenge his own spirit.

The figure suddenly sharpened, and Asmodeus stood before him, adamant as a sentry before a queen's palace. Rontrez eyed him carefully, and before he could decide on a course of action, Asmodeus stepped aside.

"Right this way," Asmodeus beckoned.

Shocked, but still on his guard, Rontrez followed Asmodeus to a room he recognized – the one where they had cracked his soul.

The whole circle was present, including Mystery. Now Rontrez understood that not only was it a setup from the very beginning, but him being in this room again at this very moment was just another part of the setup. He looked in horror at Beelzebub, Belial, Duke Mammon, Mystery, Asmodeus, and standing proudly at the head of the room, Elijah.

Rontrez pulled out the pistol Pathem had given him. "I renounce you and all that is of you, you bastard! I don't know who or what you are, but I'm going to blast you back from whence you came. It's time to pay."

With a guttural roar, Rontrez emptied his clip into Elijah. Elijah roared with pain as each bullet struck his body. When the clip was empty, Rontrez looked at Elijah, who looked tired and weak. Elijah's head slumped, and Rontrez turned his attention to Elijah's associates.

They stared blankly at him, and Bee-El made a strange, guttural noise – he began to laugh. Everyone in the room seemed to be staring at him, laughter bubbling up inside of them, like he was the stooge of some large practical joke. Suddenly, Elijah lifted his head up with a strange grin, and began to clap slowly in an awkward one-man ovation. Pathem left Rontrez's side and took a seat at the table, grinning. Rontrez's murderous rage began to fade, and he understood. Elijah's lieutenants at the table had the weapons of sins, and Pathem was not an Archangel at all, but a demon of wrath. Thus, Rontrez had been in a murderous rage ever since he had been in Pathem's presence.

Elijah looked into Rontrez's eyes and said, "For into a malicious soul wisdom shall not enter; nor dwell in the body that is subject unto sin."

Minzano stumbled through the dark, cursing. Without warning, a section of wall gave way, and Minzano ran into the long corridor behind it. Light spilled from a door at the end of the corridor, and Minzano ran toward it, not knowing what lay beyond.

"Who. . .what are you?" Rontrez asked.

"I am he that is, and was, and is to come," Elijah answered.

"You set me up from the opening, you fiendish, grimy lizard," Rontrez growled.

"Moi? I didn't set anyone up, Esau. I'm afraid it doesn't work like that."

"Yes, you did! From the beginning. From Lisa. You didn't even get Lisa's part right."

"Who cares, you didn't even know that broad. You should be thanking me anyway. You loved every minute of it. Sorry about technical incongruity in the minor details. By the way, Lisa aced her finance test," Elijah winked.

Some of those at the table barked with laughter.

"That was one of the newer employees," Elijah continued. At the time, you weren't quite ripe enough to meet the finer things in life," he grinned, gesturing towards Mystery.

"You hoaxed everyone! You came out the sky like you were something almighty. The world believed in you," Rontrez exclaimed weakly, overcome with shock.

"I didn't trick anyone. One must come to me of their own free will. It's funny how all these rules work. You'd swear I was making them up as I go along," Elijah said, letting out a sadistic chuckle. "They came to me like I was the Pied Piper. I didn't muscle anyone. They all ran to the end of the rainbow for their pot of gold."

"You're . . ."

"I am you, Esau. I am everything you have made me to be. I have done only to you what you have done to others. You have finally felt your own Excalibur."

"What are you talking about?"

"I pimped you. Just as you pimped countless women, and talked them into doing your will and believing it was for their own benefit. I did the same thing to you. You can rationalize it all you'd like, but you must realize all iniquity is a double-edged sword, the wounds of which cannot be healed. We are the same Esau Rontrez. Identical! You tasted only your own medicine."

"So you made me and everyone else your hooker? Damn you. I'm not buying the game you're spinning."

"When the ungodly curseth anything, he curseth his own soul. It's been nice."

Minzano slowed to a halt as he came to the doorway. He immediately recognized Rontrez, arguing with Elijah. Still shrouded in the darkness of the tunnel, Minzano aimed at Rontrez's chest and fired. The shot lifted Rontrez off his feet and threw him to the black marble floor. His body lay where it fell, motionless.

Minzano ran into the room to see Elijah and his colleagues still seated at the large black table inscribed with mysterious runes. Minzano recognized Archknight Asmodeus, but was shocked to see Pathem sitting among them. Ever so slightly, Asmodeus seemed to grin.

"You with them, huh?" Minzano asked, looking Pathem in the eye.

"Some call me Baphomet. Just now, you could call me the wrath behind your trigger finger." Pathem smiled, and his eyes glowed bright red for a moment.

Minzano was stunned into silence.

Minzano looked at the one of many, staring lifelessly at the ceiling. Minzano now regretted shooting Rontrez in hopes of ruining evil's plan. Among Elijah and his brethren, his actions didn't seem to have any effect.

"Congratulations. You've broken the seal," Elijah smiled.

The one of many, Minzano thought.

"The one of many indeed," Elijah repeated. "One out of many blind buzzards."

Minzano looked around at all Elijah's associates. He could not harm them, and he knew it. He didn't even know how to try.

"The arcane mystery, Vincent. The one of many," Elijah grinned into the air.

"What does it mean? One of many what?" Minzano asked.

"Sit down, Agent Minzano," Elijah gestured, "and we will talk like gentlemen – as soon as you put your gun on the table. Concealed weapons scare me, Vince."

Elijah's associates chuckled – with the exception of Asmodeus.

Minzano stared at Pathem as if he were Medusa, frozen with fear and disgust. "So he was on your side all along," Minzano mumbled.

"Sit down, Vincent. Everything is on my side now."

"I'm not on your side," Minzano growled.

"I believe you are mistaken. Put your gun on the table."

Minzano placed his pistol on the smooth marble surface, which glowed with gold runes, but he did not sit.

"The other one, too," Elijah smiled.

"Only an idiot goes in unarmed," Minzano spat. "Do I look like an idiot to you? I keep my other piece. I couldn't find trust anywhere around here even if there was a dictionary."

"Well spoken, Vincent. Declared like a genuine soldier of selfhood and individuality," Elijah said.

"Isn't that your precious one of many laying on the floor? Explain."

"I doubt you could comprehend the matter, but it is of no consequence," Elijah replied.

"What does matter is that I am aware of who you are," Minzano retorted.

"And who am I?" Elijah grinned, as if he were telling a riddle. Before Minzano could reply, Elijah cut him off and spoke again. "Oh, I must be someone called Satan. Or what is that name that everyone *loves* to call me? Oh yes, the devil. As if I am running around with an arrow tail and a pitchfork like some bastard redneck. Or is it that I am merely a man of great insight, or a being able to enlighten those in darkness?"

"I would call you Satan if I believed he existed, but the truth is, I don't know what you are or where you came from. But you have a name: Lucifer."

"Do you even know what Lucifer means, Vincent?"

"No – nor do I gave a damn."

"It means 'the shining one.'"

"Yes, you are very shiny. You light the path to Hell."

"Indeed. . . your path."

Elijah had a sickening grin on his face as he spoke his last words. By the tone of his voice, and the look on his face, with his final spoken phrase Minzano's heart sunk as he knew that killing Rontrez was the worst move he could have made. At that moment, Elijah embodied depravity.

"Vincent, you can't get upset. You don't have that right. I am just like you."

"You're nothing like me," Minzano said in protest.

Elijah's associates chuckled to themselves – with the exception of Asmodeus.

"Oh," Elijah laughed. "We're identical. I haven't done anything you haven't done before."

"I am an officer of the law. I upheld the law before you proclaimed it obsolete."

Elijah's council roared with laughter. Asmodeus again recused himself from their amusement.

"Agent Minzano, you have spent your whole life lying and deceiving. You're counterfeit. Your title within some institution changes absolutely *nothing*. You can tell yourself anything you need to, but you know the truth. You were an undercover agent, fooling others, pretending to be the bad guy. That's what you did. You fool your surroundings, Vincent. You connive your way into organizations by acquiring trust through trickery, deceit, and dishonesty, Agent Minzano. You manipulate your surroundings to present a story. You fooled everyone into thinking you were the bad guy, I fooled everyone into thinking I was something. I manipulated my surroundings, and made you think that Esau Rontrez was the keystone. We're the same. We are blood brethren, Vince. I'm just a little better than you."

"No. You're not."

"Vincent, you have come to me without knowing it."

"I've never gone anywhere without knowing it."

The table erupted with laughter, and Minzano found their heckling increasingly irritating.

"You just murdered an innocent man in cold blood, Vince. Simply unruly and inconsiderate. Contemplate your time spent in my Bloodline. Do you think you penetrated the organization by yourself? Do you actually believe that because of your ability, you fooled powers beyond this earth? Not a chance."

"I penetrated-"

"Pride!" Elijah shouted. "The love of oneself. 'I penetrated', 'I' this, 'I' that. Why did you come here by yourself, Agent Minzano? Did you really think you could take us all by yourself like some Wild West desperado? Of course not. You are here alone because of your greed. You lust for any achievement or recognition, no matter how morbid. You are so consumed within yourself that you care about nothing else. Nothing else matters to you. And that, my friend, is why you have been found guilty of the seven deadly sins. Extremely deadly, in your case."

Minzano didn't believe too much in the seven deadly sins, but he knew what they were.

"You're wrong, as evil things often are. As bad as I am, you could never reach into my life and pull out a real example of sloth," Minzano replied defiantly.

"You have to be joking. Let us float back to only moments ago." As Elijah spoke, Minzano saw a holographic image of himself sitting as clearly as if it were projected in a theater.

"We have to stop them. With every murder, evil gains another victory," Pathem said.

"Are you kidding? We can't stop them now. That cop is a dead man," Minzano replied.

"My goodness, aren't you a man of the law? You're going to leave a fellow officer to be slaughtered?"

"Tell me, oh holy one, what would you have me do? Put on a cape and go on out there in my pajamas and utility belt? Or do you want me to leave him a message? Dead men can't pick up the phone. Look, all your buddies got blasted less than a half hour after I got the phone call. It's been forty-five minutes since the hit was put out. If that man isn't dead, it's a miracle."

"Why didn't you stop it?"

"Stop it? Why didn't you stop the Holocaust, Pathem? You were here."

"Don't be ridiculous. I bet you didn't even attempt to contact him."

"Hey, don't preach to me—" the image disappeared, and Minzano was silent for a moment.

"Envy. Show me envy," Minzano dared.

"You envy all."

"I envy nothing."

"You envy those surrounding you, both in your false surroundings and in your real ones. You envied the bad boys you emulated and deceived, and that envy gave you the motivation you needed to bring them down. You had no sense of duty. No recognition of any kind of code. You had no respect for justice or equality or impartiality. No sense of honesty or integrity in your duties. You claimed to uphold some form of law, yet you let a cop be slaughtered in the streets. You took an oath to serve your country, and the only thing you served was your own envious desires for revenge. I find it scandalous. It's shameful. A crooked cop. Crooked in his ways, and even more deformed in his beliefs."

"You better pick your one of many up off of the floor. He's making a mess."

"His corpse is making just the opposite. Not a mess, but an opening. A gateway to conquest. You have seen and understood what is to come. You have acknowledged that the sides have been chosen. You have beheld the inevitable, and witnessed the deliverance of my dominion."

"You're not a bad orator, but these words don't mean anything. You're a wizard with no more spells. There is a reason I made it in here. What is it?"

"The reason you are now before your savior is to take my hand and allow me to lead you into the light."

"You're saying you want me to join you?"

"No, you have already joined me. I want you to comprehend and acknowledge your place in this new rule. I have watched you from day one. You have met Asmodeus, and you have met Pathem. They are two of my greatest assets. You will take your place beside them."

"The only place I am taking is first. Why are you doing this? Why do you want to kill everyone?"

Before Elijah could reply, Pathem hissed, "Because God has given you everything!"

"What has God ever given Man?" Minzano asked. "He's never given me anything."

"Life, freedom, choice, and unearned sovereignty over the earth. You have been favored by God over all things, even the angels," Pathem sneered.

"Don't speak to me, traitor."

"Pathem is no longer. You may now call me Baphomet. All mankind shall be restored to their proper authority: The true place of miserable ants crawling beneath our rule."

Oniva and Justes turned around from Elijah's temple to see a stranger standing beside Justes' car. There was something unusual about the man – he radiated a calmness, but there was a sovereignty in his demeanor. He met their gaze, clearly with a, peaceful quietness. He was there with a purpose. Justes approached the man and waited for him speak.

"Chris Justes and Oniva Mering. I am Gabriel, that stands in the presence of God. I have been sent to speak unto you and to bring you guidance."

"How do I know you are an angel? Everyone currently seems to be claiming divinity," Oniva asked.

"There will be no trickery or miracles. Look into my eyes and know the truth."

Justes and Oniva looked into Gabriel's eyes and knew in their hearts he was not of this earth. In Gabriel's eyes they saw truth, wisdom, and integrity.

"Gabriel, you are a messenger," Justes said humbly. "Do you bring a message?"

"I bring your direction. In the enemy's domain is where this battle ends. Enter the false temple with the shield of faith and find victory."

"Gabriel, please tell me what is going on. Who are Elijah and his men and what exactly is their plan?" Oniva asked.

"The enemies you see are leaders of evil, led by a diabolical heathen, once of the Seraphim. Those of his clan who concern themselves with humans hate them for being. The demons wish to assert their rule over all the earth, crushing humans and destroying their souls. The demons want to make the humans worship *them* instead of their Creator, offering corrupting gifts and pleasures as a reward for that worship – at first. You have seen part of evil's plan, but the worst is yet to come."

"What is the other part?"

"Elijah has two kinds of unearthly followers. The first kind you have been exposed to: the kind that wish to force the humans to revile themselves, or admit that they are as evil and corrupt as the demons themselves, to prove that they are not special in the eyes of God. Other archfiends see the potential in humans, and would rather recruit them as allies in the war against Heaven. Thus, you have what is called the Bloodline. In general, the hellions hate any human they can't exterminate, or any angel who remains unfallen. What you have not yet seen is that certain archdemons – those like Asmodeus – wish to dissect Man in order to learn the secret of his power. It is only man's power that is a reflection of God's power, for it was only humans, and not demons or angels, who were created in His image," (Genesis 1:26).

"We do have one advantage," Oniva noted.

"What is that?" Justes asked, astounded.

"We are fighting evil. It is in evil's nature to be corrupt. I think we can pretty much count on evil to betray itself. Just as Lucifer attacked the Lord in the Bible, Elijah's followers may turn on him," (Isaiah 14:12-17).

"This is true," Gabriel replied, "but even so, many demons retain a perverse sense of honor amongst themselves as a legion."

"How do we fight them – what's the plan?" Oniva asked.

"Trust is the plan. Faith is the weapon," Gabriel replied.

"I have carried the sword of Faith from day one, but I can see things getting steadily worse around here," Oniva explained.

"Yes, they are."

"This is the anti-Christ that I have studied, correct?" Justes asked.

"You can call it whatever. I would call it strictly bad news."

"Is there any good news in our near future?" Oniva asked. "Gabriel, please tell us what we have to do. You keep saying Faith and Trust, but we can't sit around trusting. I don't feel comfortable lounging around among this anarchy while Elijah and his ghouls reign. I don't see any solution available to us."

"So we fix our eyes not on what is seen, but on what is unseen. For what is seen is temporary, but what is unseen is eternal. For we wrestle not against flesh and blood, but against the rulers, against the authorities, against the powers of this dark world and against the spiritual forces of evil in the heavenly realms," (Ephesians 6:12). Gabriel put his hands together gracefully. "The adversary will soon show his true self, then terror will spread throughout its kingdom."

"When evil shows its true self, then it will succeed in destroying even the holy people, correct?" Justes gasped (Daniel 8:23-24).

"Once its patience wears thin, then its anger multiplies one thousand fold. It will cause astounding devastation and claim the lives of billions. Many of those who believe will become martyrs, those who do not will become enslaved. Go now to the temple."

Oniva and Justes entered the open door of the temple, not knowing what lay before them. The door was ajar, almost as if they were expected for dinner by a busy host. Justes took Oniva's hand as a means of comfort, though he himself felt almost none, and together they crossed the threshold. Though the outside of the temple was relatively modest, its interior corridor was breathtaking. The vast corridor expanded to its own horizon, and the spotless white walls seemed to invite them in, like children returning home.

"Welcome," a voice said from behind them.

The lights suddenly dimmed, and they turned around to face the speaker. Oniva recognized him immediately as the being that wanted her soul: Asmodeus.

We meet again, his grin seemed to say. Asmodeus eyed Oniva carefully and snapped his fingers. Two Bloodline Knights appeared out of the darkness and roughly grabbed Oniva from behind. She screamed in protest.

Asmodeus turned his gaze to Justes.

Before Justes had time to react, Asmodeus took Justes' hand and everything went black.

CHAPTER 42

When Justes regained consciousness, he was standing at the edge of the temple's olive-colored roof. One more step, and he would meet his certain death on the concrete below.

"You claim to believe in some sort of god, Chris. I wish to bestow a simple offer to you."

"I do not accept," Justes replied dryly.

"You cannot deny what has not been offered."

"I can refuse to accept anything I choose, just as you refused to accept the rightful role that was created for you. You are not supposed to be this kind of spirit. You were once part of something beautiful. Now you can never be part of the elect. You are not human, therefore you cannot be redeemed, but it is not too late to change your ways. You chose the wrong side once. Don't make it a pattern."

"Save your sermon for the sheep. I will show you, once and for all, there is no God. What you believe in is a nonentity. Pure propaganda."

"What I believe in is the truth."

"Cast yourself down from my temple. If your lord is with you, he and his mighty angels will catch you, proving me a liar and a raving madman. But if he does not, I myself will come get you, and exalt you back onto my rooftop, then you will know that I am the truth. It is written: He will command his angels concerning you, to guard you carefully; they will lift you up in their hands, so that you will not strike your foot upon a stone. Is this not what faith is all about? Just take this leap of faith. Either way, you will find the truth."

"I know the truth!"

"Then leap! Leap into revelation. Let the mystery of past and present unfold at your whim."

Out of mere humanistic tendency, Justes peered down from the temple into the night beneath his feet, and observed the unfriendly black concrete below.

He replied, "It is also written: Do not put the Lord your God to the test."

"Your babble is senseless foolery. You use these words as crutches and shields because you do not want to know the truth. You stand here now as a key. A key to unlock the gates of absolute reality. All will now know who governs the universe. You will recognize unequivocally that there is no kind of god, or any being to top me! All your life, you have put your Faith in spooks and prayers and wishful magic, each given its credentials by convenient, collective, coincidences. If you don't leap, you know in your heart the truth. . .There is no one above me."

"I will not put faith to the—"

"Leap!" Asmodeus shouted

"I will not."

"Leap! All mankind is waiting! Show the evidence of things not seen!"

"No."

Asmodeus' voice grew deep and dripped with unearthly, ominous malice. "Then die, whelp!"

Asmodeus let out a sickening roar, so loud that it drowned out all other sounds. He reached toward Justes, and crushed his skull between his skeletal hands. Justes's corpse slumped to the ground, lifeless.

Asmodeus, what have you done?

When Oniva opened her eyes, she was naked, chained to a wall in front of the table that seated Elijah and his council. Mystery stood nearest to Oniva, and Elijah stood at its head.

Mystery smiled and approached her. "You never answered my question. Do you find me attractive, Oniva?"

Oniva remained silent.

Mystery caressed Oniva's face and slowly put her lips to Oniva's.

"Don't fight, baby," Mystery cooed. Oniva's every muscle resisted and she fought to escape, but the restraints held fast.

"Do you find me attractive?" Mystery smiled, and her face began to collapse inward and drop to the floor. Where before were a woman's beautiful features, in their place was the face of a hideous reptile. The reptile dropped its arms, and the remainder of its skin fell swiftly to the ground like a discarded robe. Mystery's reptilian penis stood erect, and Oniva saw the unnatural organ had a face and a life of its own. It hissed and its forked tongue angrily whipped the air. The scaly organ extended itself toward Oniva and waved around like a furious serpent.

Elijah spoke. "Just as iniquity entered this world by the seduction a woman, the same shall deliver me all that is due from this moment forward."

Oniva screamed with terror as the serpent crept toward her midsection, writhing in anger.

Behind Mystery, Elijah's voice rang out: "Yes, Oniva. You alone have been and shall be the one of many. You alone shall be my mother, daughter and bride, and your embryo will spill upon the earth to make right what has been wrong since the creation of age. My seed shall fertilize your element, and all that is improper will become fact. It is written, so shall it be done!"

As Mystery's reptilian penis entered Oniva, she shrieked in both physical pain and in spiritual agony. Despite her clenched muscles, the snake forced its way deep inside of her, and she felt it plant its seed.

"Free will matters no more!" Elijah shouted. "All shall bow to me!"

A glimmer of light flashed before Oniva, and for an instant she saw Chris Justes's face. The light faded, and she felt a cool wind enter her.

Chris Justes knew he was no longer among the living. He remembered how he had been murdered, standing atop the temple. Strangely enough, he did not remember feeling pain. He looked around his new environment: a sea of reddish-pink, with no sound but the swish of his movements. Or was that his imagination? The only feeling he had was the overwhelming benevolence in his heart, which felt multiplied from when he last remembered.

Justes enjoyed the new feelings he possessed, and his shapeless form rushed onward.

Behind him were several tiny reptilian beings, each trying to gnaw at him tirelessly. Without effort, he cast the hideous creatures from him as if he were electric. Justes had no weapon that he knew of, but he did not seem to need one. Justes weaved through the tunnels with accuracy as precisely as someone looking at simple maze from above. Moments later, a round sphere came into view. Instinctively, he knew to stand sentry. It was eerily quiet for a moment, but then came the hideous reptiles, shrieking in anger. They seemed to attack him at light speed, concentrating on nothing but the sphere he protected.

Several enemy creatures rushed at him together, as if they were trying to ram through him entirely. Justes realized the legions of creatures were working together to penetrate the sphere. A team of countless repulsive creatures flew at him with the intent of knocking him away from his post, and a second team tried to weave around their battle to connect with the white sphere ahead of them.

It seemed impossible to keep the countless tiny monsters away from the prize, but a protective aegis formed around him and he moved faster than the speed of light, defending the sphere against those who would dare seek possession of it. As each reptilian being came into contact with Justes, it emitted a horrible high-pitched shriek and burst into flames. With each victory he gained confidence. The legions of ghastly beasts seemed to fight him with every ounce of their being. They swarmed around him like a hurricane of giant, angry gnats. Under Justes' faithful guard, not one enemy penetrated the sphere. He wondered how long he could hold off the seemingly infinite armies of miniscule reptiles, but with this doubt, the creatures seemed to grow stronger, and the fight became three times as hard. Justes became angry at himself for allowing doubt to overtake him. He summoned his strength and moved with the elegance of an angel, as fast as light to annihilate each creature he touched.

With a blinding flash, the reptilian appendage was suddenly forced out of Oniva. Mystery began to scream in excruciating pain as her true name was burned into her forehead as if etched by an invisible hand: *Mystery, Babylon the Great, Mother of Harlots and Abominations of the Earth* (Revelation 17:5). Mystery roared in anger and shook as flames burst from her body. Black, sulfurous smoke began to cloak the room in darkness, then, as if by magic, the smoke evaporated. When the smoke cleared, Gabriel appeared in its place.

Gabriel spoke in a voice that was deliberate and flawless, as if an unearthly power flowed through his very speech. **"I am Gabriel. I stand in the presence of God.** It is time. As it is written, the Son of God will send out his angels, and they will weed out of his kingdom everything that causes sin and all who do evil," (Luke 1:19, Matthew 13:41).

"And who will stop us, Gabriel? You?" Pathem grinned. "You're just a mailman."

"I pave the way for a legion of warriors, but upon you now is a legion of one."

"And who is this one?" Pathem asked with feigned curiosity. "I yearn for his destruction."

As if on cue, a small sphere appeared in front of Gabriel, suspended in midair. With a flash of light, the sphere morphed and grew into a twelve-foot figure made up of flame. Time seemed to stand still as the thunderous presence stood purposefully. All noise ceased. The only sound allowed to exist was that of the being of flame.

"I have been sent to remove all things which weed His garden."

"Lovely, a gardener," Elijah yawned.

"Hark when Gabriel sayeth: I stand in the presence of God."

The colossus extended one of its massive arms, a flaming sword extending from its very person. Though it had no visible eyes, the being seemed to glare at Pathem. It appeared to let all those in eyesight know how it felt about being impersonated. With a resounding roar, the flame being heaved back the unearthly blade and brought it crashing down.

The earth around Elijah and his men tore apart, and within it lay a chasm of fire and unendurable pain. Chains leapt up out of out of the chasm's fire and, like living snakes, wrapped themselves around Elijah and his minions. They tightened, and quickly, the chains reeled them toward the chasm. All the howling and screeching they produced could not free them from the iron bonds dragging their prey down into their prison. As each member of Elijah's clan was dragged downward, the two pieces of the earth drew nearer to each other. As the gap narrowed, Elijah himself slipped past the mouth of the pit. Clinging to the ledge, he hissed at the flame being, which held its ground as if it dared Elijah to challenge him.

With another deafening roar, a white light ran along the join, knitting the two halves of the earth together. Just as the two pieces of the realm were almost sealed, the enormous red head of a dragon burst out of the vanishing opening of the chasm. The dragon's eyes were the size of trucks, and its forked tongue angrily lapped the air. It opened its gaping mouth to swallow the being of flame. With both hands, the being of flame lifted its sword over its head. The dragon tore at the flame being with its gargantuan jaw. Unfazed by the beastly assault, the flame being brought its sword down with unparalleled force into the dragons head. The crushing blow reverberated through the ground, sending the dragon screeching back into the pit with otherworldly force. The chasm then sealed with a glimmer of white light. . . .sealed until the time.

CHAPTER 43

Oniva awoke bewildered, but refreshed. She was safely tucked into her bed in her home in Washington, DC. She threw the covers aside and dashed to the bedroom across from hers, looking for Rontrez. The guest bedroom was just as she remembered it. The bed was unmade, and his belongings were scattered about the room, but Rontrez was absent. Oniva felt a presence behind her and turned around.

There was no one there.

Slowly, she began to realize who was there.

"Reverend Justes? Is that you, is everything alright?"

Though nothing materialized in front of her like it would have in a movie, Justes replied to her with a message, sending her a feeling of peace and comfort. For a moment, she relaxed.

"Is Rontrez with you?"

The feeling of peace did not increase or decrease. Oniva asked again.

"Chris, I'm worried about Rontrez, is he alright? Please let me know something."

Justes continued to comfort Oniva's spirit, but did not answer her question. Justes's presence faded, and Oniva heard the doorbell ring. Oniva ran downstairs and looked through the peephole to see Vincent Minzano.

She unlocked the door to let him in.

"Have you seen Esau?" Oniva asked.

"Dead," Minzano replied, looking at the ground.

"Are you sure?"

Minzano nodded. "I hit him in the chest in Elijah's holy hoax house. I thought it would help things. If I took out the chosen one, I figured it would ruin things for the bad guys. Turns out it didn't matter after all. You were the key the whole time. Way to go, key. You did good."

"Where is Rontrez now?"

Minzano shrugged. "Elijah's temple is gone. That's where I saw him last."

"The whole temple is gone?"

"Every last brick. Like it wasn't even supposed to be there in the first place."

"Well, what happens now?" Oniva asked.

"The same thing that happens every time I meet a woman who seems to be of some solid moral character."

"And what's that, Vincent?"

"I go the other way, for her sake."

"Answer one question for me before you leave."

"You can ask what you want. If I answer is another issue," Minzano stated.

"Do you believe now?"

"Do I believe. . .In God?"

Oniva nodded.

"I'll tell you this. God has some explaining to do."

Oniva waited, knowing he wasn't finished.

"But you know what's funny?" Minzano chuckled.

"No, what?"

"I'm probably going to have more explaining to do when it's my time be in front of him."

Oniva did not laugh with him. "There is a reason you dropped by. You don't seem like the type for tea and crumpets, Vincent."

"You're a pretty sharp one. Surprised someone hasn't scooped you up yet."

"Maybe sometime. But what were you saying?"

"I figured out a lot of things, but I have one question."

"I don't think I could even speculate what you figured out, and I can barely begin to imagine your question."

"Though I think he needed a morgue, I dropped Justes off at the nearest hospital. The doctor says he's a goner. They called it a persistent vegetative state."

"What's that?"

"Dead. . .but now with machines hooked up to him. Just about no chance of recovery. The doctor says he would need a miracle. I passed a chapel on the way out. Something inside me wanted to go in, so I did. I sat down and started reading the book of Genesis. Easy read. Just as the serpent used Eve to get to Adam in the book of Genesis, he reversed it for his plot here, and used Adam to get to Eve. Elijah obviously used Esau to get to you. He saw you from the beginning and he wanted you the entire time. You were just outside his reach. But Esau wasn't, and he was the closest thing to you. And Pathem was playing for the other team the whole time. Saw him in Elijah's temple at the roundtable like they were old friends. That was a powerful weapon Elijah used. If people follow corrupt religious leaders like Pathem, thousands of good people from churches and communities can be lead off the cliff. Pathem tried to steer you and Justes away from what was going on. Keep you locked in that basement, using his religious title, stature, and wealth as weapons. People naturally respect and follow those things. Like the serpent in Genesis, he simply asked a question to Eve: 'Did God really tell you not to eat from any tree in the Garden of Eden?' The serpent clearly knew that it was just the one tree they weren't supposed to eat from. He just confused them to get them to eat the fruit by making it not sound so bad. Then telling them they would be like gods if they ate it. Just like Elijah confused Esau by offering him the same power. Just like the enemy tried to confuse you and Justes. Not only with fear, temptation, and Pathem's logic, but with everything else, including your friendship with Esau. Justes screwed up the whole plan by keeping you away from a spiritual and mental place where Elijah could get to you. He was a thorn in Elijah's side. A huge thorn, and evil could take it no longer and cleared him out."

"Yes. Trying to be like God got Eve, Adam, Esau, and others throughout history in serious trouble. It also got Satan himself tossed out of heaven," (Ezekiel 28 12-19).

"So that's how Elijah knew offering the power of God is something many will not resist."

"Yes. From the genesis of creation – man's and angels creation – Satan knows how strong the desire for power can be. It was the cause of his downfall, so he uses it to make others fall. I don't recall receiving the God offer, though. I just got offered a Lamborghini and an expensive pair of pair of shoes. Still glad we didn't take the bait. Your analysis is halfway fascinating. And your question is?"

"Why you? Why were you so important to Elijah's plan?"

"I'll be sure to ask him next time I see him," Oniva answered.

"At first it came to me that you were the direct genetic descendant of Eve."

"I didn't see Eve at my last family reunion. But you never know. If you think about it, that theory doesn't make any sense. Every woman is a descendant of Eve. Every person is a descendent of Adam or Eve, so your Edenic guesswork doesn't have much merit."

"I think you know why you were the key to all of this. You know something that I don't."

"I know plenty of things you don't. But I'm sorry to disappoint you. I don't know why I was in the picture."

"If you are clueless to the answer, then I was right, and I came all the way over here to make sure I was right."

"You still mean to say I am some special descendant of the original woman?"

"Possibly. We'll never know. But more important than your ancestors are your descendants."

With that, Vincent Minzano walked away without looking back. Oniva noticed the man definitely had a strange way of saying goodbye.

I hope you didn't think it was over. This trifling episode marks the beginning. The beginning of an encounter whose time is nearly upon us. As it is

written, I shall be released. When the bowels of the earth open, I shall rise and show my true being, genuine power, and veritable domain. The weak all show strength in the beginning, but the superior strength is in patient planning and one's underestimation. I do not have the element of surprise, but I have the priceless jewel of flawless timing. The best place to hide a lie is between two truths, and between the cover of two truths I wait.

A taste. This is only a small taste of what is to come. I am past persistence, and have ascended to enterprising tenacity, spiced with aggressive determination, smoothed over by observant patience. My armies have been gathered, and the pathetic scouts that have been sent before me only lull my opponent into a higher state of vulnerability. I will assert my rightful rule over all things just when it seems most impossible. No one has seen a true resurrection until they have witnessed my coming. The Coming.

Esau awoke in a green pasture, feeling refreshed. He saw sheep grazing around him and a quiet river alongside him, drifting slowly eastward. He was naked, but only the sheep were there to see him as he rose and walked quietly along the river. Across the river, there was a man tending to his sheep. He had a large stick, and the sheep seemed to be comforted by his presence, and the staff. So was Esau.

Not wanting to startle the man with his nakedness, Rontrez looked for something to cover himself with.

"No need to be embarrassed, Esau," the Shepherd said, without looking in Rontrez's direction.

"Huh?" Rontrez said in surprise.

"There are some clothes over there," the Shepherd said gently.

Rontrez looked to his left, and there were some white linen pants and a white linen shirt. After he put them on, without saying a word, the Shepherd summoned him, and Rontrez waded through the knee-deep water toward the mysterious man. The water felt soothing and comfortable against his skin. He stopped for a few seconds to enjoy it.

Rontrez looked at the Shepherd. "Where am I? Am I dead? Are you God?"

The Shepherd smiled.

Getting anxious, Rontrez continued toward the other side of the river, but more slowly than before. He spoke honestly. "I know I've done wrong. I've done some horrible things."

"Yes." The Shepherd nodded in agreement.

"I don't know how to make things right. I don't understand what happened or how I'm still alive. I get the feeling you are the man with the answers," Rontrez said humbly.

"I have a few," the Shepherd replied with a kind smile. Rontrez sensed the warmth and radiance around the man.

"May I ask a question?" Rontrez asked.

"You've already asked four," the Shepherd smiled. "Ask what you will while you are in the water. When you reach the other side of the riverbank, it will be my turn to ask a question, Esau."

"What is this place?" Rontrez asked.

"It's a quiet river. And a green pasture."

"Where am I? Geographically. Is this Heaven? Or Hell? Or Purgatory?"

"No."

"Where is Elijah?"

"That would be difficult to answer. You wouldn't understand yet. Elijah is where he belongs."

Rontrez was almost to the other side of the river, but he stopped so he could ask more questions.

"Am I dead?"

"No."

There was a calming silence. "So what do I do now?"

"Your sins can be washed away, if you allow it," the Shepherd said softly.

"In this river?"

"Not exactly, Esau. This water is clean, but... not that clean."

"Where is Oniva? Is she okay?"

"Yes. Oniva is fine. She is waiting for you. Your journeys are entwined."

Rontrez nodded and he climbed out of the river. He looked the Shepherd in the eye. There was kindness and wisdom in the man's eyes. Rontrez was mesmerized.

"I think I'm ready for your question," Rontrez said.

The Shepherd looked directly at Rontrez and asked solemnly: "Do you believe?"

"Yes."

The Shepherd looked into Rontrez's eyes for a full seven seconds in silence before nodding once. "Your table has been prepared, Esau. You know what's next."

Rontrez nodded. He started back across the comforting river.

"Goodness and love will follow you for the rest of your life," the Shepherd called out behind Rontrez.

"Surely," Rontrez said looking back. The Shepherd was gone.

• • • • •

In Columbia Community Church in Columbia, Maryland, the choir blessed the audience with its song and melody. It was the same church his mother's funeral had been in, the same church where Elijah had shown him his own surreal funeral. Clad in the white linen outfit the Shepherd had given him, Rontrez walked into his childhood church with only one purpose.

The Reverend Reginald Elliott started his sermon. He was a tall, smart man in his fifties. He had been the leader of Columbia Community Church for decades. He knew almost every member of his congregation by name. He had watched boys and girls become men and women in his church and go on to bring children of their own into the congregation. Generations of Christians learned what it meant to know God through this church. The Reverend gave Rontrez a knowing glance and a quick smile as the usher led him into the sanctuary. Reverend Elliott motioned gently to an open seat in the front row. Rontrez did not necessarily want to sit in the front row, but he didn't want to disrupt the service.

"Things have occurred that have people wondering," Reverend Elliott continued. "Some of them wondering what it means to believe in God, or something higher than what they can see. My wise and recently departed friend Chris Justes used to say, 'People spend so much time protecting the parts that they forget about the importance of the whole'. I have a feeling that in a couple days, Chris Justes will walk into this church even better than he was before his unfortunate incident. So let me explain what he meant. The body is 61% water. The part of us that is not water is composed of elements like oxygen, carbon, hydrogen, nitrogen, calcium, potassium, and other minutely trace elements, such as silver, gold, and uranium. If we calculate the dollar value of these elements if sold as individual components, we would come up with around $160. That's it. Just $160. People buy $80,000 vehicles for the $160 to ride around in. Folks buy ten million dollar homes for the $160 to live in, and spend thousands in make-up and apparel to make the $160 look like something it's not. What matters is the soul that's wrapped inside of the $160, which is priceless. You have to decide to whom your soul belongs. From there you will have perspective on what's important. If your bank account is full, but your spiritual bank is empty, you're not rich. You are poor."

With his new perspective, Rontrez couldn't agree more. His car, clothes, and everything else material was not important. Not at all. Rontrez listened intently and thought back to the Shepherd as the sermon came to a close.

"We have an old friend here," Reverend Elliott started. "The son of Rebecca Rontrez, who is no longer with us. Her son is here. He has a testimony."

Rontrez couldn't move. This wasn't why he walked into the church, and he hadn't expected to be put on the spot. He slowly stood up. Usually he liked eyes on him, but not today. He walked up to the pulpit with no idea what he was about to say to the hundreds of people now studying him. He stared at the audience blankly. "Take your time, Esau," a voice behind him said. It sounded like the Shepherd. Rontrez turned to see the Reverend nodding his head and smiling gently.

Rontrez leaned into the microphone and was immediately silenced by a deafening, high-pitched squeal from the microphone. Rontrez wanted to run off the stage and hide from the church and his sins, but he didn't. The acoustic feedback from the microphone quieted as Rontrez picked it up.

"Not big on church words," Rontrez said into the microphone. "My mom was though. She's gone now—but something she said stays with me. She told me I gotta believe. *Believe* in Him. Didn't know what she meant until today. When you have things coming from the sky, and magic tricks that look like miracles, it's easy to get confused. I lost my way. Big time. Just want to say that I realize now I haven't been much good all my life. I just thought I was because my $160 was so polished and so crisp. I was so fresh and so clean. I've done so much wrong. Bad things that they write movies about. Pimping would start off the list. Seven deadly sins would finish the list. You get it. Evil comes how you least expect it. Most of the time evil has a winning smile on its face. Comes in the form of what you want most. So a lot of people embrace evil when they reveal what they are willing to sacrifice to get whatever it is that they want most. If you believe, and hold your faith close, and understand what it is you believe in, you can't be fooled by anything. I was fooled. . .I was played like a fiddle. Not anymore. I ask this church and God for forgiveness as I re-dedicate my life to Christ."

When he finished, the church broke into a standing ovation and Rontrez received a warm hug from Reverend Elliott. "Someone is waiting for you outside," he said. "You don't want to leave too quickly, though. You have some love coming."

After he stepped down from the pulpit, Rontrez received countless hugs from members of the congregation. He felt different, almost as if he belonged there. After he was genuinely and affectionately greeted by dozens of members of Columbia Community Church, he left the sanctuary.

How in the world am I going to get home? He thought to himself, walking outside the church. He had no idea where his car was.

In his peripheral vision, he saw headlights flashing. He saw Oniva inside her Altima, waving and smiling. She leapt out of the car and ran to hug him.

"Hey, don't flash your lights at me. That's uncivilized. What do you think this is, a nightclub?" Rontrez smiled.

Oniva smiled warmly in return. "Glad you're back."

"Me too. Did you see me get called to the pulpit?" Rontrez asked.

"No, I just pulled up. And there is something different about you. So I know what happened. Congratulations on your new life," Oniva smiled.

"I feel good."

"Did you join the church? Reverend Elliott is amazing."

"No, slow down. Baby steps."

Oniva shook her head, still smiling affectionately. "I think it's time for grown man steps, Esau. You already said you were behind the pulpit just now. Use that charismatic, smooth talking, mellow aura to bring more people to a new life."

"You really think I'm cut out for the cloth?"

"You're a natural leader. You can also connect with people, are a gifted orator, and you can break complex things down into simple words. In this age, that's what many people are going to respond to – especially the youth. They can listen to *you*...or let what's on their phones and the internet minister to them."

"You're a smart lady. Someone I believe told me that our journeys are entwined. What do you think that means?"

"It means that like God, I will never leave you."

At that time if anyone says to you, "Look, here is the Messiah!" or, "There he is!" do not believe it. For false messiahs and false prophets will appear and perform great signs and wonders to deceive, if possible, even the elect. See, I have told you ahead of time.

Matthew 24:23-25